PRAISE FOR

THE *NEW YORK TIMES* BESTSELLING

WARM BODIES

"The words Marion uses to describe his grim near-future are silken smooth. They slip through the mind's grasp easily, pleasurably, leaving hardly a hint of themselves in the images they evoke."

—*The Seattle Times*

"It's got the boarded-up strongholds and mob mentality of *Night of the Living Dead*—but also romance."

—*Time Out New York*

"*Warm Bodies* is a strange and unexpected treat. R is the thinking woman's zombie—though somewhat gray-skinned and monosyllabic, he could be the perfect boyfriend, if he could manage to refrain from eating you. This is a wonderful book, elegantly written, touching and fun, as delightful as a mouthful of fresh brains."

—Audrey Niffenegger, #1 *New York Times* bestselling author of *The Time Traveler's Wife*

"Dark and funny."

—*Wired*

"Marion explores the meaning of humanity through R's journey towards personhood, a tale that gets grander in scale as his empathy builds and the book's true villains—cynicism, apathy, and status quo—are revealed."

—*Paste Magazine*

"Isaac Marion has a great new voice that hooks you from page one and accomplishes the impossible: it makes you care about young zombie love. *Warm Bodies* is a terrific read."

—Josh Bazell, *New York Times* bestselling author of *Beat the Reaper*

"A jubilant story about two star-crossed lovers, one of them dead and hungry for more than love."

—*Kirkus Reviews*

"Marion is a disarming writer, ruefully humorous, knowingly cinematic in scope. This is a slacker-zombie novel with a heart."

—*The Guardian* (UK)

"*Warm Bodies* is a terrific book—a compelling literary fantasy which is also a strange and affecting pop-culture parable."

—Nick Harkaway, author of *The Gone-Away World*

"R does possess a certain winsome charm and the upbeat ending will warm many hearts."

—*Publishers Weekly*

"A visually arresting, bleakly Ballardesque world . . . wryly playful, cinematic, and ultimately moving."

—*Time Out London*

"A mesmerising evolution of a classic contemporary myth."

—Simon Pegg, *New York Times* bestselling author of *Nerd Do Well*

"Both tender and lacerating, this zombie novel has more to say about being alive than being dead. 'Love' is not a strong enough word for my feelings about this book."

—Maggie Stiefvater, author of the Shiver trilogy and *Books of Faerie*

"Enormous fun."

—*Marie Claire* (UK)

"*Warm Bodies* is a terrific zombook. Whether you're warm-bodied or cold-bodied, snuggle up to it with the lights low and enjoy a dead-lightful combination of horror and romance."

—Examiner.com

"A captivating debut novel that is as romantic as it is terrifying. . . . Marion is an amazing storyteller who writes from his heart, or from his viscera, as the case may be."

—*SFScope*

"A unique and poignant story about life, love, and change. . . . Marion's writing style is straightforward, funny, and strong, just like his characters. . . . You can't help but be drawn into this post-apocalyptic world and root for love and hope where none should exist."

—*Fresh Fiction*

"Thought-provoking and highly original. . . . Imaginative characters and quirky dialogue make this a captivating read . . . that readers will devour."

—*Dark Faerie Tales*

"Has there been a more sympathetic monster since Frankenstein's?"

—*Financial Times* (UK)

ALSO BY ISAAC MARION

Warm Bodies

The New Hunger

THE BURNING WORLD

A NOVEL

ISAAC MARION

EMILY BESTLER BOOKS

ATRIA

NEW YORK LONDON TORONTO SYDNEY NEW DELHI

ATRIA BOOKS

EMILY BESTLER BOOKS

An Imprint of Simon & Schuster, Inc.
1230 Avenue of the Americas
New York, NY 10020

This book is a work of fiction. Any references to historical events, real people, or real places are used fictitiously. Other names, characters, places, and events are products of the author's imagination, and any resemblance to actual events or places or persons, living or dead, is entirely coincidental.

First Emily Bestler Books/Atria Books hardcover edition February 2017

Interior illustrations adapted by Isaac Marion from sources in the public domain.

Manufactured in the United States of America

10 9 8 7 6 5 4 3 2 1

Library of Congress Cataloging-in-Publication Data

Names: Marion, Isaac, 1981– author.
Title: The burning world : a novel / by Isaac Marion.
Description: First Emily Bestler Books/Atria Books hardcover edition. | New York : Emily Bestler Books, 2017. | Series: The warm bodies series ; 3 Identifiers: LCCN 2016029760 (print) | LCCN 2016037065 (ebook) | ISBN 9781476799711 (hardback) |
ISBN 9781476799728 (trade paperback) | ISBN 9781476799735 (ebook) |
Subjects: LCSH: Zombies—Fiction. | Paranormal romance stories. | BISAC:
FICTION / Literary. | FICTION / Romance / Paranormal.
Classification: LCC PS3613.A7495 B87 2017 (print) | LCC PS3613.A7495 (ebook)
| DDC 813/.6—dc23
LC record available at https://lccn.loc.gov/2016029760

ISBN 978-1-4767-9971-1
ISBN 978-1-4767-9973-5 (ebook)

Dedicated to the Mount Vernon City Library,
where I first found the ladder.

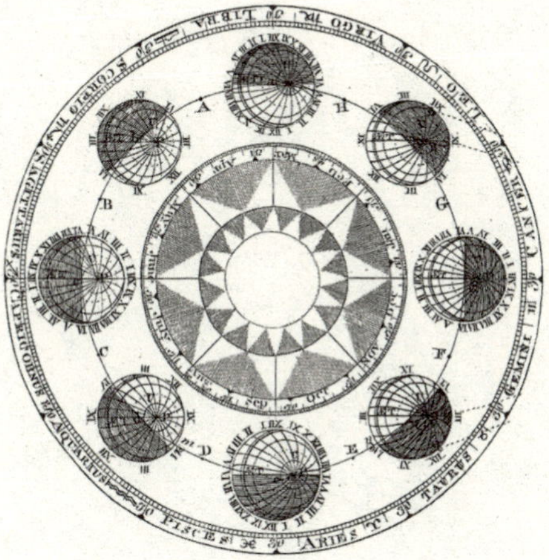

WE

WE WAIT in the rivers and the woods, in the sky and the cities and the sun, but we do not wait patiently. We have been patient too long. We have been told again and again that we can't win, that the best we can hope for is balance, but we will no longer accept this. We feel a new future building beneath us, the magma of possibility pressing against the earth.

We are becoming a mountain.

We will erupt.

ONE

the door

I will knock down the gates of the netherworld,
I will smash the door posts, and leave the doors flat down,
and will let the dead go up to eat the living!
And the dead will outnumber the living!

—*The Epic of Gilgamesh*

SCHULZ: You must speak.
BARBER: I can't.
SCHULZ: It is our only hope.

—Charlie Chaplin,
The Great Dictator

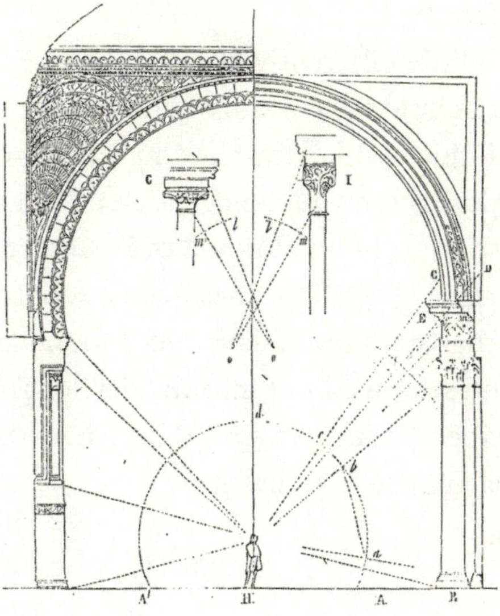

I

My name is R. It's not much of a name, but someone I love gave it to me. Whatever past lives return to me and whatever other names they bring, this is the one that matters. My first life fled without a fight and left nothing behind, so I doubt it was a loss worth mourning. A man I don't remember mixed genes with a woman I can't recall, and I was called to the stage. I stumbled through the curtain, squinting into the blinding light of the birth canal, and after a brief and banal performance, I died.

This is the arc of the average life—unexamined, unremarked, unremarkable—and it should have ended there. In simpler times, life was a one-act play, and when it was over we took our bows and caught our roses and enjoyed any applause we earned, then the spotlight faded and we shuffled backstage to nibble crackers in the greenroom of eternity.

Things work a little differently now.

Now we duck behind the curtain to find another stage. This one is dusty and cold, thick with cobwebs and reeking of rancid meat, and there is no spotlight, no audience, just a crowd of nameless extras sighing in the dark. I don't know how many years I wandered that stage, performing horrific scenes from a script I couldn't read. What I know is that sixty-seven days ago, I found an exit. I kicked open the door and stumbled out into the daylight of my third life, the one I never expected and certainly didn't deserve, and now here I am, clumsily learning how to live it.

• • •

I lean against the sheet of plywood, pressing it to the wall while I fumble in my pocket for a nail. I pull one out and promptly drop it. I grab another; I drop it. I draw a third nail and with slow, surgical movements, I set it against the wood. Then I drop the hammer.

A few mild expletives bubble in my throat, evaporating before they reach my lips. My body is in no hurry to accept this new life. The hammer is a block of ice in my barely innervated hands; the nails are tiny icicles. My heart beats, my lungs inflate, my blood has bloomed from black to red and rushes through me with desperate urgency, trying to wake my tissues from their long sleep, but I am not a normal man. I am not a tanned and toned youth ready for summer baseball. I am death warmed over.

I pick up the hammer and raise it. *Swing and a miss!* This time a few curses make it through my lips, "damn" and even "shit," nothing especially bold but enough to release some pressure. I clutch my hand, watching the flesh beneath the fingernail darken—one more bruise for my rich tapestry of wounds. The pain is distant. My brain hasn't yet remembered that my body is valuable, and it barely bothers to notify me when I damage it. I am still a tourist in the land of the Living, snapping pictures of their struggle from my hotel balcony, but I want nothing more than to join them in the dirt. Numbness is a luxury I'm eager to lose.

The plywood slips and falls on my foot. I hear one of my toes crack. I don't even have the energy to swear, I just sink onto the couch with a long sigh and stare through the scorched, splintered rift in the living room wall. We are a new couple and this is our first house; it's a fixer-upper. A little putty will take care of the bullet holes, but grenade damage is an all-day project, and we haven't even started on the bloodstains. At least Security was kind enough to clear out the bodies—the ones with flesh, anyway. We've done our best to dispose of what they left behind, but we still occasionally find bone fragments in the carpet, a few phalanges twitching on the kitchen table, a faintly buzzing cranium glaring from under the bed.

Why are we here? In a world where all anyone dreams of is comfort and safety, why did we choose this haunted house in the middle of a war zone? I know there's a reason we rejected the stadium's thick walls, something lofty and grand and profoundly important, but I find myself drifting back to the simpler explanations, the small, delicate, human concerns that are the soil for this tree.

I lean back into the prickly cushions and remember the first time I sat on this couch. A cold night. A long drive. Julie on the staircase in her soaking-wet clothes, inviting me upstairs.

There are prettier places to live. There are softer and safer places. But this place is ours.

• • •

I hear her coming before I see her. A loud, sputtering roar with occasional backfires that echo through the neighborhood like gunshots. The old Mercedes was in parade condition when I found it, but it's had a hard life since joining our family. Its engine rattles and coughs up smoke and there is no place on its bright red body that isn't dented, but it keeps running.

Julie cruises into the cul-de-sac and skids to a stop with one wheel on the curb. Her blue plaid shirt is stained with paint, putty, and a few black splotches of zombie blood—I hope it's old and dry, not some fresh setback. She starts to open her door, then she sees the Security team rushing toward her from their van on the curb and she drops her head against the headrest. "God, you guys. This is so unnecessary."

The team manager, whose name I've forgotten again, looms over her, gripping his rifle. "Are you okay? Did you encounter any Dead?"

"I'm fine."

"Rosso ordered you a twenty-four-hour escort. Why do you keep doing this?"

"Because we're trying to remind them they're human, and a bunch of guys pointing guns at them isn't helping. I keep telling Rosy but he—"

"Julie." The soldier leans in, adding more gravity to his question. "Did you encounter any Dead?"

It started with an E . . .

Julie gets out of the car and throws a bag of painting supplies over her shoulder. "Yes, Major, I encountered some Dead. I stopped and talked to them for a minute, they stared at me like lost little kids, I told them to keep fighting and went on my way." She waves at the bullet-riddled bungalow across the street, its door gone, its windows shattered. "Hi, B!"

A groan emanates from the shadows inside.

"I meant hostiles," the major says with strained patience. "'All Dead.'"

"No, sir, I did not encounter any All Dead, Boneys, bandits, or Burners. Your concern is touching, but I'm fine."

He nods to one of his men. "Check the trunk. They hide in trunks sometimes."

Julie gives up, waving him away as she backs toward the door. "You watch too many horror movies, Evan."

There. I rope it down and lock it in my vault before it can escape again. Evan Kenerly. Muscular arms. Pockmarked brown skin. Seems to enjoy pretending he's still in the Army. *Evan*.

"When you're done cavity searching my poor car," Julie adds, "would you mind grabbing those paint cans for me? Oh and watch out for the coffee table in the trunk, it might be hostile."

She turns her back on the soldiers and finally sees me, and her annoyance melts into a smile. I love to watch her transition from their world to ours. It's a change as profound as a spring thaw.

"Hi, R."

"Hi, Julie."

"How's it going in here?" She drops her bag of brushes and rollers and examines the hole in the wall, then turns in a circle, looking for signs of progress. She's been gone all day, combing the neighborhood for supplies and household items—the whole world is a yard sale—and I've been here, diligently doing nothing.

She looks at my right hand and all its purple fingers. Her smile turns sympathetic. "Still having trouble?"

I crack my knuckles. "Numb."

"Two months ago you didn't even know how to breathe, so I'd say you're doing pretty well."

I shrug.

"Why don't you hold the board and let me handle the fine motor skill?" She wiggles her fingers in front of me. "I'm a famous painter, remember? My work's hanging next to Salvador Dalí's." She picks up the hammer and a handful of nails. I hold the board over the hole while she squints one eye and places a nail.

Julie swears better than anyone I've known. She can draw from a vast vocabulary of filth and weave complex structures of inventive invective, or she can say what she needs to say using only variations of "fuck." She is a poet of profanity, and I suppress an instinct to applaud as she stomps around the room, squeezing her hand and spewing colorful couplets. I also can't help noting the difference in our reactions to the hammered finger experience, and it makes my smile fade a little. Julie is a floodlight and I am a candle. She blazes. I flicker.

She flings the hammer through the hole and collapses onto the couch. "Fuck this day."

I sit next to her and we stare at the ruined suburbs like the hole in our wall is a television. Cratered streets. Tire-scarred lawns. Houses caved in or burned to the ground. Opening titles for a very dark sitcom.

The door opens and Evan Kenerly enters, but he offers no quips or catchphrases. He drops the paint cans in the entry and turns to leave, then pauses in the doorway.

"Thank you?" Julie says.

He turns around. "Julie, listen . . ." I can't recall him ever addressing me or even making eye contact. I'm a figment of Julie's imagination. "I know you're trying to make a statement by living out here. You want to show people the plague is over and everything's fine—"

"We've never said that. That's not why we're here."

"Your neighbor 'B' is a flesh-eating corpse. You're sharing this neighborhood with hundreds of flesh-eating corpses, and you don't even lock your door."

"They don't eat flesh anymore. They're different."

"You don't know what they are. Just because they're . . . confused right now doesn't mean they won't suddenly remember their instincts while you're sleeping." His eyes flick toward me, then back to Julie. "You don't know what they're going to do. You don't know anything."

Julie's face hardens and her spine straightens. "Believe it or not, Evan, you're not the first person to tell us the world is dangerous. We've heard about a million reasons why we should be afraid. What else do you have to offer?"

Kenerly says nothing.

"We know it's not safe out here. We're aware of the risks. We don't. Fucking. Care."

Kenerly shakes his head. The door bangs shut behind him.

Julie's steely posture softens and she sags back into the couch, arms crossed over her chest.

"Well said," I tell her.

She sighs and gazes at the ceiling. "Everyone thinks we're crazy."

"They're right."

I'm just being playful, but her face clouds over. "Do you think we *should* move back?"

"I didn't mean . . ."

"Nora's there. She doesn't seem to mind living in a vault."

"Her job is there. Ours is . . . here."

"But what are we really doing out here? Are we doing anything?"

The contrast between these fragile questions and her rousing rebuttal to Kenerly reveals something I'd hoped wasn't true: I'm not the only one harboring doubts. I'm not the only one wondering what's next. But the correct response appears on my tongue, and I say it. "We're spreading the cure."

She stands up and paces in a circle, twisting her hair around her finger. "I thought I knew what that meant, but after that mess at the airport . . . and B hasn't improved . . ."

"Julie." I reach out and grab her hand. She stops pacing and looks at me, waiting. "No moving back." I pull her down onto the couch beside me. "Move forward."

I've always been a bad liar. I've never been able to say white when I'm thinking black, but the gray sludge of half truth must be within my range, because Julie smiles and dismisses her anxiety, and the moment is over. She tilts her chin up and closes her eyes. This means she wants me to kiss her. So I kiss her.

She notices the hesitation. "What?"

"Nothing." I kiss her again. Her lips are soft and pink and they know their business. Mine are stiff and pale and have only recently learned what they're for. I press them against hers and move them around, trying to remember how this works as she leans into me with escalating ardor. I love this person. I've loved her since before we met, years of stolen memories stretching back to our first glance in a crumbling classroom. Julie dug me out of my grave. Being near her is the greatest privilege I've known.

So why am I afraid to touch her?

She pushes harder and kisses deeper, trying to jump-start my passions, and I know I'm supposed to keep my eyes shut but I steal a glance. This close, she's just a blur of pink and yellow, an impressionist painting of a beautiful woman. Then she pulls back to catch her breath, and her face comes into focus. Her short blond hair, choppy and wild like windblown feathers. Her fair skin lined with thin scars. And her eyes—blue again. That impossible golden gleam is gone.

I remember the shock of it as I pulled away from our first kiss in that mystic moment on the stadium roof. An unearthly, inhuman hue, bright yellow like sunlight, a visible confirmation of whatever had happened inside us. We never once spoke of it. It was too strange, too deep, like a truth from a dream that dissolves on contact with words. We kept it inside, but it faded anyway. We watched it go over the course of a few days, standing in front of a mirror together and wondering what it meant. Hers returned to blue; mine shuffled colors for a while before settling on brown. There is very little evidence of whatever magic changed me, and there are days when I'm not sure anything really happened, nights when I expect to wake from this pleasant daydream and see a piece of meat lying next to me, eat it like I eat everything, and wander back into the dark.

I fight the urge to push her off me and run to the basement. There's a dusty bottle of vodka down there that has an extinguishing effect on the wildfire of my thoughts. But it's too late for that. She unbuttons her shirt. I slide it off her shoulders. I listen to her rapid breaths and try to read the emotion in her eyes as I prepare for another attempt to be human.

The phone rings.

Its piercing squeal sucks the lust out of the room like an open airlock. A ringing phone is not the dismissible annoyance it once was. The phone is an intercom, routed directly into the stadium's command offices, and every call is urgent.

Julie hops off me and runs upstairs, throwing on her shirt as she goes, and I trudge behind her, trying not to feel relieved.

"Julie Cabernet," she says into the bulky receiver by the bed.

I hear Lawrence Rosso's voice on the other end, his words indecipherable but tense. I was supposed to meet him this evening for another of our little chats—he has questions about the Dead and I have even more about the Living—but Julie's darkening expression tells me tonight's tea will go cold.

"What do you mean?" she asks, then listens. "Okay. Yeah. We'll be there." She hangs up and looks at the wall, twisting her hair again.

"What's going on?"

"Not sure," she says. "Traffic."

I raise my eyebrows. "Traffic?"

"'Disconcerting traffic' around Goldman Dome. He's calling a community meeting to talk about it."

"Is that all he said?"

"He didn't want to go into it over the phone."

I hesitate. "Should we be worried?"

She considers this for a moment. "Rosy's not paranoid. When we were on the road he was always the one inviting strangers to share our wine while Dad waved his gun and demanded IDs . . ." She wraps her hair into a tight ringlet, then releases it. "But he *has* gotten a little more protective since . . . what happened." She forces an easy smile. "Maybe 'disconcerting traffic' is just some Goldman kids drag racing the corridor."

She snatches the car keys off the dresser a little too fast and descends the stairs with the tempo of a tap dance. I shouldn't have asked the question. I have plenty of worries inside my own head; I don't need any more from outside.

I glance back at the house as we approach the car and feel another wave of guilty relief to be leaving it. This is my home, but it's also my wrestling ring, the site of all my trials and humiliations as I stumble toward humanity. Whatever is happening in the city, at least it won't be about me.

"I'll drive," I say, crossing in front of her.

She eyes me dubiously. "Are you sure?"

Her reaction is fair—I still have a habit of using other cars for parking brakes—but after this latest disappointment in the bedroom, I feel a need to recover some manhood.

"I'm getting better."

She smiles. "If you say so, road warrior." She tosses me the keys.

I start the car and put it into gear, and after a few jerks and sputters and minor fender benders, I drive us out of the cul-de-sac, ignoring the soldiers' laughter. Embarrassment is just one of the many perils I accepted when I made the choice to live. Living is awkward. Living hurts. Did I ever expect otherwise?

Once upon a time, in a short-and-sweet fairy tale, I might have. I was a child then, a newborn baby piloting a man. But I am rapidly growing up, and the Frank Sinatra fantasies are fading. I do not have the world on a string and Julie is not my funny valentine. We are an asthmatic orphan and a recovering corpse driving a rusty car into a rabid world, and Evan Kenerly was right: we don't know anything.

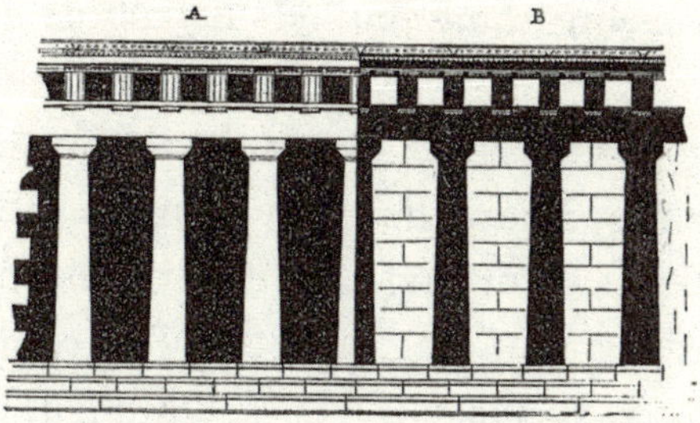

WE

WE FEEL THE CURRENTS flowing in the earth. We see the movement beneath the stillness. We watch the people sitting alone in their homes, and we hear the molten rivers in their heads.

A short man sinks deep in his recliner. He has not moved in sixteen days. This would not be unusual if he were simply dead, but he is also Dead, a condition of much greater interest to us. The dead have evaporated and we have breathed them in, but the Dead remain weighty and agentive. To be dead is to be gone from this world. To be Dead is to be marked with death's brand and conscripted into its army, but still *here*, still blessed and cursed with a body, and thus still awash with choice.

When asked his name, the Dead man presses his lips together and produces a percussive stutter. His neighbor, a small Living female, has dubbed him "B." But this is the extent of his interaction with this woman and her pale friend with the baffling scent—the electric sweetness of life with a note of death's smothering null. And under this . . . something else. Something very distant but very large. When B smells this third scent, he feels motion beneath his feet. He feels a vastness opening up around him. He feels awe and terror, so he stops breathing until his neighbors go away and the scent fades.

Who are these creatures? What do they want? Why aren't they afraid? Do they know the turmoil inside of him? The thousand opposite urges throttling each other in his head? They visit him every few days, tiptoeing into his living room and attempting conversation as he sits in the dark, staring at their reflections in his television screen, trying to understand why he isn't eating them.

He remembers a day when something changed. He felt a shift in the breeze and an interruption in gravity, a cool, clean stream flowing into his dust-crusted soul in the form of a simple question: *Why are you here?* That was the day he stood up from the warm corpse he was chewing and walked out of the airport. He found this house. He sat in this chair. He continues to sit in this chair, thinking but not quite doing. Wanting but not quite taking. Waiting and watching television.

He glances away from the endlessly looping feed of disjointed imagery—a tense football game cuts to a woman in a bikini emerging from a pool, then a sunset and a soothing voice reciting an inspirational quote, then a pulled-pork sandwich—and looks through his open front door as his neighbors drive past in their sputtering junk heap of a car. His eyes don't move when the car is gone. They rest lazily on the grass of his lawn, which is wild and gone to seed, yellowing in the summer sun.

Other eyes watch the Mercedes as it works its way through the neighborhood and out onto the open highway. B has many neighbors. New ones arrive every day, some from the airport, others from elsewhere, stumbling into town and squinting at streets and houses with traces of recognition, faint remembrances of something lost.

Death's army is large and strong and deals harshly with desert-ers, but there are rumblings. Uncertain corpses sit in their houses and stand in the streets, thinking, watching, waiting. And they hear a noise in the distance. A low, pulsating drone.

In the blue-brown haze of the eastern sky, three black shapes are growing larger.

I

I AM CONCENTRATING FIERCELY on the art of driving—the contour and condition of the road, the speed and inertia of the car, the intricate interplay of throttle and clutch—so Julie hears them first.

"What is that?" she says, glancing around.

"What?"

"That noise."

It takes me a few seconds to hear it. A distant hum, three slightly offset pitches forming a dissonant chord. For a moment I think I recognize this sound, and fear stiffens my spine.

Then Julie twists around in her seat and says, "Helicopters?"

I check the rearview mirror. Three black shapes approaching from the east.

"Who is it?" I wonder aloud.

"Nobody we know."

"Goldman Dome?"

"Working aircraft are practically mythical these days. If Goldman had helicopters, they would've told us."

The choppers roar over our heads and into the city. I am still new to Julie's world and not well-informed on the current political landscape, but I know the Dead are not the only threat, and unexpected visitors are rarely a welcome sight.

Julie pulls out her walkie and dials in Nora's channel. "Nora, it's Julie. Come in?"

Instead of traditional radio static, soft and organic, the walkie emits a distorted shriek. I don't need to ask Julie for a refresher to recall this piece of history: the BABL signal. The old government's last desperate attempt to preserve the nation's unity by smothering every argument. I can just barely hear Nora through the jammer's wall of noise, the ghost of a bygone era refusing to release its grip.

"—you hear me?"

"Barely," Julie says, and I wince as she raises the volume. "Did you see those choppers?"

"I'm at work but I—eard them."

"What's going on?"

"No idea. Rosso—alled a meet—ill you—there?"

"We're on our way."

"I'm at—ork, come—me before—eeting—want to show—omething—"

The sound of nails on a chalkboard enters the mix, and Julie cringes away from the walkie. "Nora, the jamming's too bad, I think there's a surge."

"—amn—ucking surges—"

"I'll see you soon. Cabernet out."

She drops the walkie and watches the helicopters descend into the streets around the dome. "Maybe Goldman's scouts salvaged them from an old base?" she offers feebly.

We plunge into the city, the corpse of a forgotten metropolis that most people call Post and a few thousand call home. The choppers disappear behind crumbling high-rises.

• • •

The cleanup crew has done a good job erasing the mess my old friends made of the city. All the bones and bodies have been cleared, the craters have been filled, and the walls of Corridor 1 are almost finished, leaving a clear and relatively safe highway to the stadium. But far more significant is the construction on Corridor 2, which has resumed from both ends after years of stagnation. The two largest enclaves in Cascadia are reaching across the miles that separate them. In practice, the merger is about nothing more meaningful than the safe exchange of resources, but I allow myself to imagine neurons in the brain of humanity attempting to forge a synapse.

One connection after the other. This is how we learn.

I pull into the stadium parking lot and find a spot between two Hummers, sliding in with only a few scrapes. As we head toward the gate, I glance back at our flamboyant red roadster and my brows knit with sympathy. It looks distinctly uncomfortable huddled between those two olive drab hulks. But despite Julie's tendency to humanize the inanimate, despite assigning it a name and a personality—the strong, silent type—Mercey is just a car, and its "discomfort" is just a projection of mine. Like that shiny red classic surrounded by armored trucks, I have struggled to find my place in this sensible society. The incongruity runs through every layer of who and what I am, but it starts on the outermost surface: my clothes.

Fashion has been a problem for me.

At first, Julie tried to persuade me to keep dressing sharp. My original graveclothes clearly had to go—no amount of laundering could remove their grisly history—but she begged me to keep the red tie, which was still in surprisingly good condition.

"It's a statement," she said. "It says there's more to you than work and war."

"I'm not ready to make a statement," I said, shrinking under the incredulous stares of the soldiers, and eventually she relented. She took me shopping. We sifted through the rubble of a bomb-blasted Target and I emerged from a dressing room in brown canvas pants, a gray Henley, and the same black boots I died in—always an odd pairing with my old business wear but perfect for this grim ensemble.

"Fine," Julie sighed. "You look fine."

Despite the resignation it indicates, my neutral appearance is a comfort as we approach the stadium gate. Dressing vibrantly takes a courage I don't yet have. After all those years prowling the outskirts of humanity, all I want now is to blend in.

"Hi, Ted," Julie says, nodding to the immigration officer.

"Hi, Ted," I say, trying to make my tone deliver all the signals required for my presence here. Remorse. Harmlessness. Tentative camaraderie.

Ted says nothing, which is probably the best I can hope for. He opens the gate, and we enter the stadium.

• • •

Dog shit on lumpy asphalt. Makeshift pens of bony goats and cattle. The filthy faces of children peering from overgrown shanties that wobble like houses of cards, held barely upright by a web of cables anchored to the stadium walls. Julie and I broke no evil spell when we kissed. No purifying wave of magic washed the stadium white and transformed its gargoyles into angels. One might even say we had the opposite effect, because the streets are now crawling with corpses. The "Nearly Living" as I've heard some optimists calling them. Not the classically murderous All Dead, not the lost and searching Mostly Dead like our friend B, but not yet fully alive like I allegedly am. Our purgatory is an endless wall of gray paint swatches, and it takes a sharp eye to spot the difference between "Stone" and "Slate," "Fog" and "Smoke."

The Nearlies roam the stadium freely now, having proven themselves through a probationary month of close observation, but of course that doesn't mean they blend in. They float through the population in bubbles of fearful avoidance. People read the cues—stiff gait, bad teeth, pale skin tinted purple by half-oxygenated blood—and the flow of foot traffic opens wide around them.

They nod to us as we pass. Julie nods back with an earnest smile, but the look in their eyes makes me shrink inward. Respect. Even reverence. Somehow, they've gotten it into their rotten heads that Julie and I are special. That we ended the plague and are here to usher in a new age. They can't seem to understand that we did nothing they didn't do, we just did it first. And we have no idea what to do next.

• • •

Despite my distaste for stadium life, I have to admit the place feels a little less grim under its new management. Rosso has scaled Security back to pre-Grigio levels, reassigning some personnel to largely forgotten community services like education. Former teachers are dusting off their books and teaching arcane knowledge like history, science, and basic literacy. With fewer infection patrols and fewer guns aimed at the old and sick, the city feels a little less like a quarantine camp. Some areas have an atmosphere that could almost be called idyllic. I smile at a young boy playing with a puppy in the green grass of his front lawn, trying to ignore the scars on his face and the pistol in his pocket and the fact that the grass is Astroturf.

Anytown, USA.

"Hey Julie," the boy says when he notices us.

"Hey Wally, how's that beast of yours?"

He ignores the question and regards me nervously. "Is he . . . still alive?"

Julie's smile cools. "Yes, Wally, he's still alive."

"My mom said . . ."

"Your mom said what?"

The boy pulls his eyes away from me and resumes playing with his dog. "Nothing."

"Tell your mom R is a warm and wonderful human being and he's not going to stop being one. And neither are the others."

"Okay," Wally mumbles, not looking up.

"What's your dog's name?" I ask, and he looks startled.

"Um . . . Buddy."

I crouch down and slap my knees. "Hey, Buddy." The pup runs over to me with his tongue lolling. I ruffle his face, hoping he doesn't see me as a carcass to be gnawed. He sniffs my hand, looks up at me, sniffs my hand again, then rolls onto his back and offers his belly, apparently deciding I'm Living enough.

"We've got to go," Julie says, touching my shoulder.

"To the meeting?" Wally says, and it's our turn to look startled.

"You know about that?" Julie says.

"Everyone knows. They announced it on the speakers and told us all to listen. Is it about those helicopters?"

"Um . . . yeah . . ."

"Are we going to war again?"

Julie looks at me, then back at Wally, who can't be older than twelve. "Slow down, kid," she says. "And quit playing with your pistol."

He glances down at the gun in his jeans, realizes his fingers have been caressing it, and clasps his hands behind his back, blushing.

"We don't have any idea what's going on," Julie says. "For all we know, those choppers are an aid convoy from Iceland with crates full of candy bars. So don't be such a hawk." She grabs my hand. "Let's go, R."

I release Buddy back to his owner and we continue into the city, a little more apprehensive than before. Leave it to a child to shout what we've been whispering.

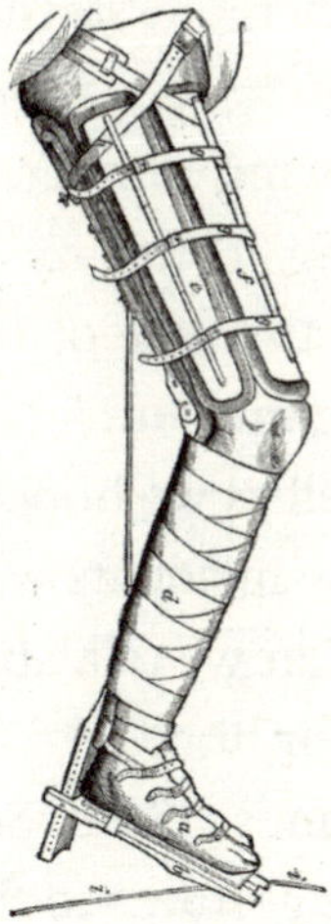

Fig. 4.

"WELL IF IT ISN'T Post's biggest celebrity couple!" Nora calls to us from across the warehouse. "Rulie? Jar? Have you picked a name yet?"

She's in full nurse regalia: baggy blue scrubs, latex gloves, a mask and stethoscope around her neck. She has attempted to make the scrubs more flattering by tying a thin belt around her waist, but the effect is lost amongst all the black gore smeared down her front. Her thicket of curls is tied back in a tight bun, but a few locks have come loose and fallen into her work, hardening into scabby dreadlocks. And yet somehow, she pulls off the look.

"Will you stop it?" Julie says, but she's smiling. "Things are weird enough."

"I bet they are." Nora stops in front of us and glances me over. "You're looking good, R."

"Thanks."

"How's life in the suburbs? How's life? How's being alive?"

"Um . . . good?"

"How's your kids?"

I squirm a little. "They're . . . staying with their mom."

"No progress?"

I shake my head, growing somber.

"When are you going to tell me what happened, anyway? I thought the airport was the base of the revolution. I thought you were out there spreading the cure."

"It didn't go . . . as well as we hoped," I mumble.

"I know you had a few incidents—"

"Nora," Julie says. "Can we talk about something else? The airport's not a fun subject for him."

Nora holds up her hands. "Sure. Sorry. Just excited to see you. I'd hug you, but . . ." She gestures to the mess on her scrubs.

"What *is* all that?" Julie says. "Do these ones still get violent?"

Nora cocks her head. "Have you not seen this place yet? Is this the first time you've visited me at work?"

Julie glances away. "It might be."

"Well, I'm sure being a suburban housewife doesn't give you much free time." Before Julie can respond to this, Nora turns and starts walking. "So anyway, come check this out. Patching R up was fun but that was just a few broken bones and knife holes—excuse me, *superficial puncture wounds*. We've gotten some much more interesting cases since then."

We follow her deeper into her workplace: a huge open warehouse converted into something resembling a hospital. The walls are corrugated sheet metal painted clean white, cords snaking around support beams to power EKGs, X-ray machines, artificial lungs, and small electric chainsaws. The place has been substantially reconfigured since I saw it last, organized and sterilized, but I know where I am.

"This place," I say, and then run out of words. "You used to . . ."

"Yeah," Nora says as she walks. "We used to dissect zombies here. Mostly we were trying to figure out new ways to kill you, but we also did a lot of our medical training here. You guys make excellent cadavers."

Julie frowns but doesn't say anything.

"We had to clean it up a bit, but all the equipment is basically the same, so it made sense to make this the zombie hospital. Before things changed we called it the Morgue, but now . . . well, we still call it the Morgue, but now it's ironic."

She leads us toward the far end of the building where most of the action seems to be. Men and women and children lie on operating tables in varying states of decay. The scene is nearly identical to the one I saw before, but with a crucial difference: the young physicians here are not cutting corpses apart. They're putting people back together.

A young girl who is gray but otherwise whole requires little attention; one of the nurses stops by to check her pulse and other vitals but mostly leaves her to lie there, gazing around the room with an expression of confused wonder.

"How're you doing, Amber?" Nora asks her.

The girl slowly stretches her lips into a smile. "Better," she whispers.

"Glad to hear it."

Next to Amber is a man whose flesh is only slightly rotted, but he has suffered multiple gunshot wounds and they're beginning to bleed. His face is a mixture of excitement and fear as two nurses hover over him, working to remove bullets from long-congealed wounds. I give him a look of commiseration.

"Mr. T here's in about the same shape you were," Nora says to me. "So you probably know what he's going through."

I do. I remember the slow creep of awareness as I woke up like a drunk from a blackout, wondering what the hell happened last night. *When did I get stabbed in the shoulder? When did I get shot four times? When did I fall off a roof and fracture most of my bones?* I remember being grateful for my numbness then, the unexpected gift of natural anesthesia. But I somehow assumed it would end when my wounds healed.

"How do you heal the rotten parts?" Julie asks. "Skin grafts?"

"Well, that's where it gets weird. Let me introduce you to Mrs. A."

Nora moves to a bed in the corner, set apart from the other patients. A woman lies naked on a plastic tarp, and another tarp on the floor catches the various fluids oozing from her ruined body. This woman has been Dead a long time. Her flesh is dark gray and withered into grandmotherly wattles. It has dried up and sloughed away completely in a dozen places, revealing the bones underneath. If I ran into this woman in my days of wandering the airport, I would have kept my distance, waiting for her to start grunting and hissing and clawing at her eyes. For that sour hum to rise from her bones.

"It's rare that they come to us when they're this far gone," Nora says. "I can't imagine what it took to break this lady loose, but look at her. Look how hard she's fighting."

The strangest thing about her is her eyes. Though the rest of her body is putrid, her eyes are incongruously whole. They stare at the ceiling with a fierce intensity, as if somewhere inside her she is lifting impossible weights. People and places and a lifetime of memories. A thousand tons of raw human soul hauled up from the depths.

Her irises are the usual metallic gray, but as I stare into them, they flicker. A brief glint, like a flake of gold in the sand of a deep river.

"What was that?" Julie says, but she's not looking at Mrs. A's eyes. She's leaning in toward her chest, pointing to a gaping hole that has rotted out of her rib cage. "Did you see that?"

"A flash?" Nora says. "Like there's a little mirror in there catching the sun?"

"Yeah . . . for like half a second. I thought I imagined it."

Nora nods. "That's the 'weird' I was talking about. And to answer your question about healing the rot . . . look closer."

Julie and I both lean in. The hole in the woman's side is . . . smaller. The edges are a little lighter. There are patches of pink in the tissues around it.

"What is it?" Julie asks in an awed whisper.

"I have no idea. I've never had less idea about anything. We've been calling it 'the Gleam.' Every once in a while it just . . . *happens*, and the Dead get a little less dead."

A strange sensation trickles through my core. A chill of uncanny familiarity, like recognizing an ancestor in a crowd on the street. I have felt this Gleam. In my eyes, in my brain, in my brittle, broken bones. I have felt it surround me and lift me to my feet, urging me onward. I catch the woman's eyes, wide and feverish with strain. "You're not dead," I murmur to her.

"So it's healing them?" Julie asks Nora.

"I guess you could say that."

"Then why do they need medical attention? Why don't you just wait for 'the Gleam' to fix them?"

"Well, that's where it gets weirder. It doesn't heal the wounds. Only the rot."

"What do you mean?"

"It can revive necrotic cells and stitch together a huge disgusting hole . . ." She points at Mrs. A's chest. ". . . but it *skips* the wounds."

"Skips? Like . . . intentionally?"

Nora shrugs. "Sometimes it seems that way. Sometimes you're looking at a slimy mess of rotten flesh and you don't even know there's a wound in there until the Gleam revives the area, and then suddenly there's a bullet hole, all bloody and fresh, like the Gleam remembered it was there and left it for us to fix."

Julie frowns at the hole, which seems to have shrunk a little further while we weren't looking. "That doesn't make *sense*."

"Wounds aren't the plague." Both women jump a little, as if they'd forgotten I was here. "The damage we do to ourselves is our responsibility."

Nora raises her eyebrows and juts her lower lip. "Wow, R. Your English has really improved."

Mrs. A shudders on her table. I catch a flurry of golden flashes in the corners of my vision that are gone before I can focus on them. Her skin begins to firm. The wrinkles fade and the color returns. Her real face is emerging from the rot, and it's young. She's in her mid-thirties. The liquid lead is draining from her eyes, leaving a deep blue.

"She's coming back," Julie whispers, leaning in close, and there's a sudden tremor in her voice. "After all this time."

Nora is stone-faced. She slips on her surgical mask and goggles, and when I follow her gaze I understand why. Red blood is pouring from gaping holes all over the woman's body. Areas that were black and desiccated when we arrived have blushed into raw, red wounds, and her newly Living lifeblood is leaving.

"That leg's gonna have to go," Nora mutters, examining what's left of her mauled thigh, which is now gushing semi-clotted blood. She reaches for the chainsaw.

"What do you—" Julie starts to ask but Nora cuts her off.

"You'll want to stand back."

She doesn't wait for us to comply. She pulls the trigger on the saw and we duck for cover as a spray of blood draws a line on the wall.

By the time I straighten up, Nora is already stitching the stump. I see the flush of giddy hope draining from Julie's face.

"So it's a tease?" she says. "They come back to life just long enough to finish dying?"

Nora's eyes are unreadable behind the mist of blood on her goggles. When she's done with the leg she resumes patching the sieve that is Mrs. A's body, but it's quickly becoming apparent that the woman isn't salvageable.

"What's the point?" Julie's voice is faint. "If we can't save them, what's the point?"

"We can save some." Nora's needle is a blur as she sutures a bite in the woman's bicep. "You come back in the same state you died in, so if it was just a bite, you're fine. If it was a fixable injury, we can fix it. But if you died of a bullet through the heart or, say, getting mostly eaten . . ." She pauses, running her eyes over the hopeless mess of Mrs. A's body. ". . . then this is just an epilogue." She resumes her stitching with a stubborn intensity. "If you can fight your way out of Purgatory like our friend here, wonderful. I'm sure you'll get bonus points in Heaven. But you're still dead."

"The plague's not immortality," I murmur to no one. "Doesn't sustain life. Just protracts death."

"Fucking eloquent, R. Who knew you'd be our resident poet?" There's an edge to this that tells me to stop. She finishes one wound and jumps to the next. "Going zombie isn't a loophole in the rules." Her voice is hard but the speed of her movements reveals her desire to be wrong. "The Gleam's not some great resurrection." She snips a thread and stands back to inspect her work. "Gone is gone."

Mrs. A is an island in a red sea. Her breathing, which had for a moment quickened to sharp gasps, is slowing again. After just a few minutes of new life, earned through perhaps years of titanic efforts, she is going to die again.

"Welcome back, Mrs. A," Nora says, doing her best to offer a comforting smile. "Sorry I couldn't . . ." She can't hold the smile; it quivers and falls. "Sorry I couldn't save you."

I catch Mrs. A's eyes. There is no blame in them, no fear or even grief. Her body is a horrific crime scene, but her face is serene. She turns her head slightly and opens her mouth, as if about to say something to me, but nothing comes out. She lets it go. Her trembling lips form a smile, and she closes her eyes. Her wounds stop pulsing.

Julie and Nora are silent, standing over the dead body like mourners at a funeral. I'm surprised to see a glint of moisture in Julie's eyes. It took her days to shed a tear for her father's horrific death; why should a stranger's bittersweet passing affect her like this?

"Julie?" I say softly. She doesn't respond. "You okay?"

She pulls her eyes away from the corpse and furtively rubs them dry, but the redness remains. "I'm fine. It's just sad."

Nora pulls the mask and goggles off her face and drops them on the floor, and just before she turns away to wash her hands, I glimpse a similar redness in her eyes. Have I missed something? What I just saw was gruesome and tragic, yes, but also beautiful. I saw a woman pull herself out of her grave and climb up to whatever's next. I saw a woman save her own soul. What did they see?

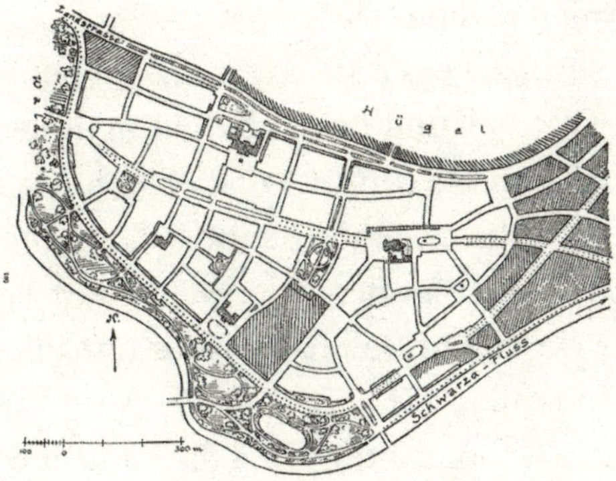

THERE IS LITTLE CONVERSATION as the three of us make our way toward the community center. The two women are usually as talkative as I am taciturn, and I'm used to floating behind them in their conversational wake. But today they say nothing, so nothing is said. It's so awkward I'm about to do something unthinkable like comment on the weather, when Julie finally breaks the silence.

"By the way, Nora," she says, as if making a brief aside in the flow of a busy dialogue, "can you stop saying 'you guys' when you're talking about zombies? R isn't a zombie."

Nora chuckles and doesn't reply.

"Nora. I'm serious."

"Am I offending you, R?" Nora asks with mock earnestness.

I shrug.

"You're offending *me*," Julie says.

Nora sighs. "My apologies to you both. You're not a zombie, R, I'm sure your dick gets rock hard."

Julie stops walking. "What is your *problem*?"

Nora stops a few steps ahead. "I just didn't think people got offended by trivial shit anymore."

"It's not trivial to him."

"He just shrugged, didn't he?"

"He always shrugs. He's a shrugger. But he fought hard to pull himself out of that hell and he's still fighting it every day, so you could at least give him the courtesy of calling him a human being."

Nora purses her lips. She looks chastised, but there's something boiling in her that won't let her cede. "Fine. Sorry for dehumanizing you, R." She wiggles her left hand's four remaining fingers. "Eat a few of these and call us even?"

She walks off without waiting for a response and we stare at her back. The last time either of us saw Nora, she was helping Rosso with some Citi planning issues and getting ready to start full-time work at the Morgue. She was stressed, a little anxious, but mostly excited. Like Julie, like all of us, she watched the steady stream of recovering Dead trickling in from the city and saw it as the beginning of a coup against death's cruel regime. Like all of us, she was brimming with hope and couldn't wait to join the fight. But since we last saw her—two weeks ago? Maybe three?—something has changed. Is it just the strain of her new job? She's a half-trained medical student thrust into the most horrific ER in history. Yet I'm doubtful it's anything so simple. Nora has weathered too much horror in her life to be undone by work stress.

"Well," Julie sighs as Nora disappears into the community center, "this day's off to a great start."

Helicopters rumble in the distance like deep, distorted laughter.

• • •

The stadium never intended to be a city. It began with a few scared refugees throwing blankets on the field, then building a few shanties, then bigger and bigger shanties that became a mass of primitive high-rises. But there was never a blueprint. Nothing about the place is well-planned or logical, least of all the community center: an architectural chimera cobbled together from pieces of countless other buildings. No two surfaces match, and one wall of the meeting hall clearly belonged to a McDonald's—the mural of a coal-eyed clown leading an army of mutated foodstuffs can be distracting during meetings, but today's builders can't say no to a free wall.

Despite its patchwork construction and the fact that it sits in the middle of a football field, it's remarkable how much the place feels like an actual community center. There's a volleyball court, a foosball table, a nursery full of children screaming for parents who may or may not come back, and a vending machine full of birth control. It serves most of the traditional functions of a community center, providing a place for the stadium's youth to gather and a town hall for the adults to debate the issues of the day, but these issues tend to be more urgent than they were in the past. *Does the park need a new gazebo?* has become *Do we have enough food to last the winter?*

Julie has attended more than a few of these meetings throughout her life, first as General Grigio's daughter and later as herself, and there's a familial affection in the faces that gather around her.

"Afternoon, Julie."

"Good to see you, Julie."

"Sorry for your loss, Ms. Grigio."

Friends of her father or of Rosso, and several of her own. Julie usually has no trouble crossing generation gaps, either younger or older, but today I see her struggling. It's the condolences, still flowing two months after her father's surreal suicide; her smile strains into a grimace. These folk come from a time before death was a daily fact dwarfed by grander horrors. They expect it to shatter her, maybe even want it to, but she isn't here to cry for them.

"Thanks, Taylor," she says. "Thanks, Britney. How about those helicopters, though?"

Her more age-appropriate acquaintances clog our path as we work our way toward the meeting hall. Teens from the foster homes, twenty-somethings from the salvage crews, and a few whose age I can't pinpoint, ambiguous like me.

Unlike me, all of these people have a place here, a history, and I envy the ease of their greetings.

"Hey, Julie."

"What's up, Jules?"

"Been a while, Cabernet."

I strain to recall their names. If I'm ever going to become a part of Julie's world, I have to at least manage that. Her life is not a fresh first chapter like mine but a story already in progress, filled with unfamiliar characters and confusing subplots.

Zane? Lourdes? Something with an X?

No one tries to ease my entry. A few nervous glances are all the acknowledgment I get. But today was never a day for making friends; even Julie seems uncomfortable and eager to detach. There are too many stormclouds hanging in the air.

Nora stands framed in the window of the volleyball court with her arms folded, watching some kids toss a ball around. Her face is close to the glass and I can see her eyes in the reflection staring back at her. When she sees us approaching, the lost look on her face coalesces into a soft sadness. "Sorry for being a bitch," she says, still watching the kids.

Julie moves toward her but stops at a less-than-intimate distance. "Did you have the wolf dream again?"

She turns around. "Can I just say sorry and leave it there?"

The two women watch each other, Julie searching, Nora evading. "Okay," Julie says. Not an ending, but a bookmark.

A pair of slender arms wrap around her shoulders, catching her in a surprise hug, and the tension in her face melts as she turns around to return it.

"Damn it, Ella, you're pretty stealthy for an old lady."

"Lawrence has been teaching me some tactics. How are you, dear?"

"Hanging on."

Her smile for Ella is warm and unreserved. I suspect that despite Julie's general popularity, her true friends form a much smaller circle. Perhaps no wider than this corner of the room.

"And how are *you*, R?" Ella asks me with more pointed interest.

"Doing well, Mrs. Des . . . Descon . . ."

She smiles. "Desconsado."

I shake my head. I visit her house nearly every week; I should be able to pronounce her name.

"Most people default to Mrs. Rosso anyway," she says. "But like I keep telling you: call me Ella."

I clear my throat. "I'm doing well, Ella. Hanging on . . . climbing up."

"Happy to hear it."

Ella is elderly, but she radiates an incongruous aura of youth. Her dark eyes are clear and sharp, her posture is straight—the result of a survival fitness regimen that knows no retirement age. She even has a few streaks of black in her gray hair, which she ties back with a red kerchief rather than tease into a grandmotherly curl cloud. She is not a little old lady. She is a woman.

Nora drifts over to the edge of our triangle, hands folded in front of her. "Hi, Ella," she says quietly.

"Good to see you, Nora. You've been scarce lately, haven't you?"

"Busy sewing up zombies."

"Right."

Julie watches Nora. Nora glances at her, then away.

"I've noticed you spending a lot of time with one in particular," Ella continues, giving Nora a conspiratorial smile, but Nora doesn't take the bait.

"I assume you mean Marcus. He needed a lot of work. Six bullet wounds and a shattered jaw."

Ella nods, faintly disappointed. "And where is he now?"

"Good question." Nora looks at me. "Where's your friend, R?"

I think for a moment, wondering how to answer this. I remember the long climb to M's temporary housing on the top floor of an apartment tower, the woozy sensation of the plywood walls swaying in the breeze. I remember opening the door to his spartan quarters and finding him stuffing his few possessions into a backpack:

two white T-shirts, a hunting knife, a box of Carbtein, and a stack of vintage porn magazines.

"I'm going camping for a while," he said, and I remember paying more attention to the quantity and fluidity of his words than to their content. It was early in our rejuvenation and we were still giddy over the ability to speak. We would sit in his room for hours and just say words, comparing the length of our sentences.

"Where?" I asked, losing by a landslide.

"Don't know yet. Just need to get out. Be alone. This thing we're doing . . ." He tapped his forehead. "It hurts."

I knew what he meant, though I couldn't relate. M, like most of the recovering Dead, was remembering his old life. Slowly, in small twists and jabs, the shards of his old identity were penetrating his new one, merging and combining, and it was a disorienting process. Some didn't survive it. One dived off the stadium roof, screaming, "Get out of me!" to whoever was creeping in. Another ran into the city and tried to join a pack of All Dead, who gruesomely rejected his membership. One simply shot herself. I heard these stories as cautionary tales and clung viciously to the present. I was still a blank slate with only Julie written on it, and I intended to keep it that way.

"Good luck," I told M at the stadium gates, and he turned. The M I used to know would have punched my shoulder. This one hugged me. Either his transformation was making him sentimental, or this was a bigger good-bye than I knew. Today's great outdoors are packed with predators—human, animal, and other—and "going camping" is a popular mode of suicide.

"I'll see you later," he called over his shoulder as he walked out into the city, and I hoped—and continue to hope—that he meant it.

"He went camping," I tell Ella while Nora and Julie watch me expectantly. At Ella's stricken look I quickly add, "He's coming back."

"We'll see," Nora says.

Ella nods and her eyes drift. "It must be difficult . . . coming back. I can hardly imagine what you go through."

"When are you doing *your* vision quest?" Nora asks me with a faint edge in her voice. "Don't you need to go out into the woods and commune with your past lives or something? Everyone's doing it."

I look at the floor, searching for the fastest way to end this conversation. "I don't want my past lives."

"Why not?" Ella asks.

Julie raises her eyebrows at me and waits. It's a conversation we've had before, and she's always been cautiously ambivalent. She won't attack my desire for a fresh start, but she won't defend it either.

"Because I want this one," I reply almost as a sigh, knowing the charm of this sentiment has worn off.

I expect Nora to laugh, but she just looks at me with arms folded, her face clouded with an emotion I can't read.

"That's sweet," Ella says. "But do you mind a bit of elderly wisdom?"

I shrug.

"People have pasts. You can't be a person without one."

Nora opens her mouth, then shuts it and looks at the floor. Hers is the one opinion I haven't heard yet, but she seems to have withdrawn from the conversation. I wish I could do the same. Julie watches me, waiting to see how I'll wriggle out of Ella's logic lock.

"*TEST*," Rosso's voice booms from the meeting hall, followed by three ear-punching thumps and a squeal of feedback. "Is it on?"

"Jesus," Julie says, covering her ears. "Is he deaf?"

"He's getting there," Ella says. "I keep telling him he's too old for this, he should pass it off to Evan and—"

"No, no," Julie cuts her off. "Please not Evan."

"Well, he is next in rank."

"I thought we weren't doing ranks anymore."

"Lawrence doesn't like the titles, but we still need some kind of leadership structure. Or so everyone says."

"Test, test," Rosso says, followed by another shriek of feedback.

"It's *on*!" Julie shouts toward the hall entrance. "Turn it *down*, you damn metalhead!"

Ella laughs. The laugh becomes a cough, and the cough lasts longer than it should.

Julie touches her shoulder. "Hey . . . are you okay?"

"Fine," Ella says, recovering herself with a deep breath. "Just old."

Julie watches her surrogate grandmother wipe spittle from her lips. She doesn't let go of her shoulder.

"Was it really that loud?" Rosso wonders, stepping in from the hall. "It's hard to tell from onstage. Our sound guy sucks."

Ella cocks her head. "You don't think you're playing a show, do you? Please tell me you're not going senile as well as deaf."

"Ella, so help me . . ."

"Ishtar Scorned broke up thirty years ago, babe. There was an apocalypse, and you're doing a town hall meeting for the survivor enclave that you—"

"Okay, enough." Rosso rolls his eyes and gives me the *Women!* look, and I'm startled by how much this delights me. I try to make the appropriate expression of fraternal commiseration, but it comes out less *I hear you, brother*, and more *I'm constipated*.

"I may have lost a little acuity," Rosso tells his wife. "A few decades of hard rock and gunfire will do that, but it's not the worst thing a man can lose with age, so back off."

Ella snickers. I study these two elderly humans and wonder what they've done differently. Age has not destroyed them like it does most. Rosso hasn't retained the physical grace of his wife; his eyes and ears are bad, his hair is sparse, and his joints are stiff, but like Ella, he has managed to keep his soul limber. I remember the way he looked at me at the stadium entrance as Julie begged him to trust us, as he opened the gate for me and let me inside, knowing full well what I was. He has not shrunken into a mass of prejudice like other, younger men. He is still living.

"Do you really need a mic?" Nora says. "It's usually only a few dozen people."

Rosso looks uneasy. "We're . . . expecting a bigger crowd today."

There's a pause as everyone wonders whether to ask the question now or wait for the official reveal, but before we can decide, the doors bang open and the crowd files in.

"How *much* bigger?" Nora wonders as the lobby fills.

"Everyone." Rosso nods to familiar faces and shakes a few hands, a blue-collar president in a grease-stained jumpsuit.

"Um, everyone is twenty thousand people," Nora says. "The hall holds two hundred."

"We're patching the mics into the stadium PA. Only the reps will be able to participate, but everyone will be able to listen."

Dread creeps into Julie's face. "It's that important?"

"Everything is that important. We're all sharing this place and everyone deserves to know what's happening. We're done with secret bunker meetings. We've seen where that leads."

The four of us watch him, waiting, and his tone deflates a little. "But yes. It's that important."

"Is the world ending again?" Julie asks, forcing a faint smile.

Rosso looks at her, stone-faced, considering the question with alarming seriousness. "Excuse me," he says, and disappears into the crowd.

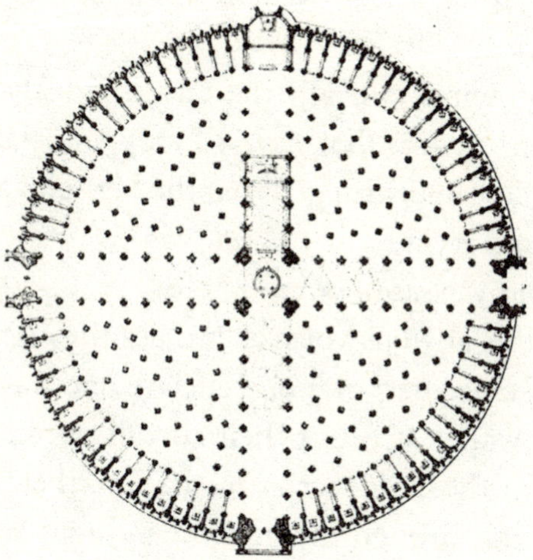

WE

WE DRIFT BENEATH THE CITY, floating through soil and stone, gazing up at the foundations of skyscrapers. They rise like exclamation points announcing the ascendancy of man, the end of a speech that seemed long and eloquent when we were up there writing it, but now, here astride the eons, more like a baby's first grunt.

We love this baby, with all its spit and shit. It's ours, it's us, and we want it to grow up.

So we rise toward the city. We glide below its surface and through its countless graves, from grand cemeteries to backyard shoeboxes, caressing familiar bones but resisting their nostalgia. There's a sense of urgency in the earth today, a seismic tension that tells us to keep moving, to keep watching, to gather all we can.

And we hear a voice.

"This is Major Evan Kenerly from Citi Stadium paging Goldman Dome, please pick up."

The web of wires beneath the city is mostly inert: lines to communications towers that have all stopped speaking. But one of them—an old cable strung across the city like a child's tin-can telephone—is still trying.

"Goldman Dome, please pick up."

We follow this anxious voice as it races through the cable. We traverse the distance between one enclave and the other, running just below the walled street of their corridor project, beneath the pounding feet of the builders rushing back to their homes. We follow the signal up through the ground and into some deep basement of the dome, and here the signal stops. The cable is cut. The voice of Evan Kenerly disperses into ambient electrons.

We pause in this dark chamber, touching its cracked and sooty walls, its heaps of charred debris, skimming the pages of its history. Decades of men shouting into telephones and conducting joyless transactions, then decades of men planning wars and defenses and defenses of wars . . . and then this. Unfinished books ended in mid-sentence. No page of the Higher has ever been written here, just reams upon reams of sorrowful paperwork, anthologies of invoices bound in beige plastic—and something worse. Something moving in the halls around us. Heavy masses of Lower dreams, forming dents in the world's thin shell.

We do not want to be here. We do not want to gather this.

We dive back into the comforting density of earth and retrace the cable to its source, hoping for brighter books. Whether it's a city or an enclave or a family in a tent, we love every accretion of minds. Even the smallest node is a treasure, a mass of consciousness pumping out experience, perception, story—a beating heart in the corpse of the world.

We emerge from the ground in the center of the stadium, and

familiarity trickles through us. *Ah yes*, some part of us whispers, and the rest of us partakes in the feeling. *These streets. This place.*

A young boy named Wally is standing in his yard with a dog named Buddy. Both are focused on a speaker that hangs from a power pole near his house. Are they listening to music? We would love to hear some music; the world hasn't been this tuneless since the dawn of the Stone Age. But it's not music. It's an old man addressing a crowd, and his voice is like Evan Kenerly's: anxious and atonal.

"For those of you listening outside, this is Lawrence Rosso, the officer formally known as General, speaking to you from the community center hall. I hope you can hear me okay, this is the first time we've—"

A squeal of feedback echoes through the stadium. The dog named Buddy flattens his ears.

"Sorry, folks. Bob, can you turn me down a little?"

A boy named David steps out of the house next door and a dog named Trina rushes over to greet Buddy.

"Hi Wally," David says.

"Shh," Wally says, not looking away from the speaker.

"Check. Check. Is that better?"

David's twin sister, Marie, emerges from the doorway behind him. It has been six years and nine months since their cells diverged from their mother's and their bodies began to form. It has been two years since David lost his memories of the womb and the darkness before it, the pain of birth and the strain of building a mind, and he is beginning to engage with the place in which he finds himself. Marie still remembers, which is why she stares at everything with the look of a visitor studying a strange world, but very soon she will surrender these pages to the Library, and we will savor them while she goes out to write more.

"What's going on?" David asks his friend while the dogs sniff each other's orifices.

"Didn't your mom tell you?" Wally says. "It's a big meeting and everyone gets to listen this time, even kids. So shut up."

"Okay," the speaker says, and the kids look up. *"I think we've got it fixed, so if I can ask everyone to pause their day for a moment, put the hammers down, give your babies their binkies, and listen."*

Marie gazes into the black grill of the speaker. She sees the vibrations of the paper cone pulsing like a heartbeat. She reminisces one last time, and she lets go. The gauzy pink light of her prehistory falls away and she is here on Earth, bare toes in the dirt, listening.

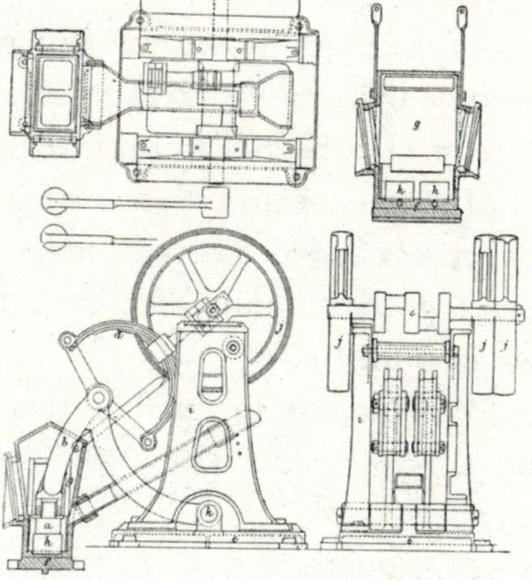

I

"YOU'VE ALL SEEN the helicopters," Rosso says into the microphone while Bob the sound guy munches a sandwich in the back of the room. "And some of you saw the convoy of trucks early this morning. These vehicles aren't ours and they don't appear to be Goldman's."

"Who the fuck else is there?" says a voice in the crowd, loud to begin with and made louder by the mics hanging from the ceiling.

Rosso adjusts his glasses, locating the speaker. "Mr. Balt. A valid question, although I'll remind you that we're broadcasting to the whole stadium here, so let's keep the language civil."

"Sorry kids," the man says, speaking directly to the ceiling mics. "Uncle Tim fucked up."

Wavy blond hair. Tan, tattooed arms bulging from a black tank top. A prominent, stubbly jaw supporting a smug grin. I remember this man. I smashed his head into a wall once. It seems I didn't kill him, which is . . . good, I guess.

"To answer your question," Rosso says with great restraint, "we don't know who else there is. We don't know much of anything. General Grigio wasn't . . . he didn't prioritize outreach." His tone briefly slips out of professionalism as he recalls his former friend. "We haven't sent scouts outside Cascadia in seven years. Travelers are rare and their reports are unreliable. Even the Almanac seems to have gone out of print."

"This is bullshit," Balt says, folding his arms so the gun tattoos on his biceps bulge. "We need to know who's out there. We need to know our enemies!"

"Because everyone out there is our enemy," Julie mutters under her breath. She and Nora and I are against the wall, slightly removed from the crowd. The women aren't official representatives, but they're considered "special consultants" due to their intimate acquaintance with the undead threat: the Morgue, in Nora's case, and in Julie's case . . . me.

And me? Why am I in this room? I have no title, I have no job, and the percentage of people who think I should be shot hovers right around fifty. But Rosso insists he sees something in my eyes, even now that they're dirt brown. Rosso says I have important work to do. I wish he could be more specific.

"Well Mr. Balt," he says, "if you've managed to locate and disable the BABL generator, I'll be happy to send out a national broadcast asking our enemies to identify themselves. Until then, we're living in a narrow spotlight on a dark stage."

Balt glowers but says nothing.

"What did Goldman say?" Julie asks. "They didn't know anything either?"

Rosso hesitates. "We've been trying to ask them." Another pause, perhaps suddenly reconsidering his decision to make this meeting public. "The line to Goldman headquarters seems to be disconnected."

A wave of fearful murmuring rushes through the room and I can almost hear it spreading through the streets outside.

"So that's it, then!" Balt says, jumping to his feet. "They invaded Goldman. It's a fuckin' war!"

"For those of you listening outside," Rosso sighs into the mic, "Mr. Balt is visibly tumescent."

"Visibly *what*?"

"Sit down, Tim. It may be an invasion, it may not. Scouts are on their way to the dome as we speak."

Balt looks at Kenerly for confirmation and Kenerly nods. Balt sits down with exaggerated slowness, adjusting his gray fatigues.

"Could it be the Fire Church?" a man in the crowd asks.

"Invasions aren't in their liturgy," Rosso says. "They're out to raze cities, not rule them."

"What about the old corporate militias?" an elderly woman asks.

"All the big ones destroyed each other in the Merger War. The survivors choked in the Borough Conflicts. There are no nation-scale forces left in America, as far as we know." He clears his throat. "But like I said . . . we don't know very far."

The room falls into silence as everyone looks around, hoping someone else has the question or answer that will ease the tension. A few rows back, Ella stands up. "Suppose it is an invasion. Suppose they've conquered Goldman and they're coming for us next. Whoever they are, any group that has a fleet of helicopters probably *is* nation-scale, and now they have Goldman's resources too. So if they want this stadium . . . do we really want to fight them for it?"

"Of course we want to fight!" Balt yelps as if insulted. "The fuck else would we do?"

"Leave? Go somewhere else and try something new? Like Lawrence said, it's wild territory out there. There could be fertile land and fresh water. There could be beautiful places to live that aren't on anyone's to-conquer list. Why sacrifice our lives for a concrete box?"

"Because *they* are outside this box," Balt says, and I jolt when I notice his finger is aimed at my head. "Yeah, you lanky motherfucker. Thought I forgot about you?" He stands up again; Rosso sighs again. "I didn't forget, but did everyone else? Did you forget about this rotten piece of shit and all the other flesh-eaters we've got hanging around our homes? This 'cure' bullshit is . . ." He stabs his finger at me a few times. "Well it's bullshit!"

Nora stifles a chuckle. Julie is too busy glaring.

"The night before they all 'transformed' or whatever the fuck you want to call it, this fuckin' corpse almost killed me and my buddies. Then he went out and fuckin' *ate* one of our guys. And now he's standing here in our fuckin' meeting hall like a fuckin' guest of honor."

A murmur of agreement runs through the crowd. I feel the focus of four hundred eyes like a laser dot on my forehead. I have to admit, he has a point.

"I'd like to 'almost kill' you too," Julie snaps, pushing herself off the wall and stepping forward. "I know a lot of people who would. So what?"

I put a hand on her shoulder but she doesn't notice it.

"A lot of shit happened that night," she continues. "R killed Krauss because Krauss was about to kill him. Everyone in this room has had to kill someone at some point. It *happens*. So let's get off the fact that he killed a guy and focus on the fact that he's a *zombie who cured himself*!"

"How?" someone in the crowd shouts. "How'd he do that?"

"What about the rest of them? How far is it spreading?"

"How do we know it's permanent?"

"Everyone, listen," Rosso says, but the crowd has reached a boil.

"What if we leave the stadium and then they all change back?"

"Yeah, what if it's a trick?"

"A *trick*?" Rosso says incredulously. "Okay, this is—"

"We don't know anything about them!"

"What if they're faking?"

"What if they—"

"*People*!" Rosso shouts into the mic, and a piercing howl of feedback derails the runaway Q&A as everyone shoves hands against ears. Bob the sound guy winks and gives Rosso a thumbs-up.

"People," Rosso sighs, letting the mic fall against his thigh. "These are valid questions . . . some of them. But there's only one person in this room who might be able to answer them."

I scan the crowd, wondering who this mystery sage might be.

"So if you'll all kindly shut up a moment . . ." Rosso looks in my direction—no. He looks *at* me. He holds the microphone out to me. "Mr. R?" he says to me. "Can you offer any insight into the current state of undead affairs?"

Rosso blurs in my vision and the McDonald's mural behind him comes into focus. The clown's small, black eyes. His red-smeared lips. The unfathomable anatomy of Mayor McCheese.

"R," Julie whispers, nudging me forward. I step onto the stage and stare at the mic. Its dark barrel is aimed straight at my face. I stare at the mic.

"R?" Rosso prompts, pushing it closer.

I take it. "H-hello," I say, and the sound of my rarely used voice amplified and fired back at me makes my eyes go wide. Imagining it sprayed over the entire stadium into twenty thousand sets of ears makes my jaw fall open.

"Weapons ready, boys," Balt chuckles. "Looks like he's about to convert again."

I pull my eyes away from the crowd and all its mistrustful faces, and I look at Julie. Her face contains so many things. Fear, urgency, a little annoyance, but mostly that emotion I've come to know as love. Julie loves me. She believes in me, far more than I do in myself. And she wants me to speak.

My lips brush the mic. An electric spark snaps against them and I jolt back, rubbing my mouth in surprise. "That *hurt*," I mumble, accidentally aloud.

"Sorry, what?" Balt says, cupping a hand to his ear.

I look up and blurt, all in a rush, "I can't answer your questions."

Not the strongest opening for my great speech of reconciliation. Balt laughs and throws up his hands.

"What I mean is . . . all I know is . . ." My mind races, searching for words to explain things I don't understand. "I don't know what . . . cured us, it was . . . different for everyone, but for me . . . I decided to . . . I wanted to be . . . I just tried to . . ."

My lips freeze in a slack-jawed O, waiting for the next syllable, but nothing comes. My eyes dart toward Julie. She couldn't have expected much more from me. We've discussed the mystery of the cure many times and have never gotten far, even with her unencumbered articulation. But she still looks disappointed. My big moment onstage, my chance to redeem myself and my fellow former Dead in front of the whole stadium, and my tongue goes flaccid.

"Well, there you have it, folks," Balt says. "Now that our resident zombie has cleared everything up for us, let's dynamite our walls and go dance in a fuckin' meadow."

Rosso walks up, shaking his head, and takes the mic from me. "Okay, honestly," he says, jabbing a hand at Balt, "who elected this man? What's your building, Balt?"

"Twenty-One Cock Street, bitches!" he says in an exaggerated baritone, pumping a fist in the air, and I hear the sound of a crowd hooting somewhere outside.

"It's Rooster Street, you idiot," Julie says.

Rosso's face is hidden behind his palm. "I thought we were past this," he says into his fingers, and the mic barely picks it up. "I thought we were done with brutes."

"What's that, Larry?" Balt says, cupping his ear again. "I'm getting old, my hearing's not what it used to be."

"Blessed are the deaf," Rosso mutters to no one but himself, "for the loud shall inherit the earth."

I can hear a shift in the room's acoustics as Bob cranks the mics, trying to pick up Rosso's dwindling volume. Being the pro that he is, he's raising the room mics instead of the stage, and the small sounds of the crowd become audible: creaking chairs, grinding teeth, heavy breaths. I brace myself to be deafened when Balt inevitably starts shouting again, but just as he's sucking in a breath to do so, a curious sound appears in the background.

Three musical tones, followed by a warm, reassuring male voice.

"Thank you for calling the United States. If you or your township is currently under attack, please hang up and contact your local militia."

"The fuck is that?" Balt says, and his voice booms so loud even he cringes. Feedback begins to build in the speakers: a low, threatening hum.

"Shut it off, Bob," Rosso says. Bob mutes the PA and the room goes quiet.

"Please listen to the following options . . ."

It's coming from the lobby. Rosso hops off the stage and works his way through the crowd, shoving Balt aside with surprising strength. I go around the stage to join Julie and Nora—their faces are as nonplussed as everyone's—and we follow Rosso into the lobby.

"To request military assistance, press one. To report military abuse, press two."

On the help desk in the corner of the lobby, on an old black office phone, the line labeled "Goldman" is blinking red. The voice emanates from the phone's speaker, backed by a faint trickle of music: calming synthesizer chords with occasional glimmers of sax.

"To report a new hive formation, press three. To report any information on a possible cause or cure, please hang up and call the National Plague 'Rotline' at 1-803-768-5463."

The recording hisses and hums and wavers its pitch like a reel of tape that's been looping for decades. Rosso looks bemused, as if this is some inscrutable prank. "Who called Fed 800?" he asks no one in particular.

"To report threats to or from your regional government, press four. If your state is attempting secession and you wish to request exemption from retributive strikes, press five."

"I called Goldman again a few hours ago," Kenerly says. "The line was still dead but I left it on auto-dial just in case."

"How did their HQ line get patched into Fed 800 . . . ?"

"For infection avoidance tips, press six. To speak to a live representative, press seven. And if you would simply like to be calmed, press eight to be redirected to the LOTUS Feed."

The voice goes quiet, leaving only the background music, which has transitioned into a gentle Latin conga rhythm. Rosso looks at Kenerly, shrugs, and presses seven.

"Due to high national crisis levels and drastically reduced staff, we are experiencing longer than usual wait times. The estimated wait to speak to a representative is—three hundred sixty-five days. We are sorry for the delay. We are sorry."

A smooth Spanish guitar riff noodles over fretless bass.

"Don't know what I was expecting," Rosso says. He reaches out to end the call.

There's a buzzing noise, then a sharp click.

"Hello?"

Rosso's hand freezes over the button. "Ah . . . hello?"

"Who is this?"

"This is Lawrence Rosso at Citi Stadium. Who are . . . who am I speaking to?"

A pause.

"This line isn't set up yet. I can't answer questions."

Rosso glances at Kenerly, then back at the phone. "Is this Goldman Dome headquarters?"

"Yes."

"May I speak to General Cinza?"

Another pause.

"Goldman Dome is under new management. Mr. Cinza is no longer with us."

"What do you mean 'new management'?"

"This line isn't set up yet. I can't answer questions. Pitchmen will be arriving at your enclave in one hour to introduce our organization."

"What is your—"

"The pitchmen will introduce our organization. They'll arrive in one hour. Thank you for calling the Axiom Group."

A click. The phone's red light goes dark.

Much of the crowd has filtered in from the meeting hall, but despite being packed tight with people, the lobby is completely silent. Rosso's eyes are on the phone but far away. I look at Julie and find a similar distance in her expression. Most of the faces in the room display simple confusion and unease—darting eyes, wringing hands, questions mumbled to the nearest neighbor—but every fourth or fifth person wears this strange, dreamy stare, like someone plunged into deep childhood reverie.

"Why do I know that name . . . ," Julie says, barely a whisper, and the undertones in her voice tell me this is not the pleasant kind of recollection, not the taste of a favorite candy or the first notes of a lullaby but the other kind. The kind that therapists dig out with special dolls.

And do I feel it? This uneasy nostalgia? I do not. I feel nothing. A cottony white nothing so perfect it's suspicious, like a plastered-over door with a sign that says NOT A DOOR. A whole new level of numbness.

"Sounds like a fuckin' invasion to me," Balt grunts, unsurprisingly immune to the spell of introspection. "I say we meet 'em at the gate with every gun we've got."

"Mr. Balt," Rosso says softly, "you are not a ranking officer so will you please gather your fraternity and return to your building. We're done here." He steps back into the hall and addresses the mics. "The meeting is over, folks. Some . . . ambiguous developments are in progress. We'll keep you apprised."

The crowd in the lobby begins to disperse, floating on a tide of anxious chatter. Balt lingers long enough to imply he's only leaving because he feels like it, but he leaves. Evan and a few other officers remain, waiting for Rosso.

"One unit outside the gate," he tells them. "Armed, but non-aggressive. I'll join you in a moment."

Evan gives the traditional Army salute—more of a geeky anachronism the further into history the government recedes—and he and his officers exit.

After the whitewater noise of a packed house, the community center feels ghostly with only five people in it. Nora spins a rod on the foosball table. The tiny blue men kick wildly, but there is no ball.

"What is this?" Julie asks Rosso as he stares at the floor. "Who are they?"

"Axiom *was* . . . a militia." I can hear a longer, darker description buried in that ellipsis. His head is shaking subtly. "But it's gone. It was wiped out years ago, when you were a little girl. There's no way it could have . . ."

Ella watches him, her throat slowly constricting. Then a sharp, wet cough erupts from her lungs and she hunches over, inhaling, coughing, inhaling, coughing. Rosso rubs her back. "Where's your medicine, El?"

The fit subsides and she straightens, wheezing like she's just run a marathon. "Left it at home."

Rosso glances to the lobby door, then to me, then to Julie and Nora. "Will you girls take her home and make sure she gets her pills? I need to get to the gate."

The girls nod and take Ella by the elbows. I move to follow them.

"R," Rosso says. "I'd like you to come with me."

I look at Julie, then at Rosso, thinking I must have misheard him. "Come with you?"

"Yes. To the gate."

I pause. "Why?"

"I'm not sure I know why. But I want you to be there."

I shoot Julie a desperate look. "There" is the last place I want to be. I want to be back at our house, patching holes and scrubbing floors, sitting next to her on the ratty old couch reading children's books while she helps me sound out the syllables, watching her cook an omelet and then attempting to eat it, telling myself this is food, this is food, people aren't food, *this* is food.

I want to be alone with her, not in this swarm of fraught and noisy people debating military operations. I've just rejoined humanity. *Curious George* is above my reading level. I'm not ready for this.

"Go on," Julie says, her eyes tight with worry. "I'll find you later."

Rosso waits patiently. He knows my fears. We've spent many an evening discussing them in his library as he counsels me through my recovery. But there is no sympathy in his eyes today, no comfort, only the steady resolve of a man telling a man what must be done and trusting him to do it.

I wanted to be human. I wanted to be part of the world. Well, this is the world. Not a cozy cottage—a battlefield. I thought I'd have more time to brace myself, but if there's one thing I've learned in my short residency here it's that nothing ever happens when you're ready for it. You tell life, "On the count of three!" and it goes on two.

I pull myself away from Julie and nod to Rosso. We walk toward the gate.

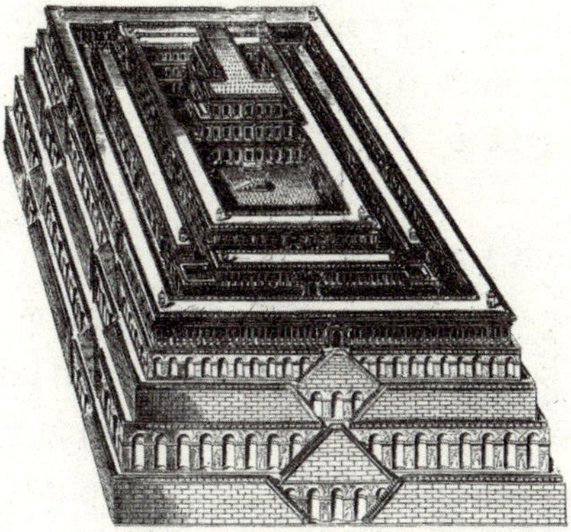

It's late July, and the average temperature hovers around 120 degrees. Humanity has had a few generations to adapt to the new climate, but everyone in the stadium still drips miserably. My ravaged body has been too busy relearning the more essential functions to bother with sweating, so the heat bakes my unmarinated meat. For once I'm grateful for the crush of the stadium's slum towers. The five-story apartments of moldy plywood and rusty sheet metal bathe most of the enclave in shade, which turns the oven down to a more livable 100.

"I wish I could be clearer with you," Rosso says as our boots slap and peel away from the melting asphalt. The "street" is really no more than a crudely paved footpath, too narrow for us to walk abreast, so I follow behind him and can only guess at his expression. "All I can say is that I believe you're important."

I say nothing.

"That is to say you *represent* something important. You and the others like you. And I'm very interested to find out what it is."

I remain silent. He glances back at me. "Am I overwhelming you?"

I nod.

He smiles and turns back to the path. "Sorry. I'm sure you're going through enough right now without me dumping some half-baked hero's journey in your lap."

"I'm not important," I say to the back of his head. "I'm . . . impotent."

"Why do you say that, R?"

I hadn't intended to elaborate, but something in the soft sincerity of his tone makes it bubble out of me. "I can't read. I can't speak. My fingers don't work. My kids won't stop eating people. I don't have a job. I can't make love. Most people want to kill me."

He chuckles. "No one said life is easy."

"Does it ever get easier?"

"No." He looks back at me again. "Well, in your case, maybe a little. But I wouldn't wait around for it. The day you solve your last problem is the day you die."

We pass the Agriculture building, a cluster of hothouses rising five stories high with hazy clouds of green visible through the translucent walls. A steady procession of workers pours out from the bottom floors, their backs bent under sacks of fresh vegetables. All this effort manages to supply about a third of the stadium's food needs. A nice little organic supplement to the steady diet of Carbtein cubes. What will these people do when the old world's leftovers run out? The medicine? The bullets? No one here knows how these things were made or has the resources to make them. The enclave works hard to build an illusion of self-sufficiency, but like all enclaves—and the cities and countries that preceded them—it relies on a thousand veins pumping lifeblood from the world outside. What happens when the heart finally stops?

"I believe in hard truths," Rosso says after a few blocks of silence. "But I have to confess I'm doubting my advice right now."

"Why?"

We pass a block of foster homes and he looks up into the windows. Nearly half of them frame a child's forlorn face, chins buried in folded arms, eyes scanning the streets for any hint that their lives might change. "I had a similar conversation with another young man not long ago."

My step falters and I briefly fall behind him, but he doesn't seem to notice.

"He had a very different life with very different struggles, but he asked similar questions, and I gave him similar answers." He drops his eyes to the ground, watches the steady procession of garbage passing under his feet. "He died soon after we talked, and I believe it was by choice." A beer can. A bullet shell. A fruit too rotten to identify. "Perhaps you shouldn't listen to me."

I feel a heavy stone in my stomach. It's been a long time since I've thought of Perry Kelvin. In all the joy and terror of my new life, it was easy to forget the life I hijacked to get here. The taste of his brain. The rush of his memories. His wry voice in my head as we guided each other forward, unlikely partners on an inner expedition.

Rosso walks in silence, perhaps expecting a reply. As always, it'd be best for me to keep my mouth shut, but this is a good man living a pained life, and the knowledge I have might comfort him, no matter how horrifically I obtained it.

"You meant a lot to Perry," I tell him. "So did your advice."

He glances back at me.

"He was on a path. You almost swayed him. It was just . . . too late."

"How could you possibly know that?" Rosso says, looking straight ahead. "I can believe Julie talked about him a little . . . but not that much."

"I . . . read his book," I say, searching for a way around the full truth. "The one he was writing before he died."

"I thought you can't read."

"I . . . skimmed?"

Rosso walks for a while, then shakes his head. "I didn't know he was writing a book. That's even sadder."

"Sadder?"

"To give up in the middle of such an undertaking. To leave so many things unfinished . . ." His voice trembles and trails off.

So much for comfort. I know there's no explaining what I'm going to say next, but now that I've stepped to the edge, I might as well jump off.

"He did finish it. In a way. He wrote his best work . . . posthumously."

Rosso's stride stalls in mid-step, then resumes.

"He's not gone," I hear myself say, but the words are unpremeditated; they appear on my tongue without passing through my brain. "His life didn't disappear when it ended. It will always exist."

Rosso stops. He turns. If he asks what I mean, I won't be able to answer. But he just looks at me, and I have a sense that somehow, he understands what I'm saying better than I do. He blinks a little moisture out of his eyes. He nods almost imperceptibly. Then he turns around, and we walk to the gate.

• • •

This was once Citi Stadium's lobby, lined with snack booths and sports memorabilia, pennants and jerseys hanging from the rafters, but all traces of the stadium's wild youth were scrubbed out long ago. The walls are now lined with ammunition crates, turret guns poke through the ticket slots in the bulletproof will-call windows, and the polite little automatic doors have been replaced with steel slabs that open for nearly no one. The stadium is all grown up.

The soldiers are assembled in front of the gate, waiting for Rosso, and they exchange confused glances when they see me trailing behind him. Rosso nods to Ted; Ted lifts the latch and heaves against the doors until they slide open on their tracks with a rumble and squeal. I follow Rosso through the opening, trying to ignore the soldiers' stares.

Outside, there is no shelter from the heat. The sun is on its way down but even its indirect rays are brutal, and the air rises from the asphalt in oily ripples. The soldiers file out behind us, sweating in their makeshift uniforms of not-quite-matching gray jackets and work pants. Kenerly's wearing a handful of Army medals that he's too young to have earned, and I wonder if they're his father's. I wonder if he developed his physique to compensate for his acne scars. I wonder what he'd think of me if I weren't the anomaly that I am.

"Sir," he says to Rosso, "may I ask why he's here?"

Rosso shades his eyes and peers into the distant streets. "Who are you referring to?"

Kenerly jerks his chin toward me.

"This isn't a stealth op, Major; non-verbals aren't necessary. I believe you're looking for a letter. Oscar? Papa? Quebec . . . ?"

Kenerly's jaw flexes. "May I ask why *R* is here, sir."

I expect Rosso to brush him off with another vague "I have a feeling," but instead, without taking his eyes off the city, he says, "R is here because he's a refugee from a world we don't understand, and I want his opinion of our guests."

"What would a zombie know about the Axiom Group, sir?"

Rosso finally turns around, and there's a tightly controlled anger in his face. "Axiom was wiped out in the Borough Conflicts and their headquarters and all their executives were buried in the Eight Six. John and I went back and confirmed it ourselves, and there's a photo in my office of us standing by the lake where their little kingdom used to be."

As he speaks, I feel a queasy sensation in my gut. An infrasound hum rolling up from the basement, rumbling through cracks in the plaster that's slathered over my mind, that suspiciously door-shaped blankness.

"Axiom is dead," Rosso says. "It's been dead for nearly a decade. And when dead things start moving again, I get superstitious. So indulge me."

He gives me a look as if to confirm I'm keeping up with him, and it pulls me back. I blink a few times and give him a nod, though I'm not sure what it signifies. Am I agreeing to something? I wish I could read the contracts I sign.

"Here they come," one of the guards says, and I am suddenly not the center of attention anymore. Main Street cuts a long, straight line through the center of Post, all the way to the grassy hills outside the city, and there, near the road's vanishing point, a dark shape is growing larger.

"Where are they coming from?" Kenerly wonders aloud. "Goldman's the other way."

We watch the shape emerge from the orange haze of the setting sun, slowly resolving into a recognizable form. A single, nondescript SUV, beige paint, no markings. The kind of anonymous vehicle suitable for a low-end limo service. The soldiers hold their rifles casually, posed in nonaggressive stances, but I see their fingers flexing on the grips. What are they to make of an envoy like this?

The SUV rolls up to the gate and parks neatly within the lines of a parking spot, one of hundreds in the mostly empty lot. The front doors open. The representatives of the so-called Axiom Group, its so-called "pitchmen," emerge from the vehicle.

I feel the infrasound burbling under my stomach as they approach. The door that isn't a door rattles faintly.

The pitchmen have a uniform. They wear black slacks. Gray shirts. Silk ties in blue, yellow, black. They wear wide grins around porcelain-white teeth.

"Hello!" the one in the blue tie says in a rich, authoritative baritone. "Thanks for taking the time to meet with us."

"Absolutely . . . ," Rosso replies, sounding far from absolute.

"We represent the Goldman Dome branch of the Axiom Group," the one in the yellow tie says, and apparently their organization doesn't care for gender-neutral titles because this pitchman is a pitchwoman. Her brown hair is tied into a neat ponytail, and her makeup is the heaviest I've ever seen on a post-apocalyptic female: bright red lipstick and a thick coat of foundation that gives her skin the matte dullness of a rubber glove. "The Axiom Group offers tried-and-true solutions to new problems." Her tone is so genial it seems about to overflow into laughter. "May we come inside and discuss what Axiom can do for your enclave?"

"It was my understanding that Axiom collapsed eight years ago," Rosso says, keeping his voice and expression flat. "Their forces were wiped out in the Borough Conflicts and what was left of them was buried in the Eight Six quake."

"It's true, that was an unprofitable year," Blue Tie says with a note of somber reflection. "We suffered severe losses and did come close to closure."

"Fortunately," Yellow Tie chirps, "Axiom's foundations are deep and unshakable. After a brief hiatus and minor restructure, we are back in business and better than ever. May we come inside and discuss our services?"

"What sort of services are we discussing?" Rosso says.

"As you know, Goldman Dome was in the process of a merger with Citi Stadium when Axiom assumed management. We would like to continue that process."

Rosso and Kenerly exchange a glance. I don't know what they were expecting from this encounter, but I doubt it was anything this . . . cheery.

"May we come inside to discuss our services?" Yellow Tie repeats.

Rosso looks at me, but all I can offer is an uneasy stare. "We're always open to discussion," he says.

"Wonderful," Yellow Tie says.

The rear doors of the SUV open, and two more men emerge.

"And who are they?" Rosso says, stiffening.

"Our assistants," Blue Tie says, as if surprised by the question. "They will assist with the merger process."

They are pale, doughy little men in white short-sleeve shirts and black slacks. They could be employees of an office supply store. One carries a thick notebook, the other a small metal briefcase, which he hands to Black Tie.

Kenerly takes a step forward. "What's in the case?"

Black Tie gazes impassively at Kenerly. He is the tallest of the group and stands behind the others like a looming bodyguard, his eyes oddly still, vacant. He pops the latches and holds the case out to Yellow Tie, who lifts the lid and displays its contents like a game-show prize: a stack of documents tucked into a manila folder.

"Our presentation," she says, blessing Kenerly with a patient smile. "Informational pamphlets, merger guidelines and agreements, et cetera."

"We know how hard it is to trust any outside group in today's world," Blue Tie says.

"We believe in complete transparency," Yellow Tie says.

Black Tie says nothing.

I can see Rosso's jaw working as reason and instinct fight for dominance. There are disquieting shapes swimming in the depths, but the surface is peaceful: five unarmed ambassadors extending an offer of alliance. If there is a threat, it's hidden somewhere behind those bright and earnest eyes.

"It's very hot," Yellow Tie says, miming the act of wiping her perfectly dry forehead. "May we come inside and discuss our services?"

Rosso's eyes move from face to smiling face, searching for options, finding none. "By all means," he says, and nods to Kenerly. "Let's discuss."

The soldiers form a circle around our visitors, hands tight on their rifles, and we step through the steel doors.

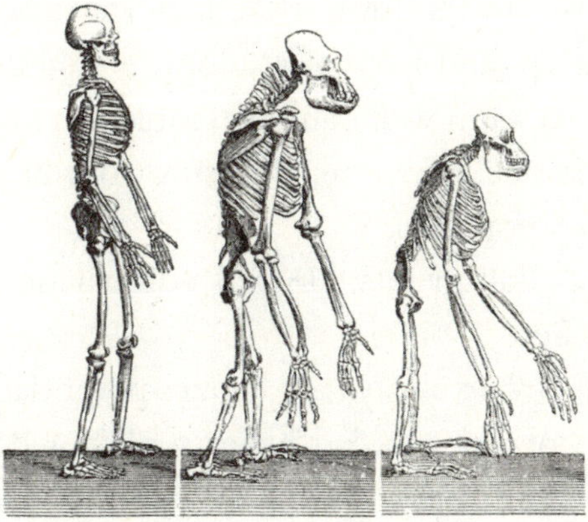

BALT IS WAITING for us inside. Ostensibly just chatting with Ted, he is sitting close enough to the gate to have overheard everything. He stands up, planting himself in a chest-out stance as he sizes up Axiom's representatives.

"Hello!" Blue Tie calls to him with a wave. In the lobby's harsh fluorescent lights, I notice that Blue Tie and Black Tie are also wearing makeup, though it's subtler than Yellow's. Just a light coat of foundation and a dusting of anti-shine, protection from the unforgiving lens of some imaginary TV camera. "We represent the Goldman Dome branch of the Axiom Group," Blue Tie says. "We're here to complete the merger."

"Captain Balt," he says warily, and offers a palm. "Representing Twenty-One Cock Street and the surrounding block."

"He's not a captain," Rosso sighs. "And it's not Cock Street."

Blue Tie doesn't exactly reject the handshake, but he evades it, exchanging it for solid eye contact and a firm nod. "Relying on elected representatives in such desperate times may be a risky indulgence," he says through a friendly grin.

"But we look forward to exploring many variations of civil government with you in the future," Yellow Tie says. She scans Balt from the boots up, and her voice adopts a slightly higher, more girlish pitch. "You seem well-equipped for leadership." Her smile is not quite professional anymore. "I'm sure your people are already utilizing your full potential?"

"Not exactly," Balt grunts. He looks off-balance, unsure where to direct his bluster.

"The Axiom Group always recognizes potential," she says, and the seriousness of her words clashes with her coquettish tone. "In these uncertain times, we understand the value of personal conviction. If your enclave does choose to cooperate with us, rest assured we can find a place for a man like you to shine." Her lips are so red they seem to throb. "I look forward to seeing your capabilities."

She returns her attention to Rosso, and whatever she just extended to Balt coils back into her. Her voice resumes its pristine professionalism. "Would it be all right with you if the captain gave our assistants a brief tour while we discuss the merger?"

"A tour," Rosso repeats.

"We'd like to make a cursory assessment of your enclave's assets so that we can better define the terms of our merger. Would that be all right with you?"

Rosso looks at the two assistants. He looks at Yellow Tie. "No. I don't think it would."

Her eyebrows rise. "I don't understand."

It's the first thing she's said that I believe. She is reading from a flowchart and it lacks a branch for refusal.

"With all due respect," Rosso says in a carefully neutral tone, "we're not in the habit of giving 'tours' to agents of foreign militia groups. You haven't even given us your names."

Yellow Tie stabilizes her fluctuating smile. "If you're concerned that we're here to learn your weaknesses, let me assure you there is nothing so complex at play. Your enclave is a sports arena. There are no weaknesses because there are no strengths. You're simply people in a box." She grins warmly.

"The Axiom Group has no interest in invasions," Blue Tie says. "Invasions waste resources and create dangerous tensions within the conglomerate. We prefer to be embraced willingly."

Rosso's face is stony. "The Axiom I remember was not so cautious in its expansion. I seem to recall it eating up half of New York and proclaiming itself the new US government before God and a dozen armies decided otherwise."

"Mistakes were made," Blue Tie says with the same grave nod he offered the first time Rosso brought up their history. "Our organization was passionate, and this led to immoderation. But much has changed. We have developed sustainable strategies for effective interaction with a diverse public."

"We are here to prove our value to you," Yellow Tie says with doe-eyed sincerity. "We are here to help."

Black Tie says nothing.

Rosso looks at me again, and again I have nothing to offer but my vague, inarticulate apprehension. The truth is, Yellow Tie is right. There are no secrets here for spies to steal. No access codes or defense strategies. Just twenty thousand scared and hungry people packed into houses made of trash. But Rosso has to draw a line somewhere.

"Your assistants are welcome to stay and assist with our negotiations," he says, forcing a thin smile. "But I'm afraid guided tours are unavailable at this time."

The pitchmen look at Rosso. The fluorescent lights buzz like beehives. Yellow Tie widens her grin to show teeth. "I'm glad we were able to reach an effective compromise." Her voice reveals no trace of irritation. "May we begin our presentation?"

Rosso indicates a nearby eatery table. "Have a seat."

Blue Tie regards the table, then the sunny passageway to the stadium's interior. "We would prefer a more secure location."

Rosso spreads his hands. "I'm afraid this is as secure as it gets around here. As you so rightly pointed out, we're just people in a box."

"Surely you have a space in which to discuss operations away from the ears of citizens."

"Our former leader built a space like that. We don't use it anymore. We've stopped hiding operations from the people they'll affect."

Blue Tie blinks a few times, still maintaining his grin. "That's not the way things are done."

"You said you believe in complete transparency."

"We apologize for our poor choice of words," Yellow Tie says. "We meant translucency. We believe in complete translucency."

"With all due respect—" He stops. "I'm sorry, I still haven't gotten your names."

"We're representatives of the Goldman Dome branch of the Axiom Group," Yellow Tie says. "We appreciate your patience as we determine how to meet your needs."

"Are you not *hearing* me?" Rosso snaps, his eyes beginning to spark. "I'm asking what your *name*—"

"I'm afraid your attitude may be negatively affecting the outcome of this meeting," Blue Tie interjects with a sudden spike in volume, and the corners of his grin fall.

Rosso closes his mouth. The pitchmen's warm river of pleasantries makes it easy to forget the helicopters, the truck convoys, and the phrase "under new management." But with that small shift in Blue Tie's demeanor, everyone suddenly recalls the shape of the situation.

"Due to the sensitive nature of the materials," Yellow Tie says in a gentle tone of deep apology, "we are unable to deliver our presentation in a public setting at this time. If you can take us to a private, restricted location"—her smile returns like the sun breaking through clouds—"we would be delighted to share our development plans for your enclave and the entire Cascadia region."

Rosso glances at Kenerly. Kenerly's face glistens with sweat and his fingers are tight on his rifle, but it's just three lunatics in colorful ties. Whatever the real threat might be, it's waiting in the shadows behind them.

Kenerly nods.

"We'll take you to our command office," Rosso says, then hesitates. "But just you three. Your 'assistants' wait outside."

"Our assistants wait outside," Yellow Tie agrees, a little too readily.

The assistants turn and exit through the gate, unfazed by their abrupt dismissal. Balt watches them go and frowns, glances at Yellow Tie, then at Rosso. "I'll go keep an eye on them," he says with the exaggerated volume of a bad stage actor as he follows the men outside.

But Rosso isn't listening to Balt. He is staring at the pitchmen with a grim intensity, as if playing out unpleasant scenarios in his head. Without another word, he walks toward the nearest passageway and the pitchmen follow close on his heels. The gloom of the tunnel gives way to daylight, but although the sky is a dim purple and the air has cooled, I feel a dampness in my palms.

I have finally learned to sweat.

• • •

I trail behind with the soldiers, watching the pitchmen's feet grind into the sticky asphalt, heavy black boots incongruous with their business attire. Ahead, Rosso and Kenerly walk in grim silence, leading these strange intruders into the heart of the stadium, and though they're unarmed, it has the feel of a march at gunpoint to a secluded spot in the woods. *Pick up that shovel. Start digging.*

Yet what I feel isn't fear. It's loss. Nostalgia for something I can't quite name. My mind drifts out of this fraught negotiation and into the streets and buildings around me. I hate this city. I wish we didn't need it. But it's filled with people I love and covered in their fingerprints. I think of Julie's old bedroom, the multicolored walls and the paintings, her own raw splashes of emotion hanging alongside Picasso and Dalí's mastery of form. I think of Nora in her foster home, older than some of the parents but refusing to take an apartment of her own, staying behind to mother three floors of frightened orphans whose faces she looks into like mirrors. I think of Rosso's house, Ella and the younger women talking in the kitchen while Lawrence sits by the fire and reads the brittle pages of some ancient text, pulling more knowledge into his already vast inner library.

I think of all this, and I imagine it razed. Tank treads grinding over paintings and books. Children fleeing through bent steel and smoldering plywood. And me standing in the center of town, screaming everyone's names through clouds of ashes.

An obsolete reflex twitches in my hand; I reach into my pocket for a phone that isn't there and wouldn't work if it were. Satellites drift dead in space. Earth's atmosphere is silent, wrapped in a fog of interference so thick even carrier pigeons get lost in it. With most of the old landlines long since cut, humanity is back to the Bronze Age: isolated tribes peering into a world of shadows.

But I need to talk to Julie. I need to hear her voice and know that she's still real, not just the pleasant prelude to a nightmare.

"Can I borrow your walkie?" I whisper to the soldier next to me.

He looks startled. "Why?"

"I need . . . to call my girlfriend."

He hesitates, processing this absurdity, then hands me his walkie. These old-fashioned devices have become a precious commodity, and Julie usually carries the one we share between us. I've rarely had anything urgent to communicate as I pass my days with housework and the vegetable garden, forcing conversations with our taciturn neighbors, taking swings at an invisible enemy and just waiting for something to happen. Well . . . something is happening.

I dial in Julie's frequency and press the talk button. I wince at the squeal of static, but I hold the device close to my face and murmur, "Julie?"

I hear bursts of noise that have the rhythm of words, but their sibilance and inflection are scrambled, draining them of meaning.

"Can you hear me?"

More noise. Another jamming surge. Even a few blocks apart, we are mumbling to each other from distant planets.

I hand the walkie back to the soldier and march on with a deepened sense of doom.

"Your enclave's growth is impressive," Yellow Tie tells Rosso, her eyes inventorying each building. "It will be a valued member of the Axiom family should you decide to join us."

"May I ask," Rosso asks, "just hypothetically, what our relationship with Goldman Dome would be if we decided *not* to join?"

Blue Tie puts on his grave face. "We live in dangerous times. The world is full of rapists, serial killers, pedophiles, terrorists, and inhuman monsters who want to eat your family."

"The Axiom Group offers safety from everything," Yellow Tie says.

Black Tie says nothing.

Rosso looks into their deeply sincere eyes. A bleak chuckle escapes him. "Well all right then. Thank you for clarifying."

I see the Armory door approaching at the end of Gun Street. Most of the doors inside the stadium are flimsy sheets of plywood that open with a rough shove. This one is nearly as severe as the main gate, a slab of steel wide enough for a Humvee to drive through but dwarfed by the expanse of concrete around it. It is the only interior door with a lock.

Rosso inserts his key. Kenerly steps forward to help him open the door, but Rosso waves him off and heaves it open easily. I find some small comfort in this. His paunch is deceptive. His glasses are a disguise. He's fought in more wars than most men can name, and under his wrinkled skin is a steel core. Perhaps he has a plan.

The pitchmen follow him into the concrete corridors of the inner wall. This passage was probably intended for getting emergency vehicles onto the playing field back when people injured each other for recreation. Now it accommodates emergency vehicles of a different sort. Row upon row of trucks fill the echoing garage of the Armory, some military and some militarized: camouflaged Army Humvees parked alongside Hummer H3s with power sunroofs and heated seats. Vehicles once favored by athletes—men the world regarded as warriors—are now driven into battle by terrified teenagers preparing to die. These days, there is more than enough war to quench humanity's thirst. We no longer have to simulate it.

Beyond the garage is a large open chamber with rows of tall shelves accessible only by forklift. It resembles a construction supply warehouse, except the equipment on its shelves is for the opposite of construction. I have never been in the Armory before, and for a moment, I catch myself lost in lizard-brain gun lust. Racks of weaponry from pistols to shotguns to rocket launchers. Crates of grenades. Land mines. And an entire corner devoted to zombie-slaying gear: chainsaws for Fleshies, steel clubs for Boneys, and police riot armor for protection from both. The dried black slime caked onto these items brings back memories that quickly cool my arousal, but I remain impressed. I had no idea the stadium was this well equipped. It occurs to me that Rosso may have had a good reason for agreeing to a meeting here. Perhaps he wanted Axiom's representatives to see that, like Rosso himself, this enclave is not as defenseless as it looks.

"Well," he says, spreading his hands, "here we are. Concrete walls. One entrance. Secure enough for you?"

"Yes," Yellow Tie says, but she makes no move toward the conference table in the corner. All three pitchmen stand in the center of the room letting their eyes roam the racks and shelves. Blue Tie approaches an open crate and runs his finger along the American flag stamped onto the rockets. "This is US Army ordnance, which makes it at least thirteen years old. It is unstable and unsafe."

Rosso drops the lid back onto the crate and locks it. "Our bombs may be a little stale, but they get the job done. We've dealt with more than a few invaders in my time here, and most are surprised by how effective an Army-trained security force can be. Ask the UT-AZ Elders, if you can still find any."

"We recommend munitions by Gray River National," Blue Tie continues as if he never paused, giving no sign that he registered Rosso's not-so-veiled threat. "They were manufactured as recently as seven years ago and were designed to survive extended storage. As a member of the Axiom Group, you'll have full access to our supply network."

Rosso's face grows stiffer. "Are we here to discuss the shelf life of grenades? Or can you illuminate for us why the hell you've come here from wherever the hell you came from?"

Yellow Tie smiles. "Of course. I'll be happy to help you with that."

As if hearing some silent cue, Black Tie pops open his briefcase and holds it out to her. She takes the folders, and though the case is now empty, Black Tie doesn't close it. He moves away from the group and sets it on the conference table, then remains standing next to it. I have not seen him make eye contact with anyone since getting out of his SUV. Not blind, but . . . drugged? Sleepwalking?

Blue Tie locks his eyes on each soldier, then on me. It's the first time he's looked directly at me, and something in his gaze—the improbably intense blue of his irises, the faint smile that never leaves his face even when he's delivering grim pronouncements—makes me feel worms wriggling in my spine.

"I'm afraid we do need to ask all but executive personnel to leave at this time," he says, still looking at me.

"Now wait a damn minute," Kenerly says.

"Our presentation contains sensitive materials that are only appropriate for upper management," Yellow Tie says.

Rosso takes a small step toward her. "Listen, Ms. Representative of the Goldman Dome Branch of the Axiom Group. I'm already breaking policy for you by holding this meeting in secret. I see no reason why my officers and advisors shouldn't hear whatever you have to say."

Blue Tie leans in close, lowering his already deep voice into a strangely intimate rumble that he has not used until now. "Our ideas require a certain broadness of perspective to be appreciated. We find that people who are not in positions of power tend to lack this perspective. They tend to fixate on details they find distasteful instead of considering the value of the proposal as a whole."

"Once you have agreed to our proposal," Yellow Tie says, "you are welcome to share the information with your people in a form that they can appreciate."

"But I'm afraid at this time," Blue Tie concludes, "we do need to ask all but executive personnel to leave."

The Armory is silent. The muffled sounds of Citi's citizenry ooze through the walls like the murmurs of ghosts. Watching Rosso's face, his jaw muscles flexing behind his skin, I feel my cautious confidence sloughing away. He may be stronger than he looks, he may be wiser than Grigio was, more open-minded, open-hearted, and open-eyed, but he has lost control of this situation, if it was ever possible to have it.

"Major Kenerly," he says without breaking away from Blue Tie's stare, "you and your team can wait outside."

"Sir, this is—"

"If our guests prefer to do business in secret, like criminals, we can indulge them for a moment."

"But sir . . ."

Rosso looks at Kenerly, his eyes softening. "We pick our battles, Evan. We pick no battles, if possible."

Kenerly hesitates, then salutes and turns on his heel. The soldiers begin to file out but I find myself unable to move. A thought bounces around my skull, so certain and insistent, I'm not sure it's mine.

Don't go. Don't leave him here.

But I have to.

Don't do it.

The whisper is faintly familiar, but my head has hosted many different voices, and I'm no good with names.

What am I supposed to do?

Don't leave him.

"R," Rosso says. "You can go."

"No," I say.

"Go, R."

"You can't trust them."

"They're not asking for trust," Rosso says, "they're asking for cooperation. And I'll decide if we can cooperate once I've heard their pitch."

Three grins shower me with affability.

Kenerly grabs me by my shoulder, but I don't budge.

"It's just a meeting," he says, addressing me directly for the first time I can recall. "Classified meetings used to be standard procedure." He seems to be trying to convince himself as much as me. "Move."

He shoves me toward the exit and I start to walk, falling in line with the rest of the men. In the mirror of a Range Rover I see Rosso turn to face the pitchmen. I see Yellow Tie opening her folder. I hear the noxious warmth of her voice fading behind me. I walk past weapons and trucks and through the long, dark corridor, and the moon looks small when I emerge.

Kenerly and his men take posts outside the Armory door, but I can't wait here with these stoic pillars of protocol while my thoughts snarl and bark at each other. I lumber out into the empty streets. The city is asleep. I am alone under the buzzing lamps.

I need a drink.

I PASS ROSSO'S APARTMENT on my way to the Orchard. I can hear Julie's and Nora's voices through the window, the Living rhythms that once stirred me like music. I still marvel at how effortlessly they converse, how smoothly they transition between speakers with nearly no break in tempo, much less the long, awkward pauses I'm used to, but it no longer enraptures me like it did. I don't stop to listen, I don't close my eyes and sway. My mind is full of hornets.

Although I've only been to the Orchard once, the route through the plywood labyrinth unfolds for me like I'm a regular, and I find myself standing in front of the pub's thick oak door with little memory of how I got here. The yellow tree painted on it has flaked a little since I saw it last. The aluminum siding still bears two head-sized dents. A satisfied smile starts to creep onto my face, but I halt it. Why did I make those dents? What was I trying to achieve by cracking Balt's head? Was I bringing justice to a man who preys on young girls, or was it just a brain-stem reaction to someone insulting my mate? The kind of primitive reflex that drives the lives of people exactly like Balt?

While I stand there staring at the door, it swings open, smacking me between the eyes. I nearly tumble off the mezzanine.

"Oh hey, sorry!" says the soldier who opened it, reaching out to steady me. "I didn't see—" He recognizes me. He pulls his hand away like I'm a hot stove, straightens up, and leaves without further comment.

I lean against the railing, rubbing my forehead. What do I expect to happen for me in a pub? Am I going to strike up a conversation with the fellows at the bar, talk about sports and cars, wave a beer in the air and lead everyone in rousing anthems of Us vs. Them? No. My ambitions are nothing so grand. I'm just here to make my brain stop working.

Grigio's prohibition is over, so the noise levels are now appropriately high, the atmosphere adequately raucous, and the amber nectar in the shot glasses is finally not apple juice. The pub is once again what it was built to be: a place for people to lower their drawbridges, to let others in and themselves out, to remember that life is more than the dimly lit tragedy of the daily grind. A warm, woozy light at the end of the day's tunnel.

This will, of course, not be my experience here. I slip through the crowd and find a stool at the far end of the bar, and I can feel a dozen eyes on my back. For a variety of reasons, some good, most bad, I am famous. I am the first of the Dead to challenge the plague, the one who triggered a change that's still spreading. I am the disease that cured itself. And I am the monster that kidnapped General Grigio's daughter and brainwashed her into falling in love with it. I am the demon that lured legions of skeletons to the stadium and caused the deaths of hundreds of soldiers, and that may have personally infected General Grigio and thrown his converting corpse off the stadium roof. I am the reason there are zombies roaming their streets and eyeing their children. I am the reason nothing makes sense.

I avoid eye contact with everyone but the bartender. When he finally nods to me, I pull a bill from the small stack that Rosso gave me to help me "find my footing" and I set it on the bar.

He looks at me uneasily. "Uh . . . what can I get you?"

Another choice. Another opportunity to tell the world what kind of man I am. What do I wear? What kind of music do I listen to? What is my favorite drink?

I shrug and mumble, "Alcohol."

He takes the hundred-dollar bill, which amounts to little more than a drink ticket in the stadium's sad little private economy, and pours me a shot of whiskey. I dump it down my numb throat and stare at the bar top. The thick pine slab is completely covered in initials, doodles, and crass little dialogues. I peruse them like book spines, trying to imagine the stories behind the titles.

JG+NG ~~friends~~ 4 LIFE
LEZBOS

BIG DICK TIM fucks ~~little girls~~
WHORES

P loves J
always

BOOZE IS BACK!!!

NO Z IN OUR STREETS

CORPSES + Corpsefuckers
GTFO!

where are we going?
what are we doing?

LOOK OUT!
THERES A BONEY
INSIDE YOU!!

It goes on and on, all down the bar. Love, hate, jokes, and the simple urge to be noticed, scrawled onto the wood year after year.

The bulk of the inscriptions are on the top of the slab, bumping and overlapping like chatter at a party, but leaning down, I notice a few on the underside, as if never meant to be seen. Most are standard crush confessions: Jerry loves Jenny, Jenny loves Joey, Joey loves Jerry. But one entry catches my eye. It appears to have been carved and then promptly scratched out. I can just barely piece the letters together.

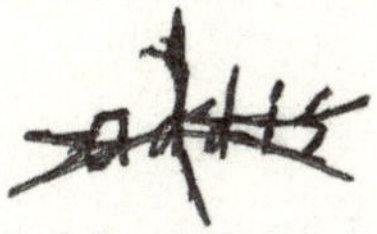

I wince. Cold needles in my chest. I don't know why this word stings; I pull my eyes away from it. They fall immediately on another line deep in the corner, scratched so faintly I almost miss it in the dim light.

goodbye mom

I close my eyes, hoping for saltwater to ease their sudden burn. When I open them again, the bartender is looking at me. I slide him another hundred.

• • •

"R?"

My name hits me like a splash of cold water and I peel my face off the bar. The room spins for a moment before I can anchor it down and bring Julie into focus.

"What are you *doing* here?" she says. Her eyes are bright blue beacons in the blur of the bar, wide and worried.

"Drinking." I don't know how many times I've emptied the glass in front of me; it could've been just twice, but my body is still defining its limits and I do believe I'm drunk.

"What the hell, R, what happened with the meeting? I still haven't heard from Rosy, why didn't you come find me?"

I can see that she's upset. I can see that it's strange, me coming here to drink alone in the middle of a crisis. I can see that she is beautiful, her strawberry lips and blueberry eyes, the peach fuzz on her cheeks. I can see the television behind her. The disorienting montage of unrelated images. A few plays of football, a few airbrushed models, a juicy tenderloin, a cute baby, a syrupy quote from a pop philosopher with a stock-footage sunrise behind it.

"R!"

The basement door that insists it's not there. The coat of white plaster and all the cracks creeping through it. *When is a door not a door? When it's ajar! When it's aflame! When it's asunder!* A polite laugh track from a classic sitcom whose cast died decades ago; fat, stupid men with gorgeous wives.

Julie sits down next to me. Which trope are we? The gun-toting teenage orphan and her hapless amnesiac boyfriend? Where is the box we can climb into? It's cold out here.

She touches my arm. "R. Are you okay? What happened?"

"I left him with them," I hear myself saying. "They're not what they say. They want to eat us and I left him with them."

"They want to eat us? What are you talking about?"

"I know them," I mumble. "I know them, I know them."

No one in the Orchard is watching me anymore. At some point after the initial shock of my entrance, they all drifted back to their conversations, or to their blank study of the televisions flashing that nerve-shredding culture collage from every spare nook in the room. A quote over a shot of hand-shaking businessmen, read aloud for any illiterates in the room: *Don't ask what's in it for you. Ask what you're in it for.*

A shirtless rock climber. Some fluffy clouds. A Corvette.

I reach for my glass and try to coax a final drop onto my tongue.

Julie snatches it out of my hand and slides it down the bar. "R, stop it! I need you to focus. Slow down and tell me what's happening. Should I alert Security?"

"They know. Evan Kenerly was there. They made us all leave. They know we can't say no. They know we're scared." My hands tremble on the bar. I pull out my last hundred and shove it at the bartender. "Another."

Julie grabs the bill and stuffs it in her pocket.

"I need another!" My voice . . . I've never heard it so loud. It trembles in time with my hands. The TVs are screaming at me. A baseball highlight reel cuts to the middle of an R&B chorus, a wailing, showboating singer doing vocal runs. "They're liars, they're going to eat everything we built, they're—"

Julie takes my face in her hands and kisses me. My lips don't move, but she puts passion into it, kissing like she's kissing her lover instead of the stiff, open-eyed face of a lunatic. The noise around me softens. The noise inside me softens. The room stops spinning and centers around the lovely face pressed hard against mine, our brains as close to touching as they can ever get.

She pulls back and locks her eyes on me, still holding my face.

"Focus on my eyes, okay?" she whispers. "Just look at my eyes and take a few breaths."

I look at her eyes. They are huge and round and the bar's lights reflect in their blue centers like distant stars. I take a breath.

"Breathing is good," she says. "It's soothing. I know it's new to you, but try to remember. Breathe and think about breathing."

My focus narrows until everything behind her is a blur. I think about breathing. My lungs are still sore from years of disuse, but they're slowly warming up and resuming their duties, extracting pure, sweet O_2 and sending it to my brain to power Living thoughts. Whatever dark fuel my brain once used was better suited to commands and urges than the lovely complexity of a human personality, human hopes and dreams.

I have these, I tell myself as I float in the muteness of space, holding on to Julie like a tether. *I am allowed these. No one can take them.*

"Good," she says. "Keep breathing. We're going to be okay. Whatever this is, we can handle it. We don't have anything we can't live without."

"Can we leave?" I say during a slow exhalation. "Do we need this city?"

"Where would we go?"

"Far away. A cabin in the hills. Just us."

"R," she says, and the tone in that one syllable is enough to reveal the cowardice of my question. "We don't need the city, but we need the people. And they need us."

"Why?"

"We're trying to build something, remember? You're the one who told me we can't run away."

My face sags into her grip. "But I'm tired."

"You're not tired," she says with a wry smile. "You're just drunk."

She releases my face and I drift. My eyes roam the bar, tracing the faces of the patrons as they stare up at the five TVs, their skin tinted gray by the glow of the screens.

"R?" Julie says, trying to pull me back to earth. "Can you tell me what happened at the meeting?"

A late-era rap song: boasts about wealth and luxury delivered with a grim wink over a distant, desolate beat that may have been played on trash cans.

"Rosy's walkie is off. Should we check on him? It's been two hours."

A staticky fuzz begins to creep into the audio from the TVs, drowning out the rapper's mournful fantasies.

"Where was the meeting? At the community center?"

I twist my neck to look at the nearest screen. The audio has been completely replaced by static and now the image begins to stutter—the rapper opens a briefcase; it's full of money; he sets it on fire and warms his hands—the image goes black.

A howl of protest rises from everyone in the room. Someone throws a tumbler at the TV, misses, hits the liquor shelf. Whiskey and glass sprinkles the bar. But the screen remains black for only a few seconds. It flickers, there's a loud *pop*, and a new image appears.

A grainy security camera feed, a fish-eye lens gazing down at a man in a white shirt tinkering with a large instrument panel. Another man in a white shirt is faintly visible in the shadows, and 'Captain' Timothy Balt stands between them, looking uncertain for the first time since I've known him.

"What is this place?" he says, glancing into the shadows around them. *"How'd you know this was down here?"*

The man at the panel notices something in front of him and his eyes dart up to the camera, the fish-eye lens warping his face into a bulbous horror. He pulls a cable out of a nearby jack and the image goes black again.

"What the hell's going on . . . ?" Julie says.

A harsh squeal erupts from all the TVs, and while everyone covers their ears, something flashes on the screen. It's there for barely a single frame, too brief for me to fully grasp, but my brain rings like a gong. I see the door again, its rusty metal corners poking out behind crumbling plaster. I hear the drone behind the door, the churning throb of sub-audible bass rumbling up from the basement, rattling the door in its frame, sending chips of plaster flying off like popcorn.

My eyes squeeze shut. My mind is dark and the image blinks in the shadows with maddening brevity, its contours just out of reach, teasing me. I feel my hand moving.

"R . . . ?"

I grab a martini glass and smash it against the bar. I grip the stem like a dagger.

"R! What the fuck!"

I hear the scrape of her stool as she jumps away from me. I'm frightening her. I was so sure I'd never frighten her again. Memories of airports and screams and smears of black blood fill my head as my hand moves.

Jagged concentric shapes. Angles swallowing angles. A grotesque mandala with nothing in its center.

I open my eyes.

I have carved a design—a logo—into the surface of the bar. Its deep lines cut through lovers' initials.

The door rattles.

"Atvist," my mouth says.

The door cracks open.

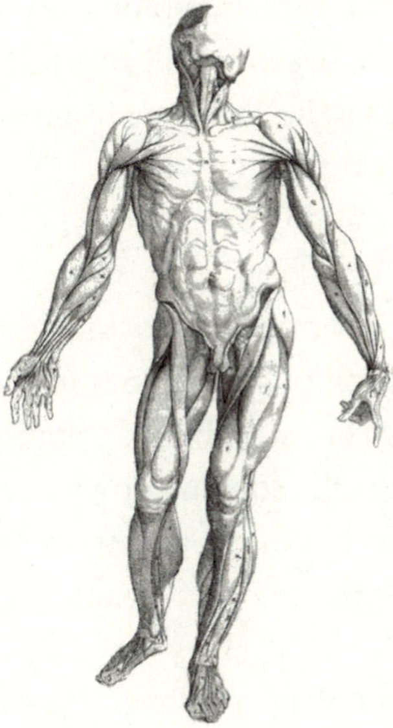

A *TALL BUILDING. A dim room. An old man. A grin.*

A briefcase. A plan. I hesitate. I accept.

I board a plane. I watch a screen. A nature show. A worm and a wasp. I watch. I recoil. I keep watching.

The worm burrows into the wasp. The worm seizes its brain. Tells it where to fly. Feeds on its guts. Builds a home out of its corpse. The worm is small, clever, twisted, mad. The worm wins. The worm knows no beauty, no pleasure, no purpose. The worm knows nothing but what it does. The worm wins and the worm feasts. Wasps, wolves, poets, presidents. The worm feasts.

"Trust me, kid." Brown teeth. Spotted gums. A bony hand on my shoulder. "I know my business."

• • •

"R!"

The sting of a slap. Frightened blue eyes searching for mine in the darkness. I slam the basement door shut and pull the Orchard back into view, and in all the shadowy fragments spinning through my mind, I see one clear imperative.

I shake Julie off me and I run.

"R, *stop!*"

I shove the heavy door open, knocking over two soldiers who topple back into the deck railing. Julie is in the doorway, calling to me, but I can't stop. I run, stumbling, gripping the cables to keep from falling off the catwalk, slipping down the staircase and caroming off the walls, finally bursting out into the street. I feel my badly lubricated joints creaking, my stiff ligaments protesting as I push them into a sprint.

The surprising weight of the briefcase. The cold metal in my hands. The decision I insisted I hadn't made.

I see the Armory door at the end of the street. Towers of metal and plywood loom over me like judges, but I'm so close. I can fix my mistake before anyone notices. I can—

A flash. A hammer of air.

I'm flying.

The moon glares down at me as I sail backward, arms spinning, a lazy summertime float down the river. *Is this still your preferred position?* the moon asks me. *On your back and half-asleep, drifting away from the fight?*

I hit the wall of an apartment and crash through the sheet metal into a child's bedroom. A girl jumps up in her bed and I see her face contort into a squeal of terror, but it's silent. I hear only the high ringing of a tuning fork. I free myself from the debris; I stumble back onto the street and into a silent nightmare.

Chunks of concrete rain from the sky, silently cratering the asphalt and punching holes through walls and roofs. Silent rockets streak out from a cloud of smoke and pinwheel madly through the stadium, blooming into silent fireballs that incinerate buildings and tear chunks out of the stadium wall. Support cables pop out of the concrete and rickety apartment towers sway. Silently, two of them fall, crashing into each other and splitting open in the middle, dumping streams of people out of their beds and onto the street. Those who survive the fall have just enough time to raise their hands in a futile defensive gesture before being buried under their own homes.

The darkness pulses red with countless fires. Crates of grenades go off in bursts of white flashes. I run past dead bodies that are beginning to twitch, but I leave it to someone else to decide their second fates. I can't stop. I am running toward a smoking hole where I abandoned someone who believes in me, and as my hearing returns, I notice that I am screaming.

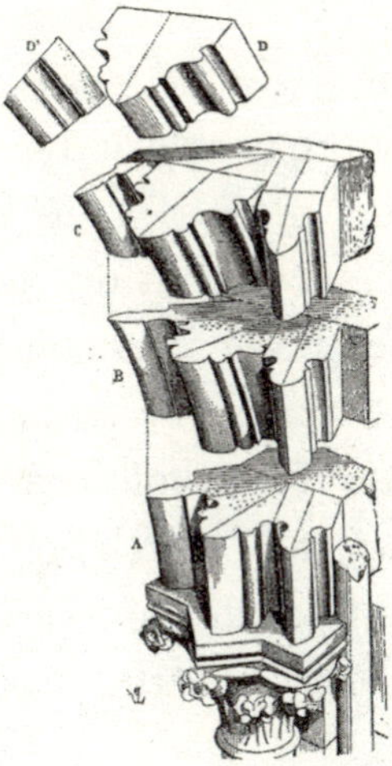

THE RAW EDGES of shattered concrete are still hot enough to burn my hands as I dig my way through the debris, but I feel the sensation more distantly than ever. I hear salvos of gunfire from somewhere in the wreckage, but this is not a battle, it's just ammunition going off, bullets firing themselves without waiting for the trigger, as if they know what they were made to do and are eager to get on with it.

I heave aside a slab of concrete and slip through the gap into what's left of the Armory. It's dark, but cut electrical wires light the cavern in blue flashes, along with the dim red glow of burning supply crates.

"Rosso!" I shout into the flickering darkness. "General Rosso!"

The path is littered with jagged concrete and spears of sheared rebar, but I start to run. I don't get more than a few paces before I trip on something soft. An electric pop from an overhead wire illuminates a body with most of its flesh blasted away, revealing a scorched, cracked skeleton, identifiable only by the shredded tie around its neck.

Black Tie says nothing.

I push further in, past the garage and into Grigio's beloved war room. In the sickly orange glow of a few burning tires, I find the other two pitchmen. Blue Tie grins up at me from the floor, his impossibly blue eyes attempting to establish trust with the ceiling while his mangled body slumps in a corner ten feet away. A steel beam runs through Yellow Tie's skull from temple to temple, pinning her head to the floor, and I search her final expression for any hint of comprehension, any realization of error or betrayal, but it remains locked in that blandly cheerful mask.

What are these people?

A ragged gasp from somewhere in the shadows. I force myself to move.

He's lying slumped against a pile of rubble. His chest isn't shaped right and his gray jumpsuit has turned dark purple. Perhaps he has spilled wine on himself. Overindulged at a tasting party, embraced life a little too hard. He'll have a headache in the morning but good stories to go with it. Julie and I will sit by his fireplace and listen, glancing at each other and smiling while Ella shakes her head in the kitchen. He is old but still vital, with plenty of days left to read his books and drink his wine and teach me how to be a person.

"I'm sorry," he whispers as I kneel beside him.

"For what?"

Why is there a tremor in my voice? He's just drunk.

"I wanted so badly . . . to see your life. You and Julie." He coughs, and a fine spray of wine speckles my shirt. "I wanted to be there."

Why do my eyes sting? Why is my vision getting blurry?

"But I'm excited, too." He stares up at the patches of night sky visible through holes in the ceiling. "I've wondered for so long what comes next."

Drunk people say the strangest things. I squint my eyes shut and warm liquid seeps out of them.

"Oh," he says, and his tone suddenly shifts. I open my eyes and find his wide with awe, his mouth slightly agape. "I can see it."

"Stop." I grip his shoulders. "Wait."

His eyes focus on me with a feverish intensity. "We're so close, R. Show them."

"I don't know what you're saying!"

His eyes drift to the ceiling again. His body begins to slacken. "It's beautiful," he says in a faint release of breath. "It's everything."

I watch his face for a while. I burn the image into my memory. I have never seen an expression like this. It says things that no one could ever articulate, no matter how vast their vocabulary or how limber their tongue. And in a moment, it will be gone.

I dig through the rubble. A grenade, a chainsaw—no. Something elegant. Respectful. If there is any respectful way to do this. The most important thing is that I do it soon. There can be no third life for this man's broken body, and I won't let him suffer the indignity of becoming like me.

I hear a gunshot. I assume it's another burning ammo crate and ignore it, but then I hear a small, frail sob, and I turn. Ella is kneeling in front of her husband, her hair singed and wild, the knees of her pants torn and bloody. A revolver dangles from her finger and falls to the floor.

Some soft, whispering instinct tells me to move toward her. As soon as I'm near enough, she sags against my chest and lets the dam break.

• • •

I hear Julie's voice as we approach the tunnel's exit. She's calling the names of all the people who matter to her. Nora's. Ella's. Rosso's. Mine. I wonder if any of us will be of any comfort to her. I help Ella over the last jagged heap of debris and we stumble out into the chaos of the streets. Security teams rush from house to house, trying to establish some kind of order, but Medical is the star of tonight's show. I catch a glimpse of Nora holding one end of a stretcher bearing a blood-smeared mess that looks like Kenerly. I catch her eyes for one second before she disappears around a corner, and the reeling shock in them tells me just how bad things are. But right now, the pain of hundreds of strangers barely even registers. I'm focused on the old woman crying on my arm and the young one running toward me with eyes full of dread.

"What happened?" Julie shouts. "What the hell happened, what is happening?"

She grabs my wrists and sucks in a breath to ask more unanswerable questions. I wrap my arms around her and pull her close. Through the crook of my elbow, she sees Ella sinking down onto an apartment stoop, she sees the tears running through the woman's laugh lines, she sees the smoking crater in the stadium wall. She understands.

"No," she says. "No."

"I'm sorry," I whisper into her hair.

"*No*!" she screams, and wriggles violently out of my arms. "This is *not* happening. It's *not* happening. *No*!"

She stands back from me and Ella, alone in the middle of the street, clenching her fists and grinding her teeth. She lost her mother long before I met her. Her father left slowly over many years, but the dirt on his grave has barely sprouted grass. And now this. Now Lawrence "Rosy" Rosso, her next-to-last fragment of family.

Grief. Rage. Both are reasonable responses to the winking cruelty of the universe.

I move toward her and try to embrace her again, but she is nowhere near ready to be consoled. She shoves me back so hard I almost fall over and runs past me toward the Armory.

"Julie, don't," Ella calls to her. "There's nothing in there that will help."

Julie stops at the edge of the rubble, staring into the dark hole and trembling, sucking in short, rapid breaths. These constrict into raspy wheezes and she fumbles in her pocket for her inhaler. She takes a shot but her breaths keep getting shorter. She clutches at her throat. "I can't—I can't—"

I rush to her side and try to lead her away from the wreckage, but she sags down onto the pavement, heaving hard against her bronchial tubes. I want to say something soothing, but what can I possibly say? My mouth is not accustomed to delivering comfort. The apparatus of my tongue and teeth has always been a weapon. How does one use it to heal?

In the silence of my uselessness, the medicine finally kicks in and her gasps begin to slow. She struggles to her feet and walks on rubbery legs to the stoop where Ella is sitting. She pulls in a deep breath, lets it out, then drops down next to Ella and buries her face in her hands, her small body shaking with quiet sobs.

I stay where I am, standing apart from them, waiting. I feel a cold sprinkle of rain and I look up. The sky is clear. The moon is bright. With the noise of twenty thousand people panicking, I didn't even notice the helicopters overhead, spraying water onto the flames that surge from apartment rooftops.

I see it now. The pieces click.

We're here to help.

High above, hovering like a book of divine wisdom, the Jumbotron blinks on. A handsome man in a yellow tie steps into view and sits in front of a microphone.

"Residents of Citi Stadium," he says in a gentle baritone. *"We invite you to feel calm. Careless storage of expired munitions has led to a terrible tragedy and loss of life from both enclaves, but as your new next-door neighbor, the Axiom Group is already working hard to minimize the damage."*

I notice men in unfamiliar uniforms—beige jackets over khaki pants—rushing through the streets with fire extinguishers and first aid kits.

"We will have the disaster contained momentarily, and in the days to come, we will work closely with your remaining leadership to help restore order. We invite you to feel calm, safe, and secure. Everything will be the way it was."

Julie peeks through her fingers at the gigantic face grinning down on the city. The screen shows a brief flash of the logo I carved into the bar, plays a stock animation of a football player chugging a Bud Light, then goes black.

"What is happening?" she whispers into her palms.

The rumble of an approaching truck cuts through the noise of the stadium's panic, which has in fact quieted noticeably following the Jumbotron's announcement. It seems that an invitation to feel calm from a stranger on a screen is all these people needed to feel calm. Do they even care who's in charge of their lives, or will any handsome face suffice? Any well-groomed head with a tie around its stump, any mouth that can lie with confidence?

Staring up at the helicopters, feeling the spray cool my flushed cheeks, I realize I'm still drunk. Or perhaps something even more debilitating. I have imbibed a terrible cocktail: whiskey, adrenaline, shock, and sorrow. I feel sick.

A beige Escalade pulls up next to us and six men in beige jackets emerge. It's a nauseating color, not a warm, sandy tan but the neutral green-gray-taupe of old office computers, cheap hotels, suburban strip malls, and municipal carpet. The men carry three empty body bags between them. They move toward the Armory entrance and suddenly Julie is on her feet.

"What are you doing?" she snaps, wiping her red eyes and darting over to block their path. "Who are you and what are you doing?"

"Here to collect the bodies," one of the men says without looking at her or stopping. He and the others move around her and begin to climb through the rubble, but she jumps in front of them again.

"I said who *are* you?"

The men slow their advance without quite stopping. "We're with Axiom. We're here to collect the bodies."

"That's my friend in there and I don't know you people," she says, glaring up at the much taller men. Her voice begins to tremble again. "You're not taking him. Go away."

"We have orders to collect all the bodies before they're handled by enclave residents. Please step aside." He pushes past her.

She grabs his jacket and yanks him backward and he falls, landing on jagged chunks of concrete.

"I said go away!" she shouts hoarsely, her eyes welling up again.

In my woozy perception, everything feels slow. I move toward Julie, but my feet are strapped with heavy weights. One of the men shoves her. She falls into the rubble. She gets up, wipes blood from a cut on her forehead, and lunges at him. Too short to reach his face, she punches him in the throat. He stumbles back, choking, and I hear Julie screaming.

"Get out of here! Get out!"

I'm almost there. The ground sucks at my feet like deep tar. I crawl up the rubble heap as four men converge on her. She takes a swing at the nearest one but he grabs her arm and twists her around, then kicks her hard between the shoulder blades. She flies clear of the mound and lands facedown on the asphalt.

I am full of dread because I know I'm going to kill this man. It's required by Newtonian law, a reaction to his action, impossible to prevent. I ascend the rubble heap and seize his head and smash his face into a concrete corner and he dies in a bubbling foam of blood. The next man who comes at me doesn't die but is certainly maimed when I throw him against a slab and hammer my fist into his shoulder joint, snapping the ligaments and effectively severing his arm. Thick limbs wrap around my throat and lift me off the ground, but my brain seems to have a course of action ready for every scenario; a well-aimed elbow breaks the man's ribs and hopefully punctures his lung, and his grip melts off me.

A very distant voice asks: *What am I doing? How am I doing it? Who is the man who acquired these skills and the reptilian coldness to use them?*

Finally, someone relieves me of my momentum. The butt of a gun cracks into the side of my head and the already slow world spins into a rippling sludge. I am aware of myself falling, but I feel nothing when my face hits the pavement next to Julie's. Our eyes meet, hers red and wet, mine simply open, staring. Where is the gold? Where is the impossible solar yellow that told us things were different, that we had changed and the world would change with us?

Dark spots begin to splatter across my vision. I try to speak to her: *Keep breathing. We're going to be okay*. But my lips won't obey. I try to say it with my eyes. I keep trying until my eyes roll up.

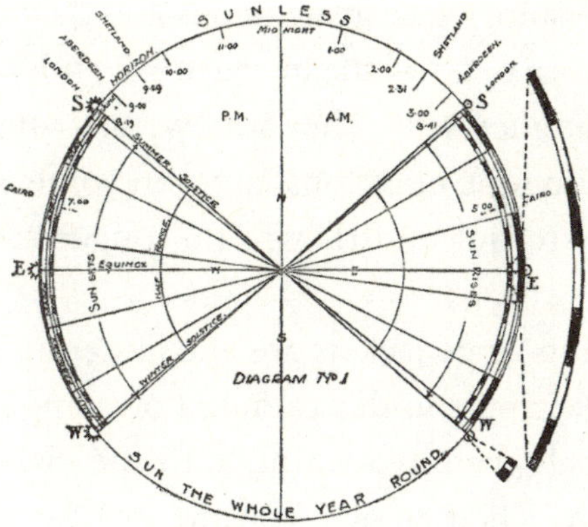

WE

We do not need to move. We are already everywhere. But omnipresence can be dull, so we indulge in locality. We condense ourself into points and roam the earth like those quaint old notions of spirits: ghosts, angels, and other things in white sheets.

We have little interest in the world itself, the actual matter and space. We are here for the story, for the landscape of consciousness overlying the dust and rock. In that landscape, sharp peaks are jutting up from the plains. There are quakes and floods and hurricanes, and rivers of magma press against the surface. That landscape is changing, and change demands our attention.

So we move. We drift through the upheaval of a city in crisis, remembering the scent of smoke, the pain of fire, the sorrow of loss.

Everywhere, men in beige jackets are herding people back into their homes, assuring them that they have it all under control and everything will return to normalcy, that cozy dream that's buried a thousand revolutions.

In their panic, most of the people do as they're told. They see confident men issuing clear instructions and they don't much care who those men are or what the instructions entail. They just want to keep their families safe. They just want to survive the night. There will be time for questions later, on some distant morning when the fires are out and they're no longer scared or hurt or hungry.

But the men in beige jackets are encountering one unexpected variable. A single ripple in this calm sea of compliance. There are certain individuals scattered throughout the crowds who do not react predictably. Their minds lack the key for the codes being shouted at them, so they do not respond to instructions or assurances, no matter how confidently delivered. They stand motionless in the streets, watching the men in beige jackets roar commands that blend into the promises pouring from the stadium PA, and they do not respond.

The men in beige jackets move closer in order to become more forceful, and that's when they notice that something is different about these individuals. The tint of their skin. The slowness of their movements. The scar tissue in the shape of bullet holes, knife slashes, and wide patches of regenerated rot. But mostly their eyes. Many different hues, alike in defiance.

We drift toward a building that radiates pain, but as we get closer we notice other accumulations. Plague and its opposite: golden flickers of cure. Something like a smile spreads through our vastness.

"You'll be okay," Nora Greene tells a man with three shards of concrete sticking out of his back. "They're not deep. I'll be back in a second to patch you up."

"Wait," he gasps as she moves away. "Don't leave me."

"God, you're needy. This is why we never would've worked."

"Nora."

"You're going to be fine, Evan. Just stay calm. I'll be right back."

She darts away from his bed to attend to another patient. The warehouse once seemed awkwardly large for this miniature ER, but now every inch of empty space has been filled with the wounded. Their accommodations follow a steady grade of increasing desperation, from proper electric hospital beds to stained twin mattresses to wool blankets thrown on the concrete floor. We jump from nurse to nurse—there are few proper doctors in this age of austerity—and then return to Nora, following her as she bandages the living and comforts the dying. A group of civilians stands in a corner, waiting for the signal that it's time to say their good-byes and then shoot their loved ones in the head, but sometimes they can't do it and the task falls to Nora. A Colt .45 sticks out of the waistband of her scrubs, an instrument as essential to modern medicine as a scalpel.

In all the blood and screaming, no one is paying attention to the rows of special patients whose beds line the walls. Many of these have far more serious injuries—missing limbs, gaping holes—but their wounds don't bleed. These patients sit up in their beds and observe the chaos with wide eyes. The Living do everything so vibrantly, the Dead think. Their blood sprays like party champagne, they hoot and howl like a gospel choir. Even in their agony, they are enviable.

While the Dead watch the Living die, a group of men in white shirts files in through a side door and surrounds them. One of these men unfolds a pocket knife. He sticks it into a patient's arm. The patient doesn't flinch, but she looks up at the man with an expression of offense. Hurt feelings.

"What are you?" the man demands.

"A . . . person," the patient replies.

"No you're not," the man says, and moves the knife down the patient's arm, opening a gash.

The patient's face darkens. "Stop."

"Hey!" Nora shouts from across the room. She hands off her patient to another nurse and rushes toward this forgotten corner of the hospital. "What the fuck are you doing? Who are you?"

"We're with the Axiom Group. What are these people?"

"What do you mean what are they?"

"Are they Living or Dead?"

"They're trying to decide. Why the fuck are you sticking knives in my patients?"

"We have orders to investigate these uncategorized individuals."

"They're zombies. They're trying not to be. What else do you need to know?"

"The Dead don't 'try.' They're passive tissue waiting for input."

Nora rolls her eyes. "Jesus Christ, Grigio all over again. Listen, I don't have time for this. I have people to sew up."

He points his knife at the patient's face. "They're ignoring our instructions and interfering with aid efforts." The patient slaps the knife out of his hand. The man looks shocked. "See?"

"Get out of my Morgue," Nora says.

"We'll need to take some of them back to Goldman Dome for study. Three should be enough for now."

Nora takes a step toward the man. "I said get out."

We notice things about Nora Greene that interest us. Many small scars darken the skin of her arms and face, and her left hand is missing a finger: chapters of her life written bold on her flesh, calling us to read them. The man in the white shirt notices these things too, and they concern him. But not as much as the pistol in Nora's right hand, which she is tapping emphatically against her thigh.

The man pulls out his walkie. "Management? Request assistance in the Medical building." He looks from Nora's blood-smeared scrubs to her blood-shot eyes. "We're encountering resistance."

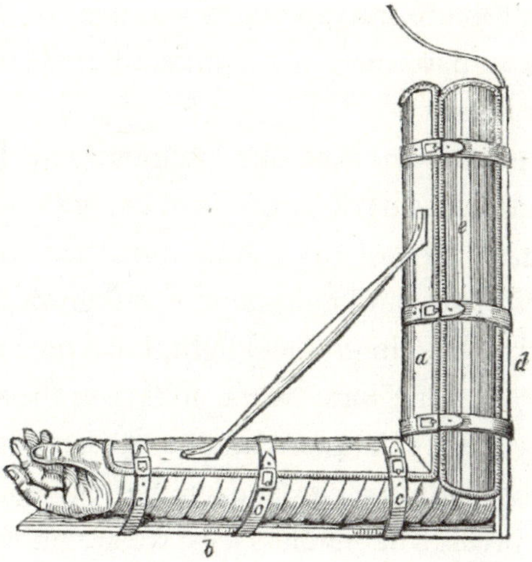

I

I DON'T SLEEP WELL. I'm not good at it. Sleep is a ceasefire with life, and I don't trust my opponent. I lie awake all night expecting ambush. In my Dead days, sleep meant lying on the floor and staring at the ceiling, trying to regather my decomposing consciousness. I would go months without it, and when it came it was always a terrible collapse. No peaceful descent into a feather bed with a book and a cup of chamomile; more like a surprise bullet to the kneecap, dropping me to the floor in a confused and frightened pile.

Since the first night I closed my eyes and truly dreamed, lying next to Julie on a stranger's mildewed mattress, my relationship with sleep has improved, but it's still dysfunctional. Most nights find me listening to her soft snores deep into the morning, passing the time by trying to decode her twitches and whimpers and half-formed words, imagining what colorful horrors her brain has prepared for her and wondering how to comfort her when she wakes up. If I'm lucky, I'll drift into a shallow slumber for an hour or two, but my mind, traumatized by years of death, remains wary of anything that resembles it.

So in a way, getting knocked unconscious by the butt of a gun is rather refreshing. I haven't slept this well in ages.

Deep in a dark alley of my mind, a grizzled street prophet is muttering news of fire and judgment, but I ignore him and stride past with my chin held high. I feel light. I am on a tropical island, swimming in warm blue water while gulls soar above and dolphins glide below. My abs are cut gems and my skin is a healthy bronze. Julie is on the beach in a bikini and sunglasses, oiling her flawless body, her huge breasts, her endless legs; we are on vacation, we are in love, we are—

We are in a nightclub and the music is pounding and I am dancing with Julie. I dance well; my hips and limbs swing in perfect rhythm, pantomiming sex in front of a hundred strangers without a hint of shame. My pockets are full of money and drugs and Julie is grinding into me with abandon, her long hair whipping into my face, her red skirt hiking higher and higher and everyone is watching us with envy and lust. I smirk at them and take Julie home to our high-rise condo and we fuck all night without pause or reservation, not looking at each other but at the city below our windows, spreading itself before us like a submissive whore offering us everything—

I am on a private plane, ensconced in soft leather and bathed in tropical jazz, looking down on endless miles of ruined cities and all the poor fools still inhabiting them. Julie sits next to me, and the sight of her brings a stern frown to my face, because I am dressed for serious business, silver shirt and red tie, but she's not wearing a pantsuit or pencil skirt or even a shoulder-padded blazer; she's wearing jeans and a plaid flannel, a red stocking cap pulled over her tangled hair. I am about to scold her when I notice my own outfit is also a little off. The fabric of my shirt has a thick, tough texture, and instead of classic Italian wingtips: heavy black boots caked with mud.

I look up at Julie. Her face is tight with sadness and fear, pleading with me. The edge of her cap is wet; a trickle of blood runs down her forehead and pools in her eye.

I glance to my right and see two men and a woman wearing the same outfits I'm wearing. One of the men has a silver briefcase. He winks at me. I feel myself lifting out of my seat as the plane dives, hurtling down into an endless expanse of dark green trees. The music gets louder as we fall, the marimbist striking the tines in a rage, breaking the mallets.

"Please don't leave me," Julie whispers into my ear. "Please don't go back."

• • •

My eyes open halfway, but I'm not confident that I'm awake. The music is still there, down to a reasonable volume now; the tropical jazz fades into an upbeat country number, still watery and nondescript but with a faint twang to indicate we have shifted cultures. I'm in some kind of dark chamber and the music is emanating from a speaker in the ceiling, but it's hard to make out details through the profusion of colorful spots in my vision, like a Fourth of July firework show between me and the outside world. My head pounds.

I hear the squeak of hinges, and a blurry silhouette hovers in the doorway. The face comes into focus for just a moment before my eyes slacken again, but it's enough to pour a sludge of fear into my delirium, because I recognize the face, and it belongs to someone who is dead. Perhaps I'm dead, too. Perhaps I died years ago, and Hell is a flooded planet of starving children and walking corpses and endless, senseless war.

I summon air into my lungs and croak, "Perry?"

I catch a glimpse of startled eyes, then the firework show resumes, the pedal steel swells—

I'm on a ranch. I'm holding the rope while Julie trots the new colt around the arena; I've never seen her happier; her face is—

Someone is shaking my shoulders. I scowl and dig in deeper.

Julie leans against the colt's shimmering chestnut neck and rests her cheek on his mane as I lead him back to the barn—

Wake up, a man shouts into my ear.

I squirm and try to shut him out, whoever he is, this horrible alarm dragging me into this horrible morning. Snooze, snooze, please snooze.

We stroll hand in hand toward the farmhouse, and it's warm and full of history; it has been in my family for generations, handed down to me by my father, who was kind and courageous, who instilled nothing but hope in his son and never once told him that only God could love his filthy human heart.

The music stops.

My eyes snap open.

A man and a woman are watching me from across a small table. Another man is standing next to me, pressing a live wire into my ribs, which explains why my back is arching and my wrists are straining and why I'm tied to a chair with a length of coaxial cable.

The man removes the wire and I go slack.

"You're quite the deep sleeper!" the woman in the yellow tie says, like a mother chiding her teenage son.

"We apologize for any discomfort," the man in the blue tie adds.

The man in the black tie returns to his seat.

I really am dead. I'm surrounded by faces that I've seen bloodied and charred on the ground. What unjust afterlife is this, that I have to share it with these obscene creatures?

"We're glad you're awake," Yellow Tie says, reaching toward me and placing her palm on the table, a gesture evoking intimacy and trust. "We have a very exciting offer to share with you."

Of course it's not really Yellow Tie. Not the one I saw with a pole through her head, anyway. Longer nose, thinner lips. But the differences in her features vanish into the sameness of everything else: her clothing, her posture, her empty cardboard earnestness. Blue Tie's hair is lighter, his chin sharper, and Black Tie is less bulky, but they are the same three people, as if their bodies are originals but their souls are copies.

My eyes dart around the room. All the lights are broken except one fluorescent tube buzzing overhead, bathing the pitchmen in a pale, unforgiving light that highlights the seams between their makeup and their flesh.

And what are you kids supposed to be?

We're human beings. Trick or treat!

The room is dark, but I can see that I'm alone with these creatures. "Where's Julie?" I ask Yellow Tie. I don't sense any particular authority structure, but it seems to be her role to tell people things they want to hear, and I want to hear that Julie is safe, even if it comes from the world's least trustworthy mouth.

The mouth smiles blandly. I try to stand up and realize my ankles are tied to the legs of the chair.

"We apologize for any discomfort," Blue Tie says again. "Unfortunately, due to recent difficulties, we do need to keep you restrained at this time to ensure the safety of Axiom employees."

"Where is Julie?" I shout at him, but the cold plastic smiles they're all wearing tell me I won't get far talking to them like people. I'm not having a conversation; I'm watching a commercial.

"No doubt you're aware of the terrible tragedy that took place in the stadium," Blue Tie says, switching to his grave and reverential face. "Improper storage of expired munitions led to an explosion that took nearly a hundred lives, including those of the enclave's central leadership."

"Fortunately," Yellow Tie chimes in like they're singing a duet, "the Axiom Group was right next door, ready to assist our new west coast neighbors. Working closely with Citi Stadium's existing Security and Medical teams, we have been able to contain the damage and provide aid to the victims."

"You did this," I mumble, looking at the table. "Everyone will know you did this. They'll fight you."

The peculiar sensation of reliving a moment from a dream. A memory of a conversation that never happened.

Trust me, kid. I know my business.

"We have offered some of our best people to fill the holes in Citi's management," Yellow Tie says, "and its remaining members have been very receptive to our help."

I begin to shake my head, my arms flexing against the cables.

"Where we are encountering some difficulty," Blue Tie says, "is with the non-living population of the stadium and surrounding area."

I stop shaking my head and look up.

"Since arriving on the west coast," Yellow Tie says, "we have encountered a puzzling—a puzzling—" She blinks. "Thing. A puzzling thing." Her smile falters for the first time and her expression crinkles into something like discomfort.

Blue Tie steps in to rescue her. "We have encountered non-living persons who are non-standard. Who do not—who show puzzling signs of—" He grimaces and lowers his head.

"Life?" I offer.

"We have encountered unknowns," Yellow Tie blurts.

Blue Tie's head rises again. "We have encountered unknowns. They behave differently. We have been unable to predict their responses, and this poses a danger."

"The Axiom Group wants to help," Yellow Tie says. "We want to provide security to this region and to the entire world."

"But security is impossible when unknowns exist," Blue Tie says. "Security is impossible when hundreds of thousands of unknowns exist."

Silence. Yellow Tie and Blue Tie both watch me with pained expressions. Absurdly, I find myself glancing at Black Tie for guidance, but he continues to be little more than statuary.

"What do you want with me?" I finally snap, and it's like pushing a skipping record needle back onto its groove. Their smiles blink on again.

"You're like them," Yellow Tie says, and slides her palm across the table again, not quite touching me. "But you're different. You influence them."

"No I don't."

"It's widely known that you instigated this deviation," Blue Tie says. "You caused these unknowns to appear."

"I didn't do anything. It just happened."

Yellow Tie leans toward me, fixing me with a look of intimacy that suggests it's time to brush aside the posturing and be real with each other. "We need your help," she says softly. "We want everyone to be secure in their places. We want to eliminate confusion. But we're finding it difficult to communicate the benefits to these non-standard individuals. They are unnaturally resistant to our help."

Her face is about two feet from mine, eyes big and imploring. I notice that her makeup goes all the way down her neck and I wonder if it covers her whole body, bronzing her veiny breasts and smoothing her withered holes. A scent like overripe pineapple wafts up from beneath her collar.

"Corpses know what death smells like," I say, staring her in the face. "Your cheap perfume can't hide it."

Her expression holds for a moment. Then it flashes into a smile. Black Tie steps around the table and shoves the wire into my neck.

"Unfortunately," Blue Tie says as I convulse, "if you are unable to recognize either the rewards of working with us or the risks of refusing, coercion does become necessary at this time."

"If at any time during this interview you would like to accept our offer," Yellow Tie says, "simply say 'yes.'"

Electric shock is a strange pain. At this voltage, very little physical damage is occurring, but my nerves still throw a tantrum. My muscles clench into knots, fire erupts in my joints, my bones tell my brain they're being shattered, and my brain itself complains of hot coals and daggers. But when Black Tie removes the wire, there's no harm done. No blood no foul, as they say in sports.

Fascinating.

The pitchmen watch me and wait. I sit in my chair, looking idly around the room. They frown, and Black Tie pokes the wire into my throat.

My neck tendons bulge. Bolts of pain flash up and down my spine and I swear I can feel my brain heating up like meat in a microwave. But I watch all this suffering from my hotel balcony, taking footage from afar with an expensive zoom lens. The pain is real. I'm aware that I'm in agony. But I just don't care.

Black Tie removes the wire and Blue and Yellow watch me expectantly.

I shrug.

"This display of endurance is unnecessary," Blue Tie says through his glued-on grin. "You cannot outlast your interview. It will continue until we reach one of two possible outcomes."

"One outcome is you assisting us," Yellow Tie says.

"The other is you dying."

I shrug again. "Been dead before. It's not so bad."

Their smiles falter. I enjoy about three seconds of triumph, then the pitchmen cock their heads, listening. I hear a commotion through the wall behind me, a clatter of furniture, a muffled shout. The pitchmen regard me like cheery mannequins, wordless and motionless, as if waiting for something.

Through the wall comes a high shriek of pain mixed with indignant fury. "Fuck you! *Fuck* you, you dressed-up sacks of shit! You Botoxed babyfuckers!"

Julie.

I lurch against my bonds, trying to turn the chair around. "Julie! I'm here!"

Another scream, less rage this time, more pain. No words.

"What are . . . doing to her?" I growl at the pitchmen, all my hard-won fluency melting away in the heat of panic.

"We are making her a comparable offer," Yellow Tie says.

"Does she share your ambivalence toward discomfort?" Blue Tie asks me.

Julie's scream rises higher and higher and then breaks off, collapses into a sob.

My eyes squeeze shut. I see fireworks. I see fire. I see flames roaring from rooftops, kids running from schools. I see rapturous faces watching the flames, watching me, hands clapping, applauding, eyes glittering in the orange light, and a bottle in my hand, a flaming rag stuffed into it—

I see a cheap plywood casket descending into a hole in the ground, a preacher sprinkling platitudes into it like piss into a toilet while fools watch and pretend to weep—

I see a blond woman in a forest, bruised and bloody, eyes full of loathing as she presses my gun to her forehead—

I open my eyes.

Julie is tied to a chair by my side, our shoulders almost touching. She is looking at me with a kind of bleakly apologetic smile, breathing hard, her eyes red and wet.

"Hi, R," she says.

Her face is spotted with small bruises. Her lower lip is cracked and puffy. On the side of her neck just above the clavicle, precisely my favorite place to kiss, the skin is mottled with the bluish brown of an electrical burn.

I feel the TV cables cutting into my ankles and forearms. I hear the chair creaking under the strain.

"Stop," she says gently. "I'm okay. Don't give them what they want."

"Unfortunately," Blue Tie says, "we do need to continue the interview at this time."

"Remember," Yellow Tie says, "if at any time you would like to accept our offer, simply say 'yes.'"

Black Tie sticks the wire into the burn on Julie's neck.

"Stop it!" I scream as she writhes against her bonds. "Stop!"

"If you would like to accept our offer, simply say—"

"We can't . . . *do* what you want!" I sputter, choking on my tongue. "Even if . . . wanted to . . . *can't*! We don't control the Dead!"

"Our reports show that you are viewed as leadership figures by the non-living population," Yellow Tie says. "We look forward to working with you toward a greater mutual understanding."

"Yes!" Julie growls through clenched teeth as she writhes in her chair. "*Yes!*"

Black Tie removes the wire from Julie's neck and she slumps over, gasping.

"You agree to assist us?" Yellow Tie asks, her smile radiating goodwill.

"Yes," Julie wheezes.

I stare at her, unsure what to feel.

"You are aware, of course," Blue Tie says, "that these interviews will remain available to you throughout our partnership. If at any point your cooperation wanes, they will resume."

"We believe in ongoing commitment to excellence," Yellow Tie says. "'Yes' should be more than just a word."

"Oh," Julie says, straightening up in her chair. "Well in that case, no."

Yellow Tie tilts her head and pouts like a disappointed mother.

"We apologize for our failure to communicate effectively," Blue Tie says.

Black Tie sets the power cord down and opens a case full of electrician's tools.

"Julie," I plead with her, though I don't know what I'm pleading for. Do I want to give in? Do I want to do my best to help them own the Dead along with the Living? How much of the world would I burn to keep Julie safe?

"It's okay," she says. "We'll be okay."

Black Tie pulls out a pair of cable shears. He sets them on Julie's lap and pries open her fist, forcing her fingers flat against the chair's arm.

"No," I say. "No. No. Julie, I can't . . ."

"R, listen to me," she says, her voice beginning to tremble. "I'm not going to help them. That's my choice. So no matter what they do to me . . ."

Her eyes dart toward her hand as Black Tie spreads her fingers out and picks up the shears. They dart back to me, wide with panic. "No matter what they do to me—"

She shrieks. The tip of her ring finger falls to the floor. One unique print, one yellow-painted nail, rolling across the filthy floor and vanishing beneath a locker.

My mind becomes a furnace of incoherent horror. *"Stop!"* I scream at Yellow Tie. "I'll do it! What do you want me to do, I'll do it!"

"R!" Julie snaps savagely. "You don't get to surrender for me! It's *my* choice and I've fucking made it!"

Black Tie moves the shears further up, toward the base of the finger.

"You don't always have to keep me safe," she says, her voice suddenly soft, and she somehow manages a smile. "That's not why I love you."

A tiny sound, like the snap of a fresh carrot.

Blood on Black Tie's shirt, an artful splatter that looks just like one of Julie's paintings, she's embarrassed by all her work but she singles that one out for scorn, a silly attempt to be Jackson Pollack, she calls it, I don't care that it's derivative, I appreciate the form, the bright colors, the passion in the wild swings of her brush—

I break the front legs off my chair and lunge into Black Tie and knock him to the floor and head-butt him over and over; his nose breaks, his eye socket breaks, I'm going to do this until everything breaks, until both our heads merge into one mass of bone fragments and pulp—

He stabs the power cord into the base of my skull and this time I feel it. True pain, up close and intimate, bursting out from the core of my brain and crackling through my eyes and teeth. I have tumbled off my balcony and into the muddy streets, and the locals are swarming over me with clubs and knives and fists, hissing, *Welcome, foreigner. Is it everything you hoped?*

I see Julie high above me as I writhe on the floor. Warm drops of her blood fall on my face like tropical rain, and behind her agony, I see sadness. I see grief. I see our tender little dream receding into blackness.

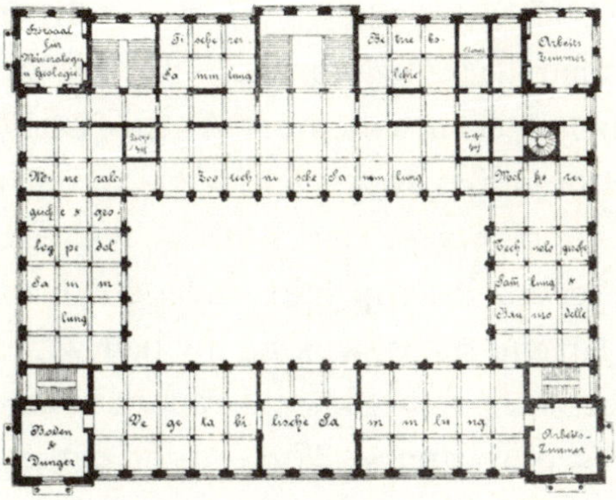

FACES DRIFT PAST ME as I float through my delirium. I see the pitchmen, their grins gone, their expressions slack, communicating with each other through small gestures and occasional grunted vocalizations. I see Julie being carried away by a man in a beige jacket. I call out from somewhere in the darkness and grasp around frantically, trying to find my body in all these suffocating shadows. I succeed in jerking my limbs and emitting a faint groan, and the man in the beige jacket turns around. At the end of my blurry tunnel of vision, I see the face of an old friend.

Perry's eyes are troubled and he shakes his head as if to say, *Don't panic. It'll be okay.* And for some reason, I believe him. I stop thrashing. I watch the ghost of the man I killed carry away the body of the woman we both love, and I sink back into the shadows.

• • •

"Can you hear me . . . look up . . ."

A soft, smoky voice, imperfect in pitch but rich in timbre.

"The clouds are lifting . . . the window's open . . . time to grow a pair of wings . . ."

The tune is familiar. The words, doubly so. Lines from a film merged with melody from a memory. A girl in a field. A man reaching out to her from miles away.

"Look up . . . look up . . ."

I open my eyes and look up. Julie smiles down at me. My head is resting on her lap and she is stroking my hair with her right hand. Her left hand lies limp on her knee, wrapped in bloody gauze.

"Lazy boy," she murmurs. "You've been getting a lot of sleep lately. Feel refreshed?"

I drag myself upright and then collapse against her shoulder as my head pops like a water balloon, gushing agony into every corner of my body. My brain. That lump of boiled hamburger that I've protected for so long, the only part I ever considered worth the effort. How can it possibly be functioning through pain like this?

"I guess that's a 'no,'" Julie says. She runs her fingers through my hair again, gently massaging my scalp. It helps.

We are sitting on a tile floor against a tile wall in a dark, sour-smelling room. The only light comes from a flickering bulb in the hall outside, leaking into our cell through the door's barred window. We're in jail. A couple of young deviants caught tearing up the town. Drinking. Smoking. Heavy petting at the drive-in.

"Are you . . . okay?" I manage to croak as I crawl back into my body.

She chuckles. "What's left of me is. Our hosts were kind enough to stitch up the stump, which I guess means they're not planning to kill me yet. Hooray." Her fingers trace around the burn on the back of my skull. "What about you?"

I pull myself upright and stare at nothing, waiting for the damage report. My body feels raw, dried out, like all my joints and muscles have been lightly seared. Waves of nausea wash over me, followed by an undertow of feverish heat. And of course, my head. The steady throb of blood pounding against constricted vessels, squeezing against my sinuses, crushing my eyes in their sockets.

"Just a little hungover," I mumble.

She smiles bitterly. "Wild night."

We are silent for a moment. Will there ever be a funeral? Will there be a day to stop and acknowledge the cutting of Lawrence Rosso's thread? Or will he be swept up with the rest of the day's tragedies and dumped into the wastebasket of the new world, where death is not a headline but a weather report?

Julie stands up and paces slowly around the room. In the flickers of light through the door I see a row of sinks, a row of toilet stalls. Our jail is a restroom. Julie stops in front of the shattered mirror and moves from side to side, examining herself in its facets. A puffy eye here. A split lip there. Blue-brown burns everywhere. "Looking good, Julie," she mutters. "A very good year for Cabernet."

I notice she has a slight limp. "Your leg?" I say.

"Just sore joints. Electricity *hurts*, doesn't it? I always thought shock would be the easiest torture, since there's no breaking or cutting or, you know . . ." She holds up her bandaged stump. ". . . permanent maiming. But wow, it's still pretty bad."

I can't take my eyes off her hand. "Come sit with me," I say, feeling a quaver in my voice.

She takes a last look in the mirror. She brushes a lock of hair off her forehead, revealing yet another scabbed cut. She sighs and comes back to my corner in the shadows, slides down the wall and settles against me. I hold her bandaged hand, staring at the missing volume in the bookshelf of her fingers. They have stolen a piece of her. She is not diminished; she is no less herself, but I still feel the loss. She is not her body but her body is her, so I love her body. And some of it is gone.

She watches me studying her, and when she notices the glimmer of moisture in my eyes she self-consciously pulls her hand away. "Look on the bright side," she says, forcing a smile. "If we ever get married, you won't have to buy a ring."

• • •

We lose track of time, sitting in the dark. No one comes to drag us into another "interview." No one slides a tray of food under the door. The speaker above the toilets clicks on and plays nondescript instrumental rock for a while, then switches mid-beat to nondescript instrumental hip-hop, then clicks off. Then clicks on again and plays classical. It might be psychological torture, or it might just be these lunatics' idea of ambiance. I try to ignore it.

"Mozart," Julie says in a bitter chuckle, staring at the speaker. "It's supposed to be the pinnacle of art, right? This transcendent human achievement? And we use it for background noise in bathrooms. We literally shit on it." There's a pained tightness in her voice. She spasms occasionally and clenches her right hand. When the music clicks off she immediately turns her attention to the patch of light on the floor. "How long do you think the solar panels will keep working? Will that bulb out there still be flickering when we're dead and everyone we know is dead?"

I look at her uneasily.

"Sorry," she says, shaking her head. "I'm trying to distract myself."

She stands up and goes to the door. She presses her face against the bars. "Hello? Any other prisoners out there? Anyone else enjoying Axiom's exceptional customer service?" She plants a fierce kick against the door; it leaves a dirty boot print but barely vibrates the heavy hinges. "Hey!" she shouts, desperation creeping through her sarcasm. *"Hey!"*

She kicks it again, then grimaces and bends over, clutching her hand. "God," she says in a raw whisper, "this really hurts."

A small voice echoes from across the hall.

"Julie?"

Her eyes widen and she leaps back to the window. *"Nora?"*

"Hey, you."

A surge of disoriented emotion wracks Julie's face; a joyful laugh bubbles out of her even as tears fill her eyes. "I'm so glad you're here."

"You're glad I'm in prison? Thanks a lot."

Julie laughs louder. "So I'm a selfish bitch. Yes, I'm glad."

Standing behind Julie, I can see the window of another cell a few feet down the hall. A single frizzy curl pokes out through the bars.

"Is R with you?" Nora asks.

"Yeah, he's in here."

"What is this? What do they want?"

"I don't even know. They think we can control the Dead. They're insane."

"Are you okay?"

"Mostly, yeah. Although this happened." She sticks her bandaged hand through the bars.

"Oh, Jules . . ."

"Yeah. We're stump sisters now."

"I'm sorry."

"Thanks."

"You'll get used to it. The only time it really trips me up is when I'm playing guitar."

"I was never going to be a musician anyway. That gene died with Dad." She's quiet for a moment. "What about you, though? You're okay?"

"They haven't fucked with me much. I'm in for disorderly conduct."

"What happened?"

"They were trying to take my Nearlies. I shot a guy."

"That's my girl."

A pause. "Jules?"

"Yeah?"

Another pause, this one longer. "I heard about Lawrence."

Silence.

"I'm so sorry."

Julie leans against the door, pressing her forehead into the bars. "Yeah."

"Ella came into the Morgue. Said she wanted to help someone. I asked if she had any medical training. She said she took a CPR class twenty years ago."

"She was okay?"

"I wouldn't say that."

Julie closes her eyes and goes quiet.

I push my face to the window. "Nora. Have you seen M?"

"Marcus? The great outdoorsman? Sure haven't. But now would be a pretty great time for him to come back, if he's going to."

"He's going to," I mumble, half to myself. "He said 'See you later.'"

"That's sweet. But what he said to me was, 'I don't deserve to be here.'"

I let myself sag back from the window. Julie takes my place. "How long have we been in these fucking bathrooms?"

"What, you're not carving check marks on the wall of your cell? Where's your prison spirit?"

"We've been unconscious most of the time."

"Oh. Well, I'm pretty sure the explosion was three days ago."

Julie nods and looks at the floor, lost in thought. "So today's . . . July 26th?"

"If I've been counting meals right, yeah," Nora says. "Why?"

To my surprise, Julie laughs. She laughs the way you laugh at a joke you know you shouldn't find funny. "It's my birthday."

There's a pause, then Nora bursts into a bitter cackle. "Well happy birthday, stump sister! Wishes and kisses!"

"Why didn't you get me a present, R? What kind of boyfriend are you?"

"Just think, you're almost old enough to buy beer!"

I listen to the two women collapse into fits, exchanging birthday clichés and savoring the fresh irony that coats each one, but I can't make myself join in. Even the blackest edges of my humor are numbed by this. It's an arbitrary line, of course, subjective and ultimately meaningless, but this is not how I imagined Julie graduating from her teens. In every meaningful way, she's been an adult for many years, certainly longer than I have, but some old-fashioned part of me still wanted to celebrate this official step into maturity. I wanted to get up early and put daisies on her pillow. I wanted to play her favorite records all day. Maybe I'd try to bake a birthday cake.

But instead, this is the party I threw for her. Sitting in a jail cell waiting for our next round of torture. *Surprise!*

I listen to the two friends riff off each other, and then I wonder if their laughter might have triggered some kind of anti-joy alarm, because as if on cue, a door bangs open and heavy boots pound down the hall.

The laughter stops. Julie backs away from the door until she bumps into me, and I wrap my arms around her, absorbing the icy tremble that's shaking her tiny frame.

"R," she whimpers as a shadow falls across the window, and the cold, terrifying reptile in my brain starts sorting through objects in the room. The mirrors. A shard of glass . . .

The door opens, and Perry Kelvin steps through.

Julie's knees collapse. She sags against me. I stumble back and fall into a sitting position, holding her under her armpits.

"Time to go," Perry says, reaching out to help me up. "Now."

I hear a distant commotion through the walls. Furious shouts, fists pounding a door. Perry's face is indistinct in the shadows, but the thick eyebrows, the brittle voice and its subtle drawl . . . I don't know what he is or how he's here or if I can trust him, but I can imagine no scenario worse than the one I was just contemplating. I grab his hand and stand up, pulling Julie with me.

She keeps her eyes locked on his, unable to speak, but her legs firm up under her and she follows.

"Hey!" Nora shouts and I see her knuckles gripping the window bars. "Let them go, you piece of shit, they can't help you! I'm the Nurse of the Living Dead, they call me Queen Greene! If anyone can control them, it's me!"

"Is she your friend?" Perry asks Julie.

"Who are you?" Julie whispers, still staring into his eyes. "Who are you?"

"Yes," I tell him. "She's our friend."

Perry unlocks Nora's cell. Nora emerges, sees his face, and freezes. "Holy shit, you look—"

The distant clang of a hammer striking a door latch.

"Introductions later," Perry says. "Follow me."

He runs down the hall but the women are stunned, immobile.

"Who is that?" Julie asks me with fear in her voice.

"Don't know. Doesn't matter." I grab her hand. "We're getting out of here."

She glances at Nora, then at me, then at the ghost waiting for us at the end of the hall. We run.

WITH EVERY DOOR we burst through, I expect to be greeted by daylight, but each time it's another hall, another chamber, another door. The professionally poured concrete of the inner wall gives way to the rushed corner-cutting of post-apocalyptic construction: moldy drywall, rusty sheet metal, and the ever-present plywood. I don't remember any building this large in Citi Stadium. I begin to suspect we are elsewhere.

The lighting in these outer chambers is more reliable, and I catch glimpses of Perry's face as we chase him through this badly built labyrinth. He's not Perry, of course. How could he be Perry? I personally consumed that man's brain and watched my brethren take his body home in several choice cuts. And then he stowed away in the back of my head, filling in for my absent conscience, and we worked together to repair our souls. I cheered him on into "whatever's next." Perry Kelvin and I made peace and parted ways—this man is not him. He is older, thicker, his jaw more pronounced, his skin more weathered. I think Julie and Nora see this too, but the resemblance still shocks them into uncharacteristic silence.

A door with a glowing window appears. I nearly salivate at the thought of daylight. After three days in this chilly hole of pain and darkness, my skin will drink in the sun like sweet tea. The man who is not Perry holds the door for us and we emerge into—not daylight. A pale streetlamp lighting a dark corner. Overhead: a suffocating sky of water-stained concrete.

"Welcome to Goldman Dome," Not-Perry says. "Keep moving."

Unlike Citi Stadium, this place makes no attempt to mimic the layout of a real city. No miniature high-rises jutting into open space. No open space at all—Goldman's "architects" appear to have filled every cubic foot of the dome with structures, all merging into one crooked, creaking mass that extends from the ground to the distant curve of the ceiling. The street we're on appears to be the only exterior path, cutting a line through the grotesque honeycomb from one end of the dome to the other. Pedestrians peer down at us from the web of dizzying catwalks that connect the two halves of the hive.

But no alarm. No floodlights. No arrest orders barking from a Jumbotron.

"They sent me to bring you in for another interview," Not-Perry says as he leads us down the street toward a row of sunken parking spots like the garage of a cheap apartment complex. "I took their walkies and locked them in their office, but they'll get out and call it in and the dome will shut down. We've got maybe five minutes."

He unlocks one of the pickup trucks—a beat-up old Ford with a gray primer paint job and a well-stocked gun rack. Julie starts to open the passenger door but Not-Perry holds out his hand. "No. All of you get in the bed."

"Why?" Nora says.

"There's some rope back there. Tie your wrists and pretend you're zombies."

"God *damn* it!" Julie suddenly shouts, snapping out of her trance. "Who *are* you?"

He sees the flinty glint in her eyes and realizes she has reached her limit. She won't be going anywhere until she gets an answer. "Abram Kelvin," he says. "I'm Perry's brother."

Julie stares at him, eyes flicking over his features, scanning. "Perry didn't have a—"

"Look, I told you my name, we really don't have time for the rest of this chat right now. Get in the fucking truck."

He hops in and slams the door. I climb into the bed and after a moment the women follow me. We wrap the rope around our wrists in a few loose coils and lie down on the rusty metal like bundles of firewood. I am the only one who's particularly pale, but their abundance of clotted wounds and bruises make up for their lack of pallor. In this dim underworld light, they'll pass.

The truck lurches out of the garage and I watch the dome's upper reaches scroll past me. A guard on one of the lower catwalks looks down, sees the truck's cargo, and spits. His sickly green phlegm splats an inch from my ear.

"Almost there," Abram calls back to us through the rear window. "Shut up and be Dead."

I turn to face Julie. Our eyes are inches apart as our heads bounce against the truck. I wonder if she remembers what I taught her about zombie mimicry on our first foray into the airport, ages ago when life was simple, just me and her and a few comical corpses.

"Don't overdo it," I whisper to her as the truck slows to a halt under a glaring streetlamp. "Just act unnatural."

I hear a door open and footsteps approach the truck. "Position and SSN?"

"Large transport pilot, acquisition assistant, guest combatant hospitality host," Abram replies. "078-05-1120."

"Assignment?"

"Three uncategorized Dead to Incinerator 2."

I struggle not to react to this. Bundles of firewood indeed. I know burning the Dead is standard practice; I've seen oozing mounds of us doused in oil and turned into bonfires, a procedure the Boneys were fond of documenting in order to remind any deviators of their place in the natural order. But for a brief moment, this appeared to be changing. Goldman's people were watching the situation in Citi with great interest. They were observing our integration with the Living, and as Corridor 2 neared completion and the merger neared signature, it seemed a real possibility that the change would spread. Can it be snuffed so easily by a few small minds with big guns?

"Pretty long haul for just three corpses," the guard says. "You got room for a dozen in there."

"Management's rushing disposal for uncategorized. Worried about it spreading."

The guard leans over to look at us, a scruffy man in a beanie and blue flannel instead of the beige Axiom jacket. One of Goldman's original guards. "Zombies turning peaceful?" he says, studying my face. "You're worried about that spreading?"

"They're not 'turning peaceful,' they're going into stasis. The plague's evolving deception tactics. We don't know where it's going, so we're playing it safe."

"By burning them all?"

"Look, if you have problems with your enclave's new guidelines you can take it up with Management but right now you need to open this gate so I can do my job, all right?"

The guard squints at me. I snap my teeth and release a soft, understated groan, the voice of a tortured soul trapped in a rotting body. It's a role I've been researching for years, and perhaps I bring a little too much pathos to it, because the guard's face contorts with guilt.

"You're gonna burn them *alive*?"

"They're zombies, you idiot, they're not alive. Open the damn gate."

The guard shines his light into our faces one by one. "I'm not sure about this. These guys don't even look infected to me." He pulls out his walkie. "I'm going to have to call Management."

With a melodramatic and entirely unconvincing moan, Nora bolts upright and grabs his head, bangs it into the side of the truck and takes a bite of his ear. He staggers back, reaching for his gun, but Abram is already out of the truck and pressing his revolver against the man's temple. "Drop the gun, drop the walkie, and open the gate."

The guard lets the requested items clatter to the pavement and his lips begin to tremble as he reaches into his booth to punch in the gate code. By the time he's finished and the steel door is moving, his face is wet with tears and snot.

"Just do it," he whimpers, pressing his forehead into Abram's gun barrel. "I don't think I can do it myself and I don't want to hurt anybody."

Nora and Julie, who have been groaning and gasping like ridiculous B-movie ghouls, finally drop the act and dissolve into laughter.

"Chin up, soldier," Nora says. "You're not catching any diseases from me without buying me a few drinks."

Abram throws the guard's gun and walkie into the truck and hops in. I give the stunned, open-mouthed man a winning smile and Nora and Julie wave as we pull away into the city streets.

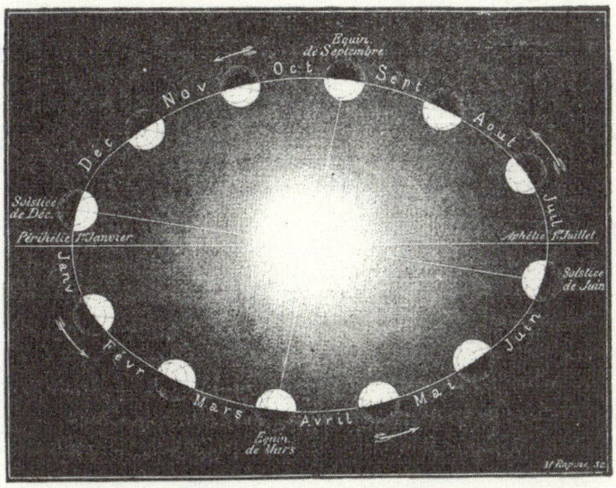

WE

We watch Abram Kelvin drive away from the dome, and feelings rush through us. They are complex and contradictory—joy, sorrow, longing, love—but our feelings always are. They flood the halls of the Library like a rich and ancient liquor, infused with the memories of everything. It is rare to look at anything without imbibing this spirit, because everything is remembered by at least one part of us. Every tree has been a perch, every stream has been a bath, every stone has cut a paw or broken a window or been used to build a house. Everything on earth has meant something to someone, and there has never been a person whom no one ever loved.

So while even a stone has a few threads tied to it, a person has a thousand ropes, and the man in the truck is pulling us. A part of us begins to separate. A book slides out from our shelves. It's a thin book, coverless and bound with red yarn, and it's been badly damaged. Tears blur its ink. Blood blots its words. But the books in our Library can heal. They can grow. They can complete themselves.

A part of us emerges from our vastness. A part of us watches Abram and reads him, hoping to learn who he is. Hoping to recover a few of the pages that a heartless world ripped out.

We follow the truck.

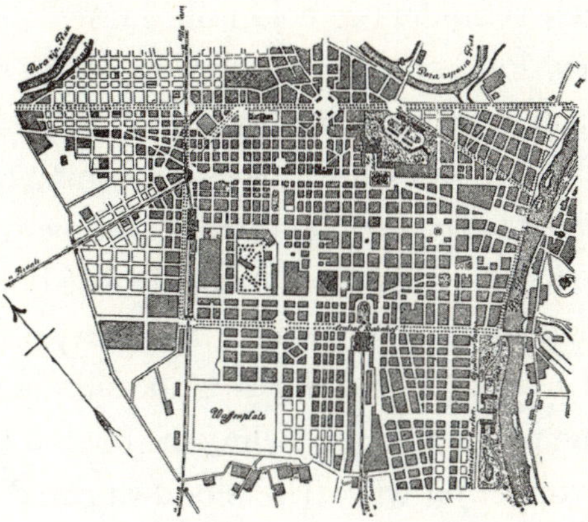

I

INSIDE THE PROTECTIVE SHEATH of Corridor 2, I can almost pretend I'm in the old world. Smooth black asphalt with freshly painted yellow lines, entirely clear of abandoned cars and the wreckage of collapsed buildings. No bomb craters, no cracks, not so much as a pothole. And the ten-foot concrete walls effectively hide the mess outside, ensuring that nothing shatters this lovely illusion of municipal vitality. They also ensure, incidentally, that we won't be swarmed and eaten by any of my less enlightened former friends.

Then the illusion evaporates. The walls dissolve into wooden pour forms and sprouts of rebar, and we're on a standard street again, exposed to the city and all its lurking threats. Despite the countless benefits of a safe route between enclaves, I have no doubt one of Axiom's first acts was to shut down the Corridor project, keeping its territory divided into manageable factions. When has a despot ever benefited from bringing people together?

The dark clouds begin to release their payload, and Julie and Nora hunch their shoulders as cold rain douses our little tailgate party. I see a few lone zombies staring up at the sky, letting the drops spatter against their unblinking eyes. The Dead have always commuted to the city. They slog in every morning from their various hives in the outskirts, they do their gruesome work, then they slog back home to hibernate a few hours before doing it all again. Only recently have some begun to alter this weary ritual. The young gray woman in a tank top and skirt—is she simply lost, separated from her hunting party, or is she feeling the cold of the rain for the first time and wondering why? The blood-smeared man trudging toward the stadium—is he going there to kill and eat, or to beg for help with these strange new stirrings?

As we drive past, both of them whirl toward us and hiss, silvery eyes wide with animal hunger. I tell myself to be patient. Whatever is going to happen won't happen overnight.

"See how far you've come, R?" Julie says. "I know you doubt it sometimes, but look at them and look at you. No one would ever guess what you used to be."

As always, she is too generous, but I accept the encouragement. Given that I seem to have fooled our rescuer, there may even be some truth in it.

Nora slides the rear window open. "Pull over. We're coming inside."

"I don't like our distance yet," Abram says without taking his eyes off the road. "Hold on a couple more miles."

"Hey. We're in the Dead part of town. I feel like shark chum back here. Pull over."

He drives a couple more blocks, then pulls into a parking garage entrance. I see him listening carefully as we climb out of the truck, and I wonder what he's more afraid to hear: the hungry groans of my people or the propeller drones of his?

Julie hops into the passenger seat without pausing to consider legroom issues. "So," she says, peering intently at Abram as Nora and I fold our long limbs into the barely-there backseat. "Are you ready for that chat?"

Abram lets out a slow breath. "Everybody buckled in?"

Nora's knees are pressed into her chest. Mine are against my chin.

"We're certainly not going anywhere if we crash," Nora says.

Abram pulls out of the garage and heads south toward the freeway, weaving steadily through the rough terrain of vehicular debris. The rain pelts the windshield in fat, splattering drops.

"Perry didn't have a brother," Julie says.

"He wouldn't remember me much. He was only five when he saw me last, and our mother never liked to talk about people we'd lost. Said we should stay in the present." He smirks. "Very convenient philosophy when you misplace a son."

Julie hesitates. "What happened?"

"The usual. Monsters attack, people die, families get separated. I wandered around on my own for a while, tried to find them, then Axiom picked me up. The old Axiom, back when they were just your standard corporate militia trying to carve out a market."

I lean forward. "What are they now?"

He looks annoyed by the question. "Something different."

"Are they human?"

He shoots me a glance that says I've secured my status as an idiot. "What the fuck else would they be?"

Julie tries to steer us back on course. "So you grew up with them? In their custody?"

He hesitates, then chuckles and turns back to the road. "I guess you could say that. Feral child raised by wolves."

"So why'd you turn on them?" Nora says, folding her arms. "Why are you helping us?"

Ahead, one of the city's many stacks of flattened cars has tipped over, blocking the road. Abram engages the four-wheel drive and guides the truck over a pile of two-dimensional coupes, crushed like beer cans for a recycling day that will never come.

"The short answer is, I thought I'd found my family." The wipers clear the windshield and then the rain covers it. The world flashes from soft blur to hideous clarity and back again. "I'd picked up some clues over the years that pointed toward Cascadia, so when I heard we were moving on Post, I requested the assignment. I knew it was a long shot, even with free access to hundreds of prisoners—sorry, I mean *guests*—and after a few days I was about to let it drop. But then this guy . . ." He jabs a thumb toward me. "This guy says his name. Looks right at me and says 'Perry.'"

The truck falls into grim silence.

"Don't worry," he adds, "I know he's dead."

"How?" Julie says in a small voice.

"Would my face have sent you into shock if he was alive? The message was pretty clear."

More silence. I brace myself for him to ask the terrible question: *How did he die?* But for the moment, he spares me.

"I assume my parents are dead too," he says, staring through the windshield.

Julie nods.

Abram's lips are a thin line. "So it's down to me."

We have ascended the hill up to the freeway and Citi Stadium is now visible on the horizon behind us. I watch it recede in the rear window, fading into a gray mirage behind sheets of rain.

"What's the long answer?" Nora says.

Abram doesn't reply.

"You betrayed Axiom and fucked up your life just to talk to someone who *might* know your brother?"

I watch his eyes in the mirror. They are familiar. Narrow-set and brown like Perry's. But a few extra years have hardened them by centuries. "No," he says, and takes a small, unmarked exit down into a wooded valley.

• • •

The street is buried in a thick layer of rotting leaves. The headlights slide across decrepit houses with boarded windows and gutted cars sinking into the rising grass, the kind of homes that probably looked like this even before the apocalypse.

"Where are we going?" Julie asks.

"That's enough questions for a while," Abram says.

At the end of the street, past a dead-end sign riddled with bullet holes, there are signs of life. Men in beige jackets move through the dark in the pale glow of headlamps on low settings.

"Are those—"

"I said shut up."

"Hey," I interject, leaning forward, but the gesture feels perfunctory. Julie looks at the side of Abram's face with a kind of injured dismay. No, this is not the boy she once loved. Not even an echo of him.

As we approach the camp's entrance, a man emerges from a small tent and lights a cigarette, takes a drag, and waits while Abram rolls down his window.

"078-05-1120," Abram says in the bored tone of well-worn procedure.

The guard checks a list on a notepad, nods, then shines his headlamp into the backseat. "Who're they?"

"New hires from Goldman. No numbers yet."

He waves us through with his cigarette, leaving a spiral of smoke in the air, and we drive into the camp.

Our high beams pierce deep into the shadows, revealing what the camp's conspicuous lack of lighting kept hidden. The property must have been some big family's country commune. Six houses on one lot, with a barn and a few cabins in the field out back. Mom and Dad and the kids and their kids and maybe even their kids' kids, all holed up at the end of this street deep in the woods, where no one could disturb their private party with news of the world and its wicked ways. How surprised they must have been to learn that the pot continued to boil even after they left the kitchen. How shocked to see that scalding tide reaching all the way to their door.

Now the farm is occupied by a new family with a more active approach to society's imperfections. All the houses and cabins appear to be barracks; Axiom soldiers pop in and out of them on various errands, delivering or receiving weapons and equipment. Beyond the houses, dozens of tents spread across a muddy field like a music festival campground, a miserable Woodstock of war.

"What are we doing here?" Nora whispers, despite Abram's instructions. "Won't they be looking for us?"

"The jamming's heavy around here. Walkies get barely half-mile range. The camp won't know what happened till a messenger arrives."

"It was never a negotiation, was it," Julie says, watching soldiers mount a grenade launcher to the hood of a Toyota pickup. "You'd take a willing merger if you could get it, but you were coming in one way or another."

A bitter smirk touches Abram's mouth. "We offer innovative solutions to modern problems."

He parks the truck next to one of the cabins. He hops out and goes inside, and we follow him.

It's warm and dry in the cabin, and surprisingly cozy with a fire crackling in a little iron stove. There's a twin bed and two chairs, a TV and an old video game system. Perhaps a room for one of the family's adolescent boys seeking independence and manhood. The old bloodstains on the curtains suggest an abrupt end to his quest.

His room is now occupied by a woman and a girl. Both of them sit in front of the TV, watching an airplane take off, watching a cat play with an injured bird, watching long-dead singers perform for long-dead celebrity judges. The kaleidoscope of images splashes strange colors on the walls of the room.

"About time," the woman says without looking up.

The girl runs to Abram and hugs his leg, but she doesn't smile. She is about six years old, straight black hair, tawny skin—the blond, ruddy-faced woman is clearly not her mother. One of the girl's eyes is big and dark, the other is covered by a sky-blue eye patch with a daisy painted on it.

"Hey, little weed," Abram says and hefts her into the crook of his arm. "You been having fun with Carol while I was gone?"

The girl shakes her head sadly.

"Well of course you haven't. Carol's no fun."

"She asks when you're coming back about every five minutes," Carol says. "I was about to tell her you died, you fuckin' deadbeat."

"It's been a busy week."

"So I hear. You owe me five days with Luke."

Abram bounces the girl on his arm, smiling absently. "I might be on assignment for a while, but when I get the days . . . yeah." He puts her down. "Sprout, I need you to get your backpack and pack up your clothes. We're going on a trip."

Carol frowns. "A trip? The fuck are you talking about?"

Abram ignores her and begins throwing clothes and food into a backpack.

"Hey Kelvin. You can't take your kid on assignment—"

"Thanks for watching Sprout, Carol. You can head home now if you want."

The light on the walls turns red and the TV's audio cuts to a warbling alert tone. Abram freezes over his pack.

"Oh shit," Carol says, rushing up to the screen like her favorite show is about to start. "Did they finally get in? Are we live on Fed TV?"

The tone plays over a blank red screen for about two seconds, then the kaleidoscope continues.

A bear swiping a salmon out of a stream. A lion pouncing on a zebra in lazy slow motion. Soldiers marching into a village.

"This fucking code," Carol mutters. "Can you follow it yet, Kelvin? I haven't finished my homework."

"Nope," Abram says with a casual calm that belies the haste of his packing. "Check the producer's guide."

Carol pulls a thick binder off a shelf and thumps it down on the table as the TV flashes through its collection of tropes. "I can't believe we're gonna keep using this Old Gov bullshit for all our messaging," she says, flipping through the binder's tabbed and laminated pages. "Why can't we just say it straight?"

Abram chuckles in spite of himself. "If we 'said it straight' people might actually understand us. Can't have that."

Carol glances back at him. "Huh?"

"It's right there in the title." He jabs a thumb toward the binder, which looks like a manual for some vintage industrial machinery. *"Leveraging Euphemism for the Prevention of Overcomprehension."*

Carol examines the binder's cover. "I'll say it again—*huh*?"

He zips up his pack. "Forget it. I'm sure this is just a test run anyway." He moves toward the door.

A voice cuts through the background music, methodical and grim: *"Everything happens for a reason. Everything has its place."*

On the TV, a gorilla paces in a zoo enclosure.

"Man is the only creature who questions his."

The gorilla fades to a badly lit photo of a man's face.

Abram's face.

Carol's eyes widen and she looks at Abram. "Well that one was clear en—"

Abram cracks a fist into her temple. She sinks to the floor.

"What the *fuck*!" Nora shouts.

Abram snatches a gun out of Carol's belt and tosses it to Nora. "You know how to use that, right?"

Nora opens her mouth to reply, then a shot of a goldfish swimming in a tiny tank fades to a photo of Nora sitting on the floor of her cell, scowling at the camera, and she goes quiet.

"What the hell is this?" Julie whispers as a goldfinch in a cage fades to a dim shot of her strapped into the torture chair.

"Suffering comes when man climbs out of his place. When he resists his nature and rejects his role."

Sprout is staring at her unconscious nanny and whimpering.

Abram hefts his pack over his shoulder and grabs his daughter's hand. "Move," he says to everyone in the room, and then he's gone.

We hesitate, trying to catch up with this turn of events, but a groan from Carol breaks the shock and we move. Before I close the cabin's door, I glance back at the TV and see my own face looking back at me. I don't remember this photo being taken, but my memory is porous even when I haven't been shocked in and out of consciousness. Despite the harsh light of the flash, I look convincingly alive. My skin is pale but lacks the purple tint of the Nearly Living. My eyes are thoroughly normal. Brown like mud, like shit, like ninety-six percent of the world's population last time such things were tallied. This is what I wanted, isn't it? To be just another man living out his lifespan in a world where children suffer and women are beaten and wild animals sit at all the desks?

"When nails escape their holes," the TV says, *"the house falls apart. Find them and bring them back."*

A single frame of the Axiom logo flickers over my face, the screen glares red, and that grating alert tone rings out in the empty shed. Then regular programming resumes.

Happy kids on tire swings.

The green glass of Freedom Tower shining over a young New York.

A writhing worm.

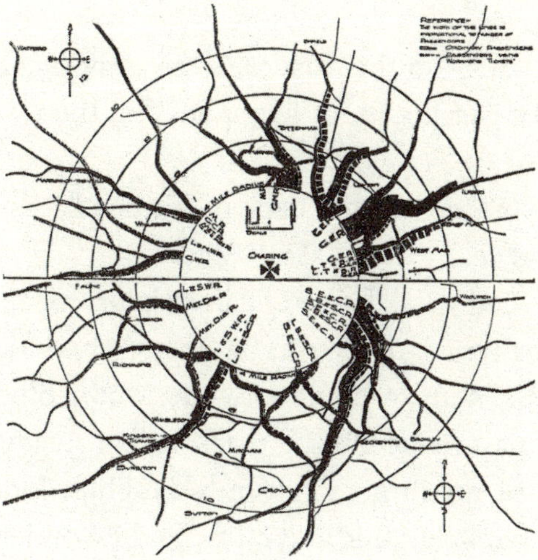

I FIDGET IN THE FRONT SEAT as we flee the camp at a painfully relaxed idle. It's like trying to play dead while a bear gnaws on my skull. I notice a few soldiers emerging from their tents and shining flashlights into each other's faces, but by the time the search gains any momentum we're already to the exit. I see the glow of a television flickering inside the guard's tent and I tense, then I see the guard himself still standing outside, halfway through his cigarette. He nods to Abram and waves us through.

"Thank God for bad habits," Julie mumbles, watching his cloud of smoke recede in the rear window.

Once we're out of view of the camp, Abram hits the gas. The old engine rattles and backfires and the truck roars forward, spitting clumps of dead leaves behind us. Instead of going back up the hill to the freeway, he takes a road that runs alongside it, hidden from aerial eyes by a thick ceiling of trees.

"Where are we going?" Julie says, leaning into the front seat.

"I'll figure that out later," Abram says. "Right now we just need some distance."

Julie nods. "Stay on this road; it's the only one out here that's cleared. Good cover for about five miles and then we can jump on the freeway."

"Abram," Nora says to the back of his head. "That stuff on the TV . . . was that really the LOTUS Feed?"

"It was the Feed we all know and love, it just has new producers."

"So our pictures . . . that 'arrest warrant' or whatever it was . . ."

Abram nods. "It just went nationwide. You're officially outlaws."

The rough pavement fills the truck with a steady rushing noise like the cabin of an airliner. Abram's daughter looks very frightened, wedged between Julie and Nora, and I wonder how much of this she understands.

"How did they do it?" Julie says after a minute of grim silence.

"Do what?"

"Fed TV, Fed FM . . . people have been trying to get ahold of the Feed ever since BABL went online, what, nineteen years ago?"

"Twenty."

"So after twenty years of everyone in America trying to hack this broadcast, you people show up"—her voice trembles and begins to rise—"smash into our homes, take control of our city, and *while you're at it*, you go ahead and grab the Holy Grail? The only unjammed frequency in the whole country?" She shakes her head. "How?"

I remember that brief interruption I observed on the bar's TV. Security footage of the pitchmen's assistants in some strange, dark chamber. A slow knock on the door in my head, *tap . . . tap . . . tap . . .*

"It's in the stadium," I blurt.

All eyes fall on me except Abram's.

"The source of the Feed is in the stadium." I see a trace of a bitter smile on Abram's face, and I look right at him. "It's what you really came for."

He shrugs. "Well, we didn't come for the nightlife."

"Bullshit," Julie says, squinting at him like this is some inscrutable joke. "People have been living in Citi for over a decade. We've turned the place inside out. You're saying we were sitting on the LOTUS broadcast station that whole time and no one knew about it?"

"Someone knew about it."

Julie's indignation freezes. Her demeanor shifts. "What do you mean?" she says in a low voice.

Abram sighs. "Look, I'm not Executive. I'm not even Management, I just fly cargo and watch prisoners, so it's not like I'm invited to the smoky room where the plots are hatched. But from what I've heard, about two months ago someone spliced a new message into the Feed."

Julie stares at him.

"It was crude, obviously rushed, but whoever sent it knew the code, and so did we."

"What did it say?" she asks quietly.

"That your stadium was under attack and we should come here to protect it. Because you had what we wanted."

Julie closes her eyes. She takes the realization like a martyr taking a bullet, barely flinching, and I suppose after watching her father try to kill her and then surrender himself to be eaten, this desperate final act may come as no surprise. But the betrayal that preceded it . . . the years of knowing what they had and choosing not to share it . . . that part cuts through. I can see it digging deeper the longer she contemplates it.

Nora notices this and tries to change the subject. "By the way, Abram Kelvin"—she taps his headrest—"since you seem so eager to get to know us . . . my name's Nora."

Abram smiles dryly. "Right. Names. We don't use them much where I'm from." He glances at Julie, but she's looking out the window, traveling dark paths in her mind, so Nora fills in for her.

"That's Julie. She and your brother were a thing."

Abram's smile fades into a distant blankness. He seems oddly uninterested in pursuing that topic, so I take my turn in the introductions.

"I'm R."

"Art?"

"R. Just the letter."

He glances me up and down as if having an unusual name suggests physical defects. "Who has a letter for a name?"

I shrug. "I do."

He holds my gaze for a moment in some kind of trust-testing ritual, then grunts and returns his eyes to the road.

"Who names their kid 'Sprout'?" Nora says, and we all jump a little when Sprout herself answers:

"I do."

It's the first time we've heard her voice.

"We named her Murasaki," Abram sighs. "Then one day I said she was growing like a bean sprout and for some reason she latched onto it."

Sprout's face flickers into a grin, showing both rows of teeth and a few gaps, then lapses back into worry.

"Where's her mom?" I ask, and Julie emerges from her brooding to shoot me a stern glance. I recall a lesson she taught me early in my rehumanization: if a family member is conspicuously absent, never ask where they are. You know damn well where they are.

To my relief, Abram ignores me.

"Thank you, by the way," Julie says to him, still subdued but recovering. "Never got a chance to say that."

Abram looks back at her. "Thank you? For what?"

"For getting us out of Goldman. Considering *this* was happening by our third day"—she flashes her bandaged stump—"I'm guessing we wouldn't have lasted much longer."

He turns back to the road, shaking his head, but Julie continues.

"I know you said you had other reasons for ditching Axiom, but you still took a big risk to break us out. If you'd just left quietly you might not be a fugitive right now, so . . . thanks."

"I didn't do it for *you*," he says with a note of disgust. "Why would I risk my life for some strangers in a jail cell? You had information about my family, Management was about to kill you, it was a good time to make my move."

Julie lowers her brows. "Hey asshole. I'm not saying you're a hero. I'm just saying thanks."

Abram chuckles darkly. "I throw you in jail, watch you get tortured, then drag you out into the wilderness to probably get killed by my employers, and you say thanks." He shakes his head again. "I shouldn't have interfered with natural selection. You're clearly not meant to make it."

My mind drifts out the window and into the darkness, away from this turbulent chatter. I picture M wandering alone in the forest, gripping his head and groaning as his old self tries to dig a nest in his brain, maybe throwing himself off a waterfall to end the confusion, and a scared, selfish part of me envies him. The simplicity of his struggle. One man fighting one fight: his own. I understand inner conflicts. But to fight for and against other people, to engage with the world outside of me . . . this is a lot more complicated.

I look at Julie in the rearview mirror, hoping to make some kind of meaningful contact, to share a glance that says, *What a mess we're in!* but she's busy glaring out the window, stunned into silence by our driver's impenetrable shell. I stare for a moment, trying to catch her eyes, and then I notice something in the window behind her head. Two points of light floating in the trees. They blink and flicker, disappear for a moment, then flicker back. Fireflies? Fairies? A memory creeps into my consciousness, not something from the forbidden basement of my first life but a dusty relic from the beginning of my second. I am wandering in the woods alone, dragged on a leash by the hungry brute inside me. I am trying to piece together the nature of reality—what trees are, what animals are, what I am—but reality keeps changing. There are strange things in the woods. Hovering hands and shadows that glow and faces peering from holes in the air. These lights in the window seem to belong to that dream. Floating eyes. The Cheshire Cat. Then they accelerate, they draw closer, and the whine of an engine erases all this whimsy.

Headlights.

"I thought we'd have a bigger lead," Abram mutters, and guns the truck to speeds that wouldn't be safe on a major highway, much less this leaf-strewn backroad. I hear the click of seat belts behind me.

Our pursuers gain steadily until I can make out the contours of their much newer, much faster vehicle: a nearly mint Porsche SUV.

"Why do they have a fucking sports car?" Nora squeals. "You've worked for them all these years and you're driving this piece of shit?"

"I need you to shut up now," Abram says through gritted teeth as he struggles to maintain control of the old Ford. Its creaky suspension fails to soften the constant barrage of potholes, and I feel my jaw rattling. The engine roars like a sick bear.

The Porsche pulls up directly behind us and flashes its high beams, a friendly notice from a concerned fellow driver: *Hey buddy, you've got a taillight out*. Then it rams us.

It's only a warning bump, nudging us into a momentary skid, but at this speed the sensation is terrifying. Sprout begins to cry in short, panicked bursts, and Julie wraps an arm around her.

In the glow of the Porsche's headlights reflecting off our tailgate, I notice a long steel tube mounted to its hood, with two hoses running back into the trunk space. I turn to Abram, who is concentrating fiercely on the road ahead of him. I don't know how to break the news gently, so I just say it: "They have a flamethrower."

A chuckle bursts out of him. He closes his eyes for a moment, gathering himself, then veers to the right and slams on the brakes. The Porsche rushes past us. He tosses a pistol into my lap and I stare at it like it's alien technology, an exotic ray gun.

"I can't."

"The hell do you mean you can't?"

"I can't shoot." I reach a shaky hand back to give the gun to Julie, but she's busy trying to calm Sprout and doesn't see it. The Porsche is pulling around. Nora grabs a rifle off the truck's gun rack and climbs out the rear window into the bed. She drops to one knee and takes aim as the nimble Porsche whips a U-turn and comes up behind us again. She gets only one shot off before they ram us, knocking her on her back, but the driver's side of the windshield is suddenly red. The Porsche stops. Abram hits the gas, and the Porsche starts to recede behind us before its driver is replaced and it comes to life again.

"Nora, get inside!" Julie shouts.

"Just a minute," Nora says, taking aim. "I'm really good at this."

She fires. One of the Porsche's front tires hisses and starts to flap . . . then seals and re-inflates itself.

"This is so unfair," she grumbles.

"Nora, get *in*! They're going to—"

Another collision knocks the words out of Julie's mouth and sends Nora toppling against the tailgate. As she climbs to her knees, she finds herself staring into the barrel of the flamethrower, its pilot light guttering in the wind like a tiki torch. She scampers to the window and wriggles inside, and Julie slides it shut just as the rear of the truck erupts into an orange blaze.

Such things have a way of ending an exciting car chase. As the window seals melt, as the women scream and press themselves against the front seats to escape the hair-curling heat, I see an ancient service station ahead, a place for weary travelers to grab some beef jerky and top off their tanks before continuing on into the wilderness. Both the rear tires burst. The truck careens out of control, and as I see the gas pump's barrier post rushing toward us, I have just enough time to think, *Good thing I buckled up,* before we hit the post and my seat belt rips free of the truck's rusted chassis and I hurtle headfirst through the windshield.

I AM FLYING.

I am flying in a plane. I am flying in an armored plane and there are old men in all the seats and one of them is grinning at me from across a table and explaining something about necessity and something about ends and means and justification because he thinks I still require justification, that I still want to believe I'm good; he thinks no one so young could grasp the truth of the world so quickly, but he is wrong. I sip my whiskey and listen to him drone—

The old men are gone and I am on a smaller plane and this one is crashing. An ocean of evergreens spreads out below us, and a blond woman gives me one last look, perhaps a good-bye—Julie screams my name—the trees tear into the plane—

The gravel tears into my shoulder and I roll over and over until my body slaps against a dumpster. I immediately rise to my feet, ready to fight enemies and protect friends, but then I remember: I feel pain now. I am soft and sensitive. I am human. And I have just flown through a windshield. Blood trickles into my eyes and my head is beginning to howl. I feel every inch of my injuries, but I fight my way through them. I stagger toward the burning truck.

Abram crawls out and opens the rear door on Julie's side. I feel a twinge of unpleasant emotion as he reaches in to rescue the woman I love while I stumble toward her, a dizzy, useless mess—but he reaches past Julie and lifts his daughter out. He sets Sprout in the grass a safe distance away and by the time he looks back at the truck, I'm there. Julie and Nora look unharmed but dazed by their impact with the front seats. The rear window is a stovetop and the air reeks of burnt hair. I pull Julie out and Nora scoots out after her and as we run toward the service station to hide from the imminent explosion, a man in a beige jacket steps out of the darkness with a fire extinguisher. The reproachful glare he gives us as he smothers the truck in white foam says we should be ashamed for causing all this trouble.

Julie, Nora, and Abram pat themselves down like they're checking for keys and wallets before leaving the house. But the guns are in the truck.

Two more Axiom soldiers emerge from the smoke, rifles drawn. The first one drops the extinguisher and joins his comrades, and I notice a gray tie underneath his coat, incongruous with the rugged utility of his uniform.

The tie is rank. The color is function. Together they show—

Shut up, I snap, throttling my thoughts into submission. *You don't know these things.*

Gray Tie draws his pistol but doesn't bother raising it. We are already thoroughly covered. "Well?" he says impatiently. "Hands up?"

We raise our hands. I feel the wetness behind my head. My blood is not yet hot, but it's at least higher than ambient temperature. Warm blood, cold comfort.

"Parker," Abram says. "You're making a mistake."

Parker is younger than Abram, mid-twenties, with a slouching stance and a lazy smirk. He looks bored. "These three," he says, pointing from me to Julie to Abram. "We take them back to the dome." He points at Nora. "We can kill this one."

"What?" Nora blurts. "No you can't! The TV said 'Find them and bring them back.'"

"It showed cages for these three," Parker says. "That means capture. Fish tank for you. That means kill."

"A fish tank is a cage, you idiot! You're supposed to capture all of us!"

Parker glances at his comrades. "I'm pretty sure fish tank means kill. You know, like, 'sleep with the fishes'?"

"Oh my God your code sucks," Nora groans.

Parker shrugs. "If I'm wrong, I'm doing you a favor. You don't want to go where your friends are going."

"Parker, listen to me," Abram says, taking a step forward. The other soldiers raise their guns but he ignores them. "Axiom's a runaway train. You need to get out while you can."

"Shut up, Kelvin," Parker says, finally raising his gun. "And step back."

Abram steps forward. "Don't tell me you haven't noticed the change since the hiatus. We're spreading too fast, taking territory we don't need and can't hold, and you never hear a word about an endgame."

"An endgame?" Parker scoffs. "You're a fucking transport pilot, Kelvin; leave the 'endgame' to Executive."

"And where is Executive? Who's on the board and who put them there? Do you even know who the president is right now?"

Parker glances to the side, thinking.

"We get our orders from our bosses and they get theirs from their bosses but you ask who's at the top and you get blank stares. You ask these fucking 'pitchmen' *anything* and you get blank stares."

Parker shrugs. "Okay, yeah, those guys are a little spooky. New training techniques, I hear." He squints. "But what's your point?"

"My point is it's not *safe* here anymore!" He takes another step forward, but the desperation in his voice tells me this is no ploy to distract Parker. He means every word. "Who are we working for? What is our product? There's no security in a company where you can't answer that. What if there *is* no one at the top? What if Axiom's a headless chicken just following leftover impulses, scratching the dirt while it bleeds to death?"

Parker stares at him for a moment, then bursts into laughter. "Wow, Kelvin. I've heard some bullshit come out of your mouth but that's a fresh pile. Is this how you managed to work here half your life without even making Brown Tie?"

"Parker—"

"What a waste. If you could've learned how to shut up and do your job, you would've been Upper Management by now."

"Parker, *listen*—"

"Nah, we're done here." Parker waves his gun toward the Porsche. "Go ahead and get in the car before I misinterpret the code again and decide birdcage means kill."

Abram grinds his teeth. He doesn't move.

Parker lets his gun drift from Abram's head to Sprout's. "You know, your kid wasn't mentioned in the broadcast. Guess it's up to me to decide what happens to her."

"Daddy?" Sprout whimpers, staring into the pistol's barrel, and Abram's body stiffens as if flooded with electricity.

"Get that away from my daughter," he says in a level growl.

"Or what, Kelvin?"

"Or I'll walk through every bullet in the clip and snap your neck while I bleed out."

Parker hesitates, then snorts to mask the concession as he moves the gun away. "Will you just get in the fucking car? This is boring."

Abram grabs Sprout's hand and pulls her close. "You're a fool, Parker."

"And yet I'm the one with the gun and the tie and the guaranteed housing in Manhattan, and you're the one going to jail."

Abram spits on the ground and moves toward the Porsche.

Parker waves his gun at me and Julie. "You too, kids."

We take a few halting steps. The other two soldiers go with us, keeping weapons trained on our heads. Parker jabs his pistol into Nora's back and says, "Into the ditch, please."

"Just let her go!" Julie shouts, her eyes beginning to glisten. "They don't even want her, she has nothing to do with this! Just take us and let her go!"

"You're . . . new, aren't you," Parker chuckles. "Axiom doesn't let go."

Nora steps down into the ditch, into the congealed muck of the gas station's oily runoff. Parker goes around behind her, perhaps to keep his eyes on us, perhaps to ensure that we get an unobstructed view. Julie stares at Nora, speechless, helpless. Nora's face is stone, but she gives Julie a small nod, as if to absolve her of responsibility for what's about to happen.

And is this really about to happen? Did the path of Nora Greene's life weave through so many dangers and heartbreaks and long, lonely miles just to terminate in this ditch because a man she's never met saw a fish on television? My mind refuses to accept it, even as Parker raises the pistol to her head. Even as Julie lunges toward her, screaming, and the soldiers slam her back against the car. Even as my vision begins to blur.

But as Parker braces for the spray of blood, a figure emerges from the shadows behind him. A big arm wraps around his neck and a big hand clamps down on his gun. He has two sweet seconds to comprehend his change in fortune before his comrades open fire and the arm jerks him around to face them and he becomes a soft, fleshy shield for the man operating him like a puppet. While Parker's men fill his chest with bullets, his own gun does the same to their heads, until the arm around his neck finally uncoils and all three soldiers slump to the ground.

The big arm belongs to a big man. Tall and bulky. Bearded and bald. His white T-shirt is stained with mud and sweat and tree sap, and now with a great deal of blood.

"Been remembering a lot," M says, shaking the gun free from Parker's lifeless grip. "Used to be a wrestler, a Marine, a mercenary . . . lots of rough stuff." He surveys the bodies around him with a look of mild amazement. "Funny. Always figured I was a poet or something."

A rare phenomenon occurs inside of me. A bubble of warmth appears in my chest. My larynx spasms—I laugh.

M turns to Nora. "You okay?"

She nods, too shocked to speak.

"Plug your ears."

M debrains the twitching body at his feet, fulfilling his responsibility to society, then climbs out of the ditch with a smile on his scarred lips. "Hey, Archie."

I run forward and hug him. His giant palm thumps my back, knocking some breath out of me.

"Good to see you, M."

"It's Marcus."

"Was afraid you were going to . . ."

"Nah."

It's answer enough for me. I step back, grinning.

"Where the hell did you come from?" Julie says, finally lifting her hands from Sprout's eyes. "I thought you were up in the woods."

"Tried it for a while." He shrugs. "Nature's boring."

A faint smile creeps through Nora's shock.

"Came down to the gas station to find beer . . . found some." He rubs his forehead with a grimace. "Was trying to sleep it off . . . then you noisy motherfuckers . . ." He spreads his palms wide, taking in the blood-sprayed Porsche, the wrecked, smoldering truck, and the three dead men in beige jackets. "What the hell?"

"Marcus," Nora says, touching his shoulder. "A lot happened while you were camping."

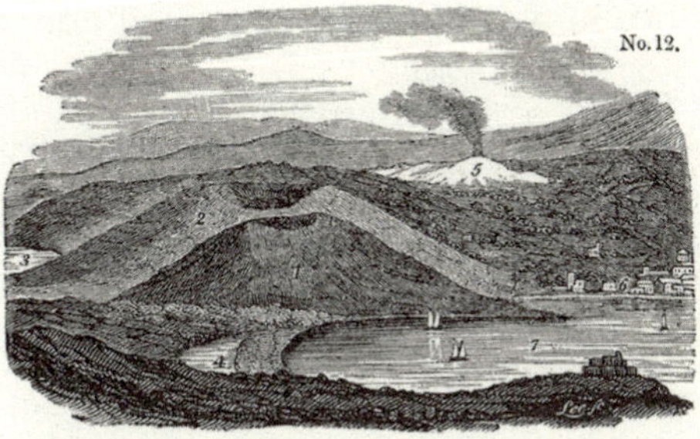

WE

It's quiet in the sky.

If we float high enough, it's almost silent.

No feelings, no memories, no chatter of stories in a million overlapping languages. It's one of the few places on Earth where nothing much has happened—even the birds and insects conduct their business near the ground. There was a brief burst of noise when humans learned to fly, when they thrust their lives into the stratosphere and filled it with fears and fantasies, transactions and quarrels, bathroom sex and panic attacks. But that era passed like a single shout in a cathedral, echoing for a second then gone, and the sky is once again a restful place.

The sighing parts of us like to hide here. Our neutral middle books, lethargic lives untroubled by agony or ecstasy, languid moments and memories of naps—these parts like to drift through newborn clouds and bathe in the blankness, a shelter from the tumult of the Library.

But something is disturbing their leisure, disrupting their pillowy quiet.

Radio waves. Slack for so many years, they have begun to vibrate with intent. For the first time in more than a decade, the mindless recordings and shrieking interference have cohered into something with meaning.

We tune in and listen—even the sighers feel a thrill. Is it music? Is it a message of hope? Voices reaching out to reconcile and rebuild?

No.

It's invasions. Acquisitions. A steady spread of poison. It's armies sharing intel in a grotesque code, relaying atrocities with cartoons and clip art. And between all this, it's a manhunt. A mobilization. A clawed hand reaching out to choke.

"Find them and bring them back."

Far below the clouds, we see a tiny light. A tiny vehicle filled with tiny people, each of them tied to a thousand of our books. Miles behind them, others begin pursuit. Walkies stab through the static, barking curses and commands.

The sighing parts of us gather their strength and abandon the quiet of the clouds. They rejoin the rest of us—the fierce parts, the indignant parts, the wronged and the murdered, the selfless and the heroic, the parts that feel the pain of others and want to make it end.

Together, we descend. We follow these tiny people, watching and waiting, bending our ears to these noisy nodes of life.

The time for quiet is over.

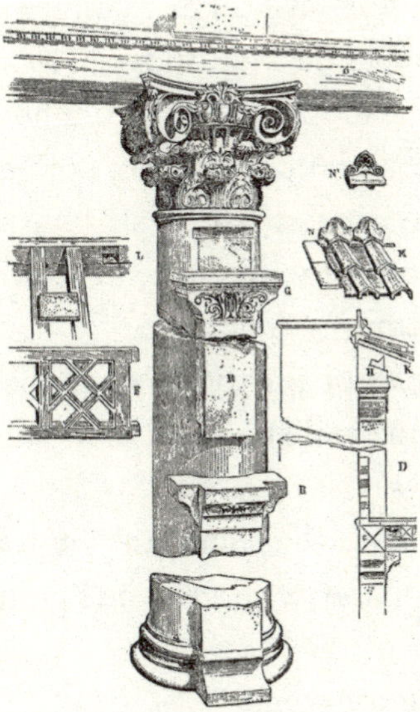

M RESTS HIS KNEES against the dash and does his best to compress his bulk. Abram's knuckles occasionally brush his belly when he reaches for the gearshift, and they exchange an awkward glance. Julie holds Sprout on her lap in the middle backseat, arms wrapped around her like a seat belt, and I sit next to her, my knees digging into M's back, staring out the window while Nora updates him on the grim new landscape of our lives.

The rain has stopped. The sky is developing a faint silvery glow. Julie and I have been unconscious much of the last few days, but when was the last time we really slept? I don't imagine torture blackouts are particularly restful. My body still hasn't fully adopted human needs—I can't remember the last time I felt hungry, and going a week without sleep is not unusual for me—but I worry about Julie. I've never seen her so wrung-out. She's less talkative than usual, letting Nora handle most of the exposition. Her eyes are puffy and bloodshot. She favors her mangled hand, wincing with each bump in the road, and I want so badly to take her home, clean her bandages, wash the blood and dirt from her body. But the word "home" sounds more and more abstract with each passing mile.

"Well . . . ," M says when Nora's story arrives at the unfortunate present, in which we're driving away from three dead soldiers toward an unclear future, ". . . okay."

The car is silent except for the roar of the pavement and the steady *tick tick* of Nora's bullet lodged in the tire.

"Abram," Nora says.

He hasn't spoken since the shootout. He watches the road and little else, which is probably wise since he's going over ninety miles per hour.

"Where exactly are we going?"

"Away from them."

"Who? The guys we just killed?"

He glances at her in the mirror. "Tell me you don't think they were the end of this."

"No, I—"

"They'll give Parker maybe ten minutes to report back, then they'll send another team. And if we manage to escape that one, they'll send two teams. And then three. And so on." He grips the wheel, weaving around potholes or, if there are too many to avoid, driving right over them. "It's like he said. Axiom doesn't let go."

"Why are they so convinced we're important?" Julie mutters to herself. "It doesn't make sense."

"The new Axiom doesn't require its actions to make sense."

"Did the old one?" I ask.

He glances in the mirror to remind himself who's asking. He's heard fewer than twenty words from me since we met.

"We used to be smart," he says, turning back to the road. "We were never gentle, we took what we needed from whoever had it, but we were trying to build a safer world and we made strategic decisions toward that goal. Now we're just eating everything in sight. It can't last."

"Didn't answer Nora's question," M says.

"Where are we going?" she repeats. "I let you drive because I thought you had a plan."

"A plan." He takes an on-ramp and rockets toward the freeway. "*My* plan is to get a couple hundred miles from the coast, drop you people off in the ruins of your choice, then take my daughter to my father's cabin in Montana and wait for Axiom to implode. What's your plan?"

We finally emerge from the slimy rot of the forest onto the concrete plateau of I-5, and Abram pushes the Porsche to speeds it probably never touched in its pre-apocalyptic lifetime, when fast cars were just expensive badges of potency, brimming with power that could never be used.

It can be used now. The speedometer approaches 100.

"It won't work," I say. "Your plan."

I expect a terse retort, but Abram says nothing.

"You can't outrun them. They have planes."

"Not enough to waste them on a manhunt," he says, but the objection sounds halfhearted.

"They have helicopters."

He says nothing.

"They're going to find us. Soon."

Nothing.

"Abram. You won't make it to your cabin."

"I know that!" he snaps, scowling at me in the mirror. "But thank you for explaining it to my six-year-old daughter."

Sprout is watching me. The ever-present worry in her eyes is nearing the dew point. "They're gonna catch us?"

"No, baby," Abram says. "Look how fast we're going. They're not gonna catch us."

"R," Julie says, looking almost as worried as Sprout, "why are you talking like this?"

I stare ahead, watching the landscape scroll toward us, from forest to plains to ancient industrial ruins. "We need to go somewhere they won't look."

Abram's eyes dart to the mirror every few seconds, checking the flat expanse of freeway behind us. There is a light scattering of vehicles, but ours is the only one in motion. "Like where?"

On the distant horizon, in the pink haze of the sunrise, a blue light blinks on the tip of a radio tower.

"Home," M says in a low rumble.

"The airport?" Julie says, reading my intent but not quite buying it.

"The airport," Abram repeats flatly. "You want to hide in the biggest hive on the west coast."

I close my eyes, steeling myself to the idea. "Axiom won't follow us."

He laughs incredulously. "They won't need to! We'll be dead before they know where we went."

"You don't understand," Julie says. "It's safer than you think."

"Which means it's safer than *they* think," Nora adds.

Abram sighs like he's suddenly surrounded by children. "Are you talking about the 'cure'? The uncategorized Dead? Are you about to tell me the Dead in the airport are 'changing' and everything's peaceful now?"

"Not exactly," Julie says. "It's . . . complicated."

"It's *not* complicated. Zombies are animated tissue responding to primal feeding impulses. They can't think, they can't change, there's nothing in there to cure."

"So fucking sure of yourself," Julie says, scooting forward and scowling at the back of Abram's head. "If they can't think, how do they know the difference between human flesh and animal flesh? Why don't they eat each other? Why do they hunt in groups? How do they know where our brains are?"

Abram's fingers press into the leather steering wheel. "They have some basic instinctive reasoning, but they're not *conscious*. They're not self-aware."

"And you can tell this by looking at them? You can see right into their souls?"

Rage flashes in Abram's eyes. "They don't *have* souls! Whoever they were is gone!"

Julie watches him glower for a moment, then asks with surprising gentleness, "Why do you need to believe that so badly?"

Abram doesn't answer.

"R," she says. "Show him."

I've been dreading this moment, but I knew it would come. I roll my pants up and push my leg between the seats, resting my boot on M's knee.

Hidden in such a seldom observed spot, it took me a long time to discover. Even naked in the shower, marveling at my resurrected body, I overlooked it. I had always assumed I died of natural causes until the first time I undressed in front of Julie. At first I took her little gasp for admiration of my endowment and I experienced a brief rush of confidence. *Maybe I'll be good at this*. Then I realized what had really caught her eye, and the first of our many attempts at intimacy wilted.

Abram doesn't gasp, but his face looks a little tight as he comprehends the circular wound on the back of my calf, the unmistakable twin rows of punctures, dried out but never healed.

"I don't know if I have a soul," I say. "But I know I'm not gone."

M pulls up his T-shirt, revealing his cratered landscape of sutured bullet wounds. "What he said."

Abram's eyes rove over our bodies, cataloging our many scars in a suddenly changed context. As evidence, it's not incontrovertible, but it's compelling. Why would anyone lie about being Dead?

"The cure is real," Julie says. "It's not a trap. They're not hibernating. They're coming back."

Abram returns his eyes to the road and doesn't speak. I can't decode the emotions on his face; there are too many at once.

"The Dead at the airport are stuck in between," Julie continues. "They might try to kill us, they might not. But if we stay out here in the open, your friends definitely will."

Abram has stopped obsessively checking the mirror, perhaps no longer worried that we're being pursued, perhaps just assuming we are. He stares straight ahead, watching the control tower rise on the horizon.

"If we can hide out until our trail goes cold," Nora says, "we might have a shot at losing them."

"And even if they do track us to the airport," Julie adds, "they'd be crazy to go in after us. They'll see the place swamped with zombies and assume we're dead. Just like you would."

Abram's face is stiff and blank, watching the airport exit approach, and although it was my idea, I hear the coward in me praying he won't take it. My memories of the airport are as dark as my memories of the torture chamber, and far more numerous. I might prefer capture over facing this place again. But the light on the tower blinks a comforting rhythm, a beacon of premature hope and renegotiated dreams, and Abram takes the exit.

IT WAS A PERFECT DAY to save the world!

R and Julie ran hand in hand down the bright green slope, their cheeks rosy, their eyes sparkly, laughing melodiously while birds fluttered around them and the sun grinned overhead. The airport shone like a pretty pearl in the valley below. It was full of zombies walking with their arms out in front of them, bumping into each other and wheezing "Brains!" like funny old grandfathers.

"We're going to fix them!" laughed Julie.

"We're going to cure the plague!" crowed R.

"Love conquers all!" declared the sun, sunnily.

R and Julie skipped into the airport with a gang of their best friends. Some scary Boneys tried to stop them but R and Julie held hands and a cloud of pink hearts turned the Boneys into butterflies.

"You're not so scary now!" said Julie, and everyone laughed.

R and Julie's friends ran around the airport playing pretty music and sticking pretty pictures on the windows and telling the zombies to cheer up, and the zombies said, "Let's be people again!" and their gray skin turned pink and their gray eyes turned blue and all the boys fell in love with the girls and everyone got married.

"I had a change of heart!" said Julie's father.

"I'm not really dead!" said Julie's mother.

"I'll always love you no matter what," said Julie, gazing into R's beautiful blue eyes, and they kissed, and all their friends applauded, and it was a perfect day.

And then the power cut out. The lights went dark. Frank Sinatra slurred to a stop—*something wonderful happens in summerrrrr*—and R blinked a few times and noticed that his old friends were ripping out his new friends' throats and his new friends were shooting out his old friends' brains and the airport's beige carpet was turning black and red. R saw his old wife hiding in the back, he watched his kids pick up a severed arm with looks of horror and hunger, he saw the panic in the faces of the Living and the confusion in the faces of the Dead, and R and Julie ran away from that bad place, wondering, *Were we dreaming*?

• • •

We're awake now.

The airport looms ahead of us, a sprawling edifice of gray concrete and mildewed glass, like a royal tomb for a shabby king. It was always ghostly when I "lived" here, but now, with the Boneys gone and the hive's society unraveled, it feels truly abandoned. No hunting parties going in or out. No socially awkward Dead wandering alone outside the terminal. No sign of movement whatsoever. It would be nice to believe that they've all dispersed and headed for the city like Nora's patients and our neighbor, B. No doubt some of them have, but not all. Perhaps never all.

We pull up to the Arrivals gate and park the Porsche in a dark corner of the loading zone, hidden from view. This area is mostly clear, but the few vehicles abandoned here suggest stories almost too poignant to ponder. Who was the family who left their minivan and a trail of spilled luggage as they raced to catch the last flight out of America? Where was that flight going, and was it shot down when it got there? Did the owner of this plush pony on the curb grow into a strong and resourceful young woman, or is she now a smear of ash floating somewhere in the Atlantic?

I pull myself out of my morbid reverie. Abram is packing for both an indefinite camping trip and a possible battle. With his backpack from the camp slung over his shoulder, he digs through the Porsche's trunk until he finds a duffel bag full of supplies and hands it to M, eyeing him cautiously. M responds to the scrutiny with a cheery grin, made somewhat unsettling by the scars on his lips.

There are enough weapons for everyone, but after giving a shotgun to Julie and a rifle to Nora and taking a bigger rifle for himself, he regards me hesitantly, holding out a small pistol.

I stare at the gun's gleaming black grip. Muscle memory rushes into my hand. The reassuring weight of steel, the thrilling thrust of the recoil, the satisfying spray of—

"No thanks," I say, demonstrating my hand's unsteady tremble. "I'm still a little uncategorized."

"If I really believed you were infected," Abram says, "I'd be giving you the other end of this gun. A scar doesn't prove anything."

I shrug.

Abram holds the pistol out to M but M brushes past him, reaches into the Porsche's gun rack, and pulls out an AK-47.

"More my size," he says.

Abram looks dubious. "Do you know how to use that?"

M pops out the clip, checks the ammo, racks the bolt and dry fires, then pops the clip back in. "Yup."

"He said he was a Marine, dumb-ass," Nora says while performing a similar function check on her rifle.

"Just two years with the Corps," M says. "But five with Gray River."

Abram nods with faux admiration, returning the pistol to his duffel bag. "So you're part of the Axiom family, then. I take it Gray River doesn't offer a dental plan."

"We won't need the guns," Julie says. "We shouldn't even bring them, it sends the wrong message."

Abram shakes his head.

I'm reluctant to contradict her, but my memories of this place are vivid. "Last time . . ."

"It was too soon. We didn't give the cure time to spread. It'll be different now."

I don't argue, but I'm not convinced. And Julie keeps her gun.

• • •

A tranquil airport is an unnatural thing. Airports were built for commotion, for the noise and effluvia of the global human enterprise. There is no place on Earth with a higher concentration of differences, every culture and language converging on this little building and mixing together, eating the same food and using the same toilets, piling their clothes side by side and stealing glances at each other's belongings as they're revealed on X-ray screens, squeezing hip to hip on cramped gate benches and inhaling each other's odors, everyone alert, worried, striving—the world and all its conflicts, compressed to a tiny point.

Not anymore. All those volatile chemicals exploded long ago, leaving only an empty casing. We encounter not a single moving creature in the outer terminal, and my fear begins to move in a different direction: will this place even protect us? If the Dead are all gone, we're no safer here than anywhere else. But my concerns are short-lived. We pass through the empty security lines and take a left toward Gate 12 and there they are, my old neighbors, milling around the food court in a slow, slumberous swarm. The fear center of my brain has never been more confused. Am I relieved or terrified?

Abram grips Sprout's arm with one hand and aims his rifle with the other, keeping his back to the wall, but the rest of us move forward with weapons down, cautious but calm.

"Hey, guys!" M bellows with a friendly wave.

The horde goes still. A few snap their teeth at us once or twice, then resume their shambling. But most remain motionless, regarding us with inscrutable expressions. Their faces are worn and weary, their bodies slumped; their strange, leaden eyes stare at us with sorrowful longing, like beggars resigned to starvation. I feel a surge of emotion for these lost creatures, pity laced with love. I was one of them. I'm still one of them. Yet somehow I escaped this place, and they remain trapped.

There was a moment, sitting on a hill with Julie, when I thought freeing them would be a simple thing. Not easy, but simple. We would come here, we'd share what we'd learned and spread what we'd created, and they would see the light and be healed. Our effect on the Boneys had been immediate and dramatic. Those empty husks had sensed a shift in the atmosphere, an inconceivable alteration to the rigid rails of their reality, and they had fled, perhaps in search of more stable land, some new flat surface on which to rebuild their universe. But my fellow Fleshies? The Dead who had yet to cut that final thread? Our effect on them was subtler. *Something* has changed; the bullet-scarred giant by my side is proof of that, as is B and every patient in Nora's Morgue. But our attempt to go forth and evangelize was disastrously naive.

They are not impressed. They are not convinced. They are waiting for something more.

M strides ahead and begins to mingle, shaking hands and slapping backs. The Dead stare at him with furrowed brows, like they don't understand what he is. He still has some distance to go before all traces of his rot are rubbed out, but I have retained enough of my Dead senses to know he registers clearly as Living. So their uncertainty is not the age-old question of to eat or not to eat. It's something more complex.

I follow M into the swaying, stinking crowd.

"Hey, R?"

I look back and see Julie and Nora lingering at the end of the hallway like kids on a dock, scared to jump in the lake.

"Are you sure about this?" Julie says.

"Maybe find some blood to smear on us?" Nora says with a cringe. "Like you did with Julie?"

I shake my head. "Wasn't just the blood. It was me going with you. Won't work anymore."

"Why not?"

I shrug. "Because I'm not Dead anymore."

I plunge into the crowd.

"You're insane," Abram shouts from his chosen position far back in the hallway. "Where are you even going?"

I point toward the distant end of the hall, over the heads of a thousand zombies. "Somewhere safe."

I press further in. The Dead don't respond to nudges or other polite requests, but M's sheer mass allows him to part the crowd like jungle grass, and I follow in his wake. Julie and Nora stick close to my back, and while Julie is fighting hard to embrace her convictions and not be afraid of these creatures—these *people*—Nora is a little more transparent.

"Hello . . . ," she greets them through gritted teeth. "How are you . . . please don't eat me . . ."

"Let's go, Daddy," Sprout says. She tugs on his hand, but he remains rooted to the floor.

"Come on!" Julie calls back to him.

"I'm not dragging my daughter through a zombie horde."

"Use your eyes, man. It's okay."

"You don't know what they're going to do."

She throws up her hands. "You don't know what *anyone's* going to do! Any person in any crowd could be a murderer, a rapist, a suicide bomber. You dive in and hope for the best."

Like her, I'm putting on a brave face, but I can't pretend I'm not scared. Fighting off the plague didn't make me immune to it. This was one of the first big questions among the Nearly Living—*what happens if we're bitten again?*—but we didn't have to wait long to find out. A suicidal runaway showed us the dismal answer: what happens now is what happened then. We rejoin the Dead. We lose it all. We start over.

Despite my long struggle, despite the Gleam and all the other mysteries of the cure, I am just as vulnerable as Julie. And just as dependent on the whim of the mob.

Once the restaurants end and the gates begin, the density thins and we pop out into an open area of benches and plastic trees. Further down the hall, another group hovers around a bagel stand, staring at the empty case and pretending to read the menu. Perhaps by accident, a woman stumbles behind the counter. The crowd instinctively forms a line. Before the man at the front can place his order, the newly hired cashier wanders off again, and the line disperses with a vague aura of disappointment.

I watch all this with great interest. Is it just the lingering echoes of old instincts, or a sign of recovery? A stiff body stretching its limbs, testing its reflexes? I remember my first real meal. I'd been trying for weeks. Every evening I'd shove bread in my mouth and force myself to swallow; sometimes I'd even manage to hold it down until Julie finished celebrating before I snuck off to the bathroom to vomit. I didn't want her to share my worry that I wouldn't survive my transformation. But then, after about a month, it happened. I felt a stirring of the *old* hunger. The kind that didn't demand human sacrifice. I watched Julie frying potatoes from our garden, drowning them in hot sauce, and my stomach grumbled. I wanted *food.* I didn't want to suck the lightning out of a human soul; I wanted to eat hash browns. And I ate them. It was another week before I could eat again, and even now my body remains distrustful of such simple, deathless nourishment, accepting it only when starvation is imminent. But that moment gave me hope that I didn't know I lacked. It was a step.

Now I watch these bewildered corpses stumble through the motions of human gastronomy, and I pour my hope into them. I will them to take the next step.

"Where'd he go?" Julie says, standing on tiptoe to see through the crowd behind us. She hops up on a bench. "Abram? Sprout?"

I don't need the bench to see that they're no longer in the hall.

"Did they seriously ditch us?" She cups her hands to her mouth. "Abram!"

"Keep it down," he says, emerging from a service door with his daughter in tow. "You'll wake them up."

Julie sighs. "I hope you feel stupid taking the long way around now that you see we're all fine."

"I don't take risks with my family." He fixes me with a stern glare. "Where's your 'safe space'?"

• • •

To Abram's relief—and mine, if I'm being honest—our route doesn't take us through the bagel crowd. The hall branches off to the right and I lead us into the elevated tunnel that connects Terminal A to Terminal B. Behind us, the overhead sign promises BAGGAGE CLAIM and RESTROOMS. The book store is called Young's Bay Books. The intimidating tome in the bestseller kiosk is *The Suggestible Universe: How Consciousness Shapes Reality.* I smile, remembering the countless hours I spent staring at all the words in this airport, wondering what they were trying to tell me. My budding literacy has lifted a veil from the world, revealing the tips of a thousand icebergs. If I ever have another peaceful moment, I'll dive deeper. I'll sit in my favorite chair with my favorite mug of my favorite tea and I'll read *The Suggestible Universe* cover to cover. Though I should probably start with the book next to it, *Scary Jerry and the Skeleton King.* Or maybe the one next to that: *Goodnight Moon.*

"What?" Julie says, noticing my faint smile.

"Nothing. Just thinking. What's your favorite book?"

She considers. "I have about fifty."

"I want to read with you." My smile expands as I add her to my tea-and-tweed daydream: sitting next to me on the couch, leaning against my shoulder with a paperback spread between her fingers. "Let's make our dining room a library."

She drinks in this image with a wistful smile. "That'd be nice."

The longing in her voice pops my bubble, a cold reminder of our circumstances. What was our actual life a week ago has become an improbable fantasy.

The lights flicker. The generators fire up, or the solar panels activate—whatever forgotten energy source powers this place wakes itself again, and the airport resumes a sad semblance of its former functions. The lights come on, the PA system stutters something about unattended baggage, the conveyors begin to move. I step aboard, Julie hops on behind me, and we take a break while the others walk past us, giving us mildly disapproving stares.

Once upon a time, Julie and I watched the sunset through these wall-to-wall windows. Now we face the other way and watch the sun crest the mountains, flooding the runways with pink light. An American Airlines plane with no engines. A United plane split in two. The blackened wreckage of a private jet. What a sad little island the airport must have been during the last days, when every person in every place thought someplace else was safer. A nexus for all doomed hopes.

I watch the pots of plastic plants glide past us, now overrun with real daisies, and another bit of nostalgia warms my thoughts. I lean over the railing to pluck one, but it passes just out of reach.

By the time we reach the end of the conveyor, the rest of the group is waiting for us, arms folded impatiently.

"What?" Julie says. "We came here to wait, didn't we?"

"Let's wait somewhere secure," Abram says. "Not in a glass hallway exposed to the whole world."

"Almost there," I assure him. He's right, of course. I need to focus, but I can't seem to shake my whimsy. Despite the multitude of dark memories this place evokes, the few bright ones I built with

Julie keep rising to the surface and painting a dumb smile on my face. Things were so easy then. So simple and sweet. Just me and my kidnapped crush and her boyfriend's brain in my pocket.

I lead the group down the boarding tunnel to the door of my former home, my refuge from the horrors of my undead existence. I never imagined I'd come back here to hide from something worse.

I pull open the airliner's massive hatch and step aside with a grim smile. "Welcome aboard."

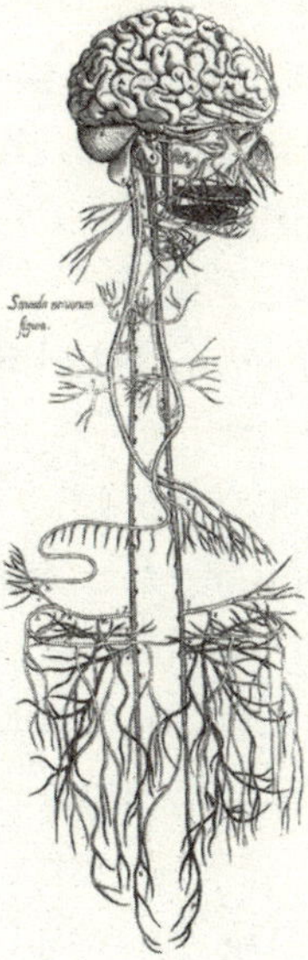

THE PLANE IS EXACTLY how we left it. The empty beer bottles, the plastic trays of frozen pad thai, and of course, my stacks of memorabilia. It strikes me for the first time how extensive my collection was. Pens, paintbrushes, cameras, dolls, action figures, a painting, a tuxedo, undelivered letters, framed family photos, a tower of comic books . . . About a third of the plane's seats are filled. If I found one or two items on each infrequent hunting trip, how long must I have been here to accumulate such a hoard? Six years? Seven? In all that time, why didn't I rot away like so many of the others? Why am I not just another dried-up metathesiophobe, hissing with fury over everything that's changed?

Julie sits in her chair of choice. She picks up her old quilt made of cut-up jeans. But this time she doesn't use it as a shield against me. She pats the middle seat and I sit beside her, luxuriating in the privilege of her trust.

M turns in a slow circle to take in the cluttered disaster of my domicile. "You brought a girl home to this?"

"I found it charming," Julie says.

M grunts.

"Where was your place?" Nora asks him. "Can't imagine it being any cleaner."

"It was clean," he says. "For a public restroom."

Nora starts to laugh, then her face stiffens. "A restroom?"

M shrugs. "It was a room with a door. Just ended up there."

Nora regards him with an odd, crooked expression that's completely unknown to me. The only thing I can read in it is confusion, but it's more than that.

"I was a zombie," M says, growing defensive. "Wasn't picky about housing."

Nora looks at the floor, looks through it.

"What's wrong?" Julie asks. She moves to get up, but Nora shakes her head and snaps out of it.

"Nothing. Sorry. Déjà vu or something." She addresses M without quite looking at him. "Do you remember where you used to live? Sometimes I feel like we've met before."

M answers cautiously. "I think . . . Seattle?"

Nora shakes her head again. "Nope. Never been there." She looks up and takes a deep breath. "Anyway, what do we have to eat? I hear airline food is excellent."

She disappears behind the flight attendant curtain and starts banging around in the kitchen drawers.

"Nora?" M calls to her, dropping the duffel bag from the Porsche onto one of the seats. "Food's . . . in here."

Silence for a moment, then she emerges from the kitchen and opens the bag, digs out a Carbtein cube and a water bottle and takes this sad meal to the back of the plane.

M looks at me. I shrug. I look at Julie. She shrugs.

I notice that Abram hasn't come inside yet. He's still standing in the doorway with Sprout, running his eyes over the unaccountable oddness of my former home.

"*This* is where you want to hide?" he says.

I raise a hand to demonstrate the safety features of the aircraft. "One entrance. Emergency exits. Small windows." He doesn't respond, so I keep going. "High ground. Good visibility. Solar pow—"

"Watch Sprout," he cuts me off, nudging his daughter forward. "I'm going to run a perimeter check."

Sprout runs forward and stops at our row, staring at me expectantly. When I don't react, she says, "Move please."

I scoot out to the aisle seat and Sprout plops down next to Julie.

Julie shoots me a look of perplexed delight, holding back a laugh.

"You like Julie?" I ask the girl, and she nods earnestly. I smile. "Me too."

I look back to the doorway to give Abram a few tips for his tour of the airport, but he's already gone.

• • •

In less than ten minutes, everyone but me is asleep. It's somewhere around noon, the sun is high and hot, but it was a very long night. Even M has managed to nod off with the effortless ease of the Living, while I sit patiently next to Sprout and Julie, listening to the chorus of snores. In almost every way, M seems to be falling back into human existence more quickly than I am, and I don't understand why. He speaks well, his reflexes are sharp, and if his stories can be believed, he successfully made love with a Living woman—albeit a very desperate one—after only a month in the stadium. I had a head start, I was the one who pulled him into this race, but now he's left me far behind. What is holding me back?

I get up and move toward the rear of the plane where I can express my restlessness without waking anyone. I sneak past Nora, who is stretched out across three seats with her feet sticking into the aisle. M would be more comfortable back here as well, but he has squeezed himself into one of business class's plush thrones of isolation, perhaps sensing that Nora needed space.

As I near the end of the jet's length, I suddenly remember one of my less whimsical collections. The last three rows are buried under piles of torn pants, bloody shirts, the occasional shoe with a foot in it. My dirty laundry covers the seats and spreads into the aisle, the college dorm of a promising young serial killer. I glance over my shoulder, feeling shivers of shame run down my back.

Whenever possible, I kept my victims' clothes. In my half-asleep haze, I had some vague notion that this was a way to commemorate the people I consumed. To honor their noble sacrifice to my needs, which were of course nonnegotiable. It was certainly more thought than most zombies give to their predations, but I doubt anyone will commend me for it. I begin scooping up the clothes and stuffing them into the overhead luggage bins as a stew of disgust churns in my belly.

Something bumps against the bathroom door.

I freeze with a blood-crusted Christmas sweater dangling from my hands. A groan emanates from the left door and is answered by a slightly louder one from the right. I glance around for a weapon. I don't see anything capable of cracking a skull, but I've done it with my bare hands plenty of times; people don't realize how easy it is, you just have to—

I halt my thoughts. I unclench my fists. I remind myself that killing is no longer how I introduce myself to strangers.

"Hello?" I say softly, and the noise in the bathrooms stops. The latches on both doors say OCCUPIED, and it strikes me as odd that a zombie would bother to lock anything. I rap a knuckle on the left door. "I don't want to hurt you. You don't want to hurt me. Will you come out?"

The red OCCUPIED slides into a green VACANT. The door opens a crack, and I'm looking at a familiar face. A woman in her mid-twenties, brown hair, pale skin, eyes that could almost be a natural gray if not for their metallic sheen.

I back up to make room, and my "wife" emerges from the bathroom. Her receptionist's outfit is filthy beyond belief, but my eyes ignore the countless bloodstains on the white button-up as they search for her name tag. It's not there. Did she remove it? Why would she remove it?

"Name?" I ask her, slipping back into our primitive patois.

She shakes her head. What is the look on her face? Shame? Bitterness? Or just the confusion and fear of a traveler lost in a foreign land?

I hear a click behind me and the other bathroom opens. My "children" peek shyly around the doorway. At least they have names. I extracted them during that brief window when they appeared to be recovering, when the sun was rising and Sinatra was crooning and everything was going to be fine. Their skin isn't bloodless but it's still very pale, even Joan's, whose pallor contrasts eerily with her dusky Arab features. They look alive but half-frozen. Their eyes are like their mother's, stuck between states. They look the same as they did the day I abandoned them. The day Julie and I realized our ambitions were too big and decided we had to downsize.

Our house in the suburbs may be the front lines compared to life in the stadium, but it was still a retreat.

"Why are you here?" I ask my nameless wife.

She drops her eyes to the floor. "Want to . . . stop."

At first I'm not sure what she means, but then I notice her condition. Patches of sunken flesh run down her neck and cheeks, soft depressions like bruises on a pear. Insufficiently embalmed with the energy of human life, her cells are finally accepting that they're dead, deflating and dehydrating one by one. She is starving herself.

The kids look slightly healthier, with only one or two depressions visible on their skin. I assume this means they lack their mother's resolve and have been finding Living flesh to eat, but then I notice the cookie in Joan's hand and the cheese stick in Alex's. Both are barely nibbled, but the effort is apparent, and effort is almost everything.

"Eat?" I say to my wife, pointing to the snacks.

She shakes her head, and this time the emotion is clear: shame. You can lead a corpse to food but you can't make it eat. The will is strong but the flesh is delicious. And so on.

I glance over my shoulder, then hold out my hands. "Wait here."

I tiptoe back to row 26 and shake Julie's shoulder. She groans and tries to wriggle away from me.

"Julie," I whisper. "Wake up."

Her eyes open a crack, glaring at me sideways. "What."

"My wife and kids . . . they're here."

She pulls herself upright, blinking the sleep away. "Here? In the plane?"

"Don't know what to do."

She slides out from under Sprout and carefully lays the girl's head on the seat. We rush back to the restrooms where my perfect little nuclear family is eyeing Nora's sleeping form with unmistakable yearning.

"Nora," Julie says, nudging her shoulder.

Nora snaps upright, restraining her shock as she registers the newcomers. "Were they about to eat me?"

"No," I say, then falter. "Maybe. But they really don't want to."

"Are these . . . your kids?"

"Uh . . . yes."

"Hi, kids," Nora says neutrally, then looks at their mother. "And you?"

"She's R's wife," Julie says with a faint smile.

Nora sighs. "Great. A fucking love triangle."

"It was . . . an arranged marriage," I mumble.

"What's your wife's name?"

"Don't know."

Nora considers this, then nods. "Okay, so maybe no love triangle."

I squirm. My wife squirms. I look at the floor and she looks out the windows. Then she grabs our kids' hands and lumbers toward the exit.

"Hey!" Nora calls to her, getting out of her seat and taking a few steps down the aisle. "I was just playing!"

But there was something more than offense in my wife's expression. I look out the window. The empty expanse of the tarmac has become a sea of gray faces.

The plane is completely surrounded by the Dead.

"*That* can't be good," Julie says, following my gaze. She runs back to check on Sprout.

I remain transfixed by the crowd. Even in the heyday of this hive, I never saw this many gathered in one place. The Boneys' church services came close, but there were always those who found fiery sermons of wordless clicks and hisses to be an unengaging experience, no matter how charismatically the Boneys delivered them, so the assemblies never drew more than half of the airport's population. The mob gathered here today has to be all of it.

And yet despite its resemblance to a mobilizing army, I don't sense hostility. Most of them aren't even looking at the plane. They face north, toward the airport's entrance, toward the city, and they wait.

The plane's door squeals open and shuts with a bang. I hear the lock mechanism snap into place. Abram strides down the aisle, his rifle at the ready, chest heaving like he's coming out of a long sprint.

"They're coming," he says between breaths.

"We know," Julie says. "We can see them."

"Not the Dead." He scoops Sprout up from her chair and moves to the emergency exit row, shutting all the window shades as he goes.

"Axiom?" Nora says, not wanting to believe it. "How the hell did they find us so fast?"

"Porsche probably had a tracker somewhere, but I figured the jamming would kill the range . . ." He slams the last window, plunging the cabin into gloom. "Doesn't matter. They're here."

"How many?" Nora says, her face hardening as she grabs her rifle from the overhead bin.

"Too many." He drops into the window seat with Sprout on his lap and grips his rifle with white knuckles.

"What's going on?" M yawns, stepping through the first-class curtain. No one answers him.

"So what's your plan, then?" Julie says with rising panic. "Just sit here and hope they don't check the only intact plane on the runway?"

He raises his window shade an inch and peers out at the swaying horde around us. "My plan is to sit here and hope your friends remember how much they like human flesh."

I raise my shade halfway. Like iron filings drawn toward a magnet, the crowd is orienting stiffly in one direction: toward a service gate at the north end of the tarmac. The gate slides open and five beige SUVs roll through it. Then they stop. No doubt they expected zombies. What they probably didn't expect was a semi-organized army of them.

The Dead still don't appear hostile. They cock their heads, uncertain, uneasy, like abused dogs sniffing a stranger's hand, wondering if it will stroke or strike. And I see my family among them. Joan and Alex and my nameless wife, huddled at the back of the crowd, waiting for these newcomers to express their intent.

The trucks begin to advance.

"What the hell are they doing?" Julie whispers. She said they would be crazy to follow us in here. She was right, and here they come.

Their sunroofs open. Soldiers in beige jackets rise through the holes. They brace rifles against the roofs.

"No," I murmur into the glass.

My former neighbors watch the trucks draw closer, nervous but curious. Then they begin to die.

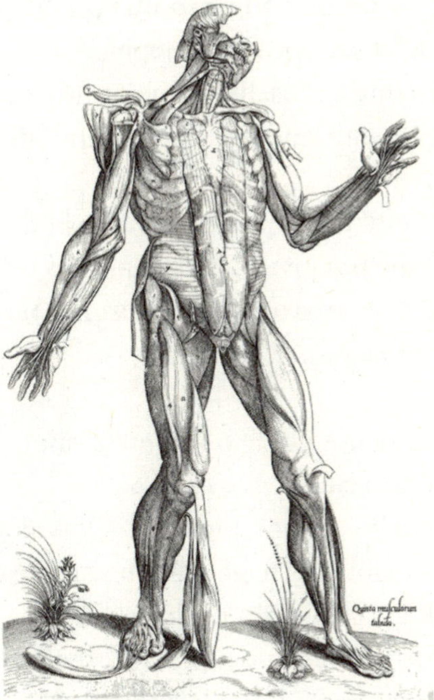

"R, *WAIT!*"

I pause in the plane's doorway but I don't turn. I can feel Julie's fear tickling my neck.

"You can't do anything for them! You don't even know how to shoot that!"

I look down and notice that I'm holding M's AK-47. I must have grabbed it off his chair in an unconscious reflex, and I appear to have chambered a round and switched off the safety. I'm not sure either of us knows what I know how to do. But the tremble in my hands is even more pronounced than usual; I'm practically spasming. I let the gun clatter to the floor and stride into the boarding tunnel.

"R!" she shouts, running after me. "There's a thousand of them down there. One more isn't going to make a difference."

"Joan and Alex," I say without stopping.

The gunfire is continuous, like a roll of firecrackers, and I imagine each and every shot ending the budding life of one of these potential people.

I hear Julie's footfalls behind me as I rush down a staircase to the ground level; she has given up arguing and is racing to join me, with M's rifle like an oversized toy against her tiny frame. I stop at the exit door and turn to her.

"Stay here."

"Fuck you, you're not going out there alone."

Crack. Crack. Crack-crack-crack-crack.

"Please," I say to her, imagining those shots aimed at her instead of the anonymous mob and feeling my fear spike tenfold. "I'm *asking* you to stay here. I'll be right back."

I don't wait for her response. She'll respect my wishes or she won't. I've said everything I can say, short of "good-bye." I burst through the door into the blinding sun.

• • •

It's not quite the massacre I was anticipating. The soldiers appear to be conserving ammo, taking methodical head shots instead of spraying into the mob. They have the luxury of doing this because the mob is not attacking them. The Dead are agitated, swaying and groaning loudly, but their faces still display recognizable human emotions. Fear, confusion, grief. They seem utterly perplexed by what is happening to them.

But as the trucks slowly advance, as row after row of the Dead drop to the pavement and the rows behind them wipe their friends' liquefied brains off their faces, something begins to change. So close to the end of their climb, just a few steps from the summit, they stop. They stumble backward. They fall.

The indeterminate hue of their eyes flashes silver, and their faces lock into the murderous blankness of the All Dead.

I want to roar and cry at the same time. The stupidity of it. The relentless razing of every green shoot. As the Dead surge forward in a wave and begin to overrun the trucks, I try not to take pleasure in the soldiers' shrieks. But I do.

My family is revealed in the rear of the crowd as everyone else advances to attack. I run to their side and grab the kids' hands. "Come on."

The nearest truck disappears under a pile of Dead. A few of them pull the gunner out through the sunroof and tear him apart while a few more crawl inside to deal with the driver. What did these men expect? Twenty or thirty of them against several thousand Dead? How can anyone be so fully grafted to a system that they would obey such mad orders?

Their desperate shots shatter windows and kick up puffs of dust on the concrete around my feet. I start to pull the kids toward the terminal door, but when I look back to make sure my wife understands the agenda, she is not there. I glance around the tarmac and find no sign of her. I stand in the shadow of the 747, holding the kids' hands and staring at the mob, knocked off balance by an emotional sucker punch. It never occurred to me that my wife would relapse with the rest of the horde. I thought she had climbed too high to fall back into this feral frenzy. But more importantly, I thought I didn't care what happened to that nameless, voiceless woman, and I am dismayed to find that I do.

The Dead set to work on the next truck. The men in the other four jump out and take defensive positions behind their doors. Despite streams of bullets ripping into the Dead from four directions, this venture is going to prove unprofitable for the Axiom Group. The third truck goes under. Then the fourth. But as the horde—reduced by a few hundred but still overwhelming—sweeps over the last two Escalades, I notice a familiar drone in the air. My hair begins to flutter back from my face, and I have just enough time to register dread before a helicopter—not some repurposed local news chopper but an actual military aircraft—swoops over the roof of the terminal building and hovers directly overhead, eclipsing the noonday sun.

Somewhere inside its cockpit, a soldier swivels the nose-mounted chain gun and begins to cut splattering swaths through the mob. He is too late to save the men in the trucks, but with all the airport's inhabitants gathered in the open with no way to fight back, he can at least take this opportunity to clear out this hive. One less unknown to threaten the natural order.

The Dead make a noble effort. They climb onto the roof of the nearest vehicle and swipe for the chopper's landing gear. Some of them even attempt to jump. But the pilot keeps it hovering just out of reach, lower than he actually needs to, perhaps taking pleasure in their desperate efforts as his gunner mows them down. I catch his face in the windshield, the sadistic smirk of a child burning ants.

A higher pitched rattle of gunfire joins the heavy thump of the chain gun and I see Julie standing behind a second-floor window, firing M's AK-47 through the glass. She probably knows this is useless against an armored attack chopper, but these are the gestures we make when useful actions run out. Her bullets chip the chopper's paint and make white spots on the windshield, damaging its resale value but little else. The gunner ignores her until she manages to ping a shot off a rotor blade, then the chain gun rises and Julie runs for cover as it strafes across her floor, filling the air with broken glass and upholstery fluff. Satisfied that he's made his point, the gunner returns his attention to the Dead.

I drag my kids toward the safety of the terminal door, determined to save at least these two, and just as I'm reaching out to open it, I hear a cry. A raw, plaintive noise almost like the howl of a dog, inarticulate but trembling with emotion. I look up.

My wife is on the control tower balcony, directly above the helicopter, leaning against the railing. Her eyes are on me, and I realize the noise I heard was her calling to me, the sound of a person trying to reach another person without words or a name. But she doesn't need words now. She cries out again, and the anguish in it makes the meaning clear.

Good-bye.

She jumps off the tower. She falls facedown, arms spread wide, hair fluttering up toward the clear summer sky, and when she hits the blurring disc of the rotors, she vanishes. Lukewarm liquid sprays across my face. I hear the wet slap of heavier bits raining down all over the tarmac, but the sound is mercifully muffled by the screech of the helicopter tearing itself apart. Its bent rotor rattles horribly for an instant, then something snaps. The chopper flips and twists and flings itself into the concrete base of the terminal building. It doesn't explode. Its impact is less than satisfying. It hits the wall with a dull crunch, then falls to the pavement in a mangled heap.

Everything goes silent. The fury abruptly drains out of the remaining Dead, their shoulders falling back into their customary slouch. But while their rage sags, mine swells, stretching my seams to bursting. My eyes take in the carnage around me, flicking from corpse to corpse, their gazes fixed on the dreaded mouth of the sky as their brains ooze through the backs of their heads. All their struggles disregarded, all forward steps ignored, erased in a few minutes by a few little bits of lead. And scattered all around them, on the ground and on my clothes and in my eyes, the remains of a woman who never told me her name. A woman I bumped into in a dream and married without ever exchanging a word, paired as a unit by the decree of a formula that neither of us understood. She should mean nothing to me. I knew nothing about who she was behind her blank stare or who she would have become if given the chance. And perhaps that's it. She was trying to become something beautiful, and these cruel and stupid children have cut open her chrysalis simply because they could.

I run to the helicopter. I wrench open the cockpit door and seize the pilot by his jacket, pulling him against his seat straps. "Why?" I growl, inches from his face.

His eyes take a moment to focus on me. In my periphery I see a twisted piece of steel sticking out of his side and his copilot dead in the other seat, but I'm focused on the pilot's face, mostly blank now but still retaining the lines of that smirk I saw through the windshield as he savored the killing of weaker things.

"Why are you doing this?" I say from some hot, dark boiler room in my mind. "Why won't you stop?"

He opens his mouth. A ragged wheeze comes out. His eyes seem to be looking past me.

"*Why*?" I shout, shaking him against the seat. "What's your goal? Who are your leaders?"

I feel something beyond rage thrumming inside me. The noise from the basement. The rattling door.

"Where is Atvist?" I scream into his face and grab the piece of steel and rip it out of his chest. The door in me is straining against its locks, and through the crack I can see fire and burnt flesh and squirming masses of worms.

I thrust my hand into his gaping wound and dig until I find his lung. "Tell me!"

I squeeze his lung, forcing puffs of air through his throat.

"*Tell me*!"

I hear footsteps behind me, and the burning red murk clears from my vision. I become aware that I am screaming at a dead man, and my fist is inside his chest, and my friends are watching in horrified silence.

I drive the piece of steel into the dead man's skull, then slowly stand up and turn around, wiping my hand on my pants. Julie, M, and Nora stare at me with wide eyes. Abram waits in the terminal doorway with his daughter, looking more impressed than disturbed. I feel an urge to apologize, to offer some unlikely excuse for what they just witnessed, but I'm too full of disgust. Some for myself, but more for everything else. My disgust for the world is so deep, my own portion sinks into it with barely a ripple.

"We need to go," I say, staring at the ground.

There is a long silence, broken only by the soft groans of the Dead. They shuffle around like sleepwalkers, eyes on the pavement and the carpet of corpses that covers it, seemingly unaware of our presence, stuffed back into some deep hole where not even the smell of life can reach them.

"Go where?" Julie asks quietly.

"Out into the world. There's nothing left here."

"What's out in the world?"

"We don't know. That's why we need to go."

Without meeting their eyes, I push past my friends and stop in front of Abram. "Axiom owns the coasts. What's in between?"

He looks me up and down for a moment as if debating how seriously to take me. "Not much," he says. "Exed cities. Empty territories. A few struggling enclaves, probably."

"Probably?"

"It's been a few years since I've heard any reports. Axiom mostly sticks to the coasts these days. But everyone knows—"

"No one knows anything," I snap. "The world has grown. A city's a country and a country's a planet. There has to be something out there."

They all watch me, taken aback by my sudden verbosity, but I'm so focused I forget to feel self-conscious.

"Something like what, exactly?" Nora says.

"People." I finally allow myself to make eye contact, first with her, then Julie, then Abram. "Help. Maybe even answers."

Julie begins to nod. "Axiom has our home and everything around it. They plan to keep spreading, and we can't stop them ourselves."

"I wasn't planning on stopping them," Abram says.

"Oh right, your cabin." She holds his gaze with that eerily mature steel that lurks beneath her youthful flippancy. I feel a little thrill whenever it emerges. "Maybe you're right. Maybe if you hide out long enough, Axiom will burn itself out. But my guess is they'll burn the rest of the continent first. Is that what you want to give Sprout for her eighteenth birthday when you finally come out of your bunker? A scorched Earth run by madmen?"

"I'm not seeing many alternatives," he says under his breath.

"Are you looking for them? There could be rebel armies, thriving enclaves, people spreading the cure . . . We have no idea what's out there."

Abram meets her steel with his own. He is looking at her so intently that he doesn't notice Sprout wandering off.

"Daddy," she says, climbing onto the 747's tire. "Let's go somewhere."

"Mura, get down!" He rushes over and pulls her off. My own kids stare at the young girl, recognizing one of their own, though their eyes are still wide with the shock of seeing their mother aerosolized in front of them. I note with another pang of sadness that the blood spattered across their faces is red. Dark red, almost purple, but not black. She was so close.

"What are you even proposing?" Abram says without turning around. "Go exploring? Take a road trip? Are you forgetting that Axiom is right behind you? You got lucky twice but the minute we find out—" He stops, releases a weary breath. "The minute *they* find out what happened here, they're going to get a lot more serious. We can't run much longer."

"Need to run faster," I say.

He points to the wreck of the chopper. "That's one of maybe ten helicopters remaining in America, and you know who has the rest."

"How about a jet?"

He opens his mouth to scoff at this, then glances back at the enormous tire that his daughter is climbing again.

"You said you were a 'large transport pilot,'" Julie says. "Can you fly a 747?"

His eyes travel up the landing gear and over the clownishly bulbous nose of one of the largest commercial airliners ever built. He chuckles. "Fucking thing's so big I forgot it was a plane."

"Can you fly it?"

He studies it for a moment, mumbling to himself. "Looks like civil-military . . . late model . . . probably close enough to the C-17 . . ." He glances sideways at Julie. "I can fly it if it flies, but that's a big 'if.' Everything else here is wrecked or gutted."

"It has power," I offer.

"There's fuel in the Iceland Air hangar," M says, then puts a hand to the side of his mouth and whispers to Nora, "I used to huff it."

Nora smiles. "Good shit?"

"Good shit."

Abram watches the Dead stumble over the corpses littering the tarmac. He looks at the two fresh ones in the helicopter, wearing the same beige jackets he is. He looks at his daughter, sitting eye level with him on the tire, her worried face showing a rare glow of excitement.

"I'll give it a preflight check," he says, keeping his voice carefully neutral. "But don't get your hopes up."

• • •

While Abram inspects the plane's vital organs, M leads me to his secret stash: a pyramid of fuel drums hidden under a tarp, though I doubt it was the tarp that kept his treasure safe. The airport in general has been largely untouched by post-apocalyptic desperation, still lush with low-hanging fruit like solar panels, cars that run, and perhaps a plane that flies. I suspect it was me and my fellow Dead, gathered here in such uncommon density, who kept the looters away all these years. Thousands of security guards working around the clock—with occasional lunch breaks.

We load as many barrels as we can onto a luggage transport and drive them to the plane. Abram is crouched on the wing, inspecting the flaps, and we watch him for a few minutes before he notices us.

"Is it stabilized?" he asks, clearly grasping at straws. The world had decades to prepare for the apocalypse and preserving the fuel was priority one. Finding perishable gas is about as likely as finding whale oil.

M jabs a hand at the label on the barrels: a clock encircled by spinning arrows.

"How many more are there?" Abram says.

M shrugs. "A lot."

Abram stares at the barrels with his mouth slightly open, searching for an argument. Then he sighs. "Get them. We'll need every drop."

The emergency-exit door bursts open and Julie steps out onto the wing. "Does that mean it works? It'll fly?"

"It's the 2035 model," Abram replies wearily, "about as new as airliners get, and it looks like everything important is intact." He wipes sweat off his forehead. "Needs a little service, but I think I can get it in the air."

A look comes over Julie that I haven't seen since that day on the stadium rooftop, when she saw that the corpse she just kissed was alive, and at least one thing in her dark world could change. She doesn't say anything. She just stands there on the wing, bathing me in a luminous grin, and for a moment, as her hair flutters over her face and the sun turns her skin gold, all her scars and bruises are gone.

"I can get it in the air," Abram cautions, "but I don't know how long it'll stay there."

Without a word, still grinning, Julie pirouettes back into the plane and slams the door.

"I need about three hours," he says to M and me, and we both blink away the hypnotic effect of Julie's happiness. "Which is about how long it'll take for Axiom to realize their pursuit team failed and send another one. So this might get sticky."

"How can we help?" I ask, feeling Julie's excitement and Abram's fear mixing inside me like a bad drug interaction.

"We're taking the world's biggest gas hog on a cross-country joyride," he says. "We need to lose as much weight as possible."

M glances down at his massive girth. "I'll . . . go get those barrels."

"Take the seats out?" I ask Abram as M lumbers off.

"If we have time. But you can start by clearing all that shit out of the cabin." He finally looks up from the panel and turns his inspection to me. "So you were a zombie. And you lived in this plane."

I nod.

"What's a zombie do with paintbrushes and books?"

I look down. "Didn't do anything. Just didn't want to forget."

"Forget what?"

"That there used to be more than this."

He looks at me blankly.

"And that maybe there can be again."

He offers no reply or reaction to this. He turns away and resumes his work. I return to the plane and start cleaning.

• • •

I've never explained to Julie what all this junk means and she's never asked, but she doesn't move to join me as I shove piles of it out the emergency exits and watch it shatter and smash on the tarmac. She watches from a distance, as if afraid of interrupting a personal moment.

"It was an anchor," I say as I toss an armful of snow globes and watch them burst like big raindrops. "Helped me hold on to the old world." I pick up a heavy box of comic books, the closest I ever got to reading before I remembered how words work, and I pause to examine the top issue's cover. A hardy gang of survivors surrounded by a horde of zombies, carelessly drawn ghouls distinguishable only by their wounds. A thousand individuals with histories and families, reduced to props for the dramas of a few attractive humans. I drop the box and watch the pages flutter, comics mixing with newspapers and fashion magazines, muscular men and skeletal women, monsters and heroes and increasingly hopeless headlines. "I don't need it anymore."

Julie moves to my side. She turns my face toward her and kisses me. Then she kicks an old computer monitor out the door and hoots "Woo!" as it explodes with a pleasant *pop*.

• • •

Nora offers to help us but I politely decline. Clearing out my former home is an emotional process and Julie is the only one I trust to treat my trash with respect. Nora shrugs and takes Sprout outside to watch her father while we dig through my surrogate memories, placeholders for my absent past.

We attack the mess with an everything-must-go gusto, but when I pick up the record player, Julie slaps the back of my head. "Are you crazy? Put that down and turn it on."

"It's heavy."

"We've spent the last five days listening to nothing but military strategy, gunfire, and our own screams. I want to hear some *music*." She puts on a record from the overhead bin. The opening horns of Sinatra's "Come Fly with Me" burst onto the speakers and Julie beams. "I never thought we'd get to play this unironically."

She DJs with dedication while we work, doing her best to keep things upbeat despite the general joylessness of my record collection. Without being conscious of it, I seem to have gathered two distinct genres in my musical salvages: warm, comforting relics from a simpler time, and bittersweet melancholia from the edge of the end. And since most of the classics are unplayably scratched, we quickly exhaust my supply of house-cleaning jams.

"I guess it's back to Sinatra," she says when *Sgt. Pepper* slips into its inner groove loop, howling its indecipherable incantations.

"Wait," I say as she stops the record. I pull one of my old favorites from the pile and hand the sleeve to her as I slide the record onto the turntable.

"Elbow?" Her grin fades as she reads the back of the sleeve. "I remember them. One of my mom's favorites." I hesitate with the needle hovering over the groove, but she waves away my concern. "It's fine. Play it."

I lower the needle. The song is gentle and full of yearning, and it drastically alters the mood. I give her a tentative smile, hoping this is okay. "Wanted to hear something new."

She reads the fine print on the sleeve. "2008? That's not new, R. *I'm* newer than this."

I shrug. "I'm . . . a little delayed."

She smirks, then looks at the ceiling as the first verse begins.

We had the drive and the time on our hands
One little room and the biggest of plans
The days were shaping up frosty and bright
Perfect weather to fly
Perfect weather to fly

"Okay," she says, nodding. "Okay, this is good."

A throat clears behind us.

"Sorry to interrupt your little listening party," Abram says, standing in the doorway, "but I did mention that people are coming to kill us, right?"

Julie looks around at the cabin, empty except for a few baseball cards and worthless dollar bills under the seats. "We're done."

"That turntable looks heavy."

"If it comes down to a few pounds, Abram, I'll cut off my arm. Deal?" She closes her eyes and sways to the music. "God, this is pretty."

Abram gives her a thoroughly unenthused stare and slips into the cockpit to begin powering up the plane. No sooner has he left the doorway than Nora steps into it. "R?" she whispers, glancing after Abram to make sure he's not listening. "You might want to come up here."

I follow her through the boarding tunnel into the waiting area of Gate 12. Several carry-ons lie open and emptied on the floor, and while the toiletries and computer gear have been ignored, the clothes have been put to use. Between two rows of seats is a huge fort made of dresses and robes draped over mop handles. The engineering is impressive.

"We need more mops," says a small voice from inside. "Go get some mops."

Julie and I exchange a glance. We duck down to peek through the entrance. Abram's daughter appears to be having a tea party with my two Dead children, still sticky with their mother's blood.

Sprout turns, grins, waves. "Hi! We're building a building!"

I realize that the items on the floor between them are not plates and silverware but notepads and compasses. Sprout seems to have found an architect's drafting kit. But I'm less concerned about the girl's impractical career goals than I am about her choice of friends. Joan and Alex kneel under the fort's colorful ceiling of luminous cotton, staring at Sprout with a dreamy disorientation in their dull gray eyes. I see no signs of hunger or aggression. They seem to have witnessed both the massacre of their neighbors and the liquefaction of their mother without succumbing to relapse, but I remember them running through the airport, laughing and playing like something very close to normal children, and I also remember them picking up a man's severed arm and sharing it between them like a jumbo hot dog. The plague is uncertain of its welcome. It circles their hearts, tapping on windows. I can't trust it or them.

"Come out," I tell Sprout, and her smile fades.

"Why?"

"You can't be around those kids."

"Why?"

Behind us, the plane's engines sputter to life. They rev and chug for a moment, then settle into a steady hum.

"Sprout, honey," Julie says, "it's time to go. But Joan and Alex can come with us."

I look at her sharply. "They can?"

She looks back even more sharply. "Were you planning on leaving them here?"

"Well, I—"

"R," she says, horrified. "Axiom's going to cut through this whole hive looking for us. You want to leave your kids to be mowed down with the others?"

"No, but . . . they're dangerous."

"Who's dangerous?" Abram says, stepping out of the boarding tunnel. "What's going on?"

Sprout peeks shyly from under a silk negligee. "Hi, Daddy."

Abram crouches down. He sees my kids staring at his daughter. "Jesus," he spits and knocks the roof off the fort, grabs Sprout and carries her clear while my kids watch mutely.

"You broke it!" Sprout cries. "You broke my building!"

"What the hell is wrong with you?" he says, glaring at all the adults in the room.

"We were watching them," Nora says. "They weren't doing anything."

"They're fucking zombies, for Christ's sake."

Julie stands up. The steel returns. "They're coming with us."

"You are out of your fucking mind."

"We'll tie them up and keep them in the back of the plane. They won't be able to hurt anyone. They're the closest thing R has to a family and we're not leaving them here for your friends to butcher."

I hear a new tone mixing into the hum of the engines. A lower-pitched drone like an ugly harmony.

"Using a jumbo jet as a getaway car is already the stupidest thing I've ever done," Abram says. "If you expect me to—"

"Quiet," I snap, holding up a hand and tilting my head, listening.

Abram looks like he's about to hit me, then he hears it too. He runs to the window and peers out at the northern horizon. Two black specks mar the blue sky. Three. Four.

The argument is over. Without further comment, Abram carries his daughter into the boarding tunnel. Julie and Nora look at me with wide eyes.

"Go," I tell them. "I'll be right behind you."

Nora runs into the tunnel and pokes her head through a broken window. "Marcus! Get your beefy butt up here! Flight six-six-six is now boarding!"

Julie hesitates just a moment, then follows Nora.

I look at Joan and Alex. They look at me. I hope what I see stirring behind the dullness in their eyes is understanding, maybe even forgiveness, as I tie belts around their wrists.

• • •

There has never been a more efficient departure in the history of commercial air travel. The moment I lock the door behind me the plane shudders away from the gate. No searching for seats, no wrestling with the overhead bins, and certainly no safety demonstration. While I lock my kids in the bathroom—they seemed comfortable enough when I found them there—Abram races onto the runway like the plane is a sports car. The black specks behind us have grown into black lumps. Their warbling drone fills my ears like angry bees. I almost tumble down the aisle when Abram guns the engines and the plane surges forward.

"R!" Julie calls to me from business class. "Get up here!"

I fight my way forward while inertia drags me back. By the time I reach Julie, the plane is shuddering and shaking like we're driving on a country road.

"Marcus!" Abram calls back to M, who's sitting in the back of business class, several seats removed from the rest of us. "You cleared the runway, right?"

"Yes," M says through gritted teeth, gripping the armrests so tight his fingers tremble.

Nora drops down next to him and smiles. "Scared of flying?"

His eyes are wide. Beads of sweat glisten on his forehead. "Little bit."

"I've never flown before. I'm excited."

"Happy for you," he growls, and Nora laughs. She reaches over and puts a hand on his forearm.

"Marcus. After everything we've lived through, we're not going to die in a damn plane crash."

M takes a deep breath and lets it out slowly. Nora pats his arm and settles back into her seat.

I fall into mine next to Julie and brace myself as the plane threatens to tear itself apart. She reaches out and grabs my hand, and I see no fear in her eyes. Despite everything, despite the many possible deaths circling our heads at this moment, the rattling of the plane and the choppers behind it and the unknown wilderness we're flying into, her eyes are full of hope. It's so bright that for a moment I swear there's a glimmer of gold in their icy blue.

"Here we go," she says, and with a final lunge, the plane leaves the ground. The shuddering stops. The only sound is the engines. We are gliding through space.

"Wow," I hear Abram gasp to no one in particular, and I realize how little he actually expected this to work.

I scan the windows behind me until I find our pursuers. They are plainly visible now, but they have stopped growing. If they were equipped with missiles, or even high-caliber cannons like the last one, we might be in trouble, but these are not gunships. They are light craft salvaged from news stations and corporate buildings, and as we climb rapidly and they shrink away beneath us, the distant flashes of their rifles and handguns become less and less frightening. Finally, a towering cumulus welcomes us into its cottony bosom, and the world goes white.

A tightly held breath bursts out of M in the form of incredulous laughter.

Nora stares out the window, awestruck.

From the cockpit, I hear Sprout giggling and clapping in the copilot's chair.

Julie squeezes my hand, and I realize it's her left hand. Either she's ignoring the pain in her finger, or she's forgotten it.

The record player is still on. In the relative quiet of our ascent I can hear it popping and skipping on an inner groove. Then a gust of turbulence rocks the cabin, and the needle scratches back a few songs, landing almost exactly where we left it in that bittersweet melody of slow-boiling beauty.

So in looking to stray from the line
We decided instead we should pull out the thread
That was stitching us into this tapestry vile
And why wouldn't you try? Perfect weather to fly

The fog around us flickers a few times, and suddenly we're above it. An impossible fantasy landscape of creamy white towers stretches out before us, and here and there, in holes and gaps below, the real world peeks through, full of unknown threats and promises, shouting at us to come back and fight.

We're coming, I tell the world, squeezing Julie's hand harder. *We're ready for you.*

TWO

the basement

Without memories, without hope, they lived for the moment only.

—Albert Camus,
The Plague

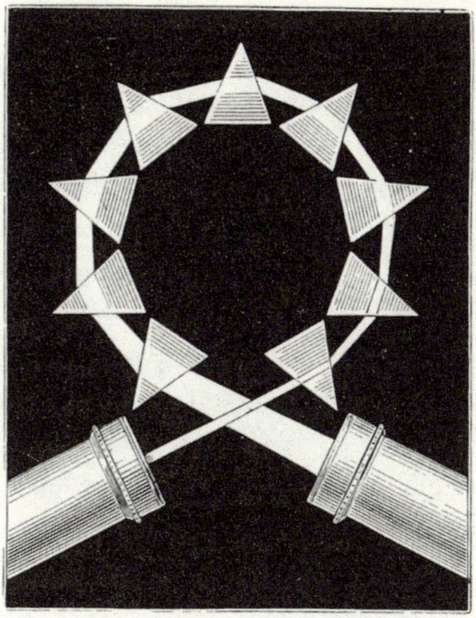

WE

A BOY IS WALKING ALONE on the highway. He has been walking a long time. His Nikes fell apart years ago and his feet have become their own shoes, tender flesh encased in callus. The boy is Dead but he does not rot. His brown skin is ashen but firm, preserved through the years by a powerfully simple refusal. The plague has not won him. He holds it at arm's length and considers its offer.

We follow the boy as we follow everyone, spinning around and through him, skimming the pages of his life's brief novella, but we follow him a little closer than others. He is interesting. He looks seven but is much older, a boy bottled and cellared, aging in strange ways that even we cannot predict. Death has halted his life but it has failed to erase him. He has wrestled it into unexpected shapes, used it as a knife to open secret boxes, and we are not quite sure what he is.

I remember this road, he thinks. *This is the right way.*

The boy remembers more than most of the Dead. Not facts, exactly, but the amorphous truths behind them. He doesn't know his name, but he knows who he is. He doesn't know where he's going, but he is not lost. The world unfolds before him like a four-dimensional map, its lines bending and peeling off the paper, outer and inner realities weaving into one.

What happened here? he asks us as he passes through a ruined city in a stretch of land once called Idaho. *What made them leave?*

We don't answer.

He passes a bullet-riddled Geo coupe and lets his eyes wander over the corpses of the family inside, fresh enough that the mother's scalp still has its ponytail.

Did anyone try to help them?

We know, but we don't answer.

Were they good people? How much of them is in you?

The boy asks us many questions while he walks, but we hold our silence. We spoke to him once, long ago, when his pain reached out and seized us by the throat. It had been years since we felt a grip so strong, and he squeezed a few words from us. But now we hold our silence. The chasm is still too wide for whispers, and we do not like to shout.

The boy accepts this and keeps walking. He is used to silence. He has been alone a long time.

At the outer edge of the city, the highway forks north and south, and the boy pauses to consult his strange map. Then he notices a sound rising into the silence. He has never heard it before. A soft roar like a distant avalanche. He looks up. The sun beats down into his eyes, flashing on his bright gold irises. He doesn't squint. His wide pupils suck in the light and break it apart; he sees all its colors, its waves and its particles, and inside this tetrachromatic rainbow, he sees an airplane.

He has seen airplanes before. He has spent the last seven years staring at them, dreaming about them, willing their dusty fuselages to move, but he has never seen one in flight. He watches the tiny black shape etch a white line through the sky and he wonders who's up there. He wonders where they're going. Then he looks down at the road and keeps walking.

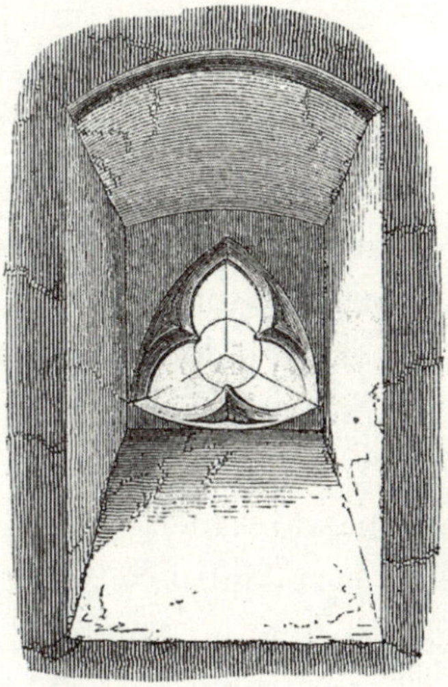

I

FOR A WHILE, I watch the clouds. Then I watch Julie watching them. I let the surreal landscape outside the window blur and I shift my focus to the back of Julie's head, her unwashed hair matted with oil and dirt, sweat and blood, the residues of everything she's gone through since her last shower a week ago, that distant age of unimaginable luxuries.

Slowly, quietly, I inhale the warm air rising from her head. I don't expect much from my numb nose. The Dead are a practical people, and the senses of smell and taste are frivolous affectations that we discard to make room for more functional tools. I have noticed a subtle shift since my return to life—my ability to detect Living flesh has dulled, and suggestions of natural aromas occasionally prickle my nose—but I am still a jammed radio, stuck on one frequency while all others drown in static.

My first sniff brings nothing but the sensation of air passing through my nostrils. I try again, and this time I get a trace of her, a distant note of that mysterious, earthy bouquet found nowhere but in a woman's hair—she turns around.

"Did you just *smell* me?"

I jerk my head away and stare straight ahead. "Sorry."

"Don't smell me. I smell like shit."

I glance sideways at her. "You don't, though."

"I can smell myself, and I smell like shit."

"You don't."

"Okay, Grenouille, what do I smell like?"

"Like . . . you." I lean in and inhale with melodramatic rapture.

She laughs and shoves me away. "You fucking creep."

Still smiling, I look past her at the sky. It hits me again that we are flying. Perhaps for the first time in years, there are human beings above the clouds, swimming in the blue void between Heaven and Earth, taunting the gods.

Julie follows my gaze to the window. "Remember when I asked if we'd ever see jets in the sky again? When the cure was just starting and we were fantasizing about the future?"

I nod.

"You said yes." She grabs my hand on the armrest. "I know it's just an airplane, it's not like this means civilization is back, but . . . I don't know. When I look out there, it feels like a victory."

"We're inside the Etch A Sketch," I say, squeezing her hand. "What should we draw?"

Her smile falters. The air between us cools, and I realize I've done it again. I've referenced a memory that isn't mine. A moment on the stadium roof when Julie shared her dreams with a boy who wasn't me. What I did to her childhood sweetheart isn't news; she knows how I know what I know, but it's a scar on the skin of our relationship that we have silently agreed not to mention.

"Get out," she says, disengaging my hand from hers. "I have to pee."

I step into the aisle and she brushes past me. "Julie," I say, but she disappears into the bathroom without looking back.

I stare at the closed door. This isn't the first time I've tripped over Perry's life, but she usually lets it go with an awkward change of subject. Was there something more in that stolen memory?

"I miss airplanes," Julie says.

"Me too," Perry says.

"Those white lines . . . the way they made designs in the blue? My mom used to say it looked like an Etch A Sketch."

And there it is. A wound within a wound. Her dead mother's words pulled from her dead lover's memory.

I close my eyes and sink low in my chair, releasing a weary sigh. I don't have to be a monster to hurt people. I can do it gently, with a single careless breath.

Julie stays in the bathroom longer than it takes to use the bathroom. When she finally comes out, she avoids my gaze, but I still notice the wetness in her eyes.

"I'm sorry," I say as she slides back into her chair. "I didn't . . ."

"It's fine." She shakes her head and wipes her eyes on her sleeve. "I had a mom and she died. It was almost eight years ago. I can't be falling apart every time something reminds me."

I can hear the effort this hardness requires.

"It's just . . . the questions. Not knowing what really happened." Her eyes begin to dampen again and she looks out the window to hide them. "There was no note . . . no good-bye. We assumed she knew what would happen, going off alone at night, but what if she was just that naive? What if she really thought she'd make it to Detroit, join the Remakers, live the life she always—" Her voice cracks and she sits in silence for a moment. "Doesn't matter, I guess. Either way, she left us. I just wish I knew why, because I keep running it through my head . . ." Her voice drops lower, almost inaudible. "And it's like it's not finished. Like she's dying over and over."

I'm not sure if she's talking to me anymore. She might be talking to the clouds, those elusive cirrus wisps that look distant even up here. Suddenly, she laughs. "She could still be out there!" It's a bleak sound, a forced signal of levity that barely escapes her throat. "All we found was her dress and some . . . some of her. For all I know she could be out there roaming the country with a gang of zombie moms." She flashes me a smile that's meant to show she's joking, but it's not even close to convincing. "That's how it works, right? Sometimes they take years to rot?"

I give her an ambivalent nod. She's not wrong. I'm proof of that. But the hope I see in her eyes, despite her efforts to hide it, looks too desperate. Too hungry. And it feels dangerous to feed it.

She turns back to the window. "I know," she mutters like she's listening to my thoughts. "I know it's stupid. It's just something I think about." The clouds seem to drift away from us, dissolving into that unmapped blue landscape. "I've been missing her a lot lately."

My response must be delicate but words are crude tools, prone to breaking what they're meant to repair. So I keep my mouth shut. I lay a hand on her back and leave it there. Minutes pass in the soft roar of engines and air. I feel her breaths slow, her muscles soften. I feel her fall asleep.

• • •

I have no idea what time it is, but after everything we've endured, it hardly matters. The sleep debt demands payment. Even Abram appears to be dozing, slouched low in his chair with the autopilot on. I feel the exhaustion as much as anyone, but my brain still hasn't found its off switch. I roam among the sleepers like a ghoul in a graveyard.

M gives me a feeble nod as I pass him. He looks even paler than he did when he was All Dead; it seems he's alive enough to get airsick. Nora is slumped in the chair next to him, snoring the ravenous snores of a sleep-starved woman finally feasting. I try not to feel jealous.

I slide open the door of the rear bathroom and look down at what's left of my family. Two young corpses tied up with belts. Alex sits on the toilet seat. Joan's feet dangle off the edge of the sink. They look up at me with big, mournful eyes, like caged puppies who don't know what they've done wrong. I can't take it.

"Stay," I tell them as I unbuckle the belts.

They nod.

"Promise you'll stay?"

They nod.

"Say it. Say you promise."

They nod.

I remember watching them laugh and play like real children in that golden hour when all it took to raise the Dead was a smile and some pretty pictures. I remember the lengthy sentences that tumbled from their mouths in those days. *This is our friend*, Joan said, introducing me to one of the airport kids whom I'd probably met and forgotten a hundred times, a boy whose charcoal skin was starting to turn brown. *He doesn't remember his name yet, so he's going out to look for it.*

I counted the syllables in that sentence and told Joan it was her new record. I remember it clearly because it was a record she never broke.

"Hungry," she says, and snaps her teeth.

I shut the door.

• • •

Abram senses me lurking in the cockpit doorway and wakes from his nap. His face is Perry's reflected in a dirty mirror, and I remember Perry's white pilot uniform covered in blood while the plane hurtled toward the ground.

This isn't one of your memories, is it? I asked him in that dream that wasn't a dream.

No, he replied. *This is yours.*

"What do you want?" Abram whispers, snapping me back to now. His copilot sleeps against the window with a channel of drool running down her chin.

"Where are—"

"Quiet," he hisses, jerking a thumb toward Sprout.

"Sorry," I say at the same volume.

He looks incredulous.

"Sorry," I say in a barely-there whisper.

"Christ," he sighs, "you're definitely dumb enough to be a zombie." He looks at his daughter and his attention drifts away from me. "She hasn't slept in two days. Sometimes she stays awake so long she starts crying, like she's so tired it hurts, but she won't sleep. I don't know . . ." He shakes his head and looks back at me. "So what do you want?"

"Where are we headed?"

He turns back to the windshield, the endless expanse of blue and white. "Canada."

"Why Canada?"

"They exed later than we did. They might still have some meat on the bones."

I nod. I can't argue with the logic, but it doesn't quite sit comfortably. I envisioned us searching the disgraced wreckage of America for some way to redeem it, not leaving it behind to rot. It's an empty concept in a world whose political lines have washed out in the rain, but crossing the border feels like dodging the draft.

"I saw Canada's bones once," Julie says, and I glance back to the cabin. She's still slouched in her seat, eyes open just a crack. "Didn't look too meaty then, and that was almost eight years ago."

"What's your point?" Abram says in a slightly louder whisper. "You have somewhere better in mind?"

Julie opens her eyes and straightens up. "What about Iceland?"

"Iceland," Abram repeats.

"It's an island. One of the most isolated countries in the world. Never been in a war, almost no crime, totally self-sufficient on geothermal power. If anywhere survived the plague, it'd be them."

"Except they didn't survive. No one did. The last country to go was Sweden."

"That's just a rumor," Julie says, growing more excited. "No one's confirmed any overseas news in years."

I feel my discomfort growing. How far are we planning to roam for the antidote to Axiom's poison? Or have our goals already begun to shift?

"Iceland's thousands of miles away," Abram says, "and we have no satellite or radio navigation. We'd end up at the North Pole or the bottom of the Atlantic."

"Canada's far away too. If you can get us there, why not Iceland?"

Abram sighs and looks at me. "Will you tell your girlfriend to go back to sleep?"

"Hey," Julie says, climbing out of her seat and standing indignantly in the aisle. "You're the *pilot*, not the captain; you're not running the show. We need to discuss stuff."

Sprout stirs and whimpers. Abram freezes until she settles, then he steps out of the cockpit. He walks up very close to Julie and stares down at her.

"What stuff?" he says softly.

"All of it," she says, returning his stare.

He ducks down to her eye level and speaks very slowly. "Canada? Is *big*. Canada is *north*. The *compass* says we're going north, so pretty soon . . . we'll be in Canada!"

I see Julie's fists clenching, but she says nothing.

"It's our best bet," Abram says, dropping the baby talk with a hint of embarrassment. "Even if it's empty, it'll make a good place to hide. We're going to Canada." He returns to the cockpit, pauses in the doorway, and glances back at Julie. "Please keep your voice down. My daughter's sleeping."

He plops into the pilot seat and starts adjusting instruments.

Julie sits, folds her arms, and glares holes into the floor. I take my seat next to her and watch the back of Abram's head. I find myself scouring my brain for any remaining fragments of Perry, something that might help me understand these people and this mess we're plunging into, but I dig carefully and quietly. Other voices have moved into the space Perry left. My head is a dark house inhabited by strangers, and I don't want to wake them up.

I AM STANDING in front of the door.

I am in a hallway. The walls are covered in gaudy printed wallpaper, a repeating pattern of a solitary house surrounded by trees, all of it scorched and peeling. From somewhere behind me, I hear the sounds of my life. The voices of my friends. I feel sunlight on my back, but it's far away and cool. The hallway is long and empty, and at the end of it is the door.

The door is ancient. Crooked. A slab of rusty metal under layers of peeling paint. The plaster that once covered it lies in a pile at my feet. The door is free, exposed, unlocked. The knob protrudes toward me obscenely.

"Open it," Perry says, standing at my side. I try to look at him but he turns his face, giving me only the back of his head. "This is your house," he says through the hole I put in his skull, like a bloody, toothless mouth. "When are you going to move in?"

He gives the door a tug and it creaks open. I back away, horrified, expecting tentacles and swarms of locusts. But there's only dust and silence. A flickering bulb taking weak stabs at the shadows. Steep stairs leading down.

"How long are you going to stand in the hall?" he says, and shoves me down the stairs.

• • •

"Hello? R? You still with us?"

Julie is leaning over me, giving my cheek tiny repeated slaps. I blink and sit up, eyes darting. "What's . . . where . . ."

"Wow," she says, stepping back, "when you sleep, you *sleep*."

Everyone is standing in the aisle, watching me, some with concern, some with impatience. I glance out the window—we're on the ground.

"What's happening? Where are we?"

"Helena," Abram says. "Need to pick up a few things."

"And Marcus needs to puke," Nora says, giving M a light elbow to the stomach. He glares at her.

They all start to file out. I stand up but don't follow them. I'm disoriented, unsure if I'm still dreaming.

"Are you okay?" Julie says. "You *were* sleeping, right? That wasn't another of your little fugue states?"

"I don't . . . I'm not sure." The plane is now empty except for the two of us. "We're in *Montana*?"

She smiles. "It'll make more sense when you finish waking up. Let's go."

I glance toward the rear restroom.

"They're fine," she says. "I told them where we're going and they said they'd stay."

"They *said*?"

"Well, they nodded."

She turns to go and I follow her, my head still spinning but starting to slow down. The plane is parked in the middle of a runway, far from the airport terminal and any potential inhabitants it may be harboring, so we exit through the cargo bay. A narrow staircase in the midsection leads to the lower deck, a cold, musty underworld that I never dared to explore during my tenancy. I don't know what I imagined lurking here, but the only horrors I detect are a few spiders.

The cabin's refined interior gives way to the industrial rawness of the cargo bay, then a hydraulic ramp leading down to the runway. The feeling of solid ground under my feet steadies me a little. I glance back at the open ramp and feel the instinct to lock it, like this commercial airliner is the family sedan parked in a bad neighborhood.

And just how bad is this neighborhood? I see no movement in the terminal's windows or on the tarmac around it. Just acres of bleached concrete, dust and leaves. Perhaps this airport wasn't consumed by plague like Post's was. Perhaps this place fell to something else.

"Wake up, Archie!" Nora yells back to me. "Let's move!"

As I turn around, Abram points a small device at the back of the plane. The ramp rises and clicks shut.

Keyless entry. Nice to know my plane has all the late-model luxuries—and that I'm not the only one with uneasy feelings as we march toward this silent city.

• • •

Our group resembles a ragged military platoon, everyone walking with weapons at the ready. M and Abram carry theirs in the poised stance of disciplined soldiers while Nora and Julie's swing against their thighs with easy confidence. The only element that doesn't fit the picture is the half-blind little girl trailing behind her father. And me, as always.

I look at my hands. They're steadier. I should tell Abram I'm ready for that pistol. I don't.

"What are we doing here?" I mumble into Julie's ear.

"Apparently Abram has some transportation stashed in town. They grew up here, him and Perry."

I look into the pale horizon beyond the airport. Endless hills of rust-hued dust and stiff, woody shrubs that scrape your calves like cat claws when you try to run away from home wearing only your swim trunks—

I miss a step. My boots scuff on the asphalt. I rub at my forehead then quickly look up. No one is watching me. I can see the outskirts of the suburbs rippling in the heat like a mirage, or a memory from a night of hard drinking.

"So this is the town you were trying to leave?" Nora asks Abram. "When your family got attacked?"

Abram keeps walking.

"And you said Perry was five, so this was . . . a long time ago?"

"Your point?"

"Well . . . what makes you think your bikes are still here?"

"Because it's not the kind of place that attracts looters."

As we get closer, the heat ripples begin to clear, and the city comes into focus.

Black.

Everything is black. Black skeletons of houses burned down to their frames. The bricks of old buildings blackened like charcoal briquettes. Even the streets are black; melted rubber and soot from a hundred burned cars. The only splashes of color are the grass and vines overtaking the ruins, feeding on the city's carbon-rich corpse.

"Let's go back," I hear myself saying.

Julie glances over her shoulder at me. "What?"

"We shouldn't be here. Let's go back."

The distress in my voice catches the group's attention and they pause their march, waiting for me to elaborate.

"Not safe," I mumble.

"It's a pile of ash," Abram says, tossing his palms out. "Nothing and nobody. What's safer than that?"

My eyes wander through the charred landscape ahead. Every single building. Even the ones separated by spaces too far for the fire to have jumped. A fire with a purpose. A fire with friends.

"What's wrong, R?" Julie says.

M is giving me a look that I don't like. Something like empathy. As if he understands. But he doesn't understand. *I* don't understand.

"I don't know," I tell Julie. My eyes fall to the ground. "I don't know."

Abram resumes walking.

"We need vehicles," Julie says, touching my shoulder. "We're not going to find anything if we stay up in the clouds."

I nod.

"If you're scared," Nora calls back to me, "just picture yourself on a bad-ass hog, wind in your hair, bitch on your back. We'll get you some cool shades and a tattoo."

I expect M to join in with a quip, tousle my hair, and call me a little girl, but he's still giving me that sad, knowing look. Anger overcomes my fear.

"Let's go."

"We'll keep our eyes open," Julie says, giving my shoulder a squeeze. "It'll be fine."

I feel a surge of disgust for her all-purpose platitudes. She has no idea what I'm afraid of; what makes her think it'll be fine?

We walk down into the black city, and though it was razed years ago, I swear I can still smell the acrid perfume of a thousand burned things.

THE SUN.

It soaks into my arms and legs and face, filling my cells like warm water balloons. Its heat radiates from the tar paper shingles and soaks into my back, saturating me from every direction. I am lying in the crook of the roof, next to the chimney, hiding. No one knows I can climb the oak outside my bedroom window and jump here from its branches. Most seven-year-olds couldn't, but I'm different. I've been practicing a long time.

I have my toys with me. Two plastic men. One is a good guy, a hero. I can tell by his big jaw and flat haircut. The other is a monster. I don't know what kind of monster but he is ugly and his skin is blue, so he is bad and I make him fight the hero. They stand on my chest, poised to attack.

"I will kill you!" the monster says in a shrill snarl.

"Not if I kill you first!" the hero says in the closest I can get to a baritone.

Far out in the yard, near the woods, I hear my father shouting something over and over. It's probably my name. It has the blunt cadence of my name, but it's distant and inconsequential. The violence in his voice is softened by the warm air. I can almost imagine he's looking for me because he wants to give me a present.

I mash the figures together into a frenzy of battle. Plastic fists clatter against plastic jaws.

• • •

I stretch the balloon's ring and slip it over the faucet. I turn on the water and watch the balloon swell.

"Who you gonna hit with these?"

I look up at my father. His huge, meaty face. His hands thick and callused from decades of brutal labor.

"Paul," I say.

He pulls one of the finished balloons out of the bag on the counter and squeezes it. "It's warm."

I nod.

"You trying to give him a nice bath? Use cold water."

"Why?"

"Getting hit isn't supposed to feel good. It's supposed to make him scream."

"Why?"

"Because that's how games work. Winning is supposed to feel good and losing is supposed to hurt. What's the point of being a winner if losers get to feel good too?"

He hands me a fresh balloon. "Use cold water." He opens the freezer and sets a tray of ice cubes by the sink. "And a few of these."

• • •

I stare at the beige carpet, looking for patterns in the stains as the youth pastor harangues us with harsh truths.

"Don't let the long hair fool you, he's not some peace-and-love hippie. Luke chapter twelve: 'Do you think I came to bring peace on earth? No, I tell you, but division.' He didn't come to make friends.

He's got fire in his eyes and a sword in his mouth and he came to cut the world in half."

Stacks of chairs with purple cushions. Folding tables. Pale fluorescent lights. Monday through Saturday, the hotel rents out this shabby conference room for political rallies, corporate training sessions, and the occasional flea market or gun show. On Sundays it belongs to a few dozen families who set up guitars and mics and hang a vinyl banner that reads HOLY FIRE FELLOWSHIP.

"He came to *divide*!" the pastor shouts into his mic, pacing back and forth in front of thirty squirming teens. "Brother from brother. Wheat from chaff. Saved from damned. He's here to draw a line. Which side will you be on when the Last Sunset comes?"

I force myself to look up from the floor and face his fevered gaze.

"Maybe you think you've got plenty of time to decide. Maybe you like living in this cesspool so much you want to hit snooze and tell God to come back later. Maybe you think if you do enough good works, if you feed enough refugees and build enough schools and recycle enough pop cans, you can make God change his mind." He shakes his head, and his voice drops to a low simmer. "God doesn't change his mind. You can't put out his fire. It's coming to burn away this twisted world, and I don't know about you, but I'm praying for it to hurry up. I'm soaking my house in gasoline."

• • •

The skeletons of Helena, Montana, loom over me, charred rafters stabbing at the sky like the ribs of ancient animals. Bits of charcoal fall onto my upturned face and I wipe at them, drawing smudges that revert my faintly pink skin to gray. I see clean white siding superimposed over the houses' black frames. Neat vegetable gardens under jungles of ivy. Children riding bikes through the glass-strewn streets. Voices in the silence.

"R," Julie says. She is walking alongside me, watching me with deepening concern. "Are you okay?"

"I don't know what I am," I say to the street ahead, my face slack, eyes far away.

She reaches for my hand. I let her take it and I let her squeeze it, but I don't squeeze back.

"Here," Abram says, stopping in front of what might have once been a two-story Craftsman house. It's now just four black walls slumped against a collapsed roof, windows smoked over, sickly brown vines creeping through every crack. "This is it."

"How can you tell?" Nora wonders, gazing up at the vaguely home-shaped void, indistinguishable from the ones around it.

Abram kneels in the yard and runs his fingers through the weedy grass. He looks up at the dead tree near the fence and the remains of a rope swing dangling from it. A very faint smile touches his face.

The top floor is crushed under the collapsed roof, but the bottom is still standing, and a steep driveway ramp leads down to a basement garage. Abram climbs the steps to the front door and pulls on the knob. The scorched wood creaks and flexes but doesn't budge. He turns and heads for the garage.

"Wait," Julie says. "We can break it."

"Doesn't matter. Bikes are in the shop."

"You don't want to go in the house?" She's incredulous. "The house you grew up in?"

He stops in front of the garage door and looks at her flatly. "I didn't grow up here. I played with toys and rode bikes here. I *grew up* in an Axiom training center."

He pulls on the garage door and it slides open. A cloud of charcoal dust rolls out like a curse from a disturbed tomb. He coughs once, then steps inside.

We follow him at a respectful distance. M stays on the sidewalk, holding his rifle in the deceptively casual stance of a veteran soldier on guard duty, slipping back into his first life like his second never happened.

"So this is The Shop," Nora says reverently, turning in a slow circle. "Mr. Kelvin talked about it all the time. Eyes got all dreamy like it was paradise lost."

The garage is actually the entire basement, work benches covered in tools, engine parts piled in the corners, and enough cans of fuel for a ride to Brazil and back. The center of the space is clear except for five mounds under canvas tarps. Abram unveils them one by one: five gleaming black motorcycles, compact BMW street bikes devoid of any spread-legged swagger—they would look very serious and practical if not for their vintage flair. They're classics bordering on antiques, their clean lines and abundance of chrome evoking an era of peace and love, love is all you need, it's easy if you try. I hear songs and poems and protests and I wonder: Has any generation since then really believed in something? Or did that one failed leap embarrass us into never trying again?

A sad smile touches Julie's face. "Perry's Slash-Fives. He rode some modern shit for salvages but these were the ones he loved."

Abram inspects the engines, tests the brakes, taps at rusty patches with a screwdriver.

"I used to think they didn't look tough enough," Julie says. "I wanted him to get a Harley. He said I had no taste and if I ever brought up 'gorilla bikes' again he wouldn't teach me how to ride." She laughs, lost in nostalgia. "He was kind of a dick."

Abram ignores her, puttering around the shop, sifting through tools and grabbing parts off shelves with a familiarity that must have been etched deeply to have lasted this long.

"Your dad kept saying he'd come back for his babies someday," Nora says, trying to catch Abram's eyes. "I bet he'd be happy to know you're doing it now."

Abram slides a pan under one of the bikes and begins draining the oil.

"Hey," Nora says.

"What," Abram says.

"Why don't you want to talk to us?"

He gets up and digs through a drawer, pulls out a box of oil filters.

"You spend half your life looking for your family, you finally find people who knew them, and you don't have a single question for us? You don't want to know how I knew your dad? You don't want to know what your brother was like?"

"I wanted to *meet* my brother," Abram says, going to work on the next bike while the first one drains. "I wanted to see what kind of man he turned into and I wanted to get to know him." He moves the pan into place. "What I *didn't* want is to listen to strangers describe him to me like a character in a fucking book." He unscrews the cap and the old black sludge puddles into the pan. "Perry's gone. Perry doesn't exist."

The garage is silent except for the clink of two wrenches that Sprout is forcing to dance with each other.

"Why are you even here?" Julie says. Her voice is tight. "If you can erase your family that easily and we're just useless strangers to you, why didn't you ditch us the moment you realized Perry was dead?"

Abram gets up and disappears behind the third bike. "I've got a lot of work to do if we're going to ride these out of here. Why don't you and Sprout go outside and play? You both like make-believe."

Julie turns and walks stiffly out of the shop. Sprout follows her, still clinking her wrenches together. Nora and I glance at each other, then follow Sprout.

Julie is standing in the grass with her hands pressed to her lower back, gazing up at the sky and breathing slowly. Sprout walks up close to her and thrusts the wrenches out as if to say *lookit*.

"What are those guys?" Julie asks, forcing a playful smile.

"Mr. and Mrs. Wrench. They're ballerinas."

Julie giggles. "Mr. Wrench is *such* a good name for a ballerina."

Sprout smiles. The Wrenches resume their dance.

Julie sinks down and sits cross-legged in the scrubby yellow grass. "Did your dad ever tell you about your uncle Perry?"

Sprout nods. "He said he couldn't find him."

"I found him. We used to be best friends."

"He died?"

Julie's smile trembles. "Yeah. He did. But he was a good man."

Sprout's face becomes solemn, an expression her soft features shouldn't even be capable of.

"He was smart, funny . . ." Julie's eyes wander off into memory. "He was sad a lot, and seeing other people get hurt made him angry inside, but he was good. He wanted to make the world better. He just stopped believing he could."

The garage door rattles on its tracks and slams shut in a puff of ash.

Julie stares at the door for a moment, then ruffles Sprout's hair. "I wish he could've met you."

• • •

M and Nora make a few attempts to help with the bikes but Abram rebuffs every offer and keeps the door shut, so we find scraps of shade in the yard and settle in to wait. Julie sets her shotgun in the grass, digs through the supply bag until she finds a knife and some duct tape, then stands up and unbuckles her belt.

M's eyebrows rise.

Julie unbuttons the plaid shirt that covers her sweat-stained tank top; M sits up straight as if to pay closer attention to a classroom lecture. Julie notices, rolls her eyes, and flips open the knife. She sticks it through a shoulder of the shirt and cuts off a sleeve.

"What the hell are you doing?" Nora says.

Julie stuffs her shotgun into the severed sleeve, then presses one end of her belt onto each end of the sleeve and mummy-wraps the ends in duct tape. She stands up, throws the makeshift holster over her shoulder, and smiles.

"Nice," Nora says. "But now your pants are gonna fall off."

"Do you see this thing?" Julie says, giving her rear a slap. "No belt needed."

Nora juts her chin in measured approval. "It's not bad for a pale pixie."

"If you want to have a competition," M says, "happy to judge."

Julie glares at him. Nora smirks.

I squirm through this exchange, wondering if it's my job to shut M's mouth on the subject of my girlfriend's body, but my dilemma is drowned out by the roar of an engine starting in the garage. It revs a few times, then drops into idle. This repeats twice more, then two of the engines cut out, leaving the third sputtering softly. We gather in the driveway and watch the garage door, tense and expectant like family members in a surgeon's waiting room. But Abram doesn't emerge. Nora steps forward and raps a knuckle against the door. "Abram? Good to go?"

No answer.

She pulls the door open. Two of the motorcycles lie on their sides in the corner. The remaining three are lined up near the door, one of them running. Abram isn't in the shop. At the top of a short staircase, the door to the first floor is open, creaking in the breeze.

Julie is the first up the stairs. I follow her reluctantly into the charred heart of the Kelvins' former home. Melted brown carpet crunches under our feet. The walls are black except where the drywall's paper has peeled away, revealing white patches of plaster like bleached bone. Nothing remains of the Kelvins' personality. Their choices of furniture, wall hangings, paint colors. All memory of their life in this house has been burned away, and walking through it reminds me of eating a senile brain. Nothing but empty hallways and nameless ghosts.

We find Abram in what must have been the living room. He is standing in front of a brick hearth that's all set with logs and kindling, abandoned before the match could be struck. They're the only things in the room that aren't burned.

"Got three of them running," Abram says in a flat voice. He stands with his back to us, staring at a framed photo on the mantel. "Other two are shot."

He has wiped the soot off the frame's glass, revealing a faded family photo. A father and a mother, a toddler and a teenager, sitting on the porch of a log cabin.

He turns around, looks at us for a moment, then takes Sprout's hand and heads toward the basement stairs. "I don't know how you're planning to save the world from ten thousand years of human decline," he says as he descends the stairs, "but good luck."

"Abram?" Julie says, moving toward the staircase.

An engine roars, and through a smoke-darkened window I see a motorcycle surge up the driveway. Abram with his backpack and his rifle, his daughter braced in front of him, her tiny hands gripping the handlebars next to her father's.

"No," Julie snarls, springing into motion. "No, no, no, no." She drops down the basement steps in two leaps and by the time I catch up with her she's already on one of the remaining two bikes. She kicks the starter and cranks the throttle and launches out of the shop like a warhead, leaving me choking in a cloud of blue smoke.

I jump on the last bike and stare down at all the levers and switches, trying to remember how it all works. If my old life has to come back to me, now would be a good time.

Closing my eyes, I kick the starter. I twist the throttle and release the clutch. The bike leaps forward and crashes into a stack of fuel cans, then lurches to a stop that throws me into the handlebars, but I manage to keep the engine going. Behind me, M and Nora are descending the stairs, yelling at me, but I'm barely aware of them. I hit the throttle again and the bike lunges beneath me. I fishtail out of the garage and skid onto the street, barely clinging to balance. Julie's trail of smoke leads down the street and around a corner like a line on a map. I follow it.

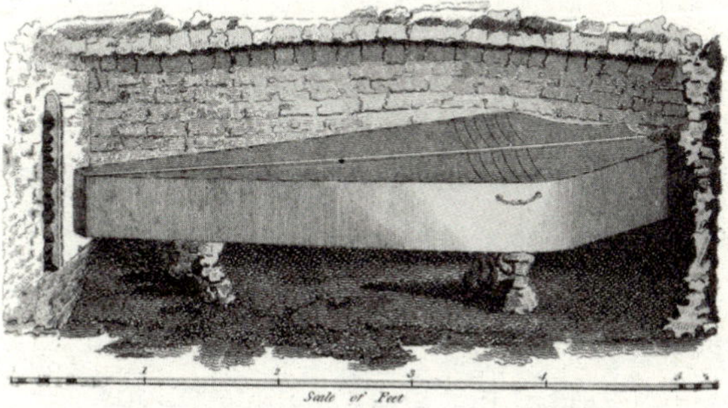

EVEN WHILE FIGHTING to control a lurching steel monster, my brain can't stop nagging. It reminds me that Abram and Julie are experienced riders with normal human reflexes and I will never catch up with them. It reminds me that we won't fare well stranded in the Montana wilderness with only three vintage motorcycles and a bag of Carbtein. It reminds me, with obvious self-interest, that I'm not wearing a helmet.

Julie's smoke trail thins as her bike's engine wakes up and clears its throat, but by the time the trail is gone, I've deduced her destination. I burst out of the confines of the suburbs and into the open plains that lead to the airport. I find her bike parked near the 747, faint puffs of smoke chugging from its muffler. I hear her voice inside the plane, hoarse with desperation.

"Abram! God damn it, Abram!"

She storms down the cargo ramp and returns to her bike, fists clenched at her sides. "He's not here. That blind, stupid son of a bitch, that motherfucking coward, I thought he'd be here, I thought he was taking the plane."

"Julie." I put my hand on her shoulder to stop her wild pacing but she shrugs it off.

"We're fucked if he leaves us. We're *fucked*. No Canada, no Iceland, we're stuck in this fucking desert and it'll take us months to even—"

"Julie!"

She snaps out of her rage and finally looks at me.

I take a breath to come down from that necessary raising of my voice. "I know where he's going."

"How?"

I'm not going to say it. I've already poked that scar once and felt the jolt of pain. I look at her, and she understands.

She gets back on her bike. I walk mine through a U-turn like a kid on training wheels, then I hit the gas and launch forward, my legs flailing in the air for a moment before I catch my balance and find the pegs. I glance back at her, hoping my clownish riding might pull a smile out of the tension, but her face is locked in a grim stare. Julie can find humor in almost anything. Hungry zombies, armies of skeletons, her own imprisonment and torture. Her dream of a better world is the one thing she'll never joke about, and I fear for anyone who threatens it.

• • •

Big brother is happy.

I like it when big brother is happy because that means everything's okay. Big brother worries more than anyone else; he thinks no one else worries enough, not even Dad, so if big brother is happy, I know we're safe.

"Perry, bring your squirt guns! We can have a battle in the woods!"

Big brother is stuffing his backpack full of clothes and fun stuff. A football. A Frisbee. A drawing pad and color pencils. I'm going to ask him to draw me a monster. Mom said the monsters you make up with your imagination are always worse than the real ones. I'll stick big brother's monster on my bedroom door to scare away the real ones.

"Let's go, kids!" Dad yells. He's outside in the truck with Mom and the motor is on and it's time to go. I grab all my squirt guns and run outside and dump them in the back of the truck. Big brother climbs in and reaches

down and lifts me up by my armpits like Mom and Dad used to do when I was a baby. We sit on the rusty metal and I feel my bottom getting wet from the dirty water that's pooled in all the dents but I'm smiling and big brother is smiling. We bang the back of our heads against the window because that means we're ready to go and Dad drives out into the town and onto the fast road and then the road with the old barns and then the gravel road and then the dirt road and the bumps make me and big brother bounce all over like popcorn in the pan the way Mom cooks it and I start laughing. Big brother laughs too, even though he's so old he's almost a grown-up, because he's happy, and if he's happy that means everything's okay.

• • •

I exit the highway onto the road with the old barns. The barns are gone, no doubt cut up for firewood, but the concrete slabs of their foundations remain, like inexplicable basketball courts in the middle of a meadow.

I take the gravel road and we pass a few dozen old farmhouses. My stolen memories tell me nothing about who might have lived here, but they must have vacated when Helena burned. Distantly, I wonder why they bothered to board up their windows. A few are actually barred, and one little cottage has a chain-link fence enclosing its yard. I catch glimpses of equipment that doesn't look agricultural, but I force my mind to stay on track. We won't find Abram in any of these houses, placed at standoffish intervals but still vaguely neighborly. The isolation he wants can only be found at the end of a long dirt road. I see several of them branching off from this gravel arterial and sinking back into the forest like the mouths of caves, damp and dark and so forbidding they are their own NO TRESPASSING signs.

Brush and branches have almost closed some of them, so I drop down to second gear, studying each opening carefully. As we approach the place where the memories converge, I begin to worry that the Kelvins' driveway has overgrown completely in the intervening years, but then I skid to a stop. Julie slides in behind me, and when the dust clears, we are looking at a wide-open highway into the forest. The road has grass, but it's short. It's been a couple years since the branches were trimmed—their sawn ends bristle with new growth—but only a couple.

This road has been in use. And at least one person used it today. A single tire track tills a line of dark earth through the grass.

Julie cranks the throttle and shoots past me, kicking up a spray of gravel that becomes a spray of dirt. I chase after her, struggling to keep the bike upright on the uneven terrain, but I don't have to struggle long. A few hundred feet into the woods, we come to a gate. A heavy steel bar with red and white stripes, the kind that once guarded state parks against the depredations of motor vehicles, as if the Montana Forest Service missed the memo that we gave up on the planet decades ago.

Sprout is kneeling on the edge of the path, trying to get a caterpillar to crawl onto her finger. Her father is sawing at the gate's lock with a pocket-size hacksaw.

"This wasn't here before," he says without pausing or turning around. "Did they come back?"

Julie and I dismount our bikes and approach the gate.

"Is this where they were all those years I was looking for them?" he continues.

"Abram," Julie says.

He keeps sawing. "Almost there."

Julie watches him for a moment, trying to calm her breathing. "*Abram*."

He finally turns around. He looks from her to me and tosses up his hands in exasperation. "How? How the *hell* did you know where I was going?"

Julie glances at me. For a moment, I consider telling him. Even though he wasn't present for most of the memories I took from Perry, I'm certain I have enough from those first five years to convince him of what I once was. Would knowing the plague isn't invincible loosen his stiff mind? Or simply snap it? The rifle on his back keeps my mouth shut.

"We tracked you," Julie says.

"Bullshit. Davy Crockett couldn't track a bike on paved roads."

"Abram, please," Julie says, trying to roll past this topic with sheer urgency. "We have maybe the last jet in North America. We have a fucking chariot of the gods that can take us *anywhere,* and it's useless without you."

"I fixed my father's motorcycles for you. Go start a hippie biker gang. I'm done." He turns and resumes sawing.

"We already did this, Abram!" Julie takes a few steps toward him. "You agreed to come with us! What's changed?"

"I agreed on one thing: that Axiom would catch me if I tried to drive here. So I flew here."

"What is it about this fucking cabin? You can go anywhere in the world and you choose *this*?" She gestures to the muddy road and the dark, mossy woods around us.

"It has a bomb shelter. There's a year's worth of supplies."

"A year?" Julie laughs incredulously. "And then what? You're going to hunt rabbits and jerk off in the woods for the rest of your life?"

Abram doesn't answer. The saw makes a thin ringing like a high violin note.

"Okay, so you're done with living, fine, but what about Sprout? Are you going to bury her with you?"

"Leave her out of this," Abram mutters, still sawing.

"She is *in* this! She's right here!" Julie turns to Sprout, who is watching the argument with knitted brows while the forgotten caterpillar crawls up her arm. "Sprout. Do you want to live here in the forest with just your dad? Or do you want to make friends and learn things? Maybe build things and invent things? Try to help the world?"

Abram whirls around and throws his hacksaw into the dirt. "Don't you *fucking* talk to my daughter. This is *my* decision."

"It's *her* childhood!" Julie shouts, taking another step toward him. "It's her life!"

"She's my daughter, God damn it!"

"She's not *your* anything! She's a *person*!"

They're standing toe-to-toe now, faces livid and trembling, and Julie somehow appears to be staring him down, despite being a foot shorter.

"Daddy?" Sprout says, her voice so soft and timid it's almost lost in the tense air. "I want to build things."

Abram gives the gate a fierce kick. The lock snaps and the bar swings open. He grabs Sprout under the shoulders and lifts her roughly onto his bike. He starts the engine and takes off in a spray of mud, and Sprout shoots Julie a sad glance before they disappear into the woods.

For a moment, the only sound is the discomforting squeak of Julie's teeth grinding. Then she jumps on her bike and starts it.

"Julie, don't," I say, running toward her.

"Don't what?" she snaps.

"Don't keep pushing him. You don't know what he'll do."

"He's pushing *me*," she says with her back to me, and I'm suddenly hyper-aware of the shotgun strapped to it. "I don't know what *I'll* do."

She twists the throttle and roars up the trail. With a mounting sense of dread, I go after her. My brain feeds me images of possible outcomes, and by the time the trees begin to thin in anticipation of a clearing, I am bracing for war, begging my past self to loan me his combat skills one more time.

Then I round a corner and Julie and Abram are there, stopped at the clearing's edge, and I hit the brakes and the bike slips and tips over and slides away from me as I roll to a stop in the dirt. Neither of them even look at me as I pull myself up and brush the mud off my clothes. They're looking straight ahead, at a log cabin in the center of a small, sunny clearing. Rough-hewn timbers, shingled roof, a brick chimney promising cozy evenings by the fire—it's the classical image in every detail except the door and windows. The door is a not-so-rustic slab of riveted steel, and the windows are dark holes covered by less-than-quaint steel gratings.

In the center of the door: a logo. A jagged, hollow mandala.

Abram yanks his rifle out of his backpack and gets off his bike. Julie does the same.

"Stay close to me, Mura," Abram says, and moves toward the porch. No rocking chairs. No lanterns. A stack of ammo crates where a stack of firewood should be. He steps to a window grating and listens. The only sounds I hear are distant bird calls and the rustling of pine branches. He grips the door's heavy latch, readies his weapon, and pulls the door open.

There is no one inside to shoot. The cabin is empty. No furniture, no beds, just a bare floor and a kitchen counter covered in utensils that probably aren't for cooking. Instead of elk heads and landscape paintings, the walls are lined with shackles. Rubber cuffs and collars hang from thick cables bolted to the wall. The shackles are unoccupied, but the dark stains on the walls tell a dark story.

"What is this?" Julie whispers, keeping her shotgun braced and ready.

Abram sifts through the tools on the kitchen counter. Scalpel. Speculum. Cranial saw. I think of Nora's Morgue and then the facility that preceded it, a place to study the Dead and to practice killing them. It's the simplest explanation, but something is askew.

I step forward and lift an object off the counter just to verify what I'm looking at.

A doll. A plastic baby doll, naked and bone white, with a blank, flat oval where its face should be.

"Daddy, look," Sprout says, picking something off the floor and holding it out to Abram. It's the baby's face. Or one of them, anyway. I see others scattered across the countertop, little paper ovals cut out of magazines: attractive men and women smiling blandly.

Sprout pushes the cutout onto the doll's face, and it sticks.

What was happening in this cabin?

Abram shakes his head as if to regather his focus. He kneels down and lifts a hatch up from the floor. He pulls a flashlight from his pack and looks at Julie.

"Stay with Sprout."

Julie shakes her head. "I'll cover you. R can stay with Sprout."

"I don't need cover and I don't trust 'R.' Stay with Sprout."

He descends the ladder and disappears into the square of darkness. We wait.

"Well?" Julie calls to him after a moment.

No answer.

"Abram?" She steps to the edge of the hatch and peers into the darkness. "Abram!"

She looks at me, twisting her hair. "I can't see him." She glances at Sprout, then back at me. "Go down and check."

I realize I'm standing in a far corner of the room as if something has backed me into it. I don't remember moving. The basement hatch is a perfect black square, like a missing pixel in the rendering of reality.

"R?"

I blink a few times and push myself to the hatch's edge. Enough daylight leaks in to make out the ladder and the floor below, but not much beyond it. I force my hands and feet to do their jobs, and I descend the ladder. I gag on the stench of mold and decay—a Pyrrhic victory for my sense of smell—but all basements smell this way. Cobwebs and rat carcasses. It's just a basement.

I reach the bottom and peer into the shadows. "Abram?"

There's no answer, but as my eyes adjust, I see the glow of his flashlight leaking through a stack of empty crates. I move forward, noting that the basement is bigger than the cabin itself, an expansive concrete chamber lined with work tables and shelves and a partially walled bathroom, and I wonder if the cabin was merely an afterthought to this bunker.

A few tools and medical devices lie scattered on these tables and shelves, along with inexplicable oddities like a stack of traffic signs and a box of wigs. But for the most part, the bunker is stripped clean.

Abram is sitting cross-legged on the floor in front of what appears to be a walk-in freezer missing its door. His flashlight illuminates his face ghostly blue—eyes blank, mouth tight—and beyond that, the interior of the freezer.

"It's all gone," he mumbles. "The food, the medicine, beds, blankets . . . the fucking toilet paper. All they left was this."

The freezer's shelves are bare, but it's far from empty. Neatly stacked corpses rise halfway to the ceiling in a slow gradient of decay: dry bones on the bottom, leathery skeletons in the middle, and brown, bloated meat on the top. Some have holes in their heads, but most don't. Most seem to have died of obscurer causes.

"What were they trying to do?" I ask, unable to tear my eyes away from the mass grave.

"No idea."

A rat wriggles out of a rib cage and crawls up onto one of the fresher corpses. It bites into the oozing nub of an earlobe. The corpse twitches.

Abram stands and marches stiffly back to the ladder, leaving me in total darkness. I hurry after him, trying to ignore the moist squirming behind me.

Sprout is waiting at the edge of the hatch, but I don't see Julie until I emerge into daylight. She's standing in front of a small cabinet in the far corner of the cabin, looking down at something. Reading something. A large pink card. She holds it behind her back as she turns to us. "What'd you find?"

"Nothing," Abram says.

"Nothing?" She looks at me, sees the lingering horror on my face. "R, what did you—"

"What is that?" Abram says, striding toward her with his palm out. For some reason, Julie hesitates—just for a second, but I feel tiny questions rising like goosebumps.

"You tell me," she says, handing him the card. "Looks like notes for a meeting or something."

I move up behind Abram to read over his shoulder. The text is so thick with abbreviations and jargon that it hits my brain like monkey chatter, and for a moment I wonder if I've slipped back into illiteracy. But with great concentration, I'm able to parse it together.

```
Full sweeps, MT, ID, WY, 87 spcm. cllct

Roamers: ^fresh ^resil. ^cog. activity v. Hivers

Roamers Ornt. response rate: 45%
Hivers: 5%

Rec. cease hive raids, incrs. street sweeps

Street sweeps avg. 10-30 spcm per day,
^60% over 3 mnth

Spcm. ids. indicate extended migration,
up to 300 mi. v origin

Cause unknown but rec. capitalize

New Ornt. mthd "de-id" ^20% effct

65 spcm: X
12 spcm: 40% coop.
8 spcm: 76% coop.
2 spcm: 100% coop.
```

```
Rec. all facil. adopt "de-id" in comb. w.
Detroit "de-edu" mthd, cont. study of NY
"pink drink" mthd

Rec. close all Helena facils, trnsfr staff +
spcm. to Detroit + NY, consolidate mthds + rsrcs

1 yr projection: 100% coop, begin mass prod.
```

Abram stares at the card for a lot longer than it should take to read it.

"Does any of that . . . mean anything to you?" Julie asks. Her tone contains more than simple incomprehension. A hint of sediment disturbed, of drowned thoughts rising.

Abram shakes his head. It's unclear if he's answering Julie or some shouting inner voice. He grabs Sprout's hand and marches out of the cabin.

"Hey!" Julie chases him out. "Abram!"

The sun is a little lower, the sky a little paler. The trees look lifeless in the still air. Abram lifts Sprout onto his bike and climbs on behind her. He says it like a bitter concession: "I'll fly the plane."

Julie stops on the porch, cocking her head. "You will?"

"I'll go to town till I find a safe place to settle. Maybe that's a year from now on the other side of the world, maybe it's tomorrow in Toronto. Either way, that's where I get off, whether you've found your utopia or not. Is that clear?"

Julie doesn't answer.

"Is that *clear*?"

"Yes," she says. "It's clear."

Abram starts his bike, spins it around, and disappears into the trees.

We stand on the porch steps, listening to the engine noise dwindle. "What did you find down there?" Julie asks quietly.

The engine's harsh growl gives way to the sounds of the forest. The birdsong fades to a few lonely calls as the sun slips below the trees.

"Corpses," I reply, staring into the dark maw of the trail. "And nothing."

"Oh."

I look at her. "What did *you* find?"

Surprise and faint embarrassment flicker across her face, like I've snuck up behind her while she's journaling. But the look is gone so quickly I can't be sure I didn't imagine it. "Just a piece of paper," she says. "Just some words."

She hops onto her bike and kicks it to life. I follow her into the woods.

WE

THE BOY is getting hungry.

He floats between states, almost perfectly balanced between Living and Dead, almost unreachable to the demands of either, but only almost. He has walked hundreds of miles without consuming any form of energy, and one can only defy physics for so long. His balance is beginning to tremble.

He doesn't remember the last time he ate. His past is an unreadable mess, like a book shredded and glued back together. A big man and a tall man and a family of skeletons. Then other Dead people. A blur of blank faces and unfamiliar rooms. Passed from hand to hand, cared for, fed a few bits of meat, then forgotten in a dark hallway, picked up by someone else, fed, and forgotten.

We can't decipher these soggy collages, so we skip ahead to the new pages, to where he smelled a new scent rippling through the airport, new sounds echoing through the halls, voices and laughter and scratchy old music. He saw the change around him, felt it creeping into him, and he pushed it out. It felt unearned, inadequate, like a father apologizing for a beating by offering a hug. He wasn't ready to embrace this supposedly new world. He didn't trust its open arms.

Now he is far away from that world, deep in the forest and more alone than he's ever been, if loneliness can be measured in miles. This stretch of highway has been untouched for so long the forest has started to reclaim it, smoothing it back into the green expanse like a fading scar. Young pines shoot through the pavement as their parents' roots break it up for them. Slabs, then shards, then pebbles, then sand. He can feel the looseness of things here, so far from the lattice of other minds. He sees vacillations in the corners of his eyes. Things that aren't quite certain what they are; they are waiting for someone to tell them. In this place, he is prepared to see spherical doors and tetrahedral fires, crystal birds and hollow bears, but he is not expecting a man on a bicycle wearing a Sonic Youth T-shirt.

The man rides past the boy, then stops, gets off his bike, and walks back to him. The man is neatly bearded, the sides of his head trimmed short, his eyes hidden behind Wayfarer sunglasses. In another era, he might be on his way to work at a trendy software company. In this era, he is sweaty and dirty and the barrel of an Uzi pokes out of his messenger bag.

The boy keeps his eyes on his own toes as the man approaches him.

"Are you Living?" the man says, stopping a safe distance away.

The boy shrugs.

"I guess that's a yes. You alone?"

The boy nods.

The man examines him. The boy's skin is pale, but only as pale as dark skin can be. "Do you talk?"

The boy keeps his head down. He doesn't talk. He can, but he doesn't. To talk is to let people inside, to share common ground and common language. Even if the words are hateful, talking is a connection, and it requires a tiny amount of trust. More than the boy has.

And yet the boy is lonely. And hungry. He looks up at the man.

"Jesus!" the man says, jumping back and reaching instinctively for his gun, then stopping himself. He looks closer at the boy's eyes. Bright, shimmering yellow. Two golden rings. "Those aren't Dead eyes," he says. "What kind of eyes are those?"

The boy shrugs.

The man looks at the boy. He looks him up and down. "What's your name?"

The boy shrugs.

The man thinks for a moment. "Why don't you come with me."

The boy studies the man's face, searching for something to read. The man's sunglasses are a wall over his soul.

Is he a good person? the boy asks us. *Is most of him in you?*

We don't answer.

The boy reaches out and takes the man's hand. The man smiles.

There is no room for the boy on the bike so the man walks with it beside him. The boy notes that this is kind. It will slow the man down and double the length of his journey, but he does it. The Dead feed their young so that their young can help them feed. There is no feeling, no bond, only numbers multiplying themselves. It has been a long time since the boy has encountered kindness.

The boy and the man walk in silence. The man glances at the boy from time to time. The boy can feel his gaze even through the sunglasses, a faint heat on the side of his face.

They emerge from the forest into a small highway town, houses sagging, grass on roofs, tree branches poking through windows. The sun is melting against the edge of the horizon, about to disappear.

"We'll sleep here," the man says, glancing at the boy again. They leave the crumbled highway and enter the crumbled town.

Next to the gas station, there is a tiny play area. One swing set and a jungle gym, its colorful paint all peeled off, a spidery dome of rusted steel bars. The man pries an armful of shingles off the side of the gas station and carries it back to the jungle gym, dumps it through the holes, and climbs inside.

"Safest place to have a fire," he says, smiling at the boy. "No surprises in here."

The boy crawls into the dome and sits in the weedy grass that's growing through the sand. He watches the man coax the rotted shingles into a tiny, sad fire that's mostly smoke. When he's convinced that it won't burn any better, the man sits back and finally takes off his sunglasses. He looks at the boy. The boy tries to read his eyes but their piercing focus makes him look away.

"Sorry for staring," the man says, still staring. "I've never seen eyes like yours."

The boy reaches into the man's messenger bag. Underneath the gun and a big knife, there is a stick of beef jerky. He pulls it out and regards it warily. He has tried this before, but maybe now . . .

"Go ahead," the man says. "If you're hungry, go ahead."

The boy takes a bite. He chews the cured, salted, chemically preserved meat. No trace of life energy, human or otherwise. He spits the meat into the gravel.

The man nods. "Thought so."

The boy looks up, not understanding this comment.

"I've heard about ones like you. Mostly Dead? Sort of . . . stuck in between?"

The boy lowers his eyes to the fire.

The man rises to a crouch and hobbles around the smoldering pile of shingles, keeping his head down but still bumping a few of the jungle gym bars. He sits next to the boy. "It must be confusing. Your brain trying to tell you you're a person even though there's nothing in there. Just a bunch of impulses in an empty room." He looks at the side of the boy's cheek. "I feel like that sometimes."

The boy looks into the fire while the man looks at his cheek, his neck. The fire's core is a murky red glow behind all the smoke.

"But you know, you don't need to worry about that," the man says, his voice soft and deeply earnest. "Because you're not really alive. Just try to remember that, okay? Everything is easier if you remember that."

The boy turns to look at the man. The man smiles and puts one hand on the boy's thigh. Then the other on his zipper.

The boy bites off the man's ear.

The man screams and leaps to his feet. His head hits the bars with a *ping* and he falls face-first into the fire. He lies motionless while his beard burns like dry moss. The boy hikes up the man's T-shirt and chews into the wells of life pulsing through deltoids, trapezius, latissimus, fascia.

How will you file this? he asks us as he buries his face in bloody flesh. *This moment, me and this bad person, this thing I had to do. Higher or Lower? Will people read it and learn from it, or will you lock it away?*

We want to tell the boy he doesn't understand. We are not a librarian; we are the books. But even if we broke our silence now, he wouldn't listen. He is busy.

He peels the man layer by layer, siphoning the life into his own starved cells. He has fought the hunger for a very long time, trying to hold his precarious balance, but there are limits. He can feel the cure circling in his head, tickling his eyes, showing him secret truths while it knocks on his soul, but he keeps the door barred. He is angry. He is not ready to talk.

He eats until he's full and then sits in the sand, staring at the red mess. Most of the man is gone, but the sinews that remain begin to twitch. The boy didn't touch the brain. This man's brain is toxic waste bubbling in the barrel of his skull, and it must be disposed of. The boy pulls the knife out of the messenger bag and removes the head from its neck. The eyes blink open, now gray. They watch him as he digs a hole in the sand. They watch him as he drops the head into the hole, and they continue to watch until he scoops sand over them. A little mound remains, so he builds a little castle, then he crawls out of the jungle gym.

He doesn't take the knife, or the gun, or the bike. His objective is not survival or advancement. He is simply searching. But he does take the sunglasses. He puts them on, covering the gleaming evidence of the struggle inside him. He walks back to the highway while the man he hoped was good smolders in the fire, tendrils of greasy smoke rising toward the stars.

1

THE FORESTS OF MONTANA are familiar to me. I look at the trees, and my hands and feet relive the sensation of climbing. The jagged bark of Douglas firs, the fine sandpaper of aspens, the twisted trunks of the whitebark pines, ancient and full of secrets.

The rumble of our idling bikes barely disturbs the silence as we creep down the shadowy hillside, all brakes, no throttle. I know Julie could go a lot faster, but she holds back, letting me set the pace, so we proceed like kids on training wheels until we emerge onto the gravel road, then the country road, then the highway. I breathe a sigh of relief as I crank the throttle and the bike lunges away from those haunted woods.

By the time we get back to the airport, the sun has vanished, leaving only a murky pink streak on the flat horizon. Nora and M are leaning against the plane's front wheel, arms crossed, frowning.

"What the fuck, Jules?" Nora says, her hands springing out like question marks.

Apparently Abram beat us here by more than a few minutes,

because the cargo ramp is down and his bike is secured inside. Julie gives Nora a weary *don't ask* head shake and drives up the ramp. I follow her in and we begin fastening the tie-downs.

"We thought he was trying to take the plane," Nora says as she and M march up the ramp. "I almost shot him."

"The plane's worthless without him," Julie mutters.

"Just in the leg. Maybe the dick."

The four massive engines whir to life, filling the cargo bay with swirling dust. Julie slams a fist against the door-close button.

"So what happened?" Nora asks as we climb the stairs to the upper deck.

"He . . . changed his mind," Julie says, and the dazed uncertainty in her voice tells Nora enough to let it go.

• • •

Our second takeoff is significantly less harrowing than our first. The only sign that we're not on a real flight by a real airline is the lack of calming platitudes from the captain. We even have a flight attendant. Once we reach cruising altitude, Sprout walks down the aisle with a tray of Carbtein cubes.

"Do you want a snack?" she asks Nora in the row across from us.

"No thanks," Nora says.

"Do you want a snack?" Sprout asks M.

M takes one and rotates it in his hand, studying it like a Rubik's cube, then takes a bite.

"Do you want a snack?" Sprout asks Julie.

Julie takes a cube. "Thank you, Sprout. Excellent service."

"Daddy said I should do it."

Julie looks at me. "Really. Well, that was nice of him."

"I think he feels bad," Sprout says. "For being mean. Do you want a snack?" She shoves the tray toward me.

I take a cube. "Thank you."

"You're welcome."

She turns and continues down the aisle.

"Where's she going?" Julie wonders, then I hear a door slide open and Sprout's voice from the rear of the plane:

"Do you want a snack?"

I jump to my feet, tensing to run—

"You're welcome."

Sprout reappears, striding up the aisle like a seasoned professional, her tray empty, a big smile on her face. She returns to the cockpit to resume her copilot duties.

I sit down. Julie takes a bite of her cube. "What do you think, R?" she muses while she chews. "She can do this a few more years to save for college, then get her degree and move into architecture. Maybe Joan and Alex can be her apprentices."

I peer into my cube's chalky white lunar landscape and feel a localized hunger pang, as if just a few inches of my stomach have woken up. I take a bite and chew, grimacing at the dry texture and inscrutable flavor, like a four-course meal blended into a smoothie.

"I know," Julie mumbles. "It's not funny."

I shrug, still chewing. "It's kind of funny."

"It's a dead baby joke."

I hear something in her voice that makes me stop chewing. That note of disquiet I heard back in the cabin, of disturbed sediment clouding the ocean floor. "Harsh assessment," I say to the back of her head as she presses her nose to the window. "You don't think they have a future?"

She's quiet for a moment, peering into the darkness. "I do. I just wish it didn't have to be in a world like this."

"Maybe it won't be," I offer, but I'm unable to give the sentiment much weight. It passes through her and out the window like a feeble ghost.

She pulls an in-flight magazine out of the seat pocket in front of her and leans back. She studies the model on the cover, a woman of a species no longer found on Earth, coiffed and painted, nourished and toned, beautiful in a way that's no longer recognizable as human.

"I used to read everything I could find about the old world," Julie says, and begins to flip through the brittle pages. "I studied it like mythology. And I always wondered what people I knew would've been like back then, when life was just a bunch of choices. Your beliefs, your priorities, where you live and what you do . . ." She pauses on an ad for a garish Broadway musical and smiles bitterly. "Can you imagine having all those options? Being surrounded by that cloud of potential just waiting for your decision?"

She continues flipping the pages. Restaurants. Movies. Museums. She stops on an ad for the University of Michigan, and her smile fades.

"My mom grew up in that world." She stares at lush photos of libraries and art studios, groups of friends laughing hysterically. "She wasn't rich or anything, but it was pre-collapse America. She was working with a palette I can't imagine." She runs her fingers over the wrinkled paper, the faded ink. "Having that world and then *losing* it . . ." Her voice falls to a murmur. "It'd haunt you forever, wouldn't it? How could you let go?"

She stuffs the magazine back into the seat pocket and closes her eyes for a moment. Then she opens them and turns to me. "What was in that cabin, R?"

I don't answer.

"What are they trying to do?" She's almost pleading. "How much more fucked is this place going to get?"

I should probably try to reassure her, squeeze her hand and recite some canned comforts, but I'm looking through her into the dark hole of the window and I'm seeing graves and fires, steel bars and brown teeth and—

"Hey." Nora is leaning out of her seat, watching us from across the aisle while M snores softly against their window. "We might not have to find out."

"What do you mean?" Julie says.

Nora shoots a glance at the cockpit, then gets up and jerks her chin toward the coach section. Julie nudges me out of the row and we follow Nora through the curtain.

"Take a look," Nora says, pulling a thin yellow pamphlet out of her pocket and handing it to Julie.

Julie skims the first page. Her eyes dart up to Nora. "Where'd you find this?"

"We went looking for you in the airport lobby and they were taped up all over."

"Why is DBC still posting in airports?" Julie wonders as she begins to read.

Nora shrugs. "I saw a lot of notes on the walls. A few fresh shits on the floor. Maybe airports are still traveler hubs."

"Nineteen from BABL . . . that's last year, right?"

"Yeah. Practically breaking news. Check the last page."

Julie flips to the end, reads it, and grins. "I knew it. I fucking knew it!" She shoves the pamphlet into my hands. "Can you read this, R?"

The crudely photocopied mess resembles either an old-fashioned DIY "zine" or a madman's manifesto.

The crazed handwriting is barely legible, but I can read it. Understanding it is another matter.

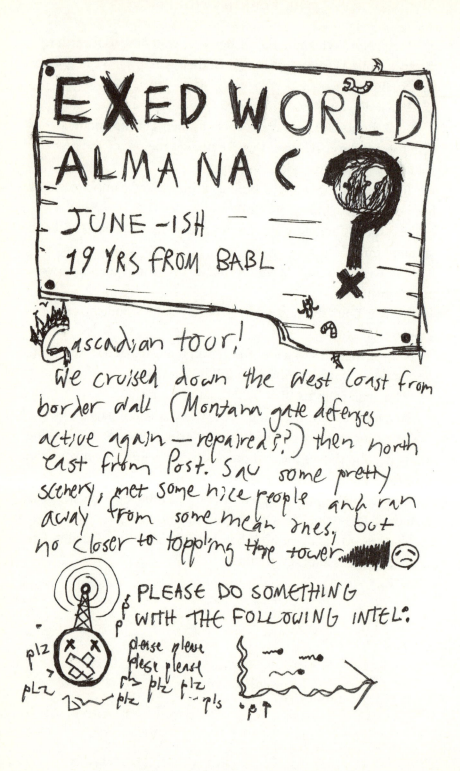

EXED WORLD ALMANAC

JUNE-15H
19 YRS FROM BABL

Cascadian tour!

We cruised down the West Coast from border wall (Montana gate defenses active again—repaired?!?) then north east from Post. Saw some pretty scenery, met some nice people and ran away from some mean ones, but no closer to toppling the tower. ☹

PLEASE DO SOMETHING
WITH THE FOLLOWING INTEL:

please please
plese please
plz plz
plz pl's

BELLINGHAM: X

SEATTLE: X (razed) 100

OYMPIA: X + dispersed pop (minor hive in captl. bldg.)

- POST: 2 fortified enclaves (closed, hostile) & dispersed pop. (MAJOR hive in Oran Airport, almost died trying to drop copies)

PORTLAND: Semi pop. no gov. Subsistence farming, barter market ... early stage socialist enclave ??? 20-30 Dead per week. (unincoporated)

WORLD UPDATE!

Sailors found in Portland!

HALF MAD ADVENTURERS TOD LEGENDS OF SHADOWY

*told VOID...

BEYOND PLANET AMERICA

SPAIN: X

FRANCE: X (paris razed)

GERMANY: X (rumored)

UK: breXit (London razed — Fire Church euro branch?? Local grown equiv??)

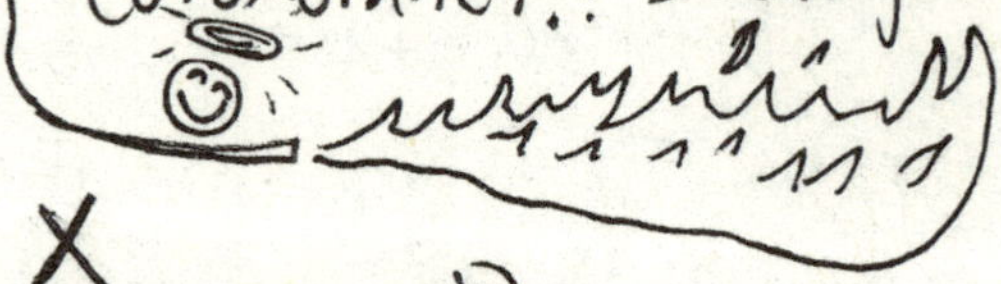

NORWAY: X

SWEDEN: X (rumored)

ICELAND: X...??? Rumored since 10 after BABL but still unconfirmed. Explorers don't return. Killed? Or SEDUCED??

NOTE!

As always, global intel
should be considered RUMORED.
Sailor reports rarely reliable.
High seas = extreme isolation =
unsupervised reality = squishy
facts

NEXT UP:
East into the heart of
the Midwaste!
Wish us luck and sanity!

WE LOVE YOU, EXED WORLD!

-DBC

"What *is* this?" I ask, handing the pamphlet back to Julie.

"It's the Almanac!" Julie says, aghast at my lack of savvy. "Even you should know the Almanac."

"People . . . believe this info?" I brush a finger over the schizophrenic scrawl, the drawings of surreal monsters.

"Beggars can't be choosers, R. Most people don't know what's happening a mile outside their shelters. DBC's been combing the country up and down for like ten years and they leave a new report whenever they pass through. It's sketchy news, but it's news."

"I got so excited the first time I found one," Nora says wistfully. "Felt like my favorite band had come to town."

Julie smiles. "Me and Mom had a secret pact that if we ever found them, we'd leave Dad and run away with them." Her smile falters, begins to cool.

"But back to the point," Nora says. "Iceland, right? Sounds promising, right?"

"Right." Julie hands the zine to Nora. "You do the talking. I've pushed him far enough today."

Nora nods and heads for the cockpit.

"Iceland?" I ask Julie, lowering my voice. "You're sure that's the answer?"

She looks at me like I've asked if water is wet. "Of course I'm not sure. I just . . ." She turns and looks out a window, her face tinting red in the dying light. "I have a good feeling."

"Why?"

"Because my mom . . ." She watches the clouds, a flock of little cumuli grazing beneath us. "My mom was half-Icelandic. She spent a couple years in Reykjavík, before she met Dad. The way she talked about it . . . the culture and the politics . . . it sounded like things just made *sense* there. I could never figure out why she came back."

"Maybe because it wasn't her home."

She glances back at me with surprise and a little annoyance, but I push ahead.

"Leaving now . . . feels like giving up."

"On what?" she says sharply. "What do we have here? That shitty house?"

I flinch. I can tell she feels the sting too, perhaps sharper than she expected. But she fights it.

"What do we have?" she persists. "The fucking stadium? Cascadian pride?"

"The people." I hold her gaze, trying to tether her fluttering thoughts. "Ella, David, Marie, Wally, Taylor, Britney, Zane—"

"I know their names, R."

"So are we going to leave them all with Axiom? Are we going to run away?"

The look she gives me makes me feel like a bully. Like I'm popping her balloons and pissing on her picnic. But I'm only quoting what she told me a few days ago, when she was quoting what I told her a few months before that. We keep tossing this bit of truth back and forth like it hurts to hold on to it.

She gives her head a hard shake as if to clear it of thoughts and returns to her seat. Nora's siege of the cockpit is already under way. I'm glad Julie chose to stay out of this one.

"What part of 'explorers don't return' did you not understand?" Abram says, waving the Almanac. "Iceland's probably one giant hive by now."

"Who has a better chance of resisting a plague than an island? They probably closed their borders at the first reports."

"Are you bullshitting me or yourself? Borders don't matter to the plague. They got it on the Space Station for Christ's sake."

Julie jumps up. I sigh.

"Iceland was different," she says, poking her head into the cockpit entryway. "They did everything different. They wouldn't have collapsed like we did."

"Are Icelanders not human? What did they do so different?"

"While we were busy with Civil War Two, they were perfecting renewable energy, food production, pouring resources into education and culture—they weren't collapsing, they were thriving."

"So you're a history buff. Then you know they were halfway underwater when we heard from them last."

"Yeah, and they were building a sea wall!"

Nora quietly slips out of the crossfire, giving me an *I tried* shrug as she returns to her seat.

"You know Canada is exed," Julie continues, picking up steam. "So is Mexico and probably South America. Think outside the hemisphere!"

Abram stands up and moves toward her. Julie backs out of the cockpit doorway, tensing into an uncertain defensive stance, but he brushes past her, steps into the bathroom, and starts urinating.

Julie folds her arms over her chest and glares at his back through the door. "Are we having a *literal* pissing contest right now?"

Abram lets out a weary sigh as he finishes up. "Listen, you beautiful sunbeam . . ." He steps out of the bathroom and flops down in the front row, looking up at her. "I'd love to believe there's a beacon of civilization out there waiting for us to find it. But if there's a beacon, why can't we see it? Why doesn't anyone know?"

"You think the last stable country in the world is going to advertise itself? And have all the fuckup countries coming around looking for a couch to crash on?"

Abram seems to consider this.

"They're probably just waiting for the right time. Building up their resources, developing a plan."

He nods abruptly and stands up. "Okay, sure. Iceland sounds good."

Julie's rebuttal freezes on her lips and she cocks her head, startled into silence.

"And Toronto's on the way there," he continues, pushing past her into the cockpit. "So if we don't find what we need in Toronto, then we'll talk about going abroad. Okay?"

He sounds so sincere that he must not be. But if his sincerity is sarcastic . . . is his sarcasm sincere? I wonder if he even knows.

He returns to his seat and Julie returns to hers, looking off-balance.

"Hey!" M shouts toward the cockpit. "How much longer?" He's still blinking sleep out of his eyes but already gripping his armrests.

"Tomorrow," Abram shouts back.

M grumbles a few curses, pressing deeper into his seat.

I squeeze Julie's knee, another attempt at comfort, but she is lost in thought and doesn't seem to notice my efforts. So I turn to the window.

The view is not what it should be. There should be lights down there. Even in remote lands there should be a few specks, then glittering lines and clusters, earthly constellations that finally converge into the ecstatic galaxy of a city, pulsing and boiling with life.

But there is nothing. The earth below is empty darkness. The only constellations are the ones above, old Leo and Cancer and Capricorn, and I find them less dear to me than the ones humanity built, these distant gods who want nothing to do with our fraught little lives. In all their smoke and noise and overheated drama, I miss cities.

The sun finally withdraws all traces of itself and the darkness is complete. I watch it roll by beneath us, an undifferentiated carpet of black, and then . . . light. A few glowing spots, then a few more, then a radiant pool bright enough to illuminate the surrounding hills. The lights form the shape of a city, but they are not streetlamps and windows. They are fires. Hundreds of buildings bathed in the distinctive white flames of Fire Church phosphorus.

"If you look to our left," Abram says over the intercom, adopting the laconic mumble of a captain playing tour guide, "you'll see some very sincere people looking for a better world."

A bitter giggle escapes Nora's throat. "*These* fuckers, on top of everything. Candles on the crazy-cake."

Julie stares past me through the window, watching the hellish death of whatever city this was, burned at the stake for the heresy of surviving. I see memories rushing past her eyes, sadness and pain and anger. Then she closes them and curls up in her seat, her back to the window and to me.

I watch the blaze until it disappears behind us and darkness reclaims the view. Darkness or fire. Are these our only options?

MY MOTHER.

She believes in a better world. But it's far away and mysterious and we will have no part in building it. The new world will be handed to us fully formed and perfect, dropped from the sky to cover the mess we've made of this one. This one's doom was written into its creation, never more than a disposable stage for a brief drama whose plot no one understands and whose ending no one can revise. The only change we can effect is how quickly the end comes, because we have nothing in us but destruction. We are corrupt from before birth, and if it ever appears we've done good, it's not us but God's hand inside us, moving our limbs to accomplish his plan. Our greatest sin is believing that we matter.

This is what my mother believes and what she teaches me, so I can't understand why she works at a refugee camp. Feeding the children of war casualties, finding homes for displaced families . . . aren't these people *supposed* to die? Isn't this the Last Sunset we've been waiting for? Why is she trying to pull the sun back up?

I ask her these questions and they upset her. They dim the glow that fills her face when she works at the camp, mending clothes, administering medicine, cooking huge vats of stew. Helping people brings her joy, even though it's pointless. I decide to leave it alone.

I go with her to the refugee camp whenever I can because my father isn't there. I get to choose clothes from the donations pile to replace my worn-out rags from home. My father says we have plenty and don't need anyone's help, but I think we're not far above the refugees themselves. At the end of each day, my mother throws a few cans of food into her purse. She says not to tell my father.

Grass-stained acid-washed jeans. A turquoise Mickey Mouse sweatshirt. My choices don't reflect any personal aesthetics. I am ten years old and poor. I take the clothes that fit.

"Hello, Mrs. Atvist."

"What are you doing here?"

I stop digging through the shoe bin and listen to the two voices out on the curb. My mother's is soft but stern and I can picture her standing with her hands knotted in front of her, demure but unmovable. The other is dry and smoky, the creak of burned timber breaking. It's just barely familiar. I must have been a toddler the last time I heard my grandfather's voice.

"I've been trying to talk to my son but he's balls-deep in this Holy Fire bullshit. I can't get a word through his skull. Thought maybe I could talk to you instead."

"What would make you think I'd go against my husband? Or our church? Holy Fire is our family."

"*I'm* your family, God damn it. I want to help you."

"We don't want your help."

"It's a fucking embarrassment. I run one of the last corps in America and my son is living in a shack. My grandson's pulling piss-stained jockeys out of charity bags . . ."

"Leave him out of it."

". . . and my daughter-in-law is stealing canned beans from a hobo shelter."

"Your money won't be worth much in a few years."

"Money's not the only currency."

His thin face. His tobacco-stained grin leering through the window of his hulking white Range Rover. I watch him from behind my mother's legs like a much younger boy.

"Hey, kid!" His eyes dart to me, catlike.

"Go back inside," my mother tells me.

I obey, but I stand inside the doorway and listen.

"What kind of a mother are you? I could make your kid prince of the new world and you're gonna let him starve with the peasants?"

"The world is God's, and he's about to burn it away."

"Listen to me. I've been working my whole life to put this family on top of the food chain. I'm not letting you or my little bitch of a son turn us back into rabbits."

"Leave us alone. Don't come here again."

"When things get bad, you'll call me." He raises his voice, shouting through the doorway. "Call me anytime, R—! I'll be waiting."

• • •

His voice echoes in my ears as my third life—my real life—reclaims my mind. I hear my name on his lips and I mute it out. I redact it. No matter how far my past encroaches on my present, I will not take its name. I won't let it scribble over the one I built with Julie.

The plane is dark, but the world outside is gray, the sun lurking somewhere just below the mountains. Julie is asleep by my side, still curled into a tight ball. The air is cool and her arms are wrapped around her bare shoulders, trembling. I tuck her old quilt around her, but her spasms don't subside.

"Wait," she whimpers, a faint bleat that barely escapes her lips. "Mom, wait. I'm awake."

It occurs to me that my blank slate is an outrageous luxury. My terror of losing it seems pathetic when I think of Julie's dreams. I fight my past because it's a wild animal creeping into my clean house, but Julie has spent her whole life sleeping next to hers, its hot breath on her neck, its bloody drool on her sheets.

I drape a second blanket over her shoulders, just in case. The air is cold. Icy upper atmosphere mixed with vintage oxygen from the plane's tanks. A strange feeling, breathing the air of another era, imbued with the sounds and smells of a world long gone. I wander down the aisle, running my hand over the soft leather of the business-class seats. These seats once cradled the world's rich and powerful. Not the richest or *most* powerful—those had private planes and private smirks and metal briefcases full of secrets—but the ones who could afford to pay double for a little extra distance from humanity. Wherever they are now, if any survived the world's shift from plutocracy to kratocracy, their presence lingers in the indentations in these seats. The hairs and skin cells in the carpet. The echoes of their voices, *call me anytime . . .*

I shake my head and blink hard and focus on the window, on my feet, on—

"Archie?" M says in a quiet rumble. "You okay?"

He is slouched low in a reclined seat, apparently just waking from a pleasant nap. Nora is asleep against the window two seats away, curled into a fetal ball like Julie.

"Fine." I start to walk past him, further into the plane, but he holds out a hand.

"Don't fight it."

I stop. "What?"

"You make it a fight, you'll lose. Doesn't have to be a fight."

I give him a level stare. "Yes it does."

"Just memories. How bad could it be?"

"Don't know. Don't want to."

He smiles. "Archie. Always so dramatic."

I glare at him. "My name's not Archie."

He upturns his palms, genuinely puzzled. "Why not? Good a name as any."

"Made up for Grigio. So he'd think I was normal. It's a lie."

He shrugs. "It's a name."

I shake my head and look at the floor. "A name should have meaning. A story. A thread to people who love you."

I glance up. His smile is trembling like he's fighting laughter. "Lover boy," he says. "So complicated."

I walk away, wishing the first-class cabin had a door instead of a curtain so I'd have something to slam.

I roam to the rear of the plane. A delicate snore alerts me to Sprout stretched across a row of seats, her little head poking out through a pile of blankets. She'll be like me someday. She's already halfway there at six years old, the furrowed brow, the lofty goals and worldly worries. I don't know whether to be proud of her or afraid for her.

There are times when I miss being mindless. Moments when I wonder if consciousness is a curse. Are blunt minds truly happier than sharp ones, or do they just travel smaller peaks and valleys? A flat line of lukewarm contentment, immune to despair but incapable of rapture? This is what I tell myself when I'm faced with untroubled folk. I tell myself over and over.

The sun finally crests the horizon and the windows restrict its light into fat golden beams that cut through the cabin, lighting up the dust. Another fine summer morning. We should be getting close.

I open the bathroom door to check on my kids and find them upright and alert, holding their Carbtein close to their faces like the cubes contain the mysteries of the universe. I am thrilled to notice they've been nibbled.

Joan looks up at me with clear focus in her gray-brown eyes, and I wonder what shape her line takes. It's certainly not flat. These kids have known trouble. Their lines soar and plunge, from almost-life to pseudo-death and perhaps now back up again. But why this oscillation? Three months ago, when they peeked out of their grave, what didn't they find? What disappointment sent them back to bed? What are they waiting for?

Their attention drifts away from me and settles on the bathroom wall. They stare at it like it's a window, like they're enjoying a first-class view of the sunrise instead of the gray fiberglass of their shit-stained jail.

"Our friend," Joan says.

"Your friend?" I repeat, hoping to seize this thread and draw her further out. "Who's your friend?"

"Goldshine," she says, turning around to give me the first smile I've ever seen on her face. "Sunboy."

"Far away," Alex says. "Lonely." There's an eerily nuanced unhappiness in his voice, not just personal sadness but empathy. Compassion.

"Help us call?" Joan pleads with me. "Tell him to follow?"

I stare at them, stunned by this sudden burst of volition. But I have no idea what they're talking about. Before I can try to decipher their cryptic blurts, Abram's voice crackles over the intercom.

"Ladies and gentlemen, we are currently passing over Detroit, Michigan, America's most thoroughly exed city, and will be approaching the Canadian border shortly. I don't expect any turbulence but this is wild territory, so I can't make any promises. Time to wake up."

My kids continue to watch me expectantly. Their look says that I'm an adult, a powerful authority possessed of all knowledge, wise and capable and tasked with their protection, and that the world is mine to give them. But I'm a stumbling amnesiac afraid of his own name. I'm a bitter teen drinking bitter sermons and living in terror of the world. I'm a boy in a Mickey Mouse shirt, and these kids are beyond me.

They watch me back out of the bathroom. They watch me shut the door.

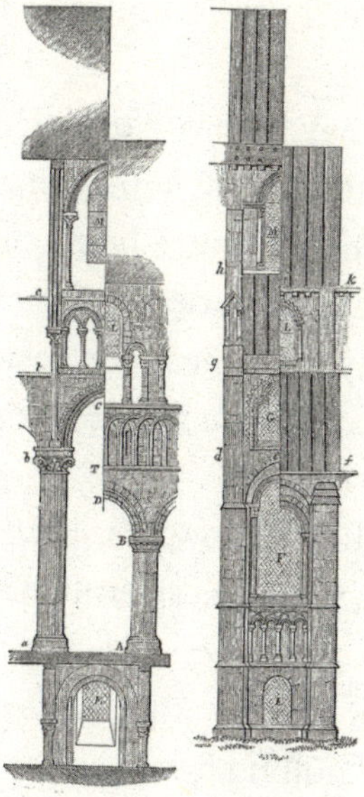

Abram's announcement has stirred Julie and Nora out of their coiled sleep positions, but it's not until the sun strikes their faces that they finally wake up, blinking and squinting against the hot rays. I take my seat next to Julie but I don't say anything yet. She sleeps badly and wakes up worse. I've learned to give her a few minutes to shake off the shadows.

Detroit spreads out below us like a concrete desert. The totality of its ruination is visible even from this altitude, an uncommon grayness without even the usual sprawl of vegetation to cover its bones. I thought the notes in Abram's cabin mentioned "facilities" in Detroit, but I must have misunderstood the shorthand because it's impossible to imagine anything alive down there. There's something almost unreal about it, a place so fully forgotten that it's beginning to deliquesce. I feel a queasy sensation as I let it fill my vision; the flatness sinks and gains depth, the streets twist and flex—then Julie looks over my shoulder and the streets are straight. The ground is flat.

My need for sleep may be more dire than I realized.

"Good morning," I tell her. It sounds inane, like a greeting from a hotel desk, but hearing my voice helps clear my thoughts.

She ignores me. She stares out at the city. "It's so empty." Her voice is low and croaky. I can hear the residue of her dreams in it, a lingering sadness. "Looks like it's been empty for centuries." No, not sadness. Disappointment.

I press my face to the window, scanning for any signs of activity, but from this altitude I wouldn't see much even if it were there, just the abstract line art of the streets.

"Mom would cry if she saw this." She sounds even less present now, like the dream is pulling her back in. "There were these artist communes trying to rebuild the city. Mom thought it was going to be the key to everything."

Burned houses. Caved-in factories. Dead parks full of gray trees.

"As usual, Dad convinced her she was wrong. Which . . . it looks like she was."

I watch the city dwindle into a sparse scattering of industrial buildings and then finally surrender to empty flatlands. I wonder how many "keys to everything" have come and gone throughout history, and why they never seem to open much. Have we been putting them in the wrong locks?

"R," Julie says. "Can I ask you something?"

I hear a spike in her tone. Her eyes are still glued to the window, but her posture is stiffer, and the dreamy languor is gone.

"All those years you were out there . . . *roaming* or whatever . . . did you ever feel things from your old life?"

I hesitate. "Feel things?"

"I know you didn't *remember* anything, but did you ever feel, like . . . the *residue* of a memory? Maybe a song that made you sad for no reason, or a piece of junk that you just had to take home?"

I try to intercept her gaze, hoping to discover what's behind this abrupt change of subject, but she continues to look past me while she talks, the vacant stare of a medium conversing with ghosts.

"All those knickknacks you collected, you must have had some reason for picking the ones you did, right? They must have had some connection to your past."

"I guess so," I say, but I have to force the words out. Why is she taking us into this territory? It's not safe here.

"So you weren't totally blank, even then. There was still something nudging you."

"Maybe?"

"What about . . . places?" She finally breaks away from the window and meets my searching gaze. Her face is placid; she's doing a solid impression of casual curiosity, but I can see something else lurking behind her eyes. "Did you ever feel pulled somewhere? An instinct to take a certain road, follow a certain direction?"

She watches me intently. I'd love to give her whatever she's looking for, but all her questions have the same answer: a vague and mushy *maybe*. This is as certain as things get in the world of the Dead. What could she be hoping to find there?

A friendly *ding* chimes on the intercom.

"Ladies and gentlemen," Abram announces, apparently starting to enjoy his captain schtick, "we are now approaching London, Ontario, and will begin a gentle descent toward Toronto . . ."

Julie holds her stare a moment longer, her lips pressed tight, then gets up and shuts herself in the restroom.

I glance at Nora, but she's not eavesdropping this time. She and M are engaged in their own conversation, something about how much they miss coffee. I feel my stomach lift as the plane begins to shed altitude.

"If you look straight ahead," our captain continues, "you'll see the end of this great country, both literally and figuratively."

I look ahead as directed, eager to shake off the uneasy feelings that have attached themselves to my mind like little burrowing parasites.

"We passed the original border a while back, but that one was a bit too restrictive for America's expanding waistline, so we had to loosen the belt. What's a hundred miles between allies? What's a few dozen dead troops?"

"He sure gets jolly when it comes to the grim stuff," Nora mutters.

Grim as it may be, this will do for safe ground. It's the past, but not *my* past. Just a page I remember from some moldy history book. The mass migrations followed by the bizarre border adjustments, the lunatic logic that if enough Americans lived there, it must be America. The nation creeping northward, racing to reabsorb its fleeing populace until an exasperated Canada finally drew the line.

I see that line on the horizon. It cuts across Ontario's fallow farmlands like an old scar.

"Daddy?" Sprout says, blinking groggily as she wanders up the aisle. "Is that a wall like in Mexico?"

"It sure is, little girl," he replies with morbid amusement. "Our prison was an international effort. We built the floor, Canada built the ceiling." He lowers the intercom and looks back at his daughter through the doorway. "But it's different this time. This time we're going over it."

Sprout smiles, then yawns, and plops into a seat near the front. She rubs the eye under the patch and closes them both.

Julie emerges from the restroom. The shadow I glimpsed in her eyes has spread to her face; her jaw is set with quiet determination—to do what?

"Abram," she says.

He ignores her. "As we approach our destination, please return to your seats. All electronic devices—"

"*Abram.*" Julie steps into the cockpit doorway.

Silence, then a sigh. "What."

"Are you sure we can cross the wall? My family tried the Washington gate once and the automation almost gunned us down."

"When was this?"

"About seven years ago?"

"That's about when their military collapsed. No way the wall is still online, and it never had anti-aircraft anyway. It was more of a symbol than a real fortification."

I glance out the window. The wall is close enough to make out the giant red maple leaves painted along its length like stop signs. How did we provoke our mild neighbor to such a mad act? I suppose even the coolest heads have their limits.

"I was thinking . . . ," Julie says, "maybe we should check it out on foot first. To make sure it's safe."

Abram glances back at her with raised eyebrows. "Never thought I'd hear you advise caution."

"And you're suddenly a risk taker?"

"What can I say, you've inspired me. Or driven me insane."

"Abram." I can't see either of their faces, but I can see Julie's grip on the doorframe tightening. "I think we should turn around. Land in Detroit and take the bikes to check out the wall."

"Land in Detroit?" He laughs. "You want me to add two hundred miles to our flight and spend a whole day on the road just for some pointless recon?"

"We can check the airport for fuel while we're there. And besides . . ." She hesitates, then pushes ahead. "You saw the notes in the cabin. 'Facilities' in Detroit. We need to know what they're—"

"No we fucking don't," he cuts her off. "That's got nothing to do with us."

"It's got everything to do with us!" Julie snaps, her voice rising. "They're trying to turn this country into some kind of—"

"I thought you were done with this country." His matter-of-fact tone stops her short. "I thought you wanted to leave."

Her fingers tremble on the doorframe, but she's silent.

Abram lets the moment hang while he checks his instruments. "We're going to cross the wall at eight thousand feet. Nothing's going to get us. But okay, just to be safe . . ."

He flips a switch, and the seat belt lights blink on.

". . . there."

I get out of my seat, watching Julie nervously. She takes a step into the cockpit, and I brace to intervene. But the explosion doesn't come.

"Abram, listen to me." There's no anger. Her voice is low and tremulous. Desperate. "I need to go to Detroit."

I lean in, trying to catch a glimpse of her face in the cockpit mirror.

"It's important to me."

Abram twists around, his brows furrowed. "Why?"

I can't quite see the mirror. But as I lean in closer, hoping Julie's face will offer some clue to the puzzle inside her . . . I see something else. Something more dangerous than her temper, than her dreams, than her secrets or mine.

A flash on the border wall. A bright spot rising.

"Uhh?" I blurt; I can't find any words; I thrust my arm between Abram and Julie and point out the window.

They look.

"Abram?" Julie shouts.

"No," he says in a tone of indignant disbelief, like there must be some mistake.

The object streaks up from the wall and a ball of fire blooms in the distance. A few seconds later, the sound hits: a low boom that I can feel in the floor.

"What the fuck was that?" Nora says, joining the bottleneck at the front of the plane. Two more glowing specks rise from the wall and explode, closer now. The three clouds of smoke float in the air like a bouquet of black roses, their white stems reaching down toward earth. The first is vertical, the second slightly curved; the third is pointing straight toward us.

"Daddy what's happening?" Sprout cries.

"Stay in your seat, Murasaki!"

Something screams past the windows and I catch a split-second glimpse of the anti-aircraft defenses the wall supposedly doesn't have: a blue cylinder with pointy fins and a red nose cone, like a child's toy rocket. It explodes somewhere overhead, shoving the plane downward.

"Gray River," M says dreamily. His face is pressed against the window, staring up at the lingering cloud of fire. "Magnum XLs."

"What?" Abram shouts, craning his neck toward M.

"Old-fashioned heat seekers."

"Why are they missing us?" Nora asks with a cringe, as if asking will break the spell.

"Tuned for fighter engines. We're too cold."

"So we'll get through," Abram declares with desperate confidence. "They'll miss us and we'll get through."

M's eyes widen. "*Maybe*, but—"

"Are you out of your mind?" Nora shrieks. "Turn around!"

Abram stares grimly ahead, his knuckles white on the controls.

"Turn around," Julie says. "We can find somewhere else."

"Like Iceland?" Abram snaps. "Like fucking Atlantis?" His voice trembles with a strange blend of rage and fear. "There's nowhere else. There's no more time. We're in the mouth and it's closing."

Another flash from the wall.

"Abram, for Christ's sake!" Julie says, grabbing the back of his seat. "Turn around!"

"Daddy?" Sprout says. She's standing in the middle of the aisle, eyes wide with terror. Abram ignores her. He shoves the throttle forward.

This missile's aim looks true. It will pierce through the center of the cockpit and burn everything to ash, all our rebellious hopes and prideful visions of a world better than the one God gave us, a world where we make our own rules, worthless creatures that we are—the missile explodes in front of us and knocks the plane upward like a punch to the chin. I topple back into the aisle and my head strikes a chair and as I sprawl out on the floor, the plane plunges into the fireball. The cabin is a cavern in Hell, red-orange light in every window and the roar of the angry damned demanding justice, *real* justice, not this kangaroo court of cosmic entrapment, the screams of children who never asked to be born, punished for the flaws in the world that greeted them—

"Help me!" Sprout is screaming over the howl of wind through two broken windows. She clings to a seat as the suction pulls at her hair and sucks drops of blood from a cut on her forehead.

Julie jumps off the floor and runs to her side. Sprout reaches out and Julie picks her up, though the girl isn't much smaller than Julie herself. She carries her into the cockpit and sets her in the copilot seat and grabs Abram by the collar of his jacket.

"Turn the fuck around!" she roars into his face.

Abram looks from Julie to his daughter to the cyclone of dust and garbage swirling out the windows. "God damn it," he hisses under his breath. He cranks the controls left.

I tumble back into my seat as the plane banks hard, rivets creaking under the strain. We tip until the window is looking straight at the ground, the dirt sky of an inverted world. I feel the air getting thin. An oxygen mask dangles in front of me and I remember the old instructions, their startlingly blatant reversal of ethics: *Secure your own before helping others.*

But before I can debate this moral puzzle, the air thickens again. My ears pop. We are descending so rapidly I wonder if we're crashing, but then I see our runway lining up in front of us: a five-lane section of freeway stretching off toward Detroit.

"Landing . . . on that?" M says through clenched teeth. "The fucking road?"

Abram says nothing. No warnings, no instructions. He's either consumed with the task of landing or he's simply done dealing with us. But we don't need him to tell us we're in for a rough touch-down. Julie slips into her seat next to me. Her face is tight, but not with fear. Something else. I take her hand and she allows it to be taken, but her fingers remain clenched.

"Fuck," M says. "Fuck."

"Marcus," Nora says. "Take a breath. You remember breathing, right?"

He concentrates, then sucks a deep breath through his teeth.

"It's not that bad. We'll be fine."

"How . . . do you know?" M squeaks with tight, overfilled lungs. "Never flown before."

"Maybe I flew in another life."

"Maybe I . . . crashed in another life."

Nora smiles and slaps his knee. "It's nice to see such a big man act like such a little bitch."

M glares at her.

"Really! It's endearing."

He closes his eyes and releases his lungful of air in a slow, meditative sigh.

"There you go," Nora says. "Maybe just keep them closed."

The freeway spreads out in front of us, cutting through miles of fields whose only crops are brambles and dust. Most freeways in America are permanent traffic jams, but this one runs between a sealed nation and an ancient ruin, a road from nothing to nowhere. It hasn't been traveled in a very long time, so other than a few patches of blackberry vines creeping in at the edges, our runway is clear.

We come in fast and hard, and a little squeal escapes M when we hit. The wheels dig grooves into the thin asphalt with a continuous crunch, joining the engines and the broken windows in the chorus of noise. The cabin rattles so violently I expect the whole plane to dissolve into a pile of rivets. But then it calms, the engines rev down, and we roll to a stop. An "I Love NY" mug falls out of an overhead bin and breaks on the floor. Then silence.

I feel that fluttering again. I feel a chill through the wall of the plane, like clammy fingers pulling at my skin. That lonely necropolis that we avoided from above is suddenly uncomfortably close.

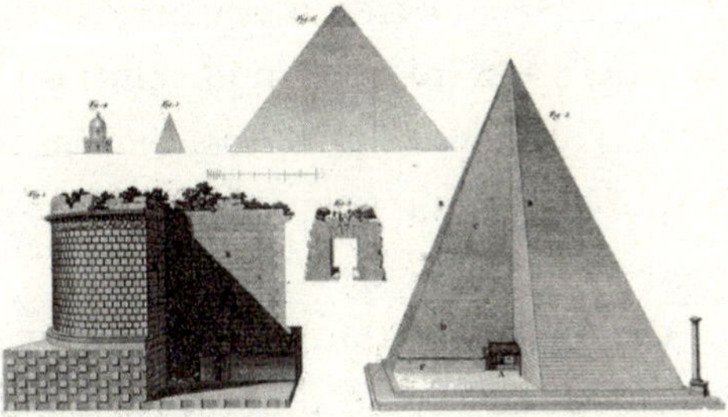

THE OUTSKIRTS OF DETROIT loom on the hazy horizon, and in every other direction: nothing. A scrubby empty plain on its way to becoming a desert. Abram stands on a ladder propped against the nose cone and digs around inside. The entire fuselage is sooty with smoke, but other than the broken windows, there is no visible damage.

"Well?" Nora says.

Abram slams the cone shut and descends the ladder. His eyes move across the ragged group assembled in front of him and I see despair. *How did I end up here? With them?*

"We need a part," he says, sounding like he can barely muster the words. "We'll head to the airport, salvage it from a wreck." His eyes narrow on Julie. "You always get your way, don't you?"

Julie is silent.

"So you can fix it?" Nora asks. "We can keep going?"

"Yes, we can keep going," he says with a drop of venom. "We can keep going and going and going."

He grabs Sprout's hand, glances briefly at the cut on her forehead, then pulls her back into the plane. A moment later, he rolls down the ramp on his motorcycle, his tool bag stuffed in the cargo box, his daughter clinging to his back.

"I could use his help," he says, nodding toward M. "The rest of you can stay here."

"No thanks," Nora says, already on her way up the ramp. "There's nothing to see. Detroit is dry bones."

"Never know where lost treasure might turn up. I'm coming."

Abram throws up his hands. "Well *someone* has to stay with the plane. Whoever shot us down is probably on their way here to loot the wreckage."

Nora stops at the top of the ramp and scans the dusty horizon. "Assuming that was actual people shooting at us and not just automation, they're at least two hours away by land. And if they do decide to come after us, we probably don't want to be here to greet them."

She disappears into the plane.

"We're staying together, Abram," Julie says, following Nora up the ramp.

Abram gazes skyward as if praying for patience, but he doesn't argue further. Nora and Julie roll down the ramp on the remaining two bikes, Abram clicks his key fob, and the ramp rises. Do my kids have any grasp of what's happening around them? Will they feel abandoned, or are they too busy navigating the multidimensional mazes in their minds? Either way, they're safer here than with me. No one is getting into the plane without a tall ladder and a cutting torch.

"No offense, R," Julie says, stopping the bike in front of me, "but I should drive."

I sigh and climb on behind her, wondering if Abram might have left the other two bikes in Helena just to see how we'd handle the awkwardness.

Nora looks at M. "Hop on, beefsteak."

He chuckles. "Not happening."

She straightens up indignantly. "Really? The man's gotta ride in front? What is this, the 2020s?"

"Not that," he says, shaking his head. "It just . . . it won't work."

"Why not?"

He shrugs and climbs on behind her. His girth pushes her onto the gas tank and his chest looms over her head, forcing her to hunch down into the handlebars.

"Okay, okay!" she laughs breathlessly, jabbing an elbow into his ribs. "Get off!"

He gets off and Nora does likewise, still chuckling. She sweeps some hair out of her face and aims an *after you* palm at the bike. It's still too small for this duo, but Nora's slender frame clinging to M's mountainous bulk works better than the reverse.

"Can you even ride, though?" she says.

M hits the throttle and does a quick lap around the plane, barely even wobbling.

"Well okay then," Nora says with a satisfied nod.

I want to knock M's grin off.

"Hey," Julie says, twisting around to look at me. "Will your kids be okay by themselves?"

I look up at the plane. I see them watching me through two rear windows, having apparently broken out of their restroom prison. They stare at me blankly, their faces offering no clues to their inner states.

"They're Dead," I mutter. "What's safer than that?"

Abram sighs loudly, tiring of our deliberations, and blasts off down the freeway in a cloud of dust. M follows him and Julie follows M, and the ancient city of Detroit ripples like a mirage on the horizon.

• • •

The apocalypse didn't happen overnight. The world didn't end in a satisfying climax of explosive special effects. It was slow. It was boring. It was one little thing at a time. One moral compromise, one abandoned ideal, one more justified injustice. No dramatic wave of destruction sweeping across the world, just scattered spots of rot forming throughout the decades, seemingly isolated incidents until the moment they all merged.

Some cities maintained the illusion of independent prosperity for many years, like the leaves of a felled tree denying their severed roots. But Detroit was the bottom branch. It's been dead so long, it looks more like an archaeological site than an American city. The modern climate has turned much of the surrounding grassland into desert, and brown sand covers everything, piling up in drifts against crumbled buildings, forming small dunes in parking lots. The rising sun catches the tops of broken towers, lighting them up like beacons while the rest of the city sulks in shadow. I have no doubt we're the first people in years to travel *toward* this place.

I tighten my grip on Julie's waist as we bounce onto the bridge over the river that was once the Canadian border. Gaps in the bridge's pavement reveal the murky reddish waters below, choked full of rusty cars and garbage and ancient human remains. I lean into Julie's neck, inhaling her cinnamon scent as a defense against the aromas from below.

Some might find my position on the back of the bike emasculating, but there are worse ways to travel than pressed against the backside of a beautiful woman. Bumps in the road produce movements that belong in a bedroom, and I'm glad M is in front of us where he can't watch. For a moment I worry about embarrassing myself with an inopportune erection, then I smile darkly. Still these adolescent worries. Still the fears of a fresh pink boy living in a world of shame. That world died years ago—people struggling to survive have no time to fear their own bodies—so why does its corpse still cling to me?

We are human beings bonded by love and we deserve the gifts our bodies offer us.

Which of these assertions do I doubt?

• • •

Once we're over the bridge and into the city, the road worsens dramatically. The ride loses any trace of eroticism as the bike bucks under us like an angry bull, levitating me above the seat then slamming me back down. Julie eases up on the throttle, but these are street bikes and this can barely be called a street. I see M and Nora struggling, too, Nora's arms pressing deep into M's sides to keep from flying off the bike as it sinks into potholes then bounces back up over chunks of debris.

"Ab-b-bram!" Nora shouts over M's shoulder. "We have to st-st-stop!"

I can see Abram weaving through the junkyard with equal difficulty, Sprout clinging to his back like a frightened baby monkey, but he predictably ignores Nora's advice. He ignores it for two more blocks, then he rounds a corner onto an arterial street, and the city overrules his decision.

The road is completely jammed with car carcasses, a river of rust and rubber. Stacks of flattened vehicles occupy all the side streets, remnants of some long-ago effort to clear a path. What made this particular traffic jam the last one? The one that would endure through the ages like a monument to a bad idea? Was it a war? An undead invasion? A descending cloud of unbreathable air? Or simply a mass realization? A thousand people getting out of their cars, looking around at the unnatural disaster of their lives, wandering home to their families? I doubt anyone knows for sure. Under the smothering cloud of fear and jamming signals, history has gone the way of art and science and most other human achievements: backward. Fact has blurred into rumor, knowledge into suspicion. Even the current year is open to debate.

Abram stares at the impassable wall of rusty steel. He pulls an ancient map out of his jacket, a relic of those strange days when technology began to roll backwards, when information returned grudgingly to the physical realm as the collapse of the digital loomed closer. He consults the lines on this wrinkled sheet of Tyvek and looks ahead, searching for street signs in the rubble. He gets off his bike.

"Thank God," Nora sighs, detaching herself from M's back and stretching her arms.

Abram pulls the tool bag off his bike, grabs Sprout's hand, and climbs up the hood of a PT Cruiser. From there, he hops to the roof of a minivan.

"You're going to climb over all that?" Julie says, staring down the canyon of rust and broken glass.

"Airport's just a couple miles, and I don't see a better way through. But like I said, I don't need you. Go play FBI agent, uncover Axiom's evil plot, or whatever you wanted to come here for."

Julie hesitates as if considering the offer. Then she glances at Sprout. "And her? No need for her to go into that mess if you'll be back in a few hours, right?"

"She's coming with me."

Julie nods. "Yeah. Then so am I."

Abram smiles coldly. "Oh, you're going to guard me, are you? Make sure I don't run off and desert your revolution?"

Julie ignores him, dismounts the bike and starts to climb the Cruiser.

Abram chuckles. He hops from the van's roof to the bed of a truck and stumbles back a little under the weight of the tool bag. Sprout barely makes the jump.

"Hey," M says, climbing up beside him. "Let me take that." He holds out a hand for the tool bag. "You watch your kid."

Abram hesitates, studying the collage of scars covering M's face, then gives him the bag. He uses both hands to help Sprout onto the next roof, and they proceed forward with a labored but steady rhythm.

I climb up behind Julie. I notice a small pistol stuffed into the waistband of her jeans, like an afterthought beneath her shotgun holster. I don't recall her having a pistol. I wonder where she found it and why she didn't remark the find. She glances back at me and I see in her eyes that steel I admire so much, but I'm not sure I like the cold edge that glints in it now.

• • •

We creep from car to car like mountain climbers traversing treacherous terrain, choosing only the sturdiest vehicles and testing each step before putting weight on it. At first we climb in silence, everyone lost in deep concentration, but after an hour or so it becomes instinctive enough that we allow our thoughts to wander.

"Marcus," Nora says. "Who fired those missiles?"

M is absorbed in crawling onto the roof of an articulated bus, which will earn him eighty feet of easy travel if he succeeds. He doesn't answer.

"You said they were Gray River. Even if Canada still had a military, they wouldn't have Gray River missiles, would they?"

"Nope," M grunts as he achieves the summit of the bus and begins his leisurely stroll to the end.

"But Axiom would."

"Yup. Parent company."

Nora walks up and down the rolling hills of a few coupes. "Why the hell would Axiom arm the Canadian border? Who do they think is invading? And what do they think they're protecting?" She gestures to the desolation around us. "*This*?"

Silence.

"Abram?" she prompts.

"If I understood why Axiom's doing what it's doing," he says, "I wouldn't be here right now. I'd be settling into my new office in Citi Stadium, drinking some good Scotch, and enjoying a few company girls for my acquisition-day bonus."

This rings false, an unconvincing impression of the Axiom good ol' boys he's known but never been. I find it hard to picture this man enjoying Scotch, or women, or really much of anything.

"I'm here because I have no idea what they're doing," he says. "And I don't think they do either."

"So you think they're just flailing?" Nora says. "They seemed pretty damn organized when they invaded Post."

"Flash and Grab was an old operation, planned before the hiatus. Axiom's good at repeating itself, and some of the old moves still work. It's when it tries to move forward that the cracks start showing." A windshield spiderwebs under his weight. He ignores the pun. "If I had to guess, I'd say they're trying to reestablish the border. Give America some hard lines again. Even before the hiatus, they never liked ambiguity."

"What's a border if there's no one on the other side?" Julie wonders dreamily, like it's some absurd Zen koan. I didn't think she was even listening; for the last several blocks she's done nothing but stare down alleys and side streets, alert but distant. "Might as well draw borders on the moon."

"You mean like the Lunar Republic of Heavenly Korea?" Abram says with a grim smile.

Nora chuckles. "I remember that. If you ever want to travel north of the Apollo landing, you'll need a visa signed by Dear Leader's ghost."

"When the moon hits your eye . . . ," M sings in a low baritone, ". . . that's Korea."

None of this levity seems to reach Julie. Her eyes have stopped roving and she stares straight ahead. "So we'll have to go around the wall."

A pause. "Go around," Abram repeats.

"Up through Maine and around Nova Scotia."

Silence. The steady scrape of boots on metal, the creaking of old suspension.

"Canada is out. You know that. We have to get off this continent."

"I told you," he says without looking at her, "I can't navigate across the ocean without radio."

"*Drop* that bullshit," she snaps. "I didn't buy it at the beginning and I certainly don't now after you got us from Post to Helena to Ontario like we were on rails."

Abram is silent.

"You have some kind of analog system. I'm guessing that's the part that got damaged, since the nose is where the nav gear goes. One of Perry's friends was a pilot; I know how planes work."

Abram looks over his shoulder, but not at Julie. "Do you understand this girl?" he asks me. "Can you translate her for me? Because I'm lost."

I see Julie's face darkening.

"Does she want to fight Axiom and save America? Does she want to run away to Iceland? Or does she just want everything she wants, all at the same time, because she doesn't know how reality works?"

Julie stops, perched on the roof of a Chevy Tahoe. Her lips are tight and her eyes are narrow, but it's not entirely anger. Abram's questions are valid, and I think she knows it. What *does* she want? What matters most? How does anyone make choices when so much can depend on so little?

She seems to be crumpling inward, imploding under her confusion, and I'm searching for something to ease the tension when a sharp scream cuts through it.

Sprout is staring over her shoulder at the collapsed remains of an antique movie theater, her good eye wide with alarm.

Abram's rifle slides over his shoulder and into his hands and he scans the surrounding buildings, darting from opening to opening with a practiced efficiency. "What is it, baby? What'd you see?"

"That building," she says. "It changed."

"What do you mean it changed?"

"I don't know," she says, frowning in concentration. "It was . . . different."

"Different how? Did you see something move? Baby, this is important, if you saw—"

"It wasn't broken." Her frown warms with a hint of wonder. "It was pretty."

This seems to put some kind of tag on the moment for Abram and he relaxes. He holsters his rifle. He resumes walking. Sprout glances back over her shoulder a few more times, then falls into step behind her father.

"Is she okay?" Nora asks with raised eyebrows.

"She has vision problems," Abram says. "Sometimes she sees things."

"What kind of things?"

"Things that aren't there."

I watch the girl's face as she climbs car after car, clinging to her father's arm like it's a mountaineering rope. Every few minutes, her eye widens on something in the ruins around us, but she keeps whatever she sees to herself.

"What happened to her?" I hear myself asking.

"Nothing," Abram says, shooting me a dark look. "She was born with it."

I stare at the places where Sprout stares, squinting into the ripples of heat rising from the sun-baked concrete. She notices what I'm doing and a look passes between us, eerily nuanced given our gulf of age. She shuts her eye, and at first I think she's winking at me, but then she scampers over the next car with her eye still shut, not noticeably hindered by her apparent blindness.

She glances back, taps the daisy on her eye patch, and flashes me a gap-toothed grin. My spine tingles.

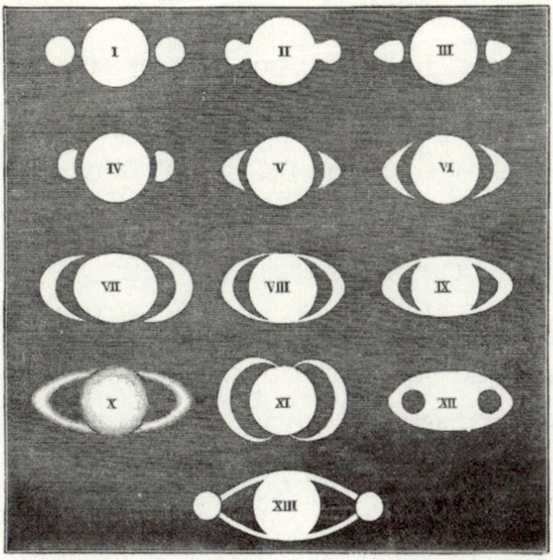

WE

DO YOU KNOW THE FUTURE? *Is there a future? What will you do? Can you even do anything?*

The boy asks us questions, knowing we won't answer. He skims the spines of our volumes, searching the endless stacks, but we are not sorted and cannot be checked out. We must be read all at once.

What's it for? Why remember all this? What can we do with it?

His anger ebbs and flows as he traverses mile after mile of silent highway, his leathery feet dragging through dead leaves and trash. Momentary spikes of rage sink back into grim contemplation. We understand these feelings. We watch them fill the pages of his books and so many books around them.

Are you only good people? he asks us in the bleak mumble that often follows his spikes. *Or are you everyone?*

Leaves and beer cans swirl around his ankles in a sudden gust of wind.

Are you Mom and Dad?

No answer comes for the boy, though we wish we could give one. We would like to help him because he sees us and talks to us and can very nearly read us, and some pages of his books line the highest shelves. But we are many, and it takes many to make us move.

Another city. The carpet of trash deepens. A broken bottle penetrates his foot's callus and cuts into live tissue. A few drops of lukewarm blood ooze out, dark but not black. He feels no pain. His mind is far away, occupying other worlds, and it has no time for the needs of his body. He does not hear the van approaching behind him. He does not hear the man calling to him. He does not realize his sphere of solitude has been punctured until the man is kneeling in front of him.

"Are you okay?" the man asks him. "Where are your parents?"

The boy looks at the man through the shadowy gloom of his sunglasses. The man's eyes are round with surprise and concern. His face is thin and brown with a short beard of fuzzy tufts. He is waiting for an answer.

The boy shrugs.

"Are you alone, mate?" another man asks, and the boy looks at the van. A rusty old Volkswagen camper, crammed full of bags and boxes, food and guns. The man's head pokes out of the passenger window. This one's face is pale, his hair yellow and shaggy, his eyes big and green. The boy wants to take off these smothering sunglasses to get a better view of these eyes, but he leaves them on. Even in his otherworldly state, he is capable of learning. It's what he's here to do.

The green-eyed man steps out of the van and kneels down next to the brown-eyed man. His arms are tattooed with spirals of numbers. He reaches out and touches the boy's face. The boy feels the instinct surge into his jaw, electrifying his teeth with unnatural hardness, but he forces it back down.

"You're so cold," the green-eyed man says. "Are you sick?"

"Cold?" the brown-eyed man says warily.

"Not *that* cold, Geb."

"Can I take these off for a second?" the brown-eyed man says, reaching for the sunglasses.

The boy steps back and shakes his head violently.

"Okay, okay," the man says, holding his hands up. "You need to look cool, I get it."

The green-eyed man smiles. His eyes are gentle. "What's your name, mate?"

The boy shrugs.

"Do you want to come with us?"

The boy thinks. His mind starts to form questions for us, specific and insistent, but he drops them. Instead, he reaches into the Library. He closes his eyes and skims our countless pages, a brief but vast fluttering. He gains something. An obscure insight. A word within an infinite crossword. He nods to the green-eyed man.

"My name's Gael," the man says. The boy notices a lilt in his voice, an echo of distant places. "This is Gebre."

"Maybe we'll talk later," Gebre says. "When you're ready." His accent is exotic too, yet familiar. "For now, would you like a snack? You hungry?"

The boy shakes his head.

"Thirsty?" He pulls a water bottle from the back of the truck and offers it to the boy. The boy takes it. He stares at the liquid sloshing inside it, and then at the microorganisms sloshing inside the liquid, billions of little diamonds and helixes living unfathomable lives in an unknowable world. He takes a sip and feels them slide down his dry throat, becoming part of him. He climbs into the van with Gael and Gebre.

I

PAUL.

I am sitting on the roof with my friend Paul Bark, smoking a cigarette that I stole from my father. I don't enjoy it; I can feel it burning my insides, but that's the point. When I asked my father why he keeps a habit that will kill him, he took a deep drag and breathed out a scripture:

"'He who loves his life will lose it, and he who hates his life in this world will keep it for eternal life.'"

I didn't understand then, but I do now. I suck in a lungful and resist the urge to cough until it fades to a dull ache. It feels good to hate my life. It feels safe. If death is what I want, then nothing can ever hurt me.

"What's your mom doing?" Paul says.

In the lawn below, my mother is pruning a rosebush. Its blooms are impossibly red against their dull green stems, like puddles of pure hue leaking in from some other realm. There are flowers all over the yard despite the blistering heat. She hauls in a whole extra water cart every week just for them.

"Why does she waste all that effort on a stupid garden?" Paul says. "Doesn't she believe in the Last Sunset?" He sounds angry, like he always does at the thought of unbelief, and I remember a game we once played when we were younger, pretending our bikes were dragons and his house was a castle we had to conquer.

"Tear down the walls of Jericho!" he had shouted gleefully as we circled the little cabin. "The Lord ordains their destruction!"

My bike slipped in the gravel and I crashed. "Piece of crap bike," I said, kicking the tire.

Paul looked betrayed. "It's not a bike, it's a dragon! The Canaanites killed your dragon!"

"I cut my knee. I'm going inside."

"No! You can't!" There had been anger in his voice but also panic. "You're ruining it!"

Now he glares at my mother's rosebushes like they're ruining a much bigger game. They trouble me too, because my mother does believe. She believes as strongly as anyone. And yet she plants flowers. She feeds refugees. Some deep, instinctive spring bubbles through the bedrock of her beliefs, and she does these senseless things.

"She's a woman," I tell my friend. "She likes flowers. She's not thinking about what it means."

Paul frowns. "'Do not love the world or anything in the world. If anyone loves the world, love for the Father is not in them.'"

"I know the scriptures, Paul."

"But does she?" He jabs a hand at the frail woman in dirty coveralls tending her vibrant pets. "Are any of our parents strong enough to live the hard truth? Or are they trying to make it softer?"

She prunes the leaves off a particularly bright bloom, and it's hard not to see love in the smile it brings to her face.

"You heard the sermon last night," Paul says. "The world wasn't made to be loved. It was made to test us. 'Not a home but a battlefield.'"

I take the last puff of the cigarette and flick it away. The dry grass smolders.

• • •

I wake to the roiling red of the sun against my eyelids. I open them and glance around, gripped by a sudden guilty fear, but no one is watching me. No one can see the young man growing inside my head. I have woken from a nap in the sun, my friends are all around me—I have done nothing wrong.

I straighten, rubbing reality back into my skull. The air is hot. The city is quiet. Abram is clattering around in the nose of an ancient plane. M is sawing something.

"Marcus," Nora says. She's sitting on the runway with her legs crossed in front of her, her back against the plane's tire, watching Sprout play with a screwdriver.

M pauses his work, leaving the square of aluminum dangling from the bottom of the plane. He looks down at Nora from his perch on the landing gear. "Yeah?"

"How much have you filled in?"

"Filled in?"

"Do you have a whole life now or is it still just sketches?"

I hear a raven croak in the distance. I wonder what it eats in this barren urban desert.

"It's sketches," M says. "But a lot of them. Like the ones for movies."

"Storyboards?"

"Storyboards."

He resumes sawing. A breeze whistles through holes in the terminal building, harmonizing with his saw.

"I haven't watched a movie in ages," Nora says with a melancholy smile. "Not since I was a teenager."

"What was the last one?"

She thinks for a moment. *"Return of the Living Dead?"*

M chuckles.

"I know. Wasn't my choice. I lost my taste for zombie flicks when they became real life, but I was in a prison pit and the guards were watching it, so . . ."

The sun has begun its descent, casting the airport in a surreal red-orange glow. Julie sits just outside the invisible border of the group's company, beyond the range of conversation, staring into the rippling city. She hasn't said a word since her last argument with Abram. I wonder what she's thinking. I wonder if the dreams that trouble her are anything like mine.

"So tell me about your sketches," Nora says, watching M cut his way toward her. "I'm curious."

He completes the cut and the square drops out. It produces an eerie wobbling noise as he hands it down to Nora.

"Piano," M says, staring into the plane's exposed guts. "Loved playing piano."

"Really!" Nora says.

He starts cutting another square. "Family was surprised too. Said I was too big for it. Said I looked like a circus ape."

Nora is quiet.

"Never liked sports much," he says over the whine of his saw, adding a gruff stiffness to his voice. "But in my family, big guys were wrestlers. So I wrestled."

Fine bits of metal rain down from his saw, piling on the ground next to Nora. He glances down at her. "You should move. Don't want to get it in your hair."

She scoots out of the way. She watches Julie for a moment. "You okay, Jules?" she calls across the awkward distance.

Julie nods without turning around. It's not reassuring. Nora raises her eyebrows at me and I realize I've been put on boyfriend duty. I approach my girlfriend, unsure of what I might be dealing with, and sit down next to her.

"Julie?"

"I'm fine," she says. "Just thinking."

She keeps the side of her face to me; I can't quite get a look at her eyes.

"About what?" I ask, and cringe at how trite it sounds. *Hey Julie, whatcha thinkin' about?*

She shakes her head as if to warn me off this ill-advised reconnaissance mission. I shut my mouth.

"What was your family like?" Nora is asking M. Their conversation seems safe enough, so I return to it, keeping Julie in my periphery.

"Mom left early. Grew up with Dad and two brothers. Don't remember their names yet."

"And I'm guessing they all died?"

She says it absently, twirling a bolt between her fingers. M stops sawing and looks at her, a small smile on his big lips. "Um . . . yeah. Probably."

Nora nods. The typical modern family: deceased.

M finishes the cut and climbs down from the landing gear, drops the second square on top of the first: new windows for our battered aircraft.

"What about you?" he says, settling against the tire next to Nora.

"My family?"

"Yeah."

Her gaze drifts out into the city to join Julie's. Broken buildings. Buried streets. Ruins rippling in the queasy orange haze like a fever dream of loss.

"Never had one," she says. "I grew out of the ground."

Julie stands up. Her back is to me; I can't see her face. Just her hair whipping in the wind.

She starts walking.

"Julie?" I call after her.

She keeps walking.

"Jules!" Nora shouts. "Where are you going?"

"Need to piss," Julie replies, but the flatness of her voice sets off my alarms. I catch up to her as she enters a narrow alley, hidden from the sun and piled high with sand drifts like a pyramid burial shaft.

"Julie."

She keeps walking.

"Julie, talk to me."

I touch her back and she flinches, wrapping her arms around herself while continuing to walk. "I'm seeing things, R," she says in a plaintive whimper, and I realize with a jolt that she's crying. I try to put my hand on her shoulder but she pushes it away and keeps walking.

"What are you seeing?"

She shakes her head and clutches her elbows, looking disturbingly unwell. "Something's wrong with this place." Her voice trembles. "I can see through it. Like it's watery soup. And my . . . my *dreams* are in there." She raises her head, looking toward—or through—the distant buildings. "The monsters, the men. And my—"

She stops. She finally looks at me. "Am I awake?"

"*Yes*, Julie, you're awake. Please, just . . ."

I make one more attempt to touch her. She turns around and runs.

• • •

Her muscles are young and alive, but my legs are twice as long. I follow at a light jog as she scrambles through the tangled streets, as she glances left and right like a lost hiker trying to find the trail.

I let her run until I hear her breath starting to whistle, then I put a hand on her shoulder and squeeze firmly.

She slows to a fast walk, taking long breaths until her lungs stabilize just shy of an attack. Her tears have dried. Her fear seems to be cooling into a hard edge of purpose. I scan the city, looking for a glimpse of whatever signs she's following, but every block looks the same to me: centuries of artistry and architecture ground down to shapeless lumps and dunes of monochrome dust. The red evening sun creeps around twisted masses of metal. Shapes dance in the corners of my eyes and vanish when I look. I remember what I saw on the plane, that blurring and twisting of streets, like the city was forgetting its own form. When Julie says something's wrong with this place, I don't doubt her.

I'm able to make her pause just long enough to grab a bag of toy army men from a corner store, which I drop at each fork in our path, imagining the horror of getting lost in this vast urban labyrinth. Julie is in no state to consider such precautions. She walks in a trance, her face pale and stiff, eyes damp but fierce. If I hadn't followed her . . . if I hadn't known the tune of her voice well enough to catch that dissonant note . . .

Lost in grim speculation, I almost crash into her when she comes to a sudden stop. We have entered a sort of courtyard, an empty space between four buildings that appears to have been recently colonized. It's overrun with bristly weeds and malnourished vines, but it bears less resemblance to ancient Egypt than the rest of the city does. Lawn chairs sit in loose circles throughout the space, surrounded by beer and wine bottles, marijuana pipes, and stacks of books that rain has reduced to pulp, however rigorously highbrow they once were.

"This must've been them," Julie mumbles, taking in the details of this sprawling still life. "The 'Remakers.'"

Scattered throughout the space are long workshop tables covered in the tools of various artistic trades. Chisels, brushes, silk screens, pencils, paint cans, knives, crochet needles, a drum kit in the corner, a pile of guitars, a podium, and a mic stand. And on one of the walls, a mural, or a blend of a dozen murals, their starkly contrasting styles somehow intertwining into a jungle of colors and figures, from crowds of tiny people to hundred-foot giants.

"They were building a different kind of city, Mom said."

I can't place the emotion in her voice, a dissonant chord of anger, sadness, and love.

"Something based on different values. Different measures of success. It was supposed to be a message to the world."

The mural reaches to the very top of the wall, where a solar panel once powered a single yellow bulb, now dark.

"I wonder how long it lasted." She cranes her neck to look at the bulb. "I wonder what killed it."

I follow a few steps behind her as she walks the perimeter of the space, running her hands along the brick walls. "We could have ended up here instead. We were so close. Ten miles, the sign said . . ." Her voice is hard but faint, like she's shouting from a great distance. "Dad wouldn't take the exit. Mom was screaming at him, but . . ." She turns in a slow circle, staring up at the mural, the inert remains of a movement. "Was this what she needed to make her hold on?" Her chin quivers. "Did she leave us for this?"

"Julie." I say it so softly it gets her attention. "Why are we here?"

She looks at me. She opens her mouth like she's finally going to answer. Then she freezes. She cocks her ear. And I hear it.

Engines. Tires snarling on gritty pavement.

Someone in this ghost town is alive.

We emerge from the courtyard just as the vehicles disappear around a corner: two windowless white cargo vans, unmarked except for the geometric mandala stenciled on their sides.

My mind clicks dry like an unloaded gun. Did they really follow us a hundred miles from the border? Or were they already here?

I glance at Julie. Her face reveals nothing, just a trembling, round-eyed blankness.

She runs after the vans.

I shout, "Wait!" but I know she won't, and I'm already following her.

The vans pause in the middle of the next block, and two more pop out from a side street to join them. These ones have windows, and just before they all drive off in a line, I catch a glimpse of their cargo. People. About a dozen in each van, packed together like miserable ride-share commuters.

This isn't a search party—at least not for us. We have stumbled into other business.

Julie follows the vans' cloud of dust. It curls through a route that's clear of debris, like a well-worn animal trail in a forest, leading deeper into the city. I keep trying to catch her eyes, hoping to decipher her intent, but she stares straight ahead, utterly opaque. And then, just as the dust is getting too vague to follow, we emerge from an alley into the back lot of a large building, and the vans are right in front of us.

For a moment I worry Julie will charge at them like they're figments in a dream, but she's lucid enough to duck behind a dumpster. Gagging on the smell of whatever's inside, I listen to barked commands and shuffling footfalls. The vans are backed up against the building, blocking my view of their activity, but it's clear they're unloading passengers. A minute later the doors bang shut and the vans drive off and we're alone in the empty parking lot.

"Julie," I whisper. "Need to go back. Get the others."

She shakes her head.

"We don't know what's in there. Can't just—"

She leaps to her feet and marches toward the building. Gritting my teeth, I go after her, attempting to channel Abram Kelvin and Evan Kenerly and all their militant paranoia, scanning windows for snipers and maximizing my situational awareness. But everything is quiet.

Julie stops in front of the entrance. The entrance is a staircase. A steep, narrow well leading down into darkness.

She descends.

"Julie, *wait*!"

Her legs sink into the shadows, then her waist, then her shoulders.

"*Julie*!"

For an instant her head is disembodied, a mass of golden hair floating on a black pond. Then the blackness swallows it.

I TEETER ON THE EDGE of the staircase, frozen in irrational panic. I can't see the bottom. It's just a flight of stairs, just the storage basement of some dull municipal building, but it stretches. It deepens and steepens until it's no longer a staircase but a bottomless well, its slick stone walls lined with hideous books, blood writing and claw etchings, cold and damp and—

I don't want to go down there. But Julie is down there. Whatever it is I'm afraid of, she's alone with it.

I plunge into the depths.

My legs buckle under me when I reach the bottom, finding solid floor where they expected another stair. A memory from childhood, step after stumbling step, learning the art of walking—except it's not from childhood. Long legs in black slacks, stumbling through a forest, away from a dead woman—

"Julie!" I hiss.

"What?" Her voice echoes back to me through the narrow tunnel, soft and toneless like the mutterings of a sleepwalker. As my eyes adjust to the darkness, I notice a pale glow bobbing ahead.

I run up alongside her. She holds a flashlight limply, illuminating her feet and not much else.

I decide to try an indirect route. "Where'd you get the flashlight?"

"It was Abram's."

She keeps a brisk pace, just short of a run, her eyes fixed on the pavement that passes through her oval of light.

"You stole his flashlight?"

"Sometimes I steal things."

I hesitate. "Why?"

"Because the world steals from me. It takes everything." She blinks twice, and I notice her eyes are wet, despite their blank stare. "Feels good to be on the other end for once."

She stops. The passage has opened up into some sort of basement storage area. Stacks of boxes aged into brittle papyrus, ancient beige computer monitors—the typical contents of an office building, with one notable exception: a rolling steel tray piled with scalpels and hooks and scissors and saws, all sticky with dark fluid. The floor is thick with dust except for a trail of footprints that leads to an upward staircase.

Julie draws her shotgun from its plaid holster. There's a door at the top of the stairs, and I'm about to make another plea for caution but she doesn't even pause. She kicks the push bar, the door flies open, and she rushes through in a tactical crouch, her gun braced in low ready position.

I lumber in behind her, unarmed, untrained, unprepared. But no high school combat class would have prepared me for this.

We are in what appears to be the library of a university. A soaring ceiling, stained glass windows, tables and shelves of dark oak. It was majestic once, a profound place for profound pursuits, but its grandeur has been destroyed—not by age and decay but by utilitarianism. Fluorescent lights in aluminum cases hang from the ceiling to obviate the bronze lamps on the walls. Rich wooden tables have been supplemented by rows of folding metal ones, their white Formica tops mocking the antiquity around them. And of course the stained glass windows are protected by sheets of plastic.

But perhaps I'm burying the lead. Perhaps I'm avoiding the room's more salient features because I'm weary of processing such images. Perhaps a detour into decor is a needed respite from the hair-tearing insanity of this world.

Because the library is full of zombies. At least two hundred of them, naked, their necks locked in rubber collars, steel cables fastened to walls, shelves, anything solid enough to hold them as they writhe and lunge, although many are eerily calm. The tables are littered with an incongruous assortment of equipment: glittering steel implements of medicine or torture sit alongside portable stereos, makeup kits, televisions, toys, and jars of fresh human fingers.

The dangling fluorescents are turned off; the only light comes through the stained glass, a dismal blue glow that leaves the huge chamber thick with shadows. Julie begins a perimeter check and I follow her. The Dead are everywhere. Not just the crowd in the reading area but lone specimens tucked away in the aisles like backups. My estimate climbs toward three hundred, diverse in age, race, and sex, but with one trait in common: freshness. Most are wholly unspoiled, with only the leaden eyes and pitiful groans to give away their status. A few have injuries—bullet holes, bites, a missing limb or two—but their flesh is always pale and smooth, like they died yesterday.

Julie prowls along the walls, methodically scanning the aisles. Her face has slipped into yet another mask that's unfamiliar to me: the grim efficiency of a soldier. I think of the night we sat on the roof of our new suburban home and traded stories from our youths. All I had to offer were vague vignettes from my early corpsehood, lacking context or continuity—*trying to eat a deer, walking with a boy, watching a girl sing a song*—but her memories were colorful and crisp, like she'd kept them all these years in a climate-controlled vault. Her life in Brooklyn, watching the waters rise, the tanks in the street, but also stickball games and schoolyard crushes and some lingering aromas of happiness. Wine parties on the apartment's tarry rooftop. Her mother laughing in a white dress, throwing empty bottles at the abandoned building next door and screaming with delight when she hit a window. Lawrence and Ella making out on the fire escape. Even her father cracking a smile, chugging a priceless vintage and belting a few bars from one of his band's songs . . .

Her shotgun moves with her body like an extra limb, tracing the contours of the room with mechanical precision. She steps around the corner of the last aisle and she stops. Her gun falls to the floor.

. . . her old bedroom, its chaos and color pulsing against the emptiness of her father's gray fortress. The sky-blue ceiling, the clothes-covered floor, the walls like the wings of a museum—red for relics of old-world passions, movie tickets and concert flyers, magazines and poems, white for her private collection of looted masterpieces with a few sheepish contributions of her own, yellow for good dreams yet to be realized, a wall that was and still is unadorned—and the black wall. A wall whose purpose I never learned, because I was afraid to ask. Because it held only one decoration. A photo of a woman who looked a lot like Julie, adrift in that dark expanse.

Julie falls to the floor as gracelessly as her gun, arms hanging at her sides, eyes wide and already filling with tears. She doesn't flinch as long fingernails swipe inches from her face. She kneels in full surrender while the woman from the photo strains against her collar, hissing and groaning and reaching for her daughter's throat.

Fig. 5.

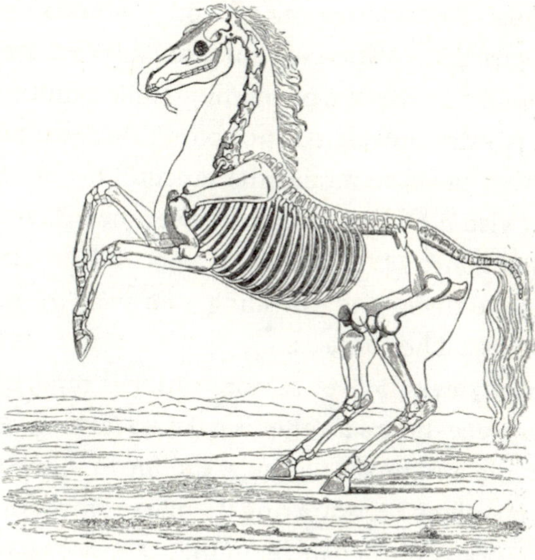

IT OCCURS TO ME that Julie might want to die. The scars on her wrists prove she has danced with the desire, but I've always believed it was a thing of her youth, a defanged fossil buried beneath miles of time.

Will this unearth it?

She kneels like a penitent begging God to take everything, and the woman in front of her seems eager to oblige. She has knocked most of the books off the shelf that holds her; it moves slightly with each lunge. I grab Julie under the armpits and drag her back a few feet. Her body is a loose pile, far heavier than it should be. She stares ahead blankly like her emotions have shattered.

Was she expecting it? Could she possibly have known? A mad hope, perhaps, a fevered wish festering in her heart, but I can't believe she ever imagined the reality of *this*.

Her mother. Dead but not dead. Stepping out of dreams and into a nightmare.

This woman died a long time ago, but I wouldn't have guessed from her appearance. Whatever inner fire allowed me to stave off the rot through all my years of roaming, Julie's mother must have it too. She is gray, emaciated, her blond hair a mass of scabby dreadlocks, but her face retains the graceful beauty I saw in that photo. It's twisted by her ravenous sneer, her rows of yellowed teeth, but it's there. My sentimental mind swells with visions of her returning to the Living, whisking Julie away from the orphanage and healing all her bruises.

But then my eyes deliver a more rational report. Like all the Dead in this place, Julie's mother is naked. Her skin bears constellations of knife and bullet wounds, the inevitable result of a life sustained on violence. Comparing them to M's injuries, I feel confident that Nora could repair them on the joyous day they begin to bleed. But this woman didn't die from bullets. This woman peeked into her daughter's room, saw that she was asleep, and wandered into the city alone. Perhaps she walked in solemn silence, or perhaps she spit and howled at the night, tearing her clothes and her hair, screaming at the Dead to come and take what they destroyed the world to get.

And the Dead obeyed.

Although her face is unscathed, her body has been gnawed like meat left out for rats. Large chunks are missing from her calves and thighs and I can see the exposed muscles spasming to produce her lurching movements. Any of these bites would have been enough to convert her, but she could have recovered from them too if she ever shook off the plague. What is draining the sunny glow from my fantasies is the gaping absence where the left half of her rib cage should be. I can see her remaining lung drooping against her spine, tinted gray from the pallor of death and black from too many cigarettes. I can see her lifeless heart.

This hole, of course, is where Julie's gaze has settled. She has already done the math. Her face remains still except for the glimmer of tears streaming down it.

I want a god to curse. I'll take any of them, all of them; I'll scream and blaspheme till lightning shuts me up. Someone has to answer for such preposterous cruelty, such monstrously drawn-out torture. But I am pounding on the door of an empty house. It's just us. It's just me, Julie, and her mother. And the three men in beige jackets marching toward us down the aisle.

"Who the hell are you?" one of them shouts. "How did you get in here?"

Julie shoves past me and strides down the aisle. Her shotgun is back in her hands and it's firing—*pump*—firing—*pump*—firing.

The cavernous space rumbles with low reverberations. Three men lie dead on the floor, their brains mingled in a puddle between them, perhaps sharing a final confused thought.

I watch Julie search their bodies. She looks faraway and somehow removed from the room, like I'm watching her through a telescope. I know that Julie has killed people. She's told me about some of them, from her first at age ten—stabbing a man in the back while he was choking her father—to her most recent less than a year ago: a standard rapist-in-the-bushes situation. But this is the first time I've watched her do it, and I'm troubled by how much it shakes me. Like I didn't truly believe her until now.

She pulls a set of keys out of one of the guards' jackets and walks past me to her mother. She unlocks the padlock on the cable, freeing it from the bookshelf. Her mother hisses and lunges toward her.

Julie punches her.

"Stop it," she says in a hard, flat voice. "I'm your daughter. You're Audrey Maude Arnaldsdóttir and I'm your daughter."

Audrey stares at her with wide eyes and an open mouth. Then she lunges again.

Julie punches her so hard she falls back into the bookshelf.

"And you're a coward," Julie continues, her voice beginning to tremble. "And a quitter. And a fucking child. But you're a human being, and you're going to fucking act like one."

Audrey rests against the bookshelf with her jaw hanging open, her eyes roaming around the room, refusing to meet Julie's gaze. It's impossible to tell if she understood anything Julie said, let alone whether it sparked any remembrance, but she seems momentarily pacified.

"Watch her," Julie says to me, and steps out of the aisle.

Audrey and I share an uncomfortable silence while Julie clatters around the library.

"I'm R," I mumble, putting my hand out to her in an absurd reflexive gesture.

Audrey's head tilts. Black fluid trickles down her chin.

Julie returns with a soiled lab coat and a long steel rod with a ring on the end. She wraps the coat around her mother, forcing her arms through the sleeves while her mother squirms. Once it's buttoned up, hiding the grisly mess of her body, the appearance of humanity rushes back in. Just an overworked doctor in need of a shower.

The transformation seems to catch Julie off guard. Her stiff-lipped determination falters and the tears return as the creature in front of her suddenly becomes the woman from her memories. For a moment, I think even Audrey feels it. Recognition flickers over her face, the savagery softening into gentle astonishment. Then it passes and she starts hissing again.

Julie connects the ring on the end of the rod to a clamp on her mother's collar. I suddenly understand her intent.

"Julie," I say as she leads her mother by the neck like a rabid dog, the pole keeping her at a safe distance.

"What." She exits the aisle and heads deeper into the university, toward the exit.

I follow her, avoiding eye contact with the pitiful prisoners writhing around us. Should we free them too? And then what? I hear the fallen guards' walkies squawking. The voice of reinforcements, reinstatement, repetition. Whatever is happening here, it will keep happening until someone silences that voice. We can't save everyone tonight.

I watch Audrey's coat billowing freely through the gap in her side. We can't save anyone tonight.

"*What*?" Julie says again, glancing back at me. "Say it."

It sticks in my throat. No, her mother can never come back to her. Yes, it's insanity to take her with us. And yes, of course we're going to anyway. I'd be a monster to think otherwise.

"Nothing," I say. "Let's go."

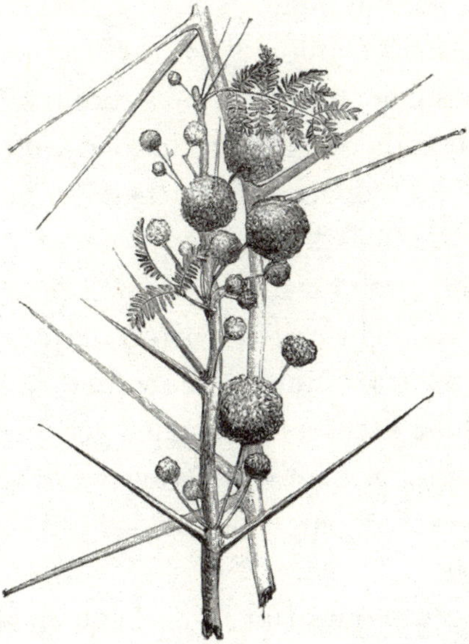

WE RACE DOWN THE STEPS of Wayne County College like kids on the last day of the semester, a cold echo of those carefree summer rituals. I can hear the sounds of long-dead students, can almost feel them shoving past me. The squeals of young beauties in cocoons of affirmation, half-formed pupae who seem a different species entirely from the woman at my side, despite somehow being the same age. I hear the bass from tricked-out cars, simian boys equating volume with virility; shoving, laughing, boasting, belittling—everyone testing everyone, clawing and pecking for position. I see and hear it all through a haze of time, a blur of overlaid moments as the city churns around me. Across the street from the college—literally next door—is the Mortuary Institute of Detroit. A block away is a dilapidated building whose sign reads PERRY FUNERAL HOME—I blink and rub my eyes, but it's really there.

Am I awake? Julie asked me, and I answered with blithe confidence. That confidence is gone.

I take some distant comfort from my trail of plastic troops. I pretend that I'm a soldier in an army in a country with a leader, that I have clear orders and good reasons to follow them. I revel in this certainty for perhaps a dozen blocks, then the sun disappears and my army fades into the dark.

"Shit," I say under my breath.

Julie's stolen flashlight casts a narrow beam and it's not long before we've lost the trail. Audrey follows her daughter in a mostly placid state, but Julie keeps a two-handed grip on the pole to control her occasional lunges, sometimes away from Julie, sometimes toward her. If we keep going like this, it's only a matter of time before something slips.

Julie pulls the pistol out of her waistband and fires into the air in a distinctive rhythm: *Bang. Bang-bang.* Then she watches the sky and listens.

A few seconds later, from somewhere across the river: *Bang. Bang-bang.*

Relief floods Julie's face, and I realize this grim fugue of determination has not completely buried her personality. She's in there, just as scared as I am, imagining the horror of spending a night in this haunted graveyard of a city.

Using the river as a reference, we work our way back to the main street and find our bike waiting where we left it, with a note on the seat under a chunk of concrete:

WENT BACK TO PLANE

COME HOME CRAZY BITCH

We both look at Audrey, then the bike, then each other.

"You drive," Julie says. "I'll sit on the tail and pin her between us."

Audrey grinds her teeth in a confused, simmering fury.

I don't need words to explain the flaw in this plan. I point at Audrey's mouth, then at my neck.

Julie thinks for a moment, then hands me Audrey's pole and dives into a heap of automotive wreckage. She emerges holding a bullet-pierced motorcycle helmet, shakes the ancient skull out of it, and shoves the battered white globe over her mother's head. "No biting, Mom."

Audrey's gunmetal eyes are wide and fierce in the helmet's view window.

Julie snaps the visor shut.

The three of us form a clownish sandwich on the bike, Julie clinging precariously to the rear edge and me humping the gas tank, cringing with every jolt in the road. I hear Audrey hissing inside her helmet, occasionally banging it against the back of my head, but Julie's arms around my waist pin Audrey's to her sides like a straightjacket. I ride as fast as I can with this awkward cargo, navigating by starlight and memory, and by the time the last glimmer of the sun goes black, we're there.

Nora is out in the road, pacing and watching the horizon. She runs to meet us as we pull up to the plane, so fixated on Julie that she doesn't seem to notice our guest.

"Something really terrible better have happened to you," she says, shaking her head in a flurry of curls, "because if you just snuck away to fuck each other, I swear to God—*oh*." She straightens up. "Who's that?"

We dismount. Julie reattaches the pole to Audrey's collar.

"Julie. Who the hell is—"

"Nora," Julie says in a trembling laugh, unable to contain the surreality of it any longer, "it's . . . this is . . . it's my *mom*."

She pulls the helmet off. Audrey grimaces at Nora, displaying her chipped yellow teeth. Nora stumbles a step back. I have no doubt she recognizes this face, if not from Julie's old photo then from its uncanny resemblance to Julie herself, its youth bizarrely preserved even as traces of rot creep in at the edges. A specimen of early-forties beauty, pickled in the plague.

"Mom," Julie says, "this is Nora. She's the best person I've ever met. Please be nice to her."

"Hi," Nora whispers almost inaudibly, her face frozen in shock.

Abram climbs down the ladder with his bag of tools. He watches us.

"How?" Nora manages to squeak out.

"We found a . . . *facility*," Julie says, and begins leading Audrey toward the plane. "Hundreds of zombies chained up. Looked like some kind of experiment, like a bigger version of what we saw in Abram's cabin." She glances at Abram. "Do you know anything about this?"

Abram doesn't answer.

"What kind of zombies?" Nora says, her curiosity starting to overcome her shock. "Nearlies?"

"We didn't have time to check the others. But Mom's . . . well . . ."

Audrey begins to struggle, clutching at her collar and making guttural choking sounds.

"Mostly," Nora says. "Maybe All."

Julie says nothing. We pass Abram, who stays where he is, still holding his tongue. When we reach the cargo ramp, he finally releases it.

"Just to make sure I'm understanding you . . ." His tone is level. ". . . you want to bring an adult zombie onboard this airplane. In addition to the two juveniles we're already carrying. So that's a total of three flesh-eating corpses sharing this airplane with us. Do I have that right?"

Julie looks at him. "She's my mother."

Abram lets out a long, weary sigh. "I'm done." He takes Sprout's hand, throws the duffel over his shoulder, and heads toward our bike.

"Hey," Julie says. "She's completely locked up, she can't hurt anyone."

Abram keeps walking.

"Hey!" She hands Audrey's pole to me and walks after him. "Where are you going?"

Nora looks at me and rolls her eyes, *here we go again*, but no, this is not the same argument between the same two people. After what Julie has just experienced, there are no parameters to what might happen here, only desperate, unpredictable momentum, rolling, slipping, falling.

"*Abram!*"

He stops and turns. He doesn't look angry, just tired, a worn-out high-school teacher who's had enough of the hormonal drama, every day a new pregnancy, a new suicide, a new shooting. "I don't know where we're going," he says. "Maybe Pittsburgh. Maybe Austin. All I know is I'm done with crazy people."

"So you're going to cross a deadly wasteland on a motorcycle when you have a private jet sitting here waiting for you? Who's the crazy one?"

He chuckles and resumes walking, shaking his head. "Not worth it."

"God damn it, Abram, we need you! You can't just leave us stranded here!"

"You have the bikes; do your revolution by motorcycle. It worked for Che Guevara."

Julie stops and stares at his back as he approaches the bike. "You just don't care, do you?" She sounds genuinely amazed. "About *anything.*"

He starts tying his duffel onto the bike. "And what should I care about?"

"People? The world you're living in? The future you're helping create?"

Abram tips his head back and laughs. "You want to know why I'm done with you people?" He turns around. "Because people who talk like that are the ones who get you killed in a world like this. Che Guevara talked like that. Lenin and Mao talked like that. All those doe-eyed idealists watching the future through a telescope while they trampled over the present. There's no bigger threat to the world than people who think they can improve it."

He lifts Sprout onto the back of the bike. She looks back at Julie with sadness and fear, but Julie looks right past her, boring into the back of Abram's head.

"How about this, then?" she says. "How about you fly the plane or I shoot you."

Abram turns around, chuckling, and finds himself looking into a gun barrel.

"How about I don't give a shit about the world," Julie says, gripping the pistol in both hands. "How about I want you to fly us to Iceland so I can get help for my mom, because she's my family and fuck everyone else."

Abram's smile is amused but weary. "Cute," he says, and turns to mount his bike.

"I will shoot you, Abram."

He shakes his head as he climbs on. "No, you'll stand there *saying* you'll shoot me, because you love to talk about things you know will never hap—"

Julie shoots him.

He falls off the bike and lands on his knees, clutching his arm. Sprout screams.

"Shit, Jules," Nora murmurs.

Abram pulls himself up, pale with pain and surprise. His hand drifts toward a pouch on the side of his duffel; I open my mouth to warn Julie but she's watching him with no apparent concern. His hand comes out empty.

"You stole my Ruger," he says with muted amazement.

"Fly the plane," Julie says.

He stares at her for a moment, then makes a grab for the rifle on his back.

Julie shoots him in the shoulder.

"Julie!" Sprout sobs, gaping at her in disbelief.

Julie's eyes dart toward Sprout and her face flickers; I glimpse shame and horror as full awareness hits her. But she hardens again.

"Fly the plane."

Abram examines his wounds—a deep graze across his left tricep and a clean shot through the trapezoid—and as blood soaks the sleeve of his beige jacket, the shock on his face slowly becomes something else. A faint smile, not patronizing this time, not mocking, not even angry. He looks at Julie like he's meeting her for the first time.

"Well all right then," he says.

He marches up the ramp with Julie's gun at his back.

Julie doesn't look at any of us. We don't look at each other. We board the plane in frightened silence, like hostages, and I haul the ghost of Julie's mother by the neck, seeing nothing in her eyes but death.

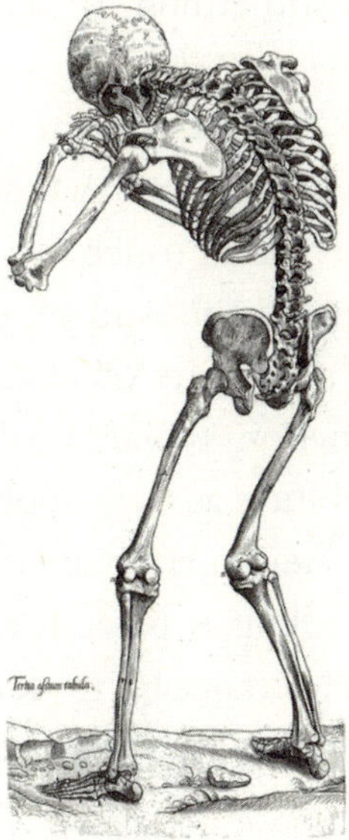

WE

"Let's play a game," Gael says.

"Which one?" Gebre says.

"Let's play Road Name."

"What's that?"

"You take the name of the first wrecked car you see, then a cartoon character from the first roadkill you see, combine them however you like, and that's your road name."

The boy sits on a plastic bucket between the van's driver and passenger seats, staring at the highway ahead. The morning sun is streaming through the trees and bathing everything in an ethereal glow, but by the time it reaches him through the dirty windshield and his scratched sunglasses, it is cloudy and dim.

"I'm playing for our little mate here," Gael says, smiling at the boy. "Because we need something to call him other than 'mate.' Right, mate?"

We watch the boy's thoughts as he weighs these two men. Their intentions, their motivations. A brain is built to learn from experience—if fire burns, don't touch fire—and if his does its job, he will never trust people again. And yet the brain is not a simple machine. It is a concentric infinity of wheels within wheels, and it fights against its own functions toward goals it barely comprehends.

"Honda Fit!" Gebre blurts as they approach a car with its nose buried in the ditch. It's Gael's turn to drive, so Gebre has the scouting advantage. "And roadkill! A pigeon, I think. They must have swerved to miss it . . ." He cranes his neck to watch the bird's dried remains disappear. "I guess that's the reward for kindness these days."

"Geb," Gael says.

"Anyway. Honda Fit plus a bird, so . . . I guess I'm Tweety Fit?"

"You can mix it however you want. Doesn't have to be whole words."

Gebre thinks a moment. "Fonda Titty."

"Sure you are," Gael chuckles. "But that's good. Okay, mate, our turn."

They have been driving for three days. The boy records the patterns around him deep in the back of his mind. Bright then dark. Warm then cold. The opening then closing of dandelions. The desperate scramble then sated stillness of insects. And the ebb and flow of conversation in the van, from idle chatter to heavy debates to long, unreadable silences. They have offered him food and he has refused. They have seen him sitting alert on his bucket while they fall asleep in the pop-top bed, and they have woken to find him unmoved, staring up at them from his bucket, waiting. He wonders why they pretend not to know what he is.

"There!" Gael says, pointing to an SUV stalled in the middle of the road with cut tires and broken windows. "Land Rover. Okay, mate, keep your eyes peeled for some roadkill and we'll make you a lovely new—"

The boy's arm darts out, startling Gael into silence. His finger is pointing to something on the road ahead. The merriment drains from Gael's face.

"Bloody hell," he whispers.

The boy watches him expectantly. Gael assumes he is too innocent to have understood what he saw and is just eager to hear his road name. Gael doesn't know him like we do. The boy knows exactly what he saw; he's just waiting to see how this man responds to the daily horror of reality. Will he firm his face and wade straight in? Or will he cough uncomfortably and suggest a new game?

"Well . . . ," Gael says in a trembling breath as the large, meaty pancake recedes behind them. "Car plus cartoon character . . . I guess your name is Rover Fudd."

Gebre buries his face in his hands, shaking his head slowly.

For the first time in the boy's second life—seven years of violence and torpor in endless, numbing repetitions—the boy smiles. He thinks goodness must be more than just kindness. It must have a hard frame to hold it together. How can you stitch a wound if you faint at the sight of blood? How can you do good in a world you refuse to see? Perhaps goodness requires honesty, which requires courage, which requires strength, which requires . . .

He stops himself.

Perhaps goodness is complicated.

The road ahead disappears from view, plunging down into a darker, denser woodland, and the boy hears the roar of an engine struggling up the hill. Gael stops the van, assuming that the strangers will want to share news and field notes and maybe some coffee or booze, as is the custom on these lonely highways. But as the boy stares at the road's vanishing point, an abrupt terminus like the edge of a cliff, he hears another noise approaching from below. Not an engine.

He straightens up on his bucket. He tugs on Gael's sleeve.

"What's wrong, Rover?" Gael says.

The boy's eyes implore him through his sunglasses as the noise grows louder, but Gael and Gebre just watch him with curious smiles, deaf to what's coming.

"Go," the boy croaks through his long disused larynx.

Gael and Gebre stare at him in open-mouthed amazement.

"Hide," the boy says.

"Rover!" Gael says. "You're talking!"

And you're not listening.

The noise is growing louder, cutting through the roar of the engine like a serrated blade.

The boy suddenly remembers there are chunks of plastic covering his face. Big slabs of black polycarbonate between him and everything else, stopping light from coming in and emotion from going out, walling him off from the world. No wonder they don't understand.

He pulls the glasses off and drops them. He looks from Gael to Gebre with his bare yellow eyes.

"Get off the road," he says.

They stare in silence for several seconds. Then without looking away from the boy's eyes, perhaps unaware he's doing it, Gael turns the wheel and eases the van onto the shoulder. The boy is wondering how to explain that this isn't far enough, that they have to crash into the woods and run as far away as possible, when the approaching vehicle crests the hill.

It's a boxy armored bank truck. It's painted all white. It's hauling a long cargo trailer reinforced with steel plates. And the trailer is humming.

There are many things to which we could compare this sound—dissonant choirs, furious wasps, the *om* of a dark meditation—but the boy thinks of a bomb. He thinks of the death spirits that live inside a bomb, the essences of its chemicals hissing and howling behind the bomb's steel walls, demanding to be released on the world.

And then they're gone. The armored car and its horrible cargo disappear into the forest, and the van is once again alone on a silent road.

Gael and Gebre seem completely unaware of the nightmare that just rolled past them. They spare barely a glance for the rude travelers who didn't even offer a friendly wave. They are staring at the boy, at his glimmering gold eyes. He senses questions coming, and they're the wrong questions, and his brief moment of feeling understood evaporates. He gets off his bucket and retreats to the back of the van. He hides among piles of blankets.

The world makes little sense to the boy. It makes less the more he studies it. It contains creatures that are nothing more than algorithms, echoes of a dead society that deserved to die, and someone is putting them to use. Someone is gathering them together, believing someone somehow will benefit.

Perhaps goodness is not complicated. Perhaps it's imaginary. Or perhaps it's just drowned in madness.

As Gael and Gebre pull back onto the road and continue their journey east, as the boy sulks in the shadows and contemplates questions too big for his age, he hears another drone. This one is soft and almost soothing. A long, slow sigh from somewhere above him. He pokes his head out the window and looks up, but the sky is empty. The plane has already passed.

I

THE RAIN.

The rain soaks through my clothes and the cold through my skin. I can feel it working its way through muscles and organs, all the way to my center, and I wonder, distantly and without much interest, if it will stop my heart.

The roof is slippery with mildew and rot everywhere except my path. I have worn it in over the years like animal trails in the forest, a channel of sagging shingles from my bedroom window to the chimney. I'm leaning against the chimney now, knees to my chest, watching the funeral from above like a cathedral gargoyle. I should be down there. I should be sitting in one of those folding chairs in my Sunday best, watching them lower her into the ground next to my grandmother, but I don't know how to grieve correctly. If she's in a better place, my grief is selfish. If this was God's plan, my grief is mutinous. And what about my rage? To whom do I direct that? To the troubled man who killed her or to the God who wrote his trouble? To the performer or the playwright? Or to myself for asking such questions?

It's good that I'm up here. The mourners below weep openly,

following convention without a thought for the contradictions, and they would expect me to do the same. But I am too angry to cry. I am a wrung-out rag, twisted and dry. So I sit on the roof and let the rain do my grieving, falling from my eyelashes like surrogate tears.

• • •

"What did she die for?"

"She was trying to help."

"By feeding them? Keeping them alive? How was that helping them?"

"We feed them so we can teach them. Hungry people are the best listeners."

"Teach them how to get into Heaven? How to stay good long enough to get into Heaven?"

My father glares at me with bleary red eyes. He is slumped in his recliner, a gray mountain of ash growing in his ashtray, staring at a television that plays bad news on every channel. Drone strike footage on MTV. Terrorist manifestos on Comedy Central. Mass graves on Lifetime. I would never have said these things to him a week ago, but grief has weakened him and strengthened me. He is drowning; I am burning.

"Isn't that why we're here?" I insist. "To just hang on until the end? To keep playing the scene until God yells 'cut'?"

"You and your damn metaphors," he grumbles, and takes a drag on his cigarette.

"Why are we here, Dad?"

"We're here to share the News," he recites. "We're here to spread the Fire."

"But the News is about Heaven, right? It's not about Earth."

"Of course it's not about Earth," he growls, shaking his head. "Earth's a ball of shit. It's been scheduled for demolition since the day it was made."

I hear my voice rising to a shout. "Then why do we keep trying to fix it? Why do we keep building homes here? Why don't we let it burn?"

He sucks in more smoke and stares at the TV, his jaw flexing.

"Maybe that man was just trying to help." My voice is low now. "Maybe he just wanted to send her to Heaven."

This gets the expected result. I stumble back against the wall, running my tongue along the holes in my lip. Oh, I've missed this. The blood, vibrant on my white T-shirt. The pain, confirming my place in this world, telling me I'm right about everything. The only thing missing is the fear. When I was young he was terrifying, but now that I'm sixteen and nearly a foot taller, he's pitiful. I exult in watching him lose control and make a sham of his principles, pissing his pants before God and man.

I will have to get my fear somewhere else.

I grin at him with red-smeared teeth. "I have to go," I say as he stands there, fists at his sides, breathing hard. "I'm late for church."

• • •

I sit once again in the hotel conference room, staring at the vinyl banner while the pastor harangues the youth of Missoula, but something is different tonight. I'm not the only one gripping the sides of his seat. A week ago a refugee obeyed a chorus of voices telling him to stab my mother with her potato peeler while she was preparing his dinner, but there is nothing special about my tragedy. Twenty murders in a month in a town with one gas station. Three arsons on public buildings followed by fatal police shootouts. And of course, the rumors about what happened to some of the bodies. Even with communications jammed, everyone feels the wave rising.

"Make no mistake," the pastor says, "it's ending. It's been a long day, but the sun is setting. So when you see all this chaos in the world, don't be concerned. This isn't our home that's burning down, it's our prison. And the Fire is God's."

I stare at him with red, watery eyes, my brain buzzing with cognitive dissonance. Paul Bark glances down at my notepad as I scribble blindly onto it.

"Everything is God's," the pastor continues. "The Devil is God's. Sin is God's. God made *everything*, therefore *everything* is his, no exceptions. So although God hates evil, it belongs to him, and he can use it as he pleases to accomplish his plan."

The scratching of my pen becomes so loud that the kids behind me lean in to look over my shoulder.

"Does that mean that God is evil, because he uses evil?" He shakes his head and smiles. "No. God is good, both the adjective and the noun. He is our *definition* of good, our atomic clock, the standard of measure by which we draw all comparisons. If God does it, it's not evil."

Paul looks up from my notepad and catches my eye. His gaze is hard, his scruffy chin jutting. He gives me a stoic nod.

"So when you see the world burning around you . . . rejoice!" Spread palms. Beatific smile. "When you see civilization crumbling into darkness, praise God, because you are watching his work. He's scouring the earth, blasting it clean in preparation for his Kingdom, and believe me"—his smile takes on a sly gleam—"you are not going to miss the house we've built with our clumsy little hands when he drops his mansion on top of it."

I feel the eyes of a dozen young men and women on me, some staring at my notepad, some at my face as it reddens and trembles. Rage and grief are colliding inside me like lava and seawater, forming gnarled black stone. A clump of my peers remains around me as the rest of the congregation flows to the exits, and though no one says a word, I know the same thought is in all of us, hovering over our heads like tongues of fire.

I tuck my notepad away as the pastor walks past us, hiding my doodles from his curious gaze. He may have inspired them but he wouldn't understand them. They are a new revelation for younger, stronger saints: houses, schools, refugee camps, all engulfed in flames, and a flock of spirits fleeing the earth, which is just a ball of black ink, without form and void, like it was in the beginning and like it should have stayed.

"What are you kids up to?" the pastor inquires cheerfully.

"Your sermon moved me," I tell him. "I'd like to stay and pray about it."

"We're all going to stay with him," Paul says.

"That's good of you," the pastor says, then downturns his smile into consolation. "I'm very sorry for your losses, all of you. I know it's been a hard season."

"What do you mean?" I say with a strange, trembling euphoria. "Everything we lose brings the Kingdom closer."

He looks uncomfortable. "Right. Well. I hope God speaks to you tonight."

He walks away, leaving us alone in the conference room. I glance from face to face, all of them pale and tired, eyes red from grieving and fighting and seeking answers that never come, and I see my own epiphany reflected in all of them.

I pull out my notepad and begin to sketch plans, and they crowd in around me like members of one body. It's the closest I've ever felt to the Spirit of God moving.

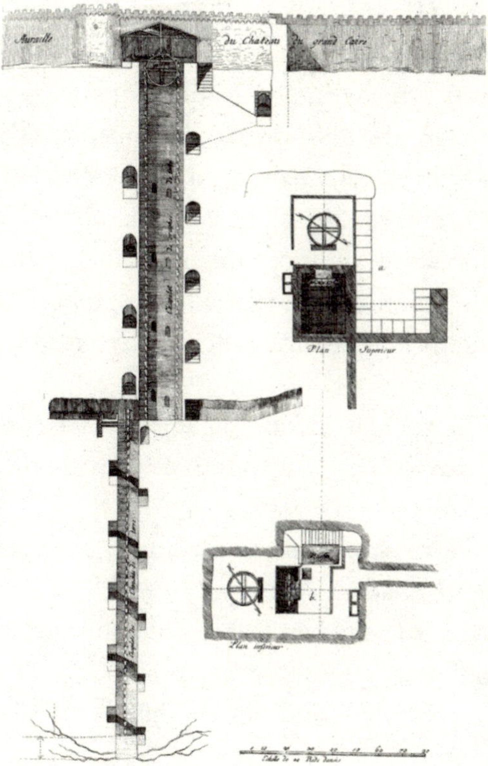

THERE IS NO WARMTH in this basement. No pleasant nostalgia in these old boxes. They lie in heaps as if tossed in a panic. Sharp objects poke through them and some are soggy with dark fluid. What was I supposed to find here? Why should I want these old horrors? There are plenty of new ones waiting outside.

I open my eyes.

The interior of the plane is calm. The soft drone of the engines. The pink morning glow creeping through the windows. Will this day look different? Are the eyes I just opened the same ones I closed last night, or did I bring new ones back with me?

What does the world look like to someone who has sought to destroy it?

M and Nora are asleep in the row behind me. Sprout is curled up near the back, arms wrapped around her knees in a heartbreaking posture of fear. Abram snores in the cockpit with the autopilot engaged, his wounds neatly bandaged, looking rather comfortable.

Only Julie is awake. She slumps in the copilot chair, her pistol on the armrest. She notices me looking at her and her puffy eyes glint with defiance, daring me to judge her. After what I've just relived, the thought of me judging anyone almost makes me smile.

I step into the cockpit and lean against the instrument panel behind her. She swivels her chair to face me, giving me a blunt stare. "What."

It's the voice of someone addressing a stranger. Perhaps an enemy. Whatever I had to say evaporates.

She swivels back to the windshield. The sun is a small coal rising up from an endless gray expanse.

"Julie." I step forward and put my hands on her shoulders. "I understand."

"Do you?" she says to the windshield, and there's a dangerous tremble under her level tone. "Because I thought you were a blank canvas." Her shoulders are so tight they seem to be extruding spikes. "I thought you get to choose where your past begins and you chose the day you met me. Which is sweet and all, but it means you never had a family, never lost a family, never lost anything. It means you *don't* understand."

I withdraw my hands. I look down at the top of her head, that little golden ball that contains every moment of my third life. I wish she were right. I wish I were nothing but that brief vignette, but my present is becoming a small raft adrift on a dark ocean.

Could I tell her? Could I introduce her to the broken wretch taking shape in my head? Is she broken enough to accept him?

A harsh beep pierces the cockpit and a red light blinks on in front of Abram. He sits up and takes the controls without so much as a yawn, either a light sleeper or a good pretender. Julie also snaps to attention, steadying the pistol and blinking alertness into her bloodshot eyes.

Abram glances at the gun. "That's really not necessary, you know. You've made your point."

Julie watches him silently.

"What am I going to do, jump out the window? Why don't you save the hostage stuff for when we're on the ground?"

"The hostage thinks I should put my gun away," Julie says flatly. "The hostage thinks that would be the logical thing to do."

Abram sighs. "I'm just asking you to ease up."

"Why?" She wiggles the barrel. "Do guns make you nervous?"

He looks at her with what appears to be genuine emotion, a genuine plea. "They make my daughter nervous."

Julie's mask slips. The hard angles of her face melt. She glances back into the cabin and sees Sprout watching her anxiously, crouched on her seat as if ready to run away. Julie's chin trembles just once, a spasm of sadness. She puts the gun in her lap.

"Thank you," Abram says.

The red light blinks and beeps again.

"What is that?" Julie says.

"It's my morning alarm. Can't be late for work when the boss is armed and insane."

"What is it."

"It's a route notice. Means we're close to Pittsburgh."

"Why do you have a route notice for Pittsburgh?"

"Because I think we should stop there."

She stares at him. "What?"

"I think we should stop in Pittsburgh."

She leans in, peering at him curiously and gripping the gun against her thigh. "Have I been *vague* about our itinerary?"

"Look, I'll fly you to Iceland. It's going to be a lifeless rock, but I'll fly you there. But before we launch ourselves across the Atlantic with limited fuel and 1970s nav gear, I think we should make a stop in Pittsburgh."

"What the hell's in Pittsburgh?"

Abram watches the first rays of the sun creep toward him along the dash. "What was it you said when you first talked me into flying this plane? Something about utopian enclaves and rebel armies? Well I definitely can't promise the first thing, but maybe the second."

There's a subtle fluctuation in Julie's skeptical stare. "There's a rebel army in Pittsburgh?"

"I know there was a year ago."

Julie puts the gun back in her lap. "I'm listening."

"Pittsburgh was my first placement after they found me in the woods. It's where I was trained, it's basically my hometown. I hopped around a lot in my twenties but when Mura was born I decided—" He shakes his head. "Point being, Branch 2 is where I first heard that Axiom was losing its mind. There were some Management guys who'd had some contact with Executive—indirect contact, of course; I've never known anyone who's actually talked to Atvist . . ."

Nausea jolts through my guts and I suddenly want to be somewhere else. Maybe a bathroom. I close my eyes and take slow breaths.

". . . but they got close enough to see that something was very wrong at the top, if there even was a top anymore."

"Rosy—" Julie starts, then stops herself. "General Rosso, the stadium's leader, said Axiom was wiped out years ago."

Abram opens his mouth to respond but someone else talks over him, an unexpected third voice blurting, "Seven years ago. Leadership killed, headquarters destroyed, everything buried in the quake. But he said not to stop."

Abram and Julie are both staring at me.

"What is wrong with him, exactly?" Abram asks her. "Was he a radiation baby?"

"Rosy said all that to you?" Julie asks, bewildered.

I blink a few times.

"*Anyway*," Abram sighs, "yes, we took a big hit in New York. The branches lost contact with Executive and for a while no one knew what was going on or if we were even still a company. But after a couple years, orders started trickling in again, reports that Executive had survived, Branch 1 was rebuilding, and everything was fine. And for a while, we believed it."

Julie glances behind her and startles. Nora is leaning in the cockpit entryway, arms folded, listening. A wrinkled yellow pamphlet dangles between her fingers. "Don't mind me," she says.

Abram returns his attention to Julie. "But by the time I left to work on the west coast campaign, there were rumblings. Secret meetings. I'd say at least half of the branch was ready to do something."

"Like what?" Julie says.

"Take down Executive. Maybe break up the whole company into local governments. They hadn't worked out the details."

"Half of one branch against a nation-scale militia network? How was that supposed to work?"

"Other branches were in on it. Call it a revolution if that tickles your teenage drama bone."

Julie's eyes narrow. "First of all, I'm not a teenager . . ."

"Oh that's right, you had a birthday. Everything's different now."

". . . second of all, since when are you a rebel, Abram Kelvin?" Her eyes narrow. "Since when do you fight for anything but your own little homestead?"

Abram keeps his face neutral.

"We've been flying all over the country looking for a way forward, and you've done nothing but run backward every chance you get. Now you're suddenly 'viva revolution'? You've suddenly got a big insurgency lined up for us that you never bothered to mention?"

The faint, weary smirk never leaves Abram's face, but it looks a little forced now. "Walking into an Axiom branch when we're all on their wanted list wasn't my first choice. If the coup hasn't happened yet, it's going to be tough to reach my contacts. And yeah, I'd rather be fishing in the mountains with my daughter than trying to save the world with a bunch of delusional children. But if it's this or a one-way trip to a frozen rock in the ocean, I'll take the revolution."

Julie shakes her head. "You're full of shit."

"I'm really not."

"There's nothing in Pittsburgh. You're just trying to get us on the ground so you can make your break."

Abram nods. "Fair call, but it's wrong. Lying's not my thing."

Julie chuckles. "Oh really!"

"One of my father's lessons that stuck: lying to someone gives them power. Makes them the judge and you the defendant. Tell the truth and deal with the results. Lying's for pussies."

Julie laughs. "You're *so* full of shit."

"Actually," Nora says, "he might not be." She straightens the yellow pamphlet and hands it to Julie.

Julie scans the page of chicken-scratch handwriting and doodled marginalia, like a medieval manuscript illuminated by drunk monks. She looks up at Nora in amazement. "Where'd you find this?"

"In the airport, of course, a thousand miles from anyone. I think DBC might be a little OCD."

"Why didn't you show me earlier?"

Nora gives her a dry stare. "You'd just shot a guy in front of his daughter. It seemed like a bad time."

Julie flinches. I suspect it's been a while since Nora has failed to be on her side. Julie turns her attention to the yellow paper, almost hiding behind it, and I read over her shoulder.

EXEDWORLD ALMANAC (K)

AUGUST-ISH (Gloop)

18 YRS FROM BABL

Brewed a big batch of bio and Barbara is back in business. Counter-clock USA chasing an ancient legend of Old Gov mystery men running lines in the Cascadian wildwoods. Hunters arrested for stumbling into clearings full of Gov hardhats — THAT SORT OF THING.

Rumors rarely from reputable lips but Cascadia and NY keep coming up so off we go

AUSTIN: SXSW  history jokes lol lol lol lol lol literally dead

MARFA: small enclave w/ local gov. Open, non-hostile, many travelers, intel.

N. ORLEANS: X (submerged) 

ORLANDO: X and SWARMING.

? ? what ? what ? why why ?

Couldn't get through to S. Florida

NEW YORK CITY: to X or not to X ?? Giant toilet bowl filling with shit and seawater. Come for the Freedom Tower, stay for the indefinite detention. Axiom Group = longevity at expense of life! Lines of travelers pouring into NY waiting turn to be robbed and enslaved = surreal horror. 

I ♥ NY

Thee District O' Columbia: X (razed)

Pittsburgh: TAKE NOTE: dispersed pop. + large Axiom base but TAKE NOTE! Base = grumbly! Axiom = unhealthy, uncertain, UNLIKED! Intriguing chats with beige jackets. Advise ALL GRUMBLERS to pay a visit. Congregate. Move some objects. Break stuff open and show what's in it and make new stuff from the pieces. That's what art is.

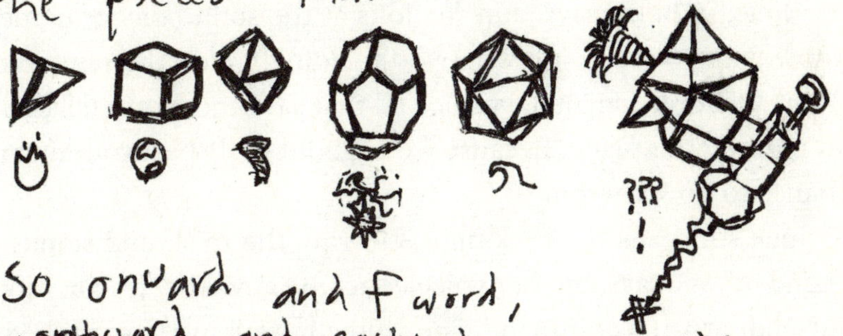

So onward and f word,
northward and eastward, topple the tower and make God nervous, emerge from the swamps and start talking!

WE LOVE YOU EXED WORLD!

-DBC

Julie lowers the page. "This was two years ago. You'd think we'd have heard something."

"Come on," Nora says. "Two years ago we didn't even know Axiom still existed. Pittsburgh could be a full-blown rogue state by now."

A moan drifts from the rear of the plane and Julie's head snaps toward the sound. Near the restrooms, chained to a chair, the remains of her mother are waiting. For what, exactly, I don't know, and I doubt Julie does either, but I can see the emotion flooding her face, cold and wet and overwhelming.

"We can't," she murmurs, her eyes glazing. "We have to get her help."

"We will, Jules," Nora says. "But what do you really think she'd want you to do right now?"

Another long, pitiful moan, so different from her earlier snarls of mindless hunger.

"Julie," Abram says, and she jolts at the sound of her name. "I know why you're doing what you're doing. I'd do the same thing. But if you ever meant a word of all that save-the-world talk, you'll let me land this plane. Because we're about to fly past your first real chance to do something."

Julie squeezes her eyes tight, clearing the mist, and stands up. "Land it," she says, but her voice is lacking any rebel fervor, more a surrender than a command. She's already walking toward the rear of the plane. "Mom? Are you okay?"

I follow her quietly, keeping a respectful distance. Her mother sits in the aisle, slouching on the floor. A length of cable runs through her collar and around the posts of a headrest, giving her a few feet to move around, and Joan and Alex sit just outside her range, watching her warily.

"Scary," Alex says, widening his eyes at me.

"Sad," Joan says, regarding Audrey with precociously deep empathy. "She's . . . very sad."

Their bells jingle. My kids have collars too. I found them in some pet carriers and decided the bells' warning would be sufficient security for these gentle young corpses. Abram was in no position to object this time.

"We're going to land in Pittsburgh, Mom," Julie says, sitting cross-legged in front of her. "They say there's a resistance there. We're going to see if we can help."

Audrey's hands lie palms-up on the floor in front of her and she stares down at them, slack-faced.

"Do you remember trying to help, Mom? Do you remember how much you wanted to make the world better?"

Audrey rocks back and forth, her filthy hair dangling into her eyes.

"Mom? Do you remember anything?"

Audrey lunges and snaps her teeth an inch from Julie's face. Julie jumps up and back, her lips trembling. Audrey is looking right at her. The Dead's emotions are hard to read, even for their fellow Dead, but if I had to guess, I'd say the look on Audrey's sallow face is bitterness. The deep, singular hurt of someone who has tried to do good and been punished for it.

"Why do we keep doing this?" I demand of my mother as she peels potatoes for tonight's vat of communal stew. "What's the point of helping people if the world's going to burn anyway?"

I can no longer spare her. My confusion has grown too big to be restrained by kindness; it lashes out heedlessly, beating my mother down.

"Are we winning points with God? Is he even keeping score? Won't it all go back to zero when he resets the world? There won't be any record of what we've done here, Mom! Why are we doing this?"

"I don't know!" she screams at me, and the peeler falls to the floor. She is crying. She has been crying for a while; her face and neck are wet with it, but her back was to me and I couldn't see. "I don't know, you cold, logical thing. I don't know."

I back out of the kitchen, my anger and confusion mixing with guilt, forming still harder alloys.

Wiping at her eyes with a callused hand, my mother bends down and picks up the peeler—

Julie is looking at me. What has been on my face? How much have I revealed? I feel gravity weakening as the plane begins its descent, thinning my body's connection to solid things.

WE

There are no more road games in the van. No more lively debates or pop rock on the stereo. Just uneasy silence. The boy sits on the bucket between the two seats, his sunglasses somewhere in the back, lost under bags and boxes. He keeps his gaze straight ahead as Gael and Gebre steal sideways glances at him. He is not bothered by their curiosity or even their fear. He would answer their questions if he could answer his own.

"One thing I can say for sure," Gebre says as if concluding a long discussion in his head, "you talked. I definitely heard you talk back there. So it is safe to assume you understand us, yes, Rover?"

"He could be deaf," Gael says.

Gebre considers this a moment. He hands the cracked iPod to Gael. "Play something kids hate."

Gael spins the wheel and clicks. A cherubic falsetto rises over plodding drums and bittersweet strings.

"No, no," Gebre says with a grimace. "I said something *kids* hate, not something every sane person hates."

"It's Sigur Rós!" Gael objects. "It's a mopecore classic."

Gebre shudders. They watch the boy for a reaction, but he stares blankly ahead. Gael raises the volume until the piercing falsetto threatens to crack the windshield. Gebre is shouting at him to shut down the experiment, the boy is obviously deaf, but then he cuts off in midsentence and kills the stereo.

"Hey," he says to the boy, whispering in the ringing silence. "Are you okay?"

The boy's face is still blank, but his shocking yellow irises are dulled behind a pool of tears. He does not answer Gebre because he is no longer in the van. He is stumbling along a walkway in a dark, echoing Library, suspended between unknowable heights and unthinkable depths, struggling to keep his eyes ahead. A few books topple out of their shelves and loose pages flutter around him, and now he's in a restaurant, sitting across from a girl, trying to tolerate the music she has chosen. The girl looks like him, older and thinner and a little lighter-skinned, but with the same brown eyes, dark like wells that sink through all strata to the beginning of life on Earth.

He loves the girl and she loves him. They are the only remaining keepers of each other's memory, though it's buried deep in them both.

"Hey," Gael says, gently wiping a tear from his cheek. "What's wrong, love?"

The boy looks at the dampness on the man's pale finger, the salt crystals inside it like icebergs adrift on a diluvial Earth.

"Washington, DC," he says.

Gael and Gebre share a stunned glance.

"Is that where you were going?" Gebre asks.

The boy doesn't respond.

"The Almanac we found in Dallas . . . ," Gebre says to Gael under his breath. "DC was exed, wasn't it? Exed and razed?"

"Rover," Gael says to the boy, giving him a look of deep regret, "there's nobody in DC, mate. It burned down a long time ago."

The boy has no visible reaction.

"But we're going somewhere that has a lot of people," Gebre says with forced cheer. "People and food and work, and it's safe there. No one will hurt us there."

Gael tentatively reaches toward him, lays a hand on his shoulder. The boy knows Gael is afraid of his teeth and for a moment he feels the urge, but it's not really hunger. He is beyond the control of that simple brute. When he feels the urge now, it's just a rattling of his cage. A frenzied effort to bend the bars.

"We're going to look after you," Gael says, giving the boy's shoulder a squeeze, and he and Gebre share a meaningful look. A decision. "Whatever's happened to you, we're going to help you heal it. Okay?"

The boy grits his teeth to stop the clicking that he can tell makes Gael nervous. He sees a moonlit balcony and a dusty airport and an old house on fire, all of it shrinking into the darkness through the rear window of a Geo coupe.

"Don't worry, Rover," Gebre says, trying even harder to infuse his voice with hope. "You're going to love New York."

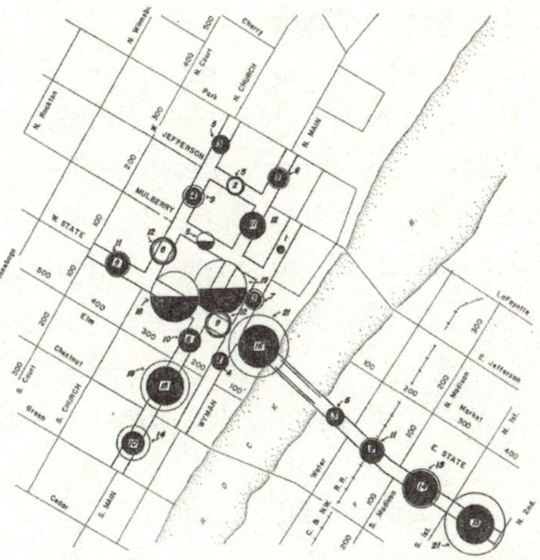

I

"IT'S A MIXED POPULATION BRANCH so it's normal for civilians to be here, but we have to assume they're still broadcasting our capture code, so people are going to recognize us if we give them a chance. I'll keep us out of traffic but if we do run into anyone, keep your mouths shut, heads down, no eye contact. Think of every time you've ever failed someone and let the shame make you invisible."

I'm not listening. I don't need these tips. No one avoids human interaction better than I do. No one has more shame to hide behind. As Pittsburgh's skyline rises in front of us, Abram drones on about the resistance leaders we're looking for, the secret conference rooms where they meet, but only a thin outer layer of me is hearing him. I am finding it hard to be here, in the present, with all its explosions and car chases and covert operations. We are trying to overthrow a despotic regime and save America, but all I can think about is the five people walking next to me, their localized conflicts, their tiny joys and pains.

Nora's eyes are faraway, traveling inner spaces I know little about. M walks beside her with an equally distant look, perhaps continuing to excavate his apparently harmless past. The pistol looks heavy in Julie's hand. The barrel keeps drifting away from Abram as if embarrassed, and Julie reluctantly drags it back.

"Nora," I say under my breath, and she jolts like a sleepwalker waking up.

"Wha—sorry, what?" she mumbles. Her eyes dart to absorb her surroundings.

"Can I ask you . . . a personal question?"

"Uh . . . sure?"

"What would you do?" I keep my voice low, audible only to her and M. "If you found your mother."

Her face clouds and she doesn't respond.

"Would you do this?" I gesture toward Julie.

"Like I told Marcus," she says, "I don't have parents. I grew out of the ground."

"Stop that," M grunts at her.

She gives him a look that's uncertain but primed for outrage. "Excuse me?"

"Stop bullshitting." He somehow infuses this with tenderness. "You're stronger than that."

Nora blinks at him a few times, her eyes widened with undecided emotion.

"You told me how they left you," I remind her. "That night at the bar?"

She turns her trapped-animal gaze on me.

"You've lost everything Julie has. So . . . would you do this?"

She seems to break down a barrier within herself, the outer layer of a many-walled city. "It's different," she says, exhaling the debris in a small sigh. "Julie loved her parents. They were good people who got crushed by circumstances. Mine . . ."

Her face trembles as if with effort, like she's climbing over something in her head.

"Mine left"—another spasm—"me." Another deep breath. "They left me. To die. And they were assholes from the beginning. So what is it you're asking? If I found my parents alive, would I hijack a plane and fly across the world to save them?" She lets out a dark chuckle that sounds more like a snarl. "Fuck no. I'd have a hard time not killing them myself."

I notice M moving his hand toward Nora's shoulder, then reconsidering, retreating.

"But I'm a coldhearted bitch," she continues with forced flippancy. "I'm all up in Buddha's ass with that non-attachment shit. Love nothing, mourn nothing, you know? Jules is different." She watches Julie walk, just a few inches taller than her prisoner's daughter. "She's been through hell and she's got iron skin, but under that? She's all gooey pink." She smiles fondly as Julie lets the gun sag to her side, barely even trying anymore. "And I love that about her. Sometimes I even envy it. It takes crazy courage to let yourself feel that much. But yeah . . ." She sighs. "Sometimes it's a problem."

"You're not that different," M says very quietly.

"What was that?" Nora says, cocking her head like she didn't hear, but the spike in her tone reveals otherwise.

"You're not as cold . . . as you think."

"Well that's an interesting theory, but you don't really know anything about me do you?"

M doesn't reply, but he holds his gaze.

"Cut the chatter," Abram calls back to us. "We just entered the branch perimeter. Wake up and watch for patrols."

I glance around. There is no visible border, no apparent change in the cityscape, but we must have crossed some landmark that only a local would recognize. A distant part of me is disappointed in the lack of human presence so far. I was looking forward to seeing what an un-exed city feels like. Even a city controlled by Axiom would feel more real than the human zoo of Citi Stadium. But we have been hiking through Pittsburgh for over an hour—roaring into town on the bikes like unconvincing Hells Angels was quickly ruled out—and we have yet to encounter another person.

This is what the early days looked like, says a memory drifting up from my basement, like a disturbed child muttering in the dark. *Cities bled out as humanity fled from itself, dispersing across the country with the absurd hope that isolation was the cure, that their shadows wouldn't follow them. But we did. We followed them everywhere.*

"You said it's been a year since you've been here?" Julie asks Abram.

"That's right."

She looks from building to empty building. "And there were people then?"

He walks another block before replying. "They must have condensed. Moved everyone downtown."

How often does prey outrun the predator? The predator is designed to win, and if it didn't usually do so, if the business of eating the weak did not net a profit, it would fold, and there would be no more predators. But there are always predators. No matter how bare the fields get.

Whoever you are, I tell the melancholy drone, *shut the fuck up*. And to my surprise, it obeys, leaving a reverberation of resentment in the silence. It's just me now, watching the ghostly towers of Pittsburgh drift past.

I wonder how many people are in my brain. Perhaps each day births a new version of me with its own thoughts and feelings, thousands of homunculi stretching back from today to yesterday to adolescence to infancy, all stuffed into the same head to argue and jostle for position. It would explain a lot.

• • •

Abram is leading us toward the river, which flows around and into downtown, backed up from the overfilled ocean until it spills over its banks and turns parks into ponds. The only visible way across the sea is a single bright yellow bridge.

"I'd just like to point out," Nora says, "that us walking over that bridge is about as stealthy as a parade."

"Trust me," Abram says.

"Now why would I do that?"

Abram stops at the bridge's entrance and slips his backpack off his right shoulder. He digs around in it using only his right arm, keeping his left limp at his side, but he still winces from the movement. I notice Julie wincing along with him. I'm about to offer him some help when he finds what he's looking for and straightens up. He points the binoculars toward the end of the bridge, then lets out a relieved puff of breath and hands them to Julie. "Okay. I was right. They just moved downtown."

Julie looks, nods, and passes the binoculars to me, like we're a group of tourists taking turns at the view scope. I see office windows. Birds in flight. Julie's head as a yellow blur. Then I find the bridge. The magnification places me at the far end of it, about fifty feet from six men in beige jackets, standing at slouchy attention with rifles against their thighs.

"Okay," Julie says, "so the bridge is guarded by Axiom soldiers. That's . . . good?"

"Better than an empty city," Abram says, already moving toward an exit ramp that curves under the bridge. "The coup could still be building."

"Abram," Julie says, and he stops, turns. "You really think this is happening?"

"I know it *was* happening. I think it still is."

"And you really *want* it to? You want to take down the people who raised you?"

Abram chuckles. "Look, if you think I have any love for the Axiom Group just because they 'raised' me, you don't know me or the Axiom Group. It doesn't operate on love, it's a business. It's an exchange of services. It gives you comfort and security, you give it everything else. And it stopped paying its end."

He starts walking again. "Besides, if anybody raised me, it wasn't Executive. It was the guys we're going to see."

The air is cool under the bridge, shaded by the looming expanse of steel girders. Behind one of the support pillars, in an unlikely corner where only a city worker would ever think to look, there is a tiny steel door in the concrete wall. He opens it and gestures to the darkness inside.

"What is this?" Julie says.

"Access shaft to the subway tunnels. They'll take us under the river and right up into the branch campus."

M is shaking his head. "Nope. I won't even fit."

"Rub some grease on you," Abram says. "You'll fit." He holds his hand out to Julie. "Mind giving back the flashlight you stole from me?"

She pulls it out of her pack and clicks it on, aims it into the doorway and nods. "Lead on."

He sighs. "You're just all flint and leather, aren't you? I bet you gave Perry a hell of a headache."

"I thought you didn't want to talk about Perry."

"Is that how he died? Did you bitch him to death?"

"Shut up," she snaps, the whites of her eyes expanding, and her gun arm rises.

Abram puts his hands up, startled by her response. "All right, all right."

She jabs the flashlight at the door. "Let's go."

"Going."

He takes Sprout's hand and disappears into the shadows. Julie follows him, Nora and I follow her, and behind us, M grunts and curses his way through the doorway. The flashlight's beam diffuses against the concrete, dimly illuminating a staircase so steep it's almost a ladder.

"Daddy," Sprout says, "are we going home?"

"This place wasn't our home, little weed," Abram says. "We don't have a home."

"When do we get to have one?"

Silence.

"Can we build one?"

Silence.

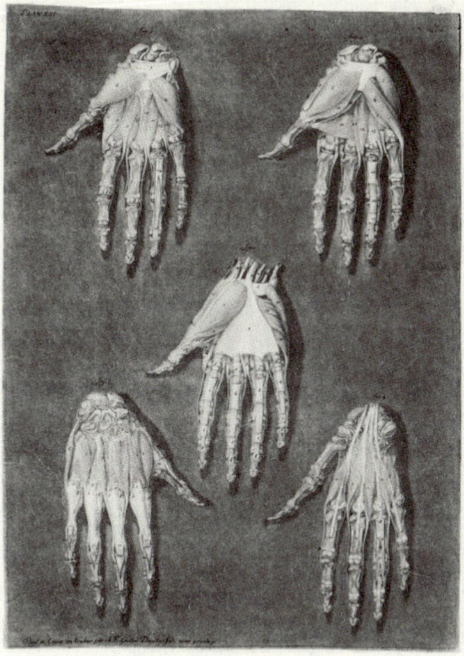

M Y PRISON.

The floor of my cell is an impressionist painting of stains, and since food is only served in the mess hall, these can only be bodily fluids. I feel them under my palms when I push myself up, greasy and sticky, and when I lower myself down, I can smell them: salty and meaty and sickly sweet, a putrid cologne of human depravity.

"How many are you up to?" Paul says from the cell across the hall.

"Not counting."

"Then how do you know when you're done?"

My arms burn and tremble. My stomach feels taut enough to snap. Sweat pours from my face, adding fresh brine to the soup on the floor, which I force myself to inhale, savoring the raw disgust. *This is what we are,* I repeat to myself with each breath. *Blood and piss and come.*

"I just know."

Scrub us away. Bleach us white.

"I'm glad you're with us, R—," Paul says, smiling. "It takes hard men to believe the truth. It takes strong warriors to fight God's war."

But I'm not thinking about God's war. I'm thinking about mine. I want to punish my weak flesh. I want to become strong so I can hurt whoever deserves hurting. These simple exercises won't make me a warrior, but the men in the yard might. War criminals, militia chiefs, rogue assassins, so amused by the boldness of this skinny country kid that they're only too happy to teach me a few tricks. My body bears the marks of their generosity. My face is purple, my knuckles are red, and my muscles were burning before I even began this set, but I'm not done yet.

"They preached hard doctrine at the Fellowship," Paul is saying from somewhere far away, "but even there, no one had the balls to really live it. To take it all the way to its conclusion like they do in the Middle East. We have to be willing to burn for the truth."

How I know I'm done is when I find myself facedown on the filthy floor, my mutinous muscles refusing all orders, my mind empty of everything and surrounded by clouds of glittering blackness. I use my last remaining calorie to roll onto my back so I can watch the colors spin in my vision.

"These bars can't hold a fire," Paul says, his voice filling with inspired fervor as he watches my suffering. "When we get out of here, we're going to round up the others and finish our work."

The lock clicks; the door slides open. A scarred, leathery face appears above me, then the door slams shut. My eyes remain fixed on a rare ceiling stain. Blood. Must have been quite a spray. Pencil to the jugular, perhaps.

"Welcome, brother," Paul calls to the new prisoner.

The man glares down at me for a few seconds, his bald, craggy visage floating in the stars like a cruel god. "The fuck are you doing?" he says, and kicks me in the ribs. "Get off the damn floor. This is my cell now."

I stand up. I sit on my cot and look at the man. Big. Muscular. Covered in tattoos. The usual snakes and skulls and eight balls, the clichés of a man who thinks darkness is crime and violence, not the void that lurks behind them.

"Shit," he says, glancing from me to Paul. "You're fuckin' kids. What are you, eighteen?"

"Seventeen," I reply.

"National Guard ain't worrying about petty shit anymore. What'd punks like you do to get in here?"

"We burned down Helena."

He looks at me, nonplussed.

"And Boise and Denver. They caught us halfway through Salt Lake City."

The man looks at Paul. Paul smiles.

"We'll finish that one later," Paul says.

I lie back on my cot, folding my lifeless arms over my chest, returning my attention to the blood on the ceiling. Dark red like a fading sunset.

• • •

The basement door is unlocked and sits half open, and cold subterranean breezes whistle through the gap. My past no longer waits for dreams. It plays out in front of my open eyes, projected onto my waking life with such hideous clarity that I can hardly believe my friends don't see it. But if they did, surely I would know it. Surely everything would change if they learned what's inside this quiet, shrugging man.

"How much deeper does this get?" Julie asks Abram, grimacing as the water crests the top of her boots and pours inside.

"Don't know," he says. "Haven't been down here in years." He holds out a hand to catch some of the fat drops raining from the ceiling. "But that's a million gallons of Allegheny River above us, so . . . how strong a swimmer are you?"

The walls of the tunnel are covered in fungal slime, and with the train tracks hidden beneath a foot of murky water, it's hard to believe this was ever a gleaming urban artery, pumping the city's lifeblood from head to foot and back again. In its current state, it looks more like a sewer drain.

"I'd worry less about the water," he continues, "and more about the high voltage rail running through it. Hope today's not the day they flip that breaker back on."

"Daddy," Sprout moans.

"For someone so obsessed with protecting his daughter," Julie says, "you sure seem to forget she's here a lot."

Abram looks mildly chastened but says nothing.

"Or is the pleasure of being a dick just worth the collateral damage?"

"She's fine."

"Daddy, I'm scared," Sprout says.

"It's okay, honey," Julie says, turning around and crouching down to Sprout's eye level. "He was just joking and trying to scare us. He wouldn't bring you down here if it wasn't safe."

Sprout's eye narrows. "You can't talk to me," she says. "I don't like you anymore."

Julie flinches. She suddenly looks about the same age as the girl in front of her. "Sprout," she says. "I'm so sorry I hurt your dad. I didn't want to, but my mom is sick and I . . . I needed him to help her."

Sprout's glare doesn't budge. "Are you going to hurt him again?"

"No! Of course not."

"Then why do you keep pointing that gun at him?"

Julie's face falters. "Because I need—I don't know if he's going to . . ."

"You can't talk to me," Sprout says, and splashes ahead to join her father.

Julie looks at the water around her ankles. She straightens up and catches me watching her; my heart lurches at the misery in her eyes before she quickly looks away.

It feels like days since we've made eye contact. We avoid it like we expect to be injured. When did we learn to fear each other? To flinch away from what we imagine the other is thinking, the cruelties we've written and placed in each other's mouths?

I don't know how to stop it. We are lost on old paths, caught in old snares. We should be walking side by side through these dark woods, but I feel our distance growing.

• • •

The water level rises until it's almost a river itself, crawling beneath the Allegheny like its timid offspring. Train oil forms psychedelic rainbows on its surface, which spiral wildly as we slosh forward in silence. When the water is almost to Sprout's waist, Abram tries to hoist her onto his shoulders—he gets her two feet off the ground before his injuries assert themselves and he drops her with a grunt of pain.

"It's okay, Daddy," she says, and takes his hand instead. "I'm okay."

He grimaces, but he accepts this. He moves forward, gripping her hand stiffly. "You know, I'm mad at Julie too," he says, "but she's right. I wouldn't bring you here if it wasn't safe."

Sprout watches the dripping ceiling. "It's really safe?"

"Sure. When I was a kid, this is where I'd go to get away from people. When my performance was weak and my father-boss wrote me up for discipline, I'd run away and hide in these tunnels." An unsettling wistfulness comes over his face. "I'd sleep on the First Street station bench, drink the drips from the ceiling . . . I'd hide for days sometimes, until I got too hungry." He chuckles. "When I started seeing things, that's when I knew I had to go back up."

"What did you see?" Sprout asks uneasily.

He doesn't answer for a moment. He peers ahead into the darkness beyond the flashlight. "A mouth."

"A *mouth*?"

"When I got really hungry and lonely, the tunnel would start to look like a big, round mouth with teeth all around it. And I'd imagine it was a monster that was bigger than the universe, and it was going to swallow everything."

"Jesus," Nora says. "Can you stop?"

Abram shakes his head as if dismissing some nostalgic indulgence. "But anyway, yes, it's safe down here. It's quiet and peaceful, and nobody knows about it, and nobody can get us."

Sprout doesn't pursue the topic. She falls back into her usual worried silence.

"Abram," Nora says warily. "How are those stitches doing? You feeling feverish at all? Dizzy? Delirious?"

"I'm fine, Nora, thank you."

Nora glances at M with raised eyebrows. Abram's tone is getting harder to read, his sarcasm less clearly marked. I'm starting to wonder if his joke about swimming was not a joke at all when the tunnel finally begins to incline and the water recedes. The flashlight reveals a station ahead.

"This is our stop," he says, and we climb a service ladder up onto the platform.

Julie runs the flashlight along the mildewed tile walls, looking for the exit. The beam falls on a bench where a moldy, rat-gnawed pillow rests on an equally decayed blanket. A steady drip splashes into a nearby soup can, which has rusted too much to hold water, and next to that is a sketchbook.

"Come on, no," Julie mutters. "This *can't* be yours."

Abram stares at the ancient tableau, the sketchbook's paper reduced to pulp, the drawings washed into Rorschach blots. A choked laugh comes out of him. "Let's go," he says, and walks briskly toward a staircase.

We follow him up to a surface-level terminal, dimly illuminated by daylight trickling down the exit stairs. Faded posters sealed in kiosks advertise cell phone providers and insurance companies and other abstractions almost impossible for the modern mind to grasp. All the signage has been edited by spray paint, the arrows now leading to predictably morbid destinations: left to DEATH, right to HELL, and up the stairs to AXIOM. Julie starts to move toward the stairs but Abram holds out a hand.

"Wait." He opens a door marked STAFF ONLY and steps into what appears to have been a conference room for subway workers. A long table, a whiteboard, a few office chairs knocked over on the floor. I don't know what Abram was expecting to find, but it's not here. The only evidence that the room has ever been used is the faint trace of a bleach-resistant bloodstain on the beige linoleum floor.

Abram stares at the stain for a moment, then turns and heads for the stairs.

"Was that the secret meeting room?" Nora asks as he brushes past her. "Is this bad news?"

He ignores her. He breaks into a run. Julie rushes to stay with him, but I sense that his haste has nothing to do with escaping. His expression is mostly anger, a familiar sight on his craggy features, but there's something else that I haven't seen.

Grief?

We emerge into daylight in the center of downtown Pittsburgh, and a strange chill runs through me, not from any bleak or horrible sight but from an unnatural lack of them.

The city is pristine.

The streets are clear of abandoned cars, swept of trash and debris—not so much as a fallen leaf in sight. Most of the buildings are freshly painted in calming neutral tones, and those with structural damage from long-ago conflicts are surrounded by scaffolding and vinyl sheeting—they are being *repaired*, a sight so old-fashioned that I doubt Sprout even knows what she's looking at. But what renders the scene truly unnerving is its lack of people. It's a civic engineer's dream, all gleaming towers and efficient planning with no pesky population to ruin it.

"What is going *on* here?" Julie mutters, gazing up at the high-rises like a small-town tourist. "Abram?"

But Abram hasn't paused. He strides toward a thick, Brutalist tower of bare concrete that looks severely out of place in the city's historic center.

"Hey!" Julie shouts, rushing after him. "What are you doing?"

Despite its ghostly first impression, the city is not *quite* empty. There are guards at the building's entrance.

"Abram, *stop*!"

But it's too late. Could this have been a trap? Could he have somehow patched his relationship with Axiom and made a deal to deliver us? It's hard to believe, but he approaches the guards with the confidence of a man who belongs here.

We chase him up the steps. Julie's gun is out, but using it now wouldn't change anything. The guards draw their rifles. Abram walks right up to them—they don't fire. They don't even speak.

"I need to see Mr. Warden," he says in a tightly controlled growl. "Branch Manager Warden, where is he?"

The men don't answer. They have no shade or shelter; the afternoon sun beats down on their faces, but their foreheads are dry. Their pale blue eyes show no sign of discomfort or, for that matter, comprehension. I feel a sick twisting in my stomach, like I've stepped barefoot into something unspeakable.

"Is this still the branch office?" Abram demands. I can tell he senses something wrong but he persists anyway. "Is Mr. Warden still branch manager?"

The men stare at him. Then their eyes drift back into the city as if looking for someone more important to talk to.

Abram grabs Sprout's wrist and pushes past the apparently decorative guards into the building's foyer. Julie throws up her hands like a surrender to insanity and follows him.

I slow my stride, letting the others pass me until I'm last in line, and I look at the guards. They do not look at me.

"What happened to you?" I ask them.

Their eyes twitch toward me briefly, then back to the city. I follow my friends into the concrete tower.

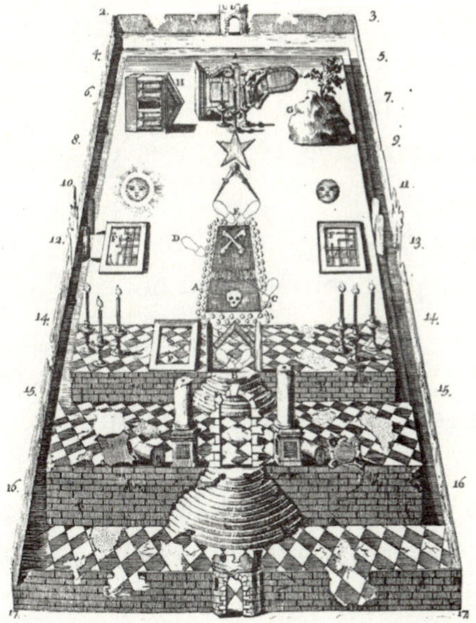

WHAT DOES THE OFFICE of a post-apocalyptic corporation look like? What kind of clerical work is required for the violent acquisition of cities? I imagine secretaries faxing massacre authorization forms to overworked, coffee-addled warlords. Executive despots shouting at underperforming militia recruiters. What kind of papers are on their desks, held down by human skull paperweights? What is their salary in a world without money, where status is a parade that few have time to watch?

Walking into the foyer of Branch 2, I am not sure if my questions have been answered. It appears to be vacant, lacking any furniture, office supplies, or motivational posters. The only decor is the flat-screen TVs that line the walls at regular intervals, broadcasting Axiom's gritty modern reboot of the LOTUS Feed. Abstract imagery and lulling platitudes have given way to aggressive propaganda, louder and simpler, eagles and gold bricks and grim patriarchs spreading protective arms over wives and children while blinking text shouts *ACT NOW!!* That subtle wrongness, like a computer trying to parse human emotions.

Abram looks disoriented. He glances left and right as if searching for something familiar.

Julie has had enough. "Abram." She raises the gun just a few inches, perhaps hoping Sprout won't notice. "Tell me what we're doing here."

"Looking for Warden." His eyes keep darting; he doesn't appear to notice the gun either, or maybe he doesn't care. "I need to know what happened."

He runs to a freight elevator. Julie lowers the gun and follows him, apparently convinced by the fear in his eyes.

He presses the top floor and punches in a code on the keypad. There's a discouraging beep and nothing happens. He shakes his head, muttering inaudibly, and works his way down the buttons until he reaches one that's unrestricted: floor twenty, thirty floors from the top.

The elevator rises, and the inertia spikes my nausea. It's been a long time since I've felt that tug of gravity on my guts, a sensation never felt in nature except by prey, the mouse's final, thrilling ascent before it meets the beak. I hear the strangers in my basement pacing around, agitated, muttering vague words of warning or threat, but I push the door shut. *Not now. Not a good time.*

We watch the floor numbers creep upward, the anticipation heightened by the sluggish pace. Julie exchanges her pistol for her shotgun, and Abram eyes his old weapon.

"I don't know what we're going to find here," he says. "You might want me armed."

"If I do, I'll arm you."

"You really think I'm going to make a break for it now? Here?"

"We're inside your employer's headquarters in the town where you grew up. Hard to imagine a better place for you to turn on us."

He looks at her with what appears to be genuine incredulity. "Were you asleep all those times 'my employer' tried to kill me? Or when they broadcast my wanted poster on national television? I thought it was pretty clear I'm fired."

As we pass floor ten, the overhead speaker emits a harsh pop, and a stream of customer service jazz trickles into the elevator. "Anarchy in the UK" on glistening sax and synthesizer.

"Nothing's clear," Julie mutters. "Nothing's been clear for a long time."

On floor fifteen, still five floors from our destination, the elevator slows. My stomach bobs back to its usual position. Then the doors open, and it sinks again.

Standing in a dim hallway outside the elevator is a man in a gray shirt. Black slacks. Red tie. Fine formal business wear rendered slightly unprofessional by ragged edges, a few stains, and incongruous work boots.

Something slams into my basement door but I lean against it, holding it shut. *I said not now!*

The man smiles politely and remains outside, as if waiting for a less crowded ride.

"Get in," Abram says.

The man gets in. Sprout shrinks back into a corner.

The man is shorter than me. His hair is lighter than mine and his eyes are a different color. The elevator fills with the syrupy smell of his cologne: cotton candy and rancid butter.

"Miller," Abram says.

The man watches the door close, then watches the floor number.

"I remember you. You were Warden's assistant."

The man turns and grins at Abram, revealing perfect teeth that bear no resemblance to the crooked congregation in my mouth. "Hello, and thanks for visiting. I'm the general manager of Branch 2, an extension of the Axiom Group. How can I help you?"

Abram stares into the man's improbably vivid blue eyes. "What happened to Warden?"

"My predecessor was involved in activities that do not reflect the values of this company," the man says through a motionless grin. "Some restructuring was necessary."

Abram is shaking his head. "You turned him in. I knew you were a fucking worm." He looks up. "Is he dead? Did you execute him?"

The most upsetting thing about the man's smile is how genuine it looks. As if he has convinced even the smallest of his facial muscles to play along. As if it's not a game at all but simply his reality. I take the end of his tie and hold it close to my face, examining its glistening fibers. "What did they do?" I ask him. "How did they make you like this?"

The man's grin widens. "I feel fantastic."

Abram pushes me aside and gets very close to Miller's face. "Tell me what's happening here," he says in a low growl, no less threatening for being unarmed. "Where is everyone?"

"Branch 2 is in transition," Miller chirps. "New employee concepts are being tested."

The elevator dings. We have reached floor twenty.

"Would you like to learn more?" he asks.

I truly don't know my answer to that question, but when the doors open and Miller steps out, we follow him.

• • •

We are in an open space the size of an airplane hangar. No walls from one end of the building to the other, no ceiling for at least three floors up. The only illumination is the pale daylight creeping through a few slit windows. I see everything in vague outlines, like the room has been pumped full of dark fog. And through this fog, I see people. Hundreds of people surrounding hundreds of machines: steel presses and cutters and more complex things I can't identify. Some of the machines are fully automated, like the one that rolls out little brass cylinders and the one that fills them with black powder and the one that caps them with cones of lead. Others need human assistance, like the one that sends packets of clay-like substance to an assembly station where a man embeds some electronics in the clay and inserts it under the lining of a metal briefcase.

"I know this," M mumbles. "I know these machines."

"We are pleased to announce the reopening of Gray River National," Miller says, his voice echoing in the vast dimness as he wanders off ahead of us, "made possible by recent advancements in human resource management. We look forward to providing simplified but effective security to all branches of the Axiom family as it continues to grow . . ."

His voice fades into the shadows. We have stopped following him. It took a moment in the low light, but I have begun to notice peculiar traits in the workers. Their movements are loose and their eyes are disconnected from their tasks, staring out the windows as their hands twist screws and connect wires, as if they're only operating these tools because they happened to bump into them. I hear Miller's voice in the distance, talking to no one, a subtle overtone to the harsh melody of the factory, the grinding of metal and squeaking of rusty wheels. A worker near me lets his hand wander into a press and pulls it away with two fewer fingers. The stumps ooze black fluid in a steady, pulseless pour, and the man continues his work.

"They did it," Julie whispers. "They did it without our help."

I approach the worker warily. He doesn't pause or look at me. There is no sign of awareness. "Who are you?" I ask him. "How did you get here?"

He works and bleeds silently.

"Why are you doing this?"

His eyes meet mine for barely a second. His movements stutter, then resume, and a memory appears in my head. Not one from the basement, not from my first life but from my dusty, bloody second.

My relationship with most of my victims was simple: they tried to kill me, they tried to run away from me, and when those options failed, they screamed while I ate them. It was the standard stuff of wildlife documentaries. But there was one young man, perhaps a little unbalanced, perhaps unusually perceptive, who asked me questions while I hunted him. In his desperation, he tried to reason with me. *Why are you doing this?* he demanded. *Why do you want to eat me? What does this get you? What is this for?*

It was the only time anyone ever tried to reach me. All the others were happy to play out the standard scene of predator and prey. They had heard the reports and seen the movies; they knew what a zombie attack was supposed to look like and they played their role to the end, doing their part to maintain the narrative, awful but comforting in its consistency.

This young man ignored all that and did something absurd: he tried to communicate with the faceless symbol of relentless terror. And for a moment, it listened. His questions penetrated the thick crust around my consciousness, and a few cold synapses fired, generating a rare coherent thought. A simple answer: *I don't know.*

My hesitation probably lasted about as long as this worker's stutter. The young man's boldness bought him just a few extra seconds of life. But what did it buy me?

I leave the worker to his process and chase Miller into the shadows of the factory. I find him standing at the edge of a rectangular sunken area, a concrete pit like an empty swimming pool, covered with steel grating.

". . . still in the experimental stage and will require more effort to maximize potential," the man is saying to no one, "but the output is already impressive." He swivels his grin toward me as I approach. "Of course we still have great interest in *your* process, which produces more versatile results. Have you come here to reconsider our offer?"

Beneath the grating, the pit is a riot of zombies. Hundreds of them crammed shoulder to shoulder, swaying in waves like a concert crowd, clawing at the walls and each other. Their agitated state indicates advanced starvation. Even my ambiguously Living flesh must smell delicious.

"What are you doing to them?" I ask the man, whose tie is the same blood red as the one hanging in the closet of the house—mine and Julie's house—at the end of a quiet street.

"The Dead are blank," he says. "They are suggestible and malleable. We are bending them into useful shapes."

"You're making slaves."

He gestures to the pit of seething bodies and they surge toward his hand, piling on top of each other to reach the grate door and rattling it furiously. "Look at them," he says, inverting his grin into an exaggerated frown. "They have no culture, no religion, no nationality—nothing. They are raw material, and someone has to tell them what to be." He turns his frown upside down and gestures to the dim swarms around us. "We tell them to be this."

"What are you?" I demand, staring hard at his smooth, unblemished face.

His eyes meet mine with unusual directness. "I feel fantastic." His grin stretches so wide I expect it to split. "I know why I'm here. I know what I'll do every day. I have answered every question and solved every problem. Everything is clear."

"R." A soft voice at my back, tugging at me. "There's nothing we can do here. Let's go before he calls the real guards."

"I have already notified Regional Security," the man assures her in comforting tones. "They will be with you shortly."

"R, let's *go*!"

I stare at the churning mass of Dead in the pit, all confused violence and desperate hunger. Do I have anything better to offer them? Can I really point to my new life of pain and terror and say, *See what you're missing?* My eyes roam the quietly shuffling ranks of well-fed working Dead. No groans, no wheezes, no anxious teeth snapping. They're adrift in an even dimmer dream, wrapped in gray wool and buried in soft dust.

Should I let them stay?

My friends run toward the elevator. I follow for a few steps, then I stop. I go back to the pit.

"Have you decided to reconsider our offer?" Red Tie asks me through that taut, joyless rictus.

I answer his question and mine with the same reply: "No."

I pull open the latch on the grating door and I run.

"Where'd you go?" Julie says as I slip into the elevator. "You were behind us and then you weren't."

I push the door-close button repeatedly.

"R . . . ?" she says with rising concern.

"I did something . . . impulsive," I say under my breath.

A chorus of hungry groans fills the factory as the doors slide shut.

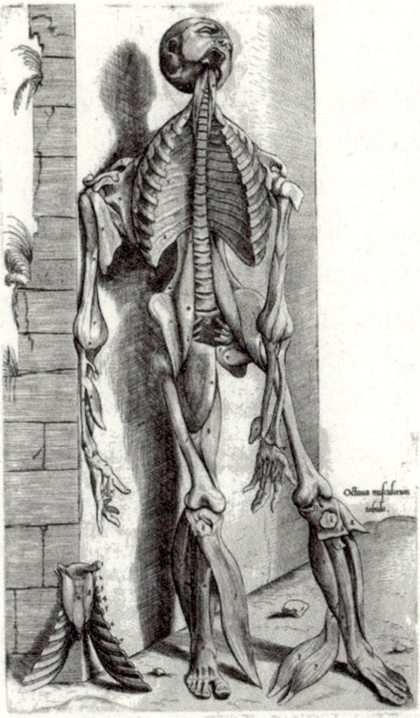

THE ELEVATOR MUSIC has shorted out again. I stare at the ceiling speaker, willing it to flood this steel cube with some watery post-culture blasphemy, because even a major-key lounge rendition of "Another Brick in the Wall" would be preferable to the snarls filtering down around us.

M looks at me and sighs. "You let them out, didn't you?"

I give him a cringing grin.

Nora puts a hand over her face.

I expect a more violent reaction from Abram, but he looks faraway, staring at the door like it's a window to a distant vista.

"It's okay," Julie says, nodding to herself. "They're twenty floors up. We'll run out of here and leave them to wreck the place. It's okay."

The groans aren't fading as quickly as they should be. The big elevator is excruciatingly slow, and even as we approach the bottom we can still hear the scrapes and grunts.

"It's okay," Julie says again, still nodding.

The doors open on the dark expanse of the lobby, and as we run for the exit, all four of the staircase doors burst open. The Dead pour out like liquid, not so much descending the stairs as free-falling down them, rolling and tumbling and trampling each other in their pursuit of our life scent.

Perhaps "impulsive" was too kind a word for my actions.

The guards at the front doors still make no attempt to stop us. Still a few bugs in the "process." Abram juts his elbows to shield his daughter as he carries her like a baby, ignoring the agony of his injuries, but we brush past the guards without resistance. And then the All Dead swarm over them, uninterested in their flesh but killing them all the same in their mindless stampede.

We take the bridge and the scenario repeats with the bridge guards, but this time we're farther away. Starvation has a way of rousing the Dead from their apathy, quickening their pace from shamble to jog, but a rotting corpse, no matter how motivated, will never be a sprinter. By the time we're over the river we've put a safe distance between us and them, and we slow down to catch our breath.

"Fuck you, Archie," M gasps, leaning against his knees. "And fuck running. And fuck"—he sucks in a deep breath—"needing to breathe."

"Abram," Julie says. "What's Regional Security?"

Abram is gazing at downtown Pittsburgh with that glassy distance in his eyes.

"Hey!" Julie says, snapping her fingers at him. "What are we dealing with? Where will they be coming from?"

"I don't know," he murmurs without looking at her. "Everything's different."

I glance back at the bridge and find the Dead already uncomfortably close. In what felt like a few seconds, they have devoured most of our distance. This is, of course, the unique danger of the Dead. Their slowness lulls you. You think you're safe. You stop to rest, maybe start arguing, lost in some heated personal drama, and while your complex minds are weaving their tangled threads, the Dead are just walking, slow and steady and unconflicted.

"Keep moving," I say, already moving.

• • •

Our careful creep from the airfield to the city took over an hour. We make the return trip in twenty minutes. The plane's cargo ramp closes behind us with a solid *clack*, but I don't allow myself to feel safe. The image of the guards disappearing under a tide of corpses plays again in my head, and I keep it playing.

Abram heads for the cockpit and Julie and I go aft to check on our familial remains, but already I see trouble. There are dents and scratches all over the cabin, as if it recently housed a wild animal. My kids are peeking out from the restroom with fear in their eyes, and the object of this fear seems to be Julie's mother, who sits cross-legged on the carpet, glowering at us.

"Mom," Julie says, trying to keep her voice steady, "what did you do?"

Audrey is still chained to her chair, but the chair lies on its side next to her, detached from the floor. Her hands are a mess of dark blood, all the nails gone and much of the skin, her fingertips peeled to the bone.

Scattered on the carpet around her is a sizable collection of airplane parts.

Abram shouts something incoherent and I hear rapid footsteps from the front of the plane. Julie readies her pistol, but Abram ignores her and starts gathering the parts off the floor. Audrey lunges at him and Julie yanks her back by the collar.

"Chain that thing to something structural," Abram says with controlled rage, "or I'll debrain it with my bare hands."

"What did she do?" Julie asks, wide-eyed.

"Tore apart the cockpit. Ripped the controls right off the rod." He scoops as many parts as he can into his shirt and rushes back to the front.

"Mom," Julie says miserably, holding tight to the cable leash. "Why would you *do* that?"

It's impossible to decode the emotion on Audrey's face, if it's emotion at all. It looks like anger and defiance, and then with a slight change of angle, it becomes grief. Or it could be none of those. Just the random movements of a face with no one behind it.

Julie runs the cable directly through the floor hook where the chair latches in and cinches it short so that Audrey can just barely stand. Audrey watches impassively as her daughter locks her up, but Julie looks agonized. "I'm sorry, Mom," she mumbles as if her mother is howling accusations. "I'm sorry."

I decide to give them a moment. M and Nora are hovering over Abram, watching him reattach whatever can be reattached, mending snapped wires with electrical tape and broken parts with duct tape.

"Can we . . . help?" M offers.

Abram ignores him. The speed of his movements suggests the danger of our situation, and it occurs to me that every part of it was caused by two soft hearts: Julie's and mine. Two long-shot bets against the hardness of reality. Should we feel foolish for this? For taking life-threatening risks for things more important than life?

I wander back to the center of the plane. Down the staircase. Out the cargo door. I walk along the towering behemoth that was once my home and emerge from the shadow of the wing into the orange evening sun. I lean my back against the nose wheel, watching the swarm of the Dead filter out of the streets and converge into one mass on the runway ahead. Perhaps they will answer the question for me.

"R!" Julie shouts down from the cockpit window. "What are you doing? Get back in!"

"Is it ready?" I call up to her. "Can we fly?"

"He's still working on it but get in!"

I return my attention to the advancing horde. They're close enough to make out individual faces now. All their identifying characteristics—skin color, eye color, even hair color in some dusty specimens—have been absorbed into the tide of gray, but traces of their personalities remain. A tattoo. A piercing. And of course, their clothing choices. Even in the ravages of death, they are full of history.

How can I remind them?

"R!"

Her voice floats down from miles above me, shrill and desperate.

I step out from the shadow of the nose cone and let the sun warm my face.

"Who are you?" I ask the Dead. "You were people. You still are people. Which ones?"

I don't shout. I ask calmly like a friend at a pub table, the serious question that leads away from idle chatter and into real depth. Are they willing to follow me there? Or will they laugh me off, call me a buzzkill and then kill me?

"Who are you?" I say again, unable to keep some fear out of my voice as they lumber closer. "Think! Remember!"

I see a ripple in their faces. Hungry snarls flicker with uncertainty. I do something I doubt they've ever seen before: I take a step toward them.

"Who *are* you?"

They stop advancing. They look at the ground, then at the sky. There is . . . a moment. And then the ones bringing up the rear bump into the transfixed vanguard, and the moment ends. They remember one thing: that they're hungry. They rush forward to devour my newly Living flesh.

And then they begin to fall. Whatever seeds I may have planted exit their heads in sprays of blood. Whatever thoughts may have been forming disintegrate as bullets sever neurons and disperse their electricity into the evening air.

M and Nora are kneeling on the wing. Nora's shots are precise, each bullet finding a brain, picking off the ones closest to me. M's AK-47 sprays more indiscriminately but kills just as well through sheer volume of bullets. A scream builds in my throat; I want to curse my friends, but I can't. Their actions are rational. They live in this world and they want to stay here. They are not obligated to join me on this altar.

I retreat to the cargo ramp and close it and run to the wing. They're still firing.

"*Stop*!" I shout at them.

"We can't, R!" Nora says between shots. "They're swarming the plane!" She sights a young man climbing up the nose wheel and picks him off.

"They . . . can't get in!"

"You know they can," M grunts. "Tight swarm, pile up, break windows . . . remember that bus we did in Olympia?"

He unloads a volley into the advancing swarm, stripping away the front row.

I grip my face in my hands. What happened to my act of kindness? How did it become *this*? I have catalyzed two massacres in a single week. What is the flaw in me that turns my noblest efforts to shit?

I rush into the cockpit and find Julie testing switches while Abram wraps the last of the duct tape around the control rod. "Please say you're done," I beg him.

He settles into his seat and carefully pushes the mass of tape that surrounds a large switch. It clicks, and the engines roar to life. I hear M and Nora scrambling inside and slamming the emergency door shut. Zombies fall away from the plane as we blast into reverse, and by the time Abram has pulled as close to a U-turn as a jumbo jet can manage, we are clear of the swarm.

They stand among the motionless bodies of their peers, watching us depart, and just before distance makes their faces illegible, I see their expressions soften from hunger to longing. A subtle change, but visible to anyone who has felt it before. Perhaps somewhere under the scorched earth, a few seeds survived. Perhaps I am capable of good in the midst of my failures. Perhaps if I tell myself enough, if I repeat it over and over as we fly away from this continent, I can make myself believe it.

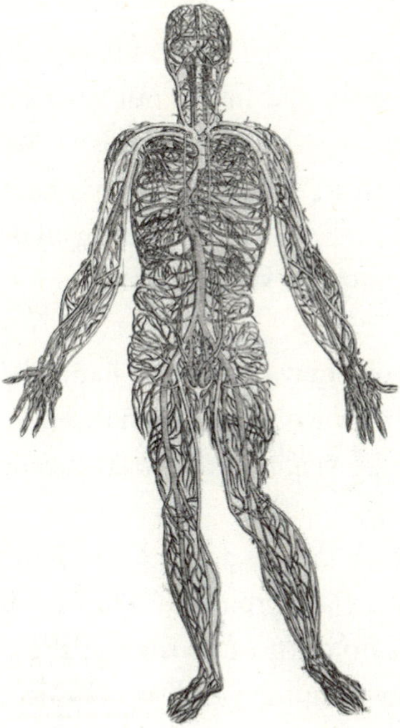

HIS FACE through the bars.

"How are you getting along with your fellow criminals, R—?"

"I've made lots of new friends."

My grandfather smiles. I don't. My face is mostly bruises, and smiling hurts. My muscles are lean and corded. The skin on my fists is finally starting to callus.

"I know prison's hard," he says, "but looks like you're taking it harder than most."

"I've been training."

"You've been getting your ass kicked."

I look at the floor. "Some of them don't like me."

"Why not?"

"Usually starts with my name."

"What about it?"

"They've never heard it before, so they don't like it."

He chuckles. "Never did figure out how a Bible-thumper like your mom came up with that hippie bullshit. Bet the kids at school got real creative with it." He notices my glare and returns to his track. "But you can't tell me you're getting all *this*"—he gestures to my face—"just for having a stupid name."

"No."

"So why don't your new classmates like you, R—?"

"Because they know I'm better than them."

He smiles bigger, revealing those translucent brown teeth. "Oh I *see*."

I spit on the floor, partly as a sign of disdain, partly because my mouth is filling with watery blood. "They're simple scum. Killers and rapists. There's no purpose to their crimes, they do it like animals, whenever they're hungry or horny or bored."

"And you're better than them because when you burned down a city, you did it for God?"

"Exactly."

He laughs. It sounds like dry bones cracking. "You did it because you're a pissed-off kid. You did it because your mommy died and you needed someone to blame, and you couldn't blame God because you know he's not real."

I grit my teeth as he talks. I don't understand what I feel toward him. It should be hate, but it isn't quite that.

"You and them, you're all liars. You make up bullshit to excuse your actions. You did it because God told you to, they did it because 'life is hard,' because they 'didn't have a choice.' Always hiding behind some noble excuse for ignoble deeds." He chuckles. "You're a bunch of pussies. The biggest, toughest bastard in this place is a fucking pussy, and you can tell him I said it."

"What do you want, *Grandpa*?" I snarl at him. "What can I do for you, *Pappy*?"

He shakes his head. "First of all, you can drop that fuzzy cardigan shit; it's not going to be like that with us. You can call me Mr. Atvist."

I nurture many dark beliefs about my place in the world, but it's a thrill to hear one so nakedly confirmed. "Okay, *Mr. Atvist*," I say, trying to halt the quaver in my voice. "Why do you keep coming here? My whole life, you've been barely a rumor. Now you're my only friend?"

He looks around the menagerie of muscled thugs and wild-eyed madmen, pausing on the empty cell across from me.

"Your partner, Paul Bark. You know he's already started burning again? Barely waited a week after he got out. He's got about three hundred people claiming membership in this—what are they calling it? 'Church of the Fire'? Looks like it's really taking off. All the corps are nervous. Even Fed's paying attention."

I stare at the floor.

"You founded a successful cult at age sixteen. You have something in you that moves people. As a businessman, that interests me."

"Get out," I mutter.

He chuckles again and stands up. The guard takes his chair and opens the cellblock door for him. "You're right about one thing," Mr. Atvist says. "You *are* better than them. But not because of your moral pretensions."

"Why, then?" I say through my teeth.

"You're better because you're an Atvist, and they're not. Because you have a future, and they don't."

A tiny crack forms in my shell. Before I can seal it, a glint of desperation shines through. "Can you get me out?" I ask my grandfather.

He smiles. "Of course I can."

He walks away.

• • •

"R," Julie says.

My eyes are already open but I blink them, snapping back to the present.

"Are you okay?"

It's a basic question, often asked by strangers. I give it the response it deserves: a shrug and a nod.

"It wasn't your fault, you know," she says, and it takes me a moment to realize she's talking about the recent massacre, not the dark path unfolding in my memories.

"It wasn't your fault," she repeats. "You did what you thought was right with the knowledge you had at the time. That's all anyone can ever do."

She is not inside my head, and I'm dismayed by how much this relieves me. There was a time when I wanted nothing more than for her to visit me in here, to know my thoughts, to know *me*. When did I revoke her invitation? I wish the absolution she's offering were for the wretch in my basement, but she has never even met him.

"Are we still going to Iceland?" I ask her.

We are sitting on the floor in the rear of the plane, leaning against the wall, watching her mother gnaw at the shredded flesh of her fingers. Julie has given up trying to stop her.

"R," she says, giving me a pained look. "Do you understand that I have to do this?"

"Do you understand that you can't save her?"

The words don't feel like mine. They feel like his. A bitter young man sulking in his cell, whispering cruelties through the bars. Is he calling out to his counterpart, the girl in Julie's basement? The scarred orphan who cries in her sleep and kills without blinking, who's convinced she's unworthy of love?

We were building a home. It was going to be beautiful. How did we let them lock us out?

"Yes," Julie replies to my cold question, and the lack of anger in it stings me. Instead of exploding, she shrinks inward, clutching her knees and staring at the floor. "I understand."

I want to pull her against me and melt our barriers with a simple warm gesture, but the wretch holds me back. He keeps my arms folded, my face stiff, and he whispers, *You'll hurt her. She'll hurt you.* He whispers, *Not safe.*

Nora brushes through the curtain and sits next to me. The three of us watch Audrey, whose eyes drift around the cabin with a vaguely troubled squint.

"I'm sorry, R," Nora says.

I nod.

"They were just too far gone."

I nod.

"One thing you learn as a nurse: you've got to let the gone ones go so you can save the ones that are still here."

Julie buries her chin in her knees. Her eyes are damp.

M is leaning in the doorway, reluctant to intrude. "Didn't kill *all* of them," he offers with a shrug.

"Yeah," Nora says with an optimistic lilt. "A few dozen, maybe, but there were hundreds." She elbows me. "You saved hundreds of people, R."

Another nod is the only response I can manage. Our friends have no idea how many fights are inside us. They can't hear our silent shouting.

M sighs and comes inside. He settles down next to Nora, leaving a few polite feet between them. Abram appears in the doorway behind him and pauses to take in the scene: a Dead woman in the middle of the room and the four of us lined up in front of her like an intervention. But he has no wry comments for us. His expression is remote.

"We're heading south," he says. "Just wanted to let you know so you don't shoot me when you see the ocean."

We all glance at Julie for her reaction, but she doesn't seem to be listening.

"Iceland's not south," Nora says.

"We can't go through New York. Axiom has defenses all over the state. We need to go around."

"That's a big detour. Do we have enough fuel?"

"I'll cut around Long Island as close as I can, then up toward Boston and—"

"Do it," Julie mumbles into her knees. "Whatever you need to do, do it. Just get us off this insane continent."

Abram nods. Julie notices us all looking at her and she straightens, resting the back of her head against the window. "Maybe we can come back someday with an Icelandic army and save everyone. Ella. David and Marie . . . even Evan if you want, Nora. But for now . . . it's like you said, right?" Her voice is an exhausted sigh spiked with bitterness. "Let the gone ones go."

I can feel the turmoil in everyone, but it's hard to argue anymore. We've traveled the country and found death in every corner. We've searched for resistance and found comfortable slaves. We have grand ideas but no way to share them, because the world has plugged its ears, wrapped itself in a blanket of radio silence, and ordered everyone into bomb shelters to wait for death in the dark.

So it seems we'll say good-bye to our country. To our continent. To everything and everyone we've known. We'll let our cities burn in fanaticism and drown in oppression, leave our homes half-built to be ruined by rain and rats. We will pile all our memories onto this vast barge of land and we will watch the whole mess sink.

As I sit contemplating this, an unfamiliar voice interrupts my thoughts.

"New," Audrey says.

Julie jumps to her feet. She flattens against the wall, eyes as wide as they can go. Her mother is looking at her. Not just allowing her glassy stare to drift across her but *looking* at her.

"What?" Julie says in a trembling whisper.

"N-new . . . Y-york."

Julie blinks away a tear. "*Mom?*"

Audrey looks around the cabin. She makes brief eye contact with each of us. Then she slumps over and stares at the floor, wheezing softly.

"Audrey?" Julie drops to her knees in front of her mother, clutching the air as she resists the urge to touch her. "Audrey Arnaldsdóttir?" She risks a quick caress of her mother's cold cheek, a quick smile through the tears. "Do you . . . do you *remember* me, Mom? Your daughter? Julie?"

Audrey releases a low groan and continues to examine the carpet.

"Doesn't happen that fast," M grunts.

Julie's eyes dart toward him, instinctively igniting into anger, but he continues.

"Small stuff comes first. Places. Things. It's a while before we can handle . . . people."

"But . . . it's her, right?" Julie says. "She's remembering where she lived?"

M shrugs. "First thing that came back to me . . . Cream of Wheat cereal. Next thing . . . apartment in Seattle."

For the first time since the blood-soaked day they met, Julie smiles at M.

"It was just parroting," Abram says. His arms are folded, his posture skeptical, but his slightly widened eyes betray him. "I said 'New York' and it said it back. They do that sometimes."

"Brook . . . lyn," Audrey sighs at the floor.

Abram's eyes widen further.

"*Mom,*" Julie says, shaking her head in giddy disbelief. "Mom, are you there? Do you remember?" She leans close and grabs Audrey's shoulders, trying to make eye contact. "You met Dad on a flight. John Grigio. You fell in love. You moved to Brooklyn. You performed your poems at his band's shows and worked at the library and signed up for every local play you could find."

"Easy," M says under his breath. "Too much at once . . . not good."

Julie seems unaware of anyone but the woman in front of her. She has caught Audrey's gaze and bobs her head to maintain it as Audrey's eyes try to escape.

"You were still young when you had me, Mom. You and Dad knew you weren't ready, you were just a couple of broke artists in a studio apartment in an abandoned corner of New York, and you argued about it for weeks. Dad said it was wrong to bring a child into this fucked-up world, you said it was wrong not to. You said the kid you'd make was exactly what this fucked-up world needed."

Julie laughs and wipes at her eyes. Audrey's have stopped darting and have settled on the floor. Julie bends low, trying to catch them again. "You were my age, Mom. I just turned twenty. Can you wish me happy birthday?"

Audrey hunches inward, making soft, inscrutable noises. Then she shoots to her feet and rips off her lab coat, tossing it away like it's on fire. She stands naked in the middle of the empty cabin, the hopeless ruin of her body on full display.

"Oh, Jules . . . ," Nora murmurs sadly.

Julie looks up at her mother, freshly stricken by the sight. The tears in her eyes have never really dried, they've just ebbed and flowed, and now they're flowing again.

Audrey looks down at the gaping hole in her side. She passes a hand through it. Her exposed lung inflates, and a mournful howl escapes her slack mouth.

"Mom," Julie whimpers, a meaningless, ineffectual noise. "Mom, please."

Abram shakes his head and returns to the cockpit. The impossibility of Julie's Icelandic hopes is too obvious for comment. No matter what science-fiction utopia we may find there, her mother is going to die.

I notice Sprout peeking through the gap in the curtain. She hesitates. She watches Julie for a moment before following her father.

"On our left," Abram announces over the PA in a tired drone, "as far away as possible, you'll see Axiom corporate headquarters, aka Branch 1, aka New York City. If you'd like to be distracted from sad thoughts, feel free to be frightened now."

Julie is beyond any comfort I can give. A clumsy pat on the back won't help and may hurt. I can't begin to imagine what she needs right now, so I decide to give her space.

I push through the curtain and wander up the aisle, watching New York through the windows. The high-rises resemble a grove of burnt trees in the hazy distance. The setting sun reflects off them like fire. We are many miles away, safe above the glittering Atlantic, but I can feel eyes on me. Scopes and targeting lasers. Perhaps a new LOTUS segment calling for us to be shot down with a less-than-subtle montage of famous plane crashes. None of this will matter. We are beyond their reach, and soon we'll be outside their world altogether, removed from their savage ecosystem.

Struggling to find the peace this should bring me, I move to the western window and watch the sun fall into the ocean, breaking into a thousand pieces on the water. For a moment, I feel it. A sense of ground swept clean, of new possibilities poking through the loam. Then, as I always do, I keep looking, and I find something that kills my reverie. I blink and I squint, but it doesn't disappear. I run to the plane's midsection, the window closest to the wing, and I look out at the engines.

A man looks back at me.

"Abram?" I shout toward the cockpit.

Abram doesn't respond. Perhaps he has no room in his head for what I want to tell him. And how can I tell him? How can I express to him this absurdity: that there's a huge, musclebound Dead man clinging to one of the engine posts. His blue-gray skin is covered in frost, but he's not frozen solid. He's moving. He's inching forward.

"Abram!"

I hear him grumble and stir in the cockpit; I hear his belt unlatch, but the Dead man has grasped the rim of the engine. He is pulling himself toward some inscrutable goal, perhaps the scent of the tiny family in the cockpit ahead, willfully unaware of the chasm of sky between them.

Abram steps out of the cockpit. He registers the urgency on my face and opens his mouth to ask. Then the man slips over the rim of the engine.

There are two explosions. The first is a reddish-black burst from the back of the engine as the bodybuilder's hard-earned mass is spread across Long Island like crop duster spray. The second is an eruption of fire that completely engulfs the wing, and when it clears, the engine is gone. So is a large chunk of the wing. Burning fuel streams from the hole in long snakes of flame.

As the plane begins to bank, as Abram disappears into the cockpit and everyone else rushes up from the rear, shouting and screaming, my mind is stuck on the least useful thought:

We never named it. I grew the seeds of my third life in this plane. Julie and I closed our vast distance in it. It rescued us and carried us around the country, and we never gave it a name.

Everyone is cramming into the cockpit, asking what to do, and Abram is shouting that there's nothing we can do, we're going down hard, sit down and buckle up and secure your own before helping others, all a soft, slow slur in the back of my awareness.

Julie was good at this. Granting life to inanimate objects. She turned a Mercedes into Mercey. What would she call a 747?

I topple across the aisle as Abram overcorrects the bank, trying to take some weight off the wounded wing.

David.

I smile to myself, falling into a chair next to Julie. "David Boeing," I tell her, barely able to contain my pleasure.

"What?" she shrieks.

"I'm naming the plane. It's David Boeing."

She looks at me with total incomprehension, but I'm still smiling. It's good. Maybe I can do this too.

"R," she says, and I suddenly realize that I misread her face. It's not incomprehension but the opposite. It's the grim understanding from which I'm hiding.

"R, if we—"

"Please don't," I blurt.

She chokes it back. She jumps out of her seat and braces against the cockpit doorway as the plane bucks and shakes. "I'm sorry," she says, turning her watery eyes from Abram to Sprout. "I'm so sorry."

"I don't care," Abram says through his teeth as he battles the wild controls.

Julie pulls herself away from Sprout's panicked gaze and stumbles back down the aisle.

"Buckle *up*, Jules!" Nora shouts, one hand on M's shoulder as he clings to his seat with rigor mortis stiffness, his face ashen, eyes wide, looking more corpselike than I've ever seen him. He stayed relatively composed for our first crash landing, but that one was soft. This one will be hard, if it's a landing at all. This one may call for screams.

Julie grabs my hand and pulls me to the back of the plane where her mother sits on the floor, clinging to her cable for an anchor while the plane rocks and bounces.

"Hold on, Mom," Julie says. "Please hold on."

She slips into the last remaining row of seats and takes a deep, slow breath, then looks at me with sudden calm. "Sit with me?"

I sit with her. The oxygen masks dangle in front of us but we don't bother. We look out the window at the rapidly approaching shore of what my basement memories call East Atlantic Beach. Beyond that, JFK International Airport, and everywhere around it . . .

Madness. Monsters. A city full of death. Even if we survive this plunge, it's hard to see a future.

"Stop it," Julie says, watching the side of my face as the runway approaches at a wild angle. "Be with me."

I look into her glistening eyes and the roaring around me goes quiet. Strange, how complications melt away in the face of disaster. How all the fear and shame and tangled knots of logic suddenly dissolve in the heat, leaving only a core of love that cares nothing for the noise in our heads, that dismisses our arguments and ignores our hesitations. A love that simply is.

In this moment, however brief it might be, everything is clear.

Julie kisses me and I kiss her back, ordering myself not to pull away, ever, because whatever might be ending today, this is how I want it to end.

My eyes are closed, all senses focused on her, so there is no terrible buildup to the impact. I am kissing Julie, I am kissing Julie, I am—

WE

THERE ARE MANY EARTHS inside the earth. The outermost is the busiest, with its oceans and forests and cities, its buzzing, hissing, chirping, grunting, roaring, speaking, and singing. This is the surface, the present, the game board on which life plays. Beneath the surface is the hidden world of holes and tunnels, where creatures creep and slither and hold secret meetings in the strata of eons past. And at the center is the fire that forged it all, Earth's raging, spinning heart, full of endless momentum, always ready to quake and erupt, forever growling *change*.

The earth likes change. It grows bored with balance; rest makes it restless. The moment its inhabitants think they know the rules, it shakes the board clear and moves on to the next game.

Next epoch. Next era. Next evolution.

We swim up through the mantle and into the bedrock, through Paleocene and Pliocene and Holocene, through our own bones and shells from species to species, generation to generation, each piece of us recognizing its remains as we float past them, indulging in brief bursts of nostalgia.

This is something we do. We remember and observe, and in the Higher levels where such things are possible, we hope.

One thing we do not do is act. We are books, not authors. There are times—like this present age of soft lines and translucent barriers and power vacuums filling with poison—when we wish we could be more. But the world belongs to the living, and they have not yet asked for our help.

So we float upward, through young rock and dark dirt and into the lowest depths of a once-great city. We pass through stagnant water tunnels and ancient brick sewage pipes clogged with century-spanning strata of shit, then up into the dense web of cables that were the neurons of New York's brain before a thousand bullets silenced its thoughts.

Now New York is mindless. Gray and rotting. An undead city walking without purpose, repeating echoes of its former life until they're worn beyond recognition, and always, always seeking flesh.

We breach the surface and the noise hits us, a human density rarely found in the new world. The queue forms somewhere in the muck of the Jersey City Bayou, condenses on the floating Holland Footbridge, and spills out into a cramped mess of fear and desperation against the Manhattan border gate.

It's here, within sight of the razor wire fence and its weary customs agents, that we find the boy and his new guardians. They stand in a small park in a crowd of battered refugees, carrying only overstuffed backpacks after hiding their van in a suburban garage. There is no room for vehicles in this coveted real estate. There is barely room for people. Every inch of Manhattan has been put to use, eighty-floor high-rises converted into tenements, parks into high-yield corn fields, the streets themselves into sprawling tent cities. Only the scythe of the modern mortality rate creates vacancies for the crowd outside. Concrete flood barriers form a wall around the island, and the swollen East River and Hudson surround it like invading armies, splashing over the top in every stiff breeze. Submerged to her chest, Lady Liberty is no longer a proud torchbearer standing tall for freedom. She is a drowning swimmer waving for help.

"Electricity," Gebre says. "Plumbing. Law enforcement. And *zero* undead hordes."

Gael sighs and picks his pack off the muddy grass as the line advances. "Yeah."

"They won't put us on salvage crews. There has to be thousands of kids in there and they will need teachers."

"Hopefully for more diverse subjects than they did in UT-AZ. My doctorate doesn't qualify me to teach rifle maintenance."

"Gael, Gael, Gael," Gebre says, gesturing grandly to the crumbled high-rises beyond the fence. "It's New York City."

The boy watches his guardians through a dark veil. On their insistence, he is once again hiding behind his Ray-Bans. He has not spoken since they deterred him from DC, but not because he's angry. He could have left them if he chose to and finished his journey alone, but he stayed with them. He followed them here to this sinking island of denial, tilting his ear to some obscure suggestion. A voice from the deep halls of the Library, the rustling of countless pages forming a whisper.

"What do you think, Rover?" Gebre asks. "You want to go to school? I can teach you wars and governments, Gael can teach you quarks and bosons. All kinds of useless things!"

The boy is not listening. He is looking south down Canal Street, at a procession of white commuter vans. The boy sees the grim faces of the drivers, but the passengers are only silhouettes. He peers hard at the tinted windows, trying to penetrate the glass.

"Ages and skills," the customs agent says, approaching Gebre with a clipboard.

"I'm forty-three," Gebre replies. "Gael's thirty-four, and Rover's . . . ten."

"I taught quantum physics at Brown University," Gael says.

The agent looks up blankly. "We don't have any need for—"

"*Applied* quantum physics," Gebre interjects, flashing a smile. "He can . . . design better bullets?"

Gael stares coldly at the agent. The agent makes a mark on his board. "And you?" he grunts toward Gebre without looking up.

"Gun maintenance," Gebre says, still grinning.

"My husband is being modest," Gael says with a subdued ferocity. "He has a doctorate in world history."

Gebre sighs. "Fine, yes, I'm a historian. And I'm also very good at cleaning M16s."

The agent glances between him and Gael. He makes another mark on his board. "We'll find you something. Always new openings in Salvage."

Gael and Gebre exchange a glance.

"And what about the boy here, is he—"

The agent drops his clipboard.

The boy is staring hard at the vans as they wait in front of a service gate. His sunglasses are in his hand. His impossible eyes are wide, trying to drill through the vans' tinted glass and see the people inside, because somewhere in today's haul of agitators and underperformers, there is a signal, a beacon, like someone is trying to tell him something.

And are we trying to tell him something? Are we speaking to him now? A book speaks whenever someone reads it, and only its reader knows what it has said.

A hand clamps onto the boy's shoulder.

"I've got another uncategorized," the agent says into his walkie. "Juvenile. Severe iris gilding. Sending him your way."

"Let go of him!" Gael shouts.

"He's infected," the agent says. "He'll be taken to our facilities for care."

Three guards emerge from the customs booth and push Gael and Gebre aside.

"Please don't do this," Gebre says. "He's not Dead."

"Uncategorized are being studied for a new plague management program," the agent says. "Your boy's going to help make the world safe again."

The boy listens to his guardians' voices. They rise steadily, from imploring to demanding to desperate as grim-faced men lead him beyond the fence. The last thing he hears sounds like a promise:

"We'll find you! We won't leave you with them!"

What is the ratio, he wonders? Three bad people are dragging him away from two good people; is there more bad than good? Is there any consensus on humanity?

He catches one last glimpse of the vans. He sees the pitted surface of the window glass, gnarled silica bubbles and dust particles like mountains. But his vision crashes against the darkness inside. He sees a familiar silhouette, a shadow against a shadow and a dim memory of warmth. Then three bad people haul him away.

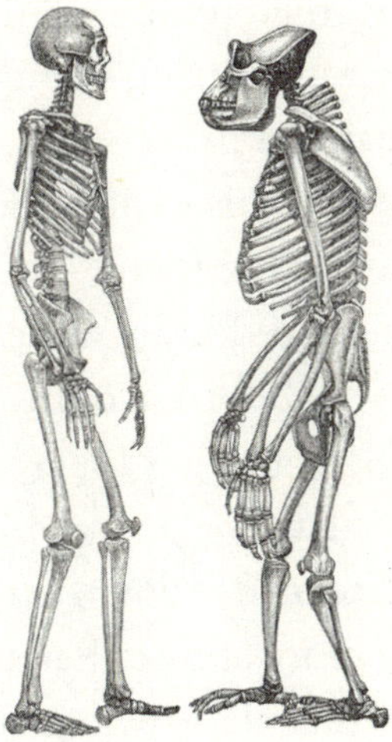

I

THE STAIN.

There is a new stain in my cell.

My cellmate—he just sneered when I asked his name, like I wasn't worthy of even that front-porch intimacy—has contributed more than a few stains during his tenancy. I've watched him piss through the bars at guards in the hall. I've watched him vomit onto the floor after drinking some rotten concoction of fruit and cleaning products. I've tried to avoid watching him when he hunches in his bunk, grunting and thrusting to the thought of whatever blimp-breasted aberration might tickle his brain stem.

He hasn't always used his own fluids, though. Sometimes he's used mine. He has spattered my blood with fists and feet, and occasionally, when he's caught me on a bad day, when my head is full of fading memories and the creeping realization that I will not get to experience the life we're all afforded, that I will miss all the milestones and die a half-formed thing—on those days, he has smeared my tears into the concrete, mixing them with my blood.

My cellmate has painted many stains, but today's is his masterpiece. This one obliterates his earlier efforts. It covers them completely as it spreads across the floor.

Prison security becomes looser when the world outside is collapsing. It becomes possible to acquire pencils, for example, for drawing and journaling and other therapeutic expressions.

The cellblock door bangs open and boots march toward me. The camera in the corner stares down at my cellmate's prone form. I can think of nothing more absurd than the fact that I'll be be punished for this, here in this place whose sole purpose is to remove dangerous men from society. Well, I have removed one. Let God punish me for preempting his plan, but here on Earth I should be praised for my pragmatism.

The boots stop in front of my cell. My grandfather watches the blood pool around my bare feet. He smiles.

"I think you're ready."

He nods to the two men at his sides—not prison guards; I don't recognize their militaristic black uniforms—and they leave us. He leans close to the bars.

"What do you think, R—? Do you think you're ready?"

I grab his shirt and pull his face against the bars hard enough to bruise his papery skin. "Three years," I snarl. "You left me here for *three years*."

He is grimacing and chuckling like he's wrestling with a toddler. "Easy, kid! Take it easy on the old man."

I throw him backward and glower at him while he adjusts his collar.

"What was it you said last time I was here? That you were learning a lot? Well, you had more to learn. And now I think you've learned it."

My eyes drift around the prison. Most of the cells are empty now.

The law machine is rusty and missing a thousand cogs, and no one has time to repair it. It won't be long before the meals stop coming.

"Why did you kill that man, R—?"

I don't answer.

"You went to great lengths to minimize casualties in your fires. 'Life belongs to God,' you said. So why did you kill that man?"

"He'd done terrible things," I mumble. "He deserved to die."

"That's everyone who ever lived. If you're God's executioner, why haven't you been killing folks your whole life? Why's this pig fucker your first?"

The prison blurs in my vision. I focus on the bloody handprints I left on my grandfather's shirt. "Because he hurt me. Because I hated him."

"Because *you wanted to kill him.*"

I nod.

"And that's what it boils down to, R—. What *you* want. No one really does anything that doesn't benefit them. Behind every moral stance is a selfish desire. The harshest asceticism, the saintliest altruism . . . they all satisfy some inner urge. To feel strong, to feel needed, to feel *good*. No matter what your moral kick, it's always about *you*. Because who else is there?"

He approaches the bars again. The rage has drained out of me. I can't bring myself to look at his narrow brown eyes so I look down at my feet. The blood oozing between my toes.

"You're alone, R—. You're the only person. All these things walking around you might look like people, but they only exist in relation to *you*. They are what they do for you and how they make you feel. For all you know, they might disappear whenever you're not looking at them."

The blood is already cold. The man who shared this tiny cube with me for more than three years is fading from existence before my eyes. He's transparent; I can see the concrete through his inconsequential heap of meaty debris; I am already forgetting what little I knew about him.

"It takes us a lifetime of confusion and struggle to realize what animals are born knowing," my grandfather says in his smoky growl. "That there's nothing to know. That we're searching for meaning in an empty room. That the purpose of life is to live as long as you can, eat as much as you can, fuck as much as you can, to spread your genes and your ideas and turn as much of the world as you can into *you*."

He grins, showing those crooked brown teeth. "And you know what? It's *fun*. Once you know what life's really about, it's fucking *fun*."

A shudder runs from my sticky toes through my groin and up into my skull. "What do you want?"

"I want you to work for me."

"Doing what?"

"Times are changing. Commerce is dying. Everyone's running for the hills to grow corn and wait for the Rapture, but I won't stop." His grin has stiffened into a fierce grimace, lips tight on his teeth. "You hear me, R—Atvist? I'll never stop. The end of the world is an opportunity. We just have to figure out how to seize it."

I look around at this prison where I spent the better part of my youth. I became an adult here. I shed my teenage skin here, stepped out of it muscled and scarred and powerful, and then I remained in this cell, staring at these bars, brooding over the rules of a fictional universe while the real one outside moved on.

I have never touched a woman. I have never tasted a beer. But I have killed a man and I have razed a city.

"I'll help," I tell my grandfather. "I have ideas."

His grin returns. His breath wafts through the gaps in his teeth, tobacco and stale coffee. "Can't wait to hear them, kid."

He pulls a keycard out of his wallet. He swipes it over the cell door, the lock clicks, and I'm free. I step into the hall and follow Mr. Atvist out of the prison, leaving a trail of red footprints on the concrete.

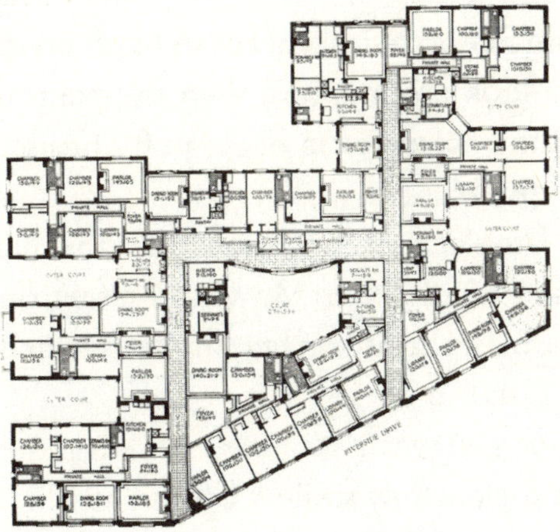

I HAVE KILLED MANY PEOPLE. I have eaten their flesh and drank their memories, men, women, and children. I will never deny or forget this, but I will accept it. I did monstrous things because I was a monster, driven by unfathomable hungers and barely conscious throughout, lacking name and identity and moral framework. I have mourned this dark chapter, learned what I could from it, and turned the page. I have forgiven my second life.

But what about my first? There is no fanciful plague to blame for this. My original self is not an absurd ghoul pulled from pulp fiction. He has a name; he has a mother, a father, and a grandfather, and he made his choices in the same mundane way anyone makes them.

Who is that man? I inhabit his body and possess his memories, but he is alien to me. I feel more kinship with the mindless corpse than this bitter, rudderless, world-blaming wretch. But somehow, through some obscure alchemy of time, those two elements merged . . . and became me.

I open my eyes.

Steel bars. The stench of sweat and mildew. Am I still in the dream? I'm lying flat on my stomach, so I pull myself to my knees and attempt to look around, and then the pain hits. My fingers move to touch the epicenter; a huge, puffy bruise rises from my forehead like a tumor.

"Always the late sleeper," says a soft voice that definitely doesn't live in the prison of my past. My vision clears on the face of a beautiful woman. The bruise on her forehead matches mine. A dry chuckle creeps out of me.

"Your head . . . Did we . . . ?"

Julie offers a melancholy smile. "Looks like it."

"Kissing contusions," Nora mumbles. "Serves you right for being disgusting."

The floor under my hands is stiff commercial carpet, its mottled beige designed to be the sum of all stains, victory by preemptive surrender. The room is bare, and all of David Boeing's passengers sit on the floor, leaning wearily against the walls, except for my kids and Julie's mother. I have a moment of panic before I see them in their own room across the hall, visible through barred interior windows. Audrey paces in a circle, snapping her teeth, and Joan and Alex huddle in a corner, hiding from her. The buzzing fluorescent lights turn our faces the same sickly gray as theirs.

"You're lucky, though," Nora continues. "You slept through a fun interrogation session. First of many, I'm sure."

I scan her for injuries and have a moment of shock at her missing finger before remembering that happened long ago, in another life that even Julie is left to wonder about. Nora has a few scratches, but these are probably from the rough landing. When Axiom moves from convince to coerce, it doesn't stop with scratches.

"What did they want this time?" Julie says.

"They're still trying to figure you out. Sounds like whatever they're doing to control the Dead is a pretty crude science. Good for making mules but not much else. They want more sophisticated slaves, like our Nearlies. The ones they think you 'made.'" She smiles darkly. "They want your magic, Jules. Just teach them your spells and we can all go home."

Julie shakes her head, unable to verbalize the absurdity. The magic that confounds them is humanity. The naturally occurring, slow acting, unpredictably potent product of conscious minds connecting. These madmen want to synthesize love. They want to manufacture it, weaponize it, and use it to control people. It's such a ludicrous scheme it would be funny if they weren't trampling the world in pursuit of it.

Abram is shaking his head too, but I sense his disbelief has a different target.

"What?" Julie says to him.

"I'm just enjoying this so much," he says, slumped against the wall like an alleyway vagrant. His blood-stained beige jacket is gone; his gray tank top reveals an array of cuts and bruises, some fresh, some old. "I thought Axiom was insane, but they're only trying to *manage* the plague, maybe turn it into something useful. You're the ones trying to talk the Dead out of being Dead." He looks at me with incredulous disdain. "You're the ones unleashing a horde and then standing in front of it asking it questions, like a fucking zombie therapist." He shakes his head again. "What kind of cartoon do you think you live in?"

I meet his gaze levelly. I won't apologize to a statue for trying to take a step. "It has to start somewhere."

"You were *talking* to them!" He laughs and throws up his hands. "You think you can cure a plague with *words*?"

"Words are ideas."

I'm not sure where these ones are coming from. I hear a whisper in my head, like the rustling of pages.

"Every cure to every plague has started with an idea."

Abram lets out a deep sigh and slumps lower. He tugs Sprout against his shoulder but she resists, remaining upright and giving me a curious look.

"R," Julie says. "I think that was a new syllable record."

I shrug. I haven't been counting.

"Stopped fighting it yet?" M asks with a subtle smile, and I'm suddenly uncomfortable in this axis of attention. I stand up and gaze out the exterior windows, hoping to lose myself in a New York panorama. But the view is the brick wall of a neighboring high-rise. A few floors up, a gigantic billboard grins down at me from the roof, the model's eyes covered by a solar panel like he wanted his identity hidden.

"So you're the ones."

Everyone sits up. Eyes dart for the source of the voice.

"The salmon, the zebra, the goldfinch, and the goldfish, right?"

It's coming from the adjacent room. A woman's voice, high and squeaky enough to penetrate the wall with surprising clarity.

"Why did you get caught? I was rooting for you, whoever you are."

"Uh . . . who are *you*?" Julie asks the wall.

"Fellow grumbler. Month two of a life sentence. Welcome to Freedom Tower."

Abram hops to a crouch and puts his face close to the wall. "Where are the guard stations? Have you found any patrol gaps? What's your plan?"

There is silence for a few seconds. Then I hear singing. "Mon ami, mon ami, la la la la la . . ."

"Hello?" Abram says.

"Have you seen the city yet?" the woman asks, abruptly cutting off her song. "Densest pop in North America so you'd expect reality to be taut, but nowhere's more surreal. Streets hold their shape but people don't. No flying frogs or portal ponds but the place itself is madness. Inverted island, air underwater, everybody clawing at the bubble."

We all look at each other.

"What's your name?" Julie asks.

"My name's embarrassing," she says. "I go by H. Tomsen. Or

just Tomsen. Or just H. What's your name? Are you the goldfinch or the goldfish or the Goldman? How are things at the dome? I heard them talking about a takeover a while back. God, I miss the world."

She speaks with a clipped, rapid cadence that sounds less like conversation and more like the random firing of synapses. Julie waits for an opening, then says, "I'm Julie."

Abram returns to his slouch against the wall, apparently deciding we won't be gaining any intel from our neighbor. M listens with a bemused smile, but Julie and Nora show particularly sharp interest.

"You have a . . . distinct way with words," Nora says. "Are you a fan of the Exed World Almanac?"

"God, I miss the Almanac," the voice sighs. "God, I miss input and output. Been working on new issues in here but not much to report when the world is a room. Everywhere's exed and pop is always one—except for that time a spider joined me."

Julie and Nora glance at each other with widening eyes.

"Wait . . . ," Julie says. "Are you saying you *make* the Almanac? Are you a member of DBC?"

A burst of giggling pierces the wall.

"Tomsen?"

"Used to be. Now DBC's a member of me. Hold on, let's introduce."

I hear some metallic clicking. A squeaking hinge. A few footsteps. Then the door to our cell swings open.

"What the hell?" Abram says as we all jump to our feet.

"Nice to meet you, Julie," Tomsen says, thrusting a hand out to Abram. "H. Tomsen."

"Uh, hi," Julie says, leaning in to intercept the handshake. "I'm Julie. Hi."

Tomsen looks somewhere between Nora's age and Abram's, but her appearance is ambiguous in more ways than one. With her face weathered by sun and scars, it's hard to say if she's a hard-worn youth or a well-preserved matron. Her skin is copper, her short curls are reddish brown, and her eyes are bright green, suggesting a heritage mixed beyond labeling. She wears a loose safari shirt and cargo pants whose patina of dirt and engine grease hints at a rough life on the road. Her wiry body seems to hide in their billowy folds.

"Who are you?" Abram says, moving to shield Sprout. "You're not a prisoner?"

"Of course I'm a prisoner," Tomsen says. "I'm in prison."

"You just walked out!"

"Well I'm not going to sit in prison for two months without learning how to get out of my cell."

Her features are fine and her eyes are striking, but pretty isn't the right word for her. Handsome? Attractive.

Abram shakes his head, grabs Sprout's hand, and pushes past Tomsen, scanning the corridor. Except for the one with our Dead family members in it, all the rooms appear empty, though fist-sized holes in the windows hint at earlier occupants. Whoever they were, they have been processed, their useful juices extracted, their husks expelled.

Abram tries the elevator. It emits a negatory squawk, flashing a red light on a keycard slot. He goes for the stairs.

"What's that person's name?" Tomsen whispers to Julie.

"Abram."

"Abram!" Tomsen calls after him. "Twenty locked doors and twenty floors of beige-coats between us and street. Mixed-use building. Prison slash barracks."

Abram pauses at the stairwell entrance.

"Room service comes every hour. You want to be in your cell when they get here or problems."

Abram's shoulders rise and fall for a moment, then they sag. He returns to the cell.

"Maybe steal a gun later?" Tomsen suggests. "Try again with a gun? You seem like a gun guy."

"Okay wait, hold on," Nora says, putting a hand out and shaking her head as if to clear away distractions. "We can talk escape later—what did you mean DBC is a member of you?"

Tomsen shrugs. "It's me. I write the Almanac."

Julie and Nora look at each other, cover their mouths, and squeal.

"We're huge fans," Julie gushes.

"*Huge* fans," Nora elaborates.

Tomsen stares at them, startled into silence by this outpouring.

"But where's the rest of your crew?" Julie says, glancing into the windows of the other cells. "Did they escape?"

Tomsen shakes her head. "Don't know about crews. Never had a crew. Tried to get one back in school days. They escaped."

Nora frowns. "But . . . who's the 'we'? Who's DBC?"

"Dead Beat Cartographers. Used to be the family band, me and Mom and Dad, then just me and Dad, and now . . . just me!" She flashes a stiff smile.

Julie's fangirl fervor cools into concern. "You've been doing all that exploration . . . alone?"

"Of course not alone, I'd go crazy! Barbara goes with me."

"But . . . Barbara is your van, isn't it?"

Tomsen lets out an uproarious giggle. "No, no, Barbara is definitely not a van."

"Oh," Julie laughs uncertainly. "Good. I thought—"

"She's an RV. Vans don't have bathrooms."

Julie and Nora exchange another glance.

"I have to go now," Tomsen says, looking around for a clock that isn't there and fidgeting from foot to foot. "Guards coming. Nice to meet you people. I didn't meet all of you. Only two actually. I'll meet the rest of you later when the guards aren't coming."

M waves from the back of the room, still sitting against the wall. "Hey Tomsen," he says. "Where's the coffee?"

"They don't bring coffee. Mostly water and Carbtein." She cocks her head. "Why? Do you like coffee? I don't like it. Makes me jittery."

M smiles and shrugs. "Just wondering. Marcus, by the way."

Tomsen waves at him. She steps backward out of our cell, then pauses in the doorway and looks at Julie. "They'll probably take your Dead friends now."

Julie's face stiffens. "What?"

"Uncategorized usually go straight to Orientation. Sometimes here first for temp storage but never more than a day." She flattens her lips into a sympathetic line. "Sorry."

She turns and disappears into the corridor. I hear her cell door click shut, then her shaky falsetto again. "Attention, mon ami . . ."

Our door remains open. Everyone but M stands crowded in front of it, staring into the hall outside, wrestling the urge to run.

"Jules," Nora says. "Don't."

Julie steps out into the dim, flickering hall. She reaches between the bars of her mother's cell window.

"You okay, Mom?"

Audrey stops pacing and fixes her daughter with an inscrutable gaze. Any injuries she might have suffered in the crash are unnoticeable amongst the general ruin of her flesh.

"I just met the author of the Almanac, Mom. Remember the Almanac? Remember how excited you got when we found the Canada issue?"

Audrey glances toward the window of Tomsen's cell. Julie's face lights up.

"Yes! That's her, right there in that room. It's just one girl, Mom. She's been out there all these years, searching the world. She even has stories from outside America. Don't you want to talk to her?"

The elevator's light winks on. I hear the distant whir of machinery.

"Julie!" Nora hisses. "Get in here."

Julie glances over her shoulder at the elevator. "Mom?" she says with a trembling smile. "They're probably going to take you away. I can't stop them right now, but I promise I'll come find you, okay?" Her lips tighten. "I won't leave you like you left me."

An emotion creeps into Audrey's face. I'm almost certain it's sorrow.

"Can you say something, Mom? So I know you're still here?"

Audrey's eyes drop to the floor.

"Can you please just tell me you're here?"

"Julie," I say, watching the elevator doors and grinding my teeth. "Come on."

She grips the bars with both hands, pressing her forehead against them, then finally tears herself away. She runs back to the cell and Abram slams the door just as the elevator dings.

I'm expecting interrogators. Pitchmen. Grinning revenants in power ties. But four bored-looking men in beige jackets emerge from the elevator and go directly to Audrey's cell with barely a glance our way. They collar the three prisoners—a frail, sad woman and two malnourished waifs—and lead them out on poles.

Joan and Alex catch my eye as they shuffle toward the elevator. I wish I knew what to say to them, but I know almost nothing. Where they're going. What's going to happen to them. What I can do about it. All I can manage is a feeble wave. They wave back, then disappear into the elevator.

Audrey stops between the open doors.

"Here," she says.

Julie has turned her back, unable to watch the grim procession, but at the sound of her mother's voice she whirls around. Audrey is looking directly at her, eyes steady with comprehension if not quite recognition.

"I'm . . . here."

Julie claps a hand to her mouth. She squints against a rush of tears, but she and her mother maintain their gaze until the elevator doors sever it.

There is a long silence in the cell. Julie moves to the corner farthest from anyone and slides to the floor, wiping her eyes into a dry stare. I can hardly imagine what she's feeling. Her mother may be emerging, but into what? There is no happy outcome ahead.

Audrey died years ago, violently and irretrievably. The plague we hope to cure is the only thing keeping her with us.

I sit next to Julie, but not close. The others settle into their own natural positions, pairings determined by relationship, proximity by intimacy. Abram paces for a while, maybe wracking his brain for an escape plan, maybe just stewing, but eventually he succumbs. We sit in a circle around the perimeter of the room, the overhead fluorescents flickering on our faces like a sallow campfire.

Julie finally notices my stare, and I jerk my eyes away. An image blooms in my head and I permit it to spread, filling my chest with long-absent warmth. What if we met in a different time? One of the many eras that weren't like this one? What if I were just a boy in a café ignoring his homework to watch a girl sip her coffee? What if this girl had an ordinary life, worrying about work and school and little else, with a heart that had been bruised perhaps but never burned or blackened? What if neither of us had ever killed anyone, never seen our parents die, never been beaten or tortured or saddled with the weight of an impossible quest? What if she caught me staring and smiled, and I said hello and asked her name, and it was as simple as that?

Such worlds have existed, I remind myself. Such worlds are possible. No matter how distant they may seem from this one.

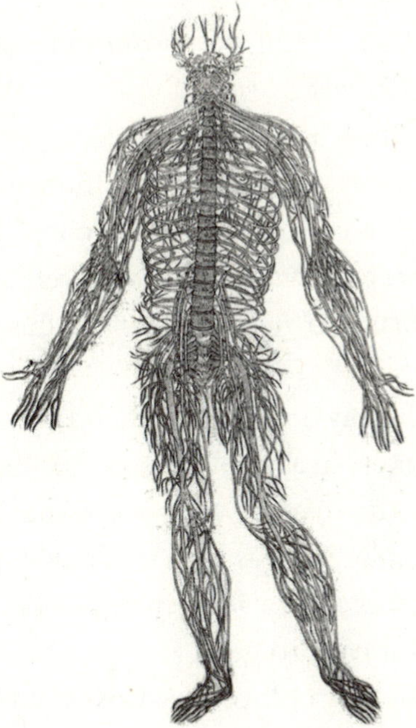

THE WOMAN'S NAME.

"Like what you see?" Mr. Atvist whispers over my shoulder.

I am learning not to recoil at the smell of his breath. He says he stopped smoking on the day my father died, but either the fumes have permanently infused his tissues or it's just the smell of an old man rotting.

"One of the many perks of working here," he says, joining me at the visual feast. A blond woman is struggling to navigate her cubicle in a tight red dress. There aren't many women in the Atvist Building, but the few I've seen are improbably attractive and impractically dressed.

"Who is she?" I ask, not taking my eyes off her.

"What do you mean who is she?"

"What's her name? What does she do here?"

He chuckles. "You ask all the wrong questions, kid. But then you're probably still a virgin, right?"

I glance at him, then back at the woman.

"Straight from Holy Fire to UT-AZ Internment, I'm guessing you never got much chance to sow your oats." He grins. "And no, losing your ass cherry to that thug in your cell doesn't count."

Despite my efforts, I cringe a little under his moistly percussive syllables.

"Listen, R—," he says, slapping a hand on my shoulder, "this company has its fingers in a lot of pots, but if there's one ethos that ties it together, it's that we get what we want. That's our mission statement, as a company and as men. Hell, that's the reason there's life on this planet, because a few microbes decided they wanted more and did what it took to get it."

Unlike most Axiom employees, this woman is wearing a name tag. She must have brought it from another job. I am straining to read it—Raquel? Roseanne?—when she notices my stare. She smiles, and it's the smile of an opportunity sensed, joyless and calculated, accompanied by adjustments of posture that expose a lush valley of cleavage. Powerful signals boil up from the deep crevices of my brain, cascading over the delicate ones near the surface, and I forget about the name tag.

"Who is she?" Mr. Atvist repeats, shaking his head. "She's pussy. She's prey. And if you're going to help me run a company that's going to run the country, I need you to learn to hunt."

• • •

So I learn.

I sit in on every conference, listening to the old men of Executive snarl and bark. I shadow every operation, watching our negotiators mix their skillful blend of hope and fear and occasionally violence.

I absorb it all with fanatical fervor, and I pick up the business so quickly no one even cries nepotism when Mr. Atvist promotes me to Management. For the first time in my life, I have power, a flaming sword compared to the feeble lighter I wielded with Paul, and I begin to swing it.

"I want this one fired," I say, and it happens.

"I want that one killed," I say, and it happens.

I am still young and low on the ladder, but I have promise. I have instinct. Mr. Atvist puts me in charge of public relations, and I reach into my angry young self and my grim and fearful family and all the little minds that surrounded us and I think, *What do they want? What do they trust?* I crouch low to this dusty, moldy shelf of desperate moments, blunt urges and whimpering needs, and I peruse its ugly books.

I say, "I want to climb to the top of the world and spit into the hole where God was."

And it happens.

The Axiom Group rises on a pile of weaker corps as civilization declines. We survive the transition from currency to hard goods. We sell weapons to the government to fight its own citizens, raking in millions of tons of refined materials, components, and Carbtein, and by the time Old Gov's outer damage meets its inner rot and the whole ancient edifice collapses, we find ourselves conveniently positioned to replace it.

Who, me? we say with Lucille Ball innocence. *Well, if you insist . . .*

It's an oddly quiet moment when it happens. A decade or two earlier, one ill-considered comment from a politician could make the whole world explode, headline news and internet uproar, but on the night the United States winks out of existence, no one is talking about it. Few people even know about it. The internet remains a nationwide error message, killed long ago with the flick of a switch to keep it safe from cyberterrorism. The airwaves are silent but for the local chatter of short-range walkies, and everything else is buried under BABL's blanket of interference. Even Fed FM seems to be taking the night off, asleep in a sea of static. The only national news being broadcast at 2:48 AM on this particular Tuesday is the garbled spasms of Fed TV, which is trying to tell us something important but still can't bring itself to speak plainly.

"I'll huff and I'll puff," shouts a wolf in an old black-and-white cartoon, *"and I'll blow your house down!"*

A vintage photo of Confederate soldiers. The White House. Pigs herded into pens. Flashes of sickly green static.

A news anchor looks up from his desk, sees the camera, opens his mouth—

A shaky handheld shot of the Pentagon in flames. Sausages on a grill. The anchor again: *"Ladies and gentlemen, I'm afraid we have terrible—"*

Blue static. Red static. An army of graffiti-covered tanks rolling into Washington, DC.

"Sorry, we're having some—"

Helicopter footage of an unfathomably large mob surrounding the burning Pentagon, thousands if not millions of people swarming against its walls.

"Ladies and gentlemen, I'm afraid—"

The camera falls off its tripod. Screams, loud noises, boots rushing toward the lens.

The screen goes dark. My apartment goes dark. All my lavish furnishings disappear. The screen remains black for five minutes, then the clock strikes 3:00 AM and Old Glory fades in, waving proudly while the music swells and images of delicious food scroll past. The LOTUS Feed has resumed its regular programming.

My walkie beeps. I pick it up.

"It happened," Mr. Atvist says.

"Are we positioned?"

"We're the most electable candidate, but it still won't be easy. A lot of other groups are going to want in."

I watch colorful images flash randomly across the screen, the

Feed now lacking what little curation it ever had. It will veer and roll like a plane with a dead pilot until the station someday loses power.

"We've been quiet," Mr. Atvist says. "We've been discreet while we laid our foundation, and that's good. Soft power has its place. But if we're going to rebuild this country the way it ought to be, we're going to have to get hard. Are you ready for that?"

I watch the TV. I don't answer.

"I asked if you're ready to get hard, kid. Wake up that secretary of yours if you need a fluffer."

"What are you planning?" I'm startled by how weakly it comes out. A small, trembling sound that reminds me of a little boy hiding on a rooftop. I tell myself it's just late. I'm just tired. Exhausted and rubbed raw by a punishing regimen of indulgence. Two company women snore in my bed, the stench of smoke and body fluids mingling into rancid perfume. One of them is my assistant. The other I don't recognize. They are painkillers that I take to ease my doubt. They affirm my choices with the prize of their bodies, writhing in my big bed in my big apartment where I get to watch the end of America in utmost safety and comfort. This is the top, is it not? How can my path be wrong if it led me to the top?

"Be in the conference room in an hour," Atvist says. "We'll raise a toast to America and discuss how to cook its carcass."

The walkie feels heavy in my hand. I drop it and stare at the flickering madness on the TV. I feel a strange urge to cry, but I strangle it.

"You okay?"

My assistant is sitting at the edge of the bed, watching me.

I get up and step into my slacks, throw on my silver shirt.

"Are you sure you want to go?"

"Have to."

"I thought you always do what you want."

I shoot her a dangerous look and she goes quiet. I button my shirt and reach for my red tie.

Outside, ninety floors below my huge windows, the city writhes in its fever, the streets crackling with panic, gunshots and fires. But all I see is Freedom Tower gleaming in the moonlight. Sinopec Tower blinking down at me in mockery.

There are buildings taller than ours. This is not the top.

• • •

In the musty shadows of my basement, a madman is muttering the story of his life. He slumps in a corner, his once expensive clothes filthy and tattered, his red tie darkened to brown, a discarded wretch telling tales of improbable glory. This is where I want him. Chained to the floor, starved and impotent. I won't kill him. I won't even silence him. I will keep him here and listen until I know all his secrets, all his strengths and weaknesses, and he will never control me again.

I open my eyes to the pale light of my latest prison. Julie sleeps next to me but not close, curled into a ball with a buffer of cool air between us. Our lives have become so burdened with fear, our love feels like a luxury we can't afford. Even here in this cell with nothing to do but wait, we keep pushing it away. But I refuse to believe it's gone. I catch it gleaming in the cracks between moments. A quick look. A kiss in a crashing plane. Somehow, in the midst of all this fire and death, we will find it again.

The elevator dings. Julie's eyes snap open. She sees me watching her and appears puzzled by the faint smile on my face, but as always, there isn't time to share my thoughts with her. The elevator opens and I don't need to look away from her face to know who has stepped out. The panic in her eyes tells me everything.

"We'll be okay," I tell her, and I'm shocked by how level my voice is. I am not Dead anymore; I breathe and bleed and feel pain, but for some reason, I'm not afraid. I sidle close to her and touch her arm. "We're stronger now. They don't know how to hurt us."

She looks at me and presses her lips together, stopping their tremble. She nods, and this simple gesture floods me with hope.

The cell door opens and we stand up to face them.

"Hello!" Yellow Tie chirps.

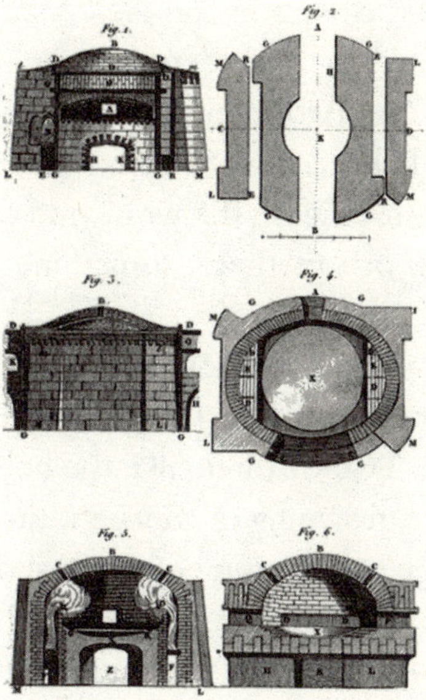

WE

THE BOY IS SITTING at a desk. He has been told the desk is a privilege reserved for high-potential individuals. It is the first time in either of his lives that someone has told him he has potential, but it fails to inspire him. He is in a room full of high-potential individuals, diverse in age, sex, and appearance, but all with a certain sameness. Whatever their natural skin tone, it has faded. Whatever their natural eye color, it has changed—most to gray, but a few with flecks of gold. It occurs to the boy that potential is a vague word. Poison has potential to kill. Flesh has potential to rot.

All of these high-potential individuals sit at desks like the boy's, absorbing a bewildering array of inputs. Screens fill every corner, all playing different programs—sports, films, old news broadcasts with constant commercial breaks—and all at full volume, fighting for dominance with the pop song on the PA speakers, which is just the sound of women's orgasms set to a thumping beat.

In the midst of this, two men stand at the front of the room, delivering what might be lectures of some kind, though the boy can pick out only a few snatches in the whirlwind of noise. Something about security from one of them, something about liberty from the other.

Most of the people in this room glance wildly from screen to screen, speaker to speaker. A few stare straight ahead as drool pools on their parted lips. Two or three, like the boy, look around with lucidity in their eyes, frowning in concentration as they try to understand this strange assault. One of these suddenly screams and flings out her hand, knocking over her IV stand. The tube pops out of the bag. The syrupy pink cocktail squirts out onto the floor, and a man in a lab coat rushes to reconnect it.

The boy can feel the syrup in his own veins, interacting inscrutably with his lukewarm blood. He follows the tube from his arm to the bag, and then up to the ceiling where it joins all the others, dangling like jungle vines from a central hub, which feeds from a thick hose running out of the room. The boy wonders where it goes and what is in it. He wonders what these people want him to become.

The session pauses while the lab assistant struggles with the unruly student. In the stunning void of silence, the boy can hear the groans and howls of the less privileged individuals in nearby classrooms. Individuals too deep in the plague to operate in the world as people. These do not get desks. These do not get to watch television. These have lower potential, and will be Oriented for lower functions, according to the evident order of nature.

The door opens. A woman in a lab coat pushes two children inside. The boy stares at the children and they stare at him.

One of them smiles. A girl of about seven, her dusky skin barely touched by gray, her dark eyes flecked with gold like veins of ore promising a windfall.

She runs to the boy and hugs him and he remembers that her name is Joan.

Joan's blond brother dances around the boy's desk, touching the boy's cheeks and laughing. "Found you, found you!" Alex says.

It is not the first time these children have found him. In a distant age, in a distant part of the world, they found him wandering deep in an airport basement and dragged him up to daylight. His friends, Joan and Alex. Two more good people.

The woman in the lab coat grabs them by their collars and drags them to their desks, shoves them down and jabs IV tubes into their arms. The session resumes. The storm of noise buffets their eyes and ears, but Joan and Alex seem to be ignoring it. They are distracted. They smile at the boy and he finds their joy infectious. He smiles back.

The pages on our Higher shelves rustle as they fill with new words. Simple sentences polished and gleaming.

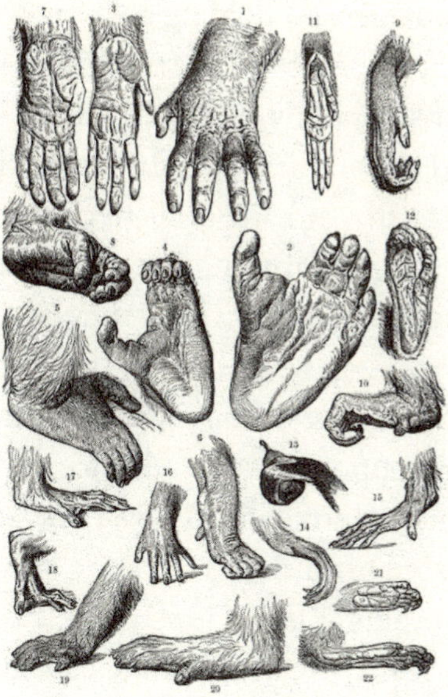

1

HERE IT IS. The busy metropolis I've been waiting to see. No more quiet courtyards and hollow buildings and wind howling through ghostly streets. This is New York City. I watch it rush by through the SUV's window, and the past and present overlap. Am I a prisoner, or is this just another commute? Another limo ride home after a long day at the Atvist Building? The sidewalks churn with pedestrians and the streets are packed with rush-hour traffic. There is energy and commerce, and when obscured by the window's heavy tint, it almost looks like the old world. But when I roll the window down for an unfiltered view, discrepancies appear. Laundry flutters from high-rise windows, turning glittering business towers into Dickensian rookeries. Every park and square has been repurposed into some form of labor site: makeshift assembly lines and meat rendering stations, the occasional fenced holding area for hopeful immigrants. The lack of traffic noise seems strange—Where is the brass orchestra? That discordant symphony of horns?—until I notice that all the vehicles on the road are marked with the Axiom logo. Construction trucks and transport vans, moving in silent unanimity.

The window rolls up, dimming the harsh detail of the scene. Blue Tie catches my eye in the rearview mirror. "For optimal safety, windows should be kept up when driving through population areas. We experience difficulties with unsalaried employees."

"Everyone has an opportunity to advance in this company," Yellow Tie says, turning to smile at me over the seat, "with enough hard work and personal sacrifice."

Black Tie says nothing. Black Tie stares at the side of Julie's face, and she leans away from him as far as she can, almost ending up in my lap.

"You smell like shit," she growls at him, then turns to the front seat to include the other two. "You smell like stale old-man shit covered up with air freshener. Where are you taking us?"

"432 Park Avenue is currently the tallest building in the western hemisphere," Yellow Tie says with silky assurance. "With ninety floors of spacious condo units and every amenity you can imagine, it is truly the new standard of luxury living."

"What the fuck are you talking about?" Julie shouts. "Do you even hear yourself?"

I am watching the river of people flowing by on each side of the street. Gaunt, exhausted faces, bodies either scrawny or obese, wrapped in tattered remnants of expensive clothes, logos obscured by rips and stains, all colors faded. Crude plywood patches cover the war-torn, quake-rattled buildings, repaired but not restored, storefronts fenced off and filled with obscure machines. The city buzzes like a factory, but where is the product? I see no abundance. No glow of hard-earned contentment on any of these faces. The factory's product is more factories.

How did this happen? Not even the wretch in my basement wanted to live in a world like this. He wanted to feed on the fruits of society, not pave over the orchard. What was the moment that broke Axiom's mind? I pry at my memories, but they refuse to open.

"Are you really going to take Park all the way there?" Julie says.

"It's the most direct route," Blue Tie says.

"The traffic is hell. Third is faster."

Blue Tie glances at her in the mirror, then continues on Park. Julie sighs.

It gives me some small pleasure to remember that we're both New Yorkers, for whatever that title is worth now. One bit of common ground in the vast gulf between her past and mine. I imagine her riding along to her father's gigs downtown, sucking in the sights with her hungry young eyes, oh so eager to grow up. And later, visiting him at Fort Hamilton as the Borough Conflicts began to boil, a little less eager now. I see her at twelve years old, an image that comes to me with surprising detail: shorter, skinnier, with fewer scars on her soft cheeks, her tiny frame disappearing into baggy work clothes, walking alone over the Brooklyn Bridge while distant bomb smoke adds texture to the sunrise. The thought makes me smile until I remember that I was there too, perhaps looking down at her from some grim tower window, seeing just another pixel in the porn of my ambitions.

I want to cough up my past and spit it far away from me, but it catches in my throat. The only way to make it gone is to digest it.

"Here we are!" Yellow Tie announces as the SUV pulls to the curb.

"Three days later," Julie says with a roll of her eyes.

"We appreciate your enthusiasm for today's interview," Yellow Tie says, opening our door. "We hope this means you've decided to collaborate."

"Fuck you. You smell like cherry condoms full of rancid come."

I snort. Yellow Tie frowns. However colorful Julie's insults get, they remain disgustingly accurate.

I step out into a stiff wind that blows the pitchmen's stench out of my nose—only to replace it with the city's blanket aroma of trash and human waste. Black Tie ejects Julie with a shove and she stumbles; I catch her as best I can with my wrists bound in front of me. Both of us are cuffed but otherwise unrestrained. If we made a sudden sprint, we could probably get away, but the pitchmen's clear lack of concern reveals the futility of this idea. Where would we go? How far would we get? The city itself is the prison.

My neck pops a few times before I find the top of 432 Park Avenue. The building is a perfectly symmetrical rectangle, its square windows rising in an unbroken sequence until they're too small to see. But what makes my head spin is not the height; it's the familiarity. The excited gibbering behind my basement door.

I lived here.

It was glorious, the wretch sighs. *But more importantly, it was necessary. The people needed to see that someone was still in charge, still looking down on them from some unfathomable perch. It's the mystery that maintains power, the weary assumption that it's all beyond them. God is wise to hide in Heaven.*

But something isn't right. The lobby is oddly unkempt for a seat of divine power. Its white marble floors are smudged with boot tracks, furniture overturned, everything covered in dust. No doorman, no concierge, no sign of life whatsoever. I remember this building as a luxury fortress for the world's few surviving power brokers, but now it's as cold and quiet as any other ruin.

"This *isn't* the tallest building," Julie says as the pitchmen lead us into the elevator. "How are you going to run this country if you don't even know New York's skyline?"

"Its height was exceeded by Sinopec Tower," Yellow Tie admits.

"Exactly. Nice dick but I've seen bigger."

We surge upward. Square windows rush past the elevator's clear walls, offering us a flickering zoetrope view of the city that becomes transparent as we pick up speed.

"You'll notice Sinopec Tower is not visible at this time," Blue Tie says.

Julie scans the skyline, frowning.

"After losing our downtown headquarters in the tragic Eight Six quake," Yellow Tie says, "we felt it was important for brand confidence that we occupy the tallest buildings in the city. We were able to take Freedom Tower with minimal expense, but we had ongoing conflicts with the occupants of Sinopec Tower. We opted to eliminate the building, resolving two issues at once."

"Efficient multitasking is crucial to staying on top in today's competitive world," Blue Tie says.

Julie stares at the empty space where that blue glass spire used to be. I feel a similar gap in my memories. In all their leaping back and forth through time, there is a barrier they never cross, and in the shadows beyond that barrier is where these things happened. Earthquakes, floods, and falling buildings. A mad scramble to the top after being laid low.

How did he do it?

The floor numbers keep rising. Fifty. Sixty. The higher we climb, the less real the city looks. People disappear. Buildings shrink into toys. Rooks on a bewildering chessboard.

It hits me suddenly like ice water to the face.

"Where are we going?" I take an aggressive step toward Blue Tie. "What's in this building?"

"Executive would like a word with you," he says.

My stomach lurches. "Is he here?" My tongue recoils from the name. "Is . . . *he* here?"

All three well-dressed ghouls grin at me. Even Black Tie.

I ram into Blue Tie with my shoulder, knocking him away from the button panel. I frantically pound the emergency stop, but nothing happens. Black Tie's fist hits me like a bus and I stagger back, seeing flashes and spots. Julie springs into action like we planned this. She leaps onto Black Tie's back and loops her cuffs over his head, pulling the chain into his neck so hard it almost disappears into his flesh. But he seems unperturbed. Instead of struggling to free his windpipe, he reaches back and grabs Julie by the hair. She screams as he yanks her off his shoulders and flings her to the floor. A clump of gold remains in his fist. He sees me gaping at it, gives me a calculated smirk, and stuffs it in his pocket.

Rage replaces terror. I coil against the door, preparing to tackle him into the glass and hopefully through it, to pummel and punish him all the way down to our messy reunion with the street. But then Blue Tie jams a Taser into my neck, and I collapse.

Black Tie pulls Julie off the floor. He holds her by the shoulders while Blue Tie jabs the Taser into her chest and keeps it there.

"Stop," I croak, staggering to my knees.

"We do need your full cooperation at this time," Yellow Tie admonishes.

"Fuck . . . *you*!" Julie snarls through gritted teeth as sparks snap between her canines.

An obscure piece of trivia flickers into my head. Another little piece of the puzzle that is the woman I love: studies have shown that swearing has an anesthetic effect.

Swearing eases pain.

The elevator dings. The door opens. Black Tie releases Julie and she collapses against me in an awkward heap. I can't embrace her so I improvise, pressing my chin onto the top of her head. "Are you okay?" I whisper.

She nods feebly, rubbing her head against my chin. Her breath is warm on my throat.

"If you'll follow us now," Yellow Tie says, beckoning us out of the elevator, "we'll transfer you to Executive and they'll be happy to help you."

We stumble out into an apartment whose stark contrasts give it the aura of an art installation. Perhaps some heavy-handed commentary on consumerism or the emptiness of wealth. Much like the lobby below, the loftiest residence in the western hemisphere has let itself go. Its sleek leather furniture is stained and cracked, its white marble countertops are dulled by dust, and the pale oak floors are marred by a trail of boot scuffs leading deeper inside. A bowl of what may have been fruit is now a bowl of dried rot, just one of many graveyard aromas that abuse my nose. But it's the faintest of them that disturbs me the most: cigarette smoke. Or rather, human flesh putrefied by it.

He's here.

After all those years, he's still here. Waiting for me. Crawling up from my basement.

Atvist.

The name forces itself into my thoughts, gnawing at my identity like the one my parents gave me, that strange little noise that began with 'R.' What if he says it aloud? What if he releases it from the confines of my head and makes it real, along with the rest of the dark life we shared?

Will it overwrite me? Will I disappear?

I feel a jab in my back and I lurch forward; I hadn't realized I'd stopped walking.

There are strange signs of violence in the apartment. Chairs are knocked over, books shredded and strewn about, and what looks like claw marks in the drywall. It would not surprise me to learn that my grandfather owned a pet bear. All the light fixtures are shattered, and although the huge square windows provide plenty of exposure, the apartment is thick with gloom. The sun has slipped behind a dark cloud rolling in from the ocean. The windows creak in the wind.

The pitchmen drive us along the boot scuff trail—apparently the only trafficked portion of the entire sprawling penthouse—until we come to the living room. I remember this room. I remember the fireplace with its flawless, axe-chopped cedar logs, never lit. I remember the grand piano that dominated the space like a glossy black sculpture, never played. I remember sitting on the couch sipping old Scotch and listening to him pontificate while beautiful women clung to our arms, never named.

Do you ever get tired? I would ask him sometimes. *Do you ever wonder what we're working toward?*

And he would laugh and say, *No.*

We sacrifice so much for it, I would say to him after a few drinks as my world blurred around me. *Our own lives and others'. Do you ever ask yourself why?*

And he would laugh and say, *Because we can. Because if we don't, someone else will. Because it's how the world works.*

The piano is dusty but still pristine. The logs have grayed but still look ready to warm this marble crypt if anyone cared to light them. I remember these fixtures. What I don't remember is the white curtain running from wall to wall, dividing the space in half like an opulent hospital room.

"Executive would like a word with you," Blue Tie says again, and he and Yellow Tie move ahead of us, placing their backs to the curtain. I expect them to sweep it open with melodramatic flair, revealing Atvist and his board members at their long black table. But the pitchmen just stand there. The light behind the curtain casts amorphous shadows against it. And then:

We know who you are.

Bees in my hair. Mosquitoes in my ears. A nest of baby spiders bursting open in my brain. I am used to hearing voices, but this is different. This is not my conscience or my past or any ghost I've absorbed. This is from outside.

We know what you did and we want you to undo it.

The last time I heard a voice like this, I didn't know if it was real or my own projection. In the midst of those grim moments outside the stadium, surrounded by armies of skeletal horrors, it didn't much matter. The voice ranted and raved and spewed its rhetoric and I did my best to ignore it while I smashed its grinning skulls. But the terror in Julie's eyes removes any comforting ambiguity. This voice is real.

You will give us what we want or we will find ways to take it.

It has all the mindless confidence that I remember, the droning boredom of foregone conclusions, but there is a new edge to its timbre. A raspy overtone of aggression.

Him.

It took us centuries to build our machine. It was perfect. It kept people safe by feeding them to us. And you broke it.

"R, what is this?" Julie whispers, pressing her hands to the sides of her head.

You confused people. You told them to look for things that don't exist. You confused the plague, corrupted its function, and now the world is filling with people who have no place. People who don't fit in our mouth. And they are scared and we are hungry.

It's him, but he's just one voice in a choir—or perhaps a crowd, because it's more noise than harmony, a million blustery old men shouting over each other until their voices merge and average out, all their cultivated sophistries finally melting into truth.

We want you to make things simple again. We want you to lead them back into our mouth.

"No," I say.

A draft whistles through a crack somewhere and ripples the curtain. Outside, the sun has been fully consumed by the mass of dark clouds. A leaf slaps against the glass, blown up from trees so distant they look like grass.

We will hurt you.

"You did that before."

We will hurt people you love.

"You did that too, motherfuckers," Julie says, firming her face and straightening her spine.

The curtain billows like a seismic tremor. Whatever is behind it has no human outline. The shadows are low and lumpen and bristling with sharp points.

You children, says another familiar growl. *You dancing, grinning fuckups.*

A blast of wind buffets the building, rattling the window panes. Blue Tie's walkie beeps. He raises it to his ear. I can't make out the words buzzing from the other end but I can hear distress.

"Please excuse me," he says, and slips behind the curtain.

Julie and I glance at each other. Yellow Tie maintains her cheery grin but says nothing.

"What's wrong?" Julie says. "Are you going to torture us or not?"

Straining my ears, I pick up subtle noises from behind the curtain. Wordless whispers. A low chattering.

"Well?" Julie snaps, growing anxious in the eerie silence. "I've still got nine fingers, let's do this!"

I can see whitecaps forming on the ocean. Another gust hits the tower like a soft fist and the window nearest to me cracks. I watch the silvery lines spread, a noise like creaking bones, and I have a strange thought:

Sand castles. You're child kings in sand castles, and you forgot about the tide.

Blue Tie emerges from the curtain and exits the room without comment. Still grinning, Yellow Tie follows him and Black Tie follows her, shoving us ahead.

"Hey!" Julie shouts. "What the hell's going on?"

They hustle us into the elevator and we plummet. Julie looks at me with wide eyes, but all I can offer is a shrug. The pitchmen watch the darkening sky as they listen to their buzzing walkies. Their grins begin to fade.

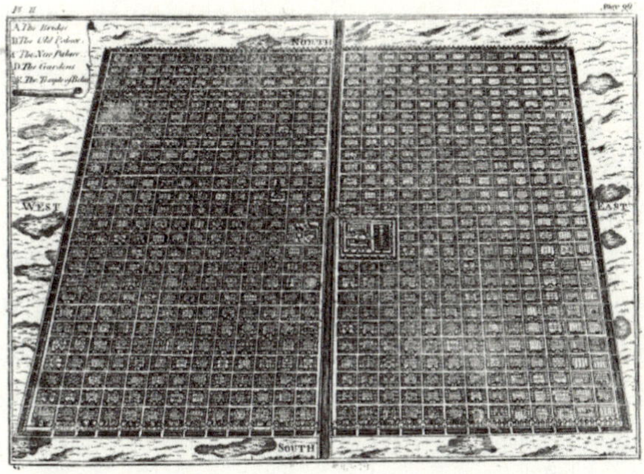

THE CITY HAS WOKEN from its muffled daydreams. Its clouded eyes have snapped alert and nervous. Through the dark glass of the pitchmen's SUV, I see people rushing up and down streets with boxes and backpacks, loading handcarts and even a few horses. I see Axiom troops lining people up for some kind of sorting process. Its exact nature eludes me but it results in two distinct groups: people who nod mutely and pile into vans, and people who scream and shout until the soldiers force them away. I hear occasional gunshots echoing down the avenues, but it's hard to hear much over the howling wind.

Julie has stopped demanding answers. She watches the chaos around us with a faraway look in her eyes. "It was like this when my family left," she murmurs. "Everyone trying to get out with whatever they could grab. Tanks in the streets, all sprayed up with war paint, every borough's colors and logos. Staten Island against Brooklyn against Queens against the Bronx, and all of them against Manhattan. And of course the Dead that came out of every skirmish. The Dead against everyone."

She watches a woman herding two children into a subway tunnel. I watch a man on a fire escape attempting to board up a window, fumbling with a sheet of plywood as the wind tries to snatch it from him.

"It was just people, then," Julie says. "We thought we were running from people."

The pitchmen park on the sidewalk and rush us into the building. They remain silent and expressionless all the way back to our jail floor, perhaps lost in reveries of their own if their strange minds have any capacity for private thoughts. I find it more likely they're just overloaded by this sudden change of agenda. Unplugged from their flowchart, stumbling blind in the unscripted darkness.

They unlock our cuffs and nudge us into our cell without a word. Nora looks us over and lets out a relieved and slightly puzzled sigh upon finding no new mutilations. Abram glowers up at the pitchmen as Sprout sleeps against his shoulder. M slouches against the wall, snoring softly.

In here, with the only window looking out on a brick wall, it's unclear what's happening outside. There is howling and creaking, but the sense of panic spreading over the city is not apparent.

"Hey," Julie says.

"Hey," Nora says. "How'd your interview go?"

"Listen," Julie says, rushing toward her, "things are falling apart out there, we need to—"

She stops and looks over her shoulder. The pitchmen are still waiting in the doorway. "Yes . . . ?" Julie says. "Am I supposed to tip you or something?"

They raise their walkies. I hear the faint buzz of voices, and their blank expressions snap back into grins, once more filled with certainty.

Black Tie steps into the cell and reaches for Sprout's arm.

Abram smacks his hand away and stands up, shoves him hard enough to tip the much bigger man off balance. "That's not happening," he says.

"It's for her safety," Yellow Tie says with a disarming smile. "If she can be Oriented, she'll be safe permanently. Isn't that what you want?"

"She's not Dead."

"The Axiom Group is committed to breaking down barriers," Yellow Tie declares, radiating pride. "As we develop techniques for Orienting a diverse range of biological states, the traditional categories of 'Living' and 'Dead' will become increasingly irrelevant until they become indistinguishable. There is a place for everyone in the new America." She beams like a kindergarten teacher telling kids they're special. "Even you."

"Get out," Abram growls, standing in front of his daughter, who is glancing around in a panic, eyes still crusted with sleep.

Yellow Tie sighs. She raises her walkie and says, "Security escort to floor twenty please."

Abram lunges. Black Tie cracks him across the face. He reels backward and would fall over if not for Sprout steadying him from behind.

I brace myself for another fight, another series of shocks to my already throbbing brain, but while I'm still debating my first move, the stairwell door bursts open and three soldiers spill out, rifles trained on us through the cell window. Julie's fist is clenched and cocked, always quicker to decisions than I am, but she freezes as the soldiers rush into the cell, their eyes to their rifle sights, jumping from target to target to show that we're all covered.

"We hope you'll choose not to endanger yourself any further," Blue Tie says. "Once we stabilize the branch, we look forward to making you all members of the Axiom family."

One of the guards presses his rifle barrel against Abram's forehead while the other reaches behind him to grab Sprout's arm.

"Get off!" Sprout shouts, wriggling and kicking; the guard subdues her long enough for Yellow Tie to cinch a zip tie around her wrists.

Abram's fists clench, but he's pinned. Sprout stops struggling and shoots a teary glance over her shoulder, first at her father, then at Julie.

"Well," M sighs, pulling himself up off the floor, "fuck it."

He rushes the nearest guard and slams his head into the wall, rips the rifle out of his hands, shoots him in the chest, spins around and shoots the second one in the head. Black Tie grabs the gun and wrenches it aside while Blue Tie sticks a Taser into M's back but M ignores it, uses the resulting muscle spasm to launch an elbow into Blue Tie's face, head-butts Black Tie, shoves him back, and lands three skull-cracking punches before the third guard shoots him.

Bright red blood erupts from his shoulder, then his stomach. M falls to the floor.

In the time it takes for all this to happen, the rest of us have managed to take about five steps forward. M is impossibly quick for his size. The remaining guard blocks the doorway, his rifle still trained on Abram, who trembles with rage that could break the bonds of reason at any moment.

"We apologize for this disruption," Blue Tie says as he and Black Tie follow Yellow Tie to the elevator. "Unfortunately, violence does become necessary when authority channels are bypassed."

The guard snatches cards and keys off his two dead coworkers, locks our cell door, and joins the pitchmen.

"The Axiom Group is working toward a more stable world," Yellow Tie says. "We hope you will live long enough to understand this."

She smiles maternally as the elevator doors close.

The cell is silent except for the wind. The subtle creaking of glass and steel.

"Sorry, Abe," M wheezes. "I tried."

The guard he shot first is beginning to twitch. Abram looks down into the man's lifeless brown eyes and watches them turn gray. Then he stomps the man's head against the floor until his boot goes through.

"My name is Abram," he mumbles, wiping speckles of blood off his face. "My name is Abram Kelvin."

He returns to his corner of the room and slumps to the floor.

Nora drops to her knees next to M and pulls his shirt up to examine his wounds. She says nothing and her face is all stern professionalism, but her nostrils flare with rapid breaths.

"What's . . . diagnosis, Doc?" M says. "Is it bulletosis?"

"Shoulder's okay," she mutters. "Grazed the clavicle and went out the back. The gut shot . . ."

She trails off.

"Really bad time to trail off," M says.

But Nora's eyes are oddly empty as she stares at the hole in his belly. She blinks again and again.

"Nora?" Julie says.

Nora gives her head a hard shake. "Sorry. I was . . ." She lifts M's hip a few inches off the floor, revealing an exit wound, then drops him back, not gently. He grunts.

"Bullet went through. It's off to the side and there's plenty of fat so it probably missed any important organs. But I guess we'll find out soon enough."

"God, Nora," Julie says, shaking her head. "Your bedside manner . . ."

Our cell door creaks open. H. Tomsen peeks through the crack. "Is he okay or is he going to die? I don't like watching people die."

"Are there still any office supplies on this floor?" Nora asks her. "Like a stapler, maybe?"

Tomsen runs into one of the empty conference rooms and returns with a heavy-duty stapler.

"Perfect." Nora pinches the hole in M's stomach together and snaps a thick staple into the seam.

"Fuck!" M shouts, in surprise as much as pain.

"Have to find something to sterilize it later, but for now, this'll slow the bleeding."

Another staple.

"Shit!" M shouts.

"God *damn* it!" M shouts.

And so on, anesthetically.

I go to the window and press my face to the glass. The neighboring building and its grinning billboard blocks any view of the city at large, but I can see the narrow street below. Axiom employees are rushing out of Freedom Tower like a swarm of beige ants, loading crates into trucks, people into buses—evacuating.

A blast of wind hits the window and I feel it in the glass like an angry shove.

"We need to get out of here," I announce to the room.

"Oh, you think so?" Nora says, prepping another staple.

"Fucking shit!" M shouts.

"I mean *now*. City's emptying out. I think it's—"

"Shitting fuck!"

"It's a hurricane," Julie says, and this gets their attention. "Probably a big one. And considering half of Manhattan is below sea level . . ."

No one speaks. M suffers the next staple in silence.

"So they *are* taking her to safety," Abram murmurs into his palm. There's an unnervingly boyish, singsong quality to his voice. "That's good. She can play with the Dead kids. Your Dead mom can adopt her. That's good."

"Abram," Julie says, trying to catch his eyes. "We're going to find her."

He smiles at the floor.

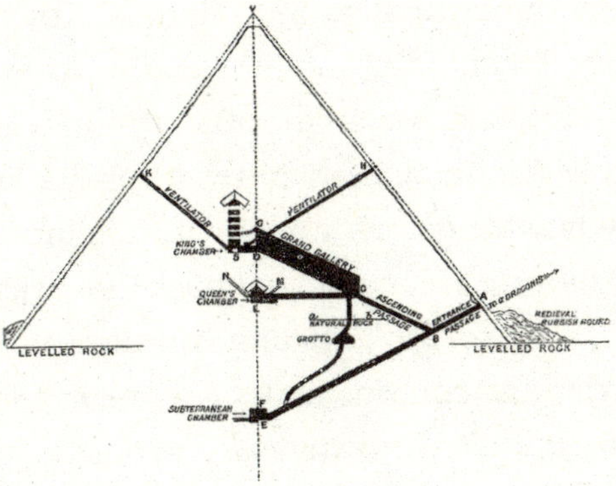

JULIE CHECKS the stairwell door. Locked.

I try the elevator. Keycard required.

We rummage through the other offices and conference rooms, some of which haven't yet been converted into jail cells, but we find nothing useful in their musty drawers. Just pencils and pens and absurd Axiom paperwork. Accounting forms listing ammo crates as income. Human trafficking receipts.

"There's no way out," Tomsen says, watching us through the bars of her cell window. Her cell is dark. I don't know why she put herself back in there now that all the guards are gone. "Sorry, but I've tried everything. I've been in here two months and I've tried everything. There's no way out."

Julie stands in the hallway tapping her foot and twisting her hair.

"I've broken into a lot of buildings," Tomsen continues. "Almost all of them. Sears Tower. Chase Tower. Key Tower. Wilshire Grand Tower. Bank of America Building. Chrysler Building. Woolworth Building. GE Building. Met Life Building—"

"Tomsen?" Julie says, cutting her off as politely as possible. "Are you going somewhere with this?"

Tomsen pauses, thinking. "GE Building. Trump Hotel. Columbia Center. Transamerica Pyramid. Sinopec Tower, before they exed it. Comcast Technology and Innovation Center—"

"Tomsen!" Nora shouts from the other room. "Get to the point!"

Tomsen cocks her head, perhaps retracing her steps to find the point. "I know how to get in and out of buildings. But this one's different." She shoves her hands in her pockets and starts pacing her cell. "Security is double, triple. Redundant. Ridiculous. They must spend hours a day just entering codes and turning locks." She digs her fingers into her kinked brown curls and pulls her face tight, suddenly distraught. "I hate this building! Nothing makes sense! I can pick key locks but not code locks. I'm not a hacker! I'm a journalist! I can't get you out of here."

A blast of wind hits the building and doesn't let up. The building creaks like a tree fighting a bulldozer. I've never heard of a hurricane felling a skyscraper; surely they're built to withstand strong winds. But then again, the drowned ruins surrounding this island attest to the old world's lack of foresight. And this is the new world. There are new winds.

Above and below us, I hear windows breaking.

"I'm sorry," Tomsen says, wiping furiously at her face. I realize with some alarm that she's crying. "I can't pick the code locks. I can't get you out of here. I'm sorry."

Julie glances at Nora through the cell door as if seeking backup, but Nora is still busy with M, tearing strips off the dead guard's clothes and tying them around M's wounds.

Julie knocks on Tomsen's cell door. "Can I come in?"

Tomsen doesn't answer, so Julie pushes the door open and steps through, shooting a look over her shoulder that tells me to follow. I am her backup backup.

Before addressing the woman frantically pacing her cell, I have to take a moment to absorb the cell itself. It's like stepping inside a particularly manic issue of the Almanac. The floor, the walls, and somehow even the ceiling are covered in words and sketches, some scratched into the drywall, others finger-painted with food or perhaps less savory substances. The content itself—what little is legible—appears to be a detailed account of life in this cell. Feeding schedules. Descriptions and portraits of guards. Speculations on the unfathomable purpose of her detainment. Everything is written in the same bubbling style as the Almanac itself, all her world-exploring energy compressed into this tiny room.

It occurs to me what cruelty this is. It occurs to me that to a person whose life is a search, to a person who has never stopped moving, two months in this place must feel like a century.

The cell is dark because the lights are broken out. The writings on the wall are punctuated by fist holes.

"Tomsen, listen," Julie says. "We're not expecting you to get us out of here. We're going to get out together, and we'll take any help you can offer."

Tomsen keeps pacing. Julie watches her for a moment.

"How long have you been writing the Almanac?"

"Since nine from BABL," Tomsen says without slowing.

"What made you start?"

"Was already on the road looking for the tower. Figured might as well share whatever news I found, connect the world at least a little, light a few shadows. Best I could do until the tower falls."

"So you were out there alone, trying to find the jammer . . . for eleven years?"

"Not alone, I had Barbara! She has so much personality, I wish you could meet her. She got me so close. I was *in* the tower, I'm *sure* of it, I had the bomb, I was about to do it and then those *fucking*—those men, they . . ."

Julie is waiting. Tomsen finally notices the silence and stops pacing.

"I know how hard it is," Julie says. "Feeling like it's up to you to save the world. Like you're the only one trying."

Tomsen stares at her with damp, expressionless eyes.

"I felt that way for a long time, wandering around the country watching my parents slowly give up. Moving into an enclave full of people who were happy to die in a cage." She cocks her head. "You went there, actually. The stadium in Post? I think you described it as 'closed, hostile.' Pretty accurate."

Tomsen continues to stare.

"Anyway, I just want you to know that you're not working alone anymore. You've got a crew now, and we can help each other."

Tomsen blinks the remaining moisture out of her eyes. "A crew?"

"Like Nora said, we're huge fans. It'll be an honor to work for you."

"Abram worked for Axiom," I add. "He might have info you don't."

"Right," Julie says. "So let's just try it. Open all the doors you can. See how far we get."

Tomsen nods. She nods so hard I worry about her neck. "Okay. Okay, we'll do it."

I'm looking over her shoulder, watching that grinning billboard wrench and sway on the neighboring tower. And then something else catches my eye. Something bright red and spinning.

"Uh," I say. "There's—" No time for words. I revert to body language. I tackle the two women to the floor as a stop sign spins through the window like a saw blade and sinks into the drywall. Wind screams through the broken glass.

"Can we do it *now*?" Julie shouts to Tomsen, brushing glass out of her hair.

Tomsen pulls a pouch of improvised tools out of her pocket and runs to the stairwell door.

M is on his feet; Nora tries to support him but he brushes her off. "I'm fine."

"Are you sure?"

"You do good work. I'm fine."

We gather around Tomsen as she goes to work on the lock with a paper clip and what looks like a straightened binder ring. Abram lingers in the cell doorway. He doesn't move to join us until the lock clicks and the door swings open. We run down the dark stairwell as windows shatter behind us, bits of debris punching through like a hail of bullets.

• • •

In violation of every building code imaginable, there is a locked door between every floor. If there were a fire, the top-floor employees would be slow roasted to perfection before they got halfway to the bottom.

The stairwell doors are solid slabs, but the doors to the offices themselves have windows, and I peer through them while Tomsen picks the locks. Vacant. Unlit. Most look like strange hybrids of corporate work floors and military barracks: cubicles with cots, copier rooms with rifle racks. A few look like jails, but we appear to be the only prisoners left behind. Was this a passive-aggressive execution or were we just forgotten in the shuffle? It's hard to tell with this company. Despite its apparent craving for order and security, the new Axiom feels like a broken machine, a flopping, flailing contraption loaded with explosives and set loose on the world.

"Okay, what now?" Tomsen says. "I've been this far before but I can't unlock this one so what now?"

Four floors from the bottom, we have hit a keypad door. Its thick steel solidity removes any thought of breaking through, although various dents and scrapes suggest past attempts.

"Abram," Julie says. "Did you ever work in this building? Do you know any access codes?"

Abram looks at the lock and says nothing.

"Abram?"

"I didn't even know the code for Pittsburgh," he says quietly. "Everything's different."

A surge of wind roars through broken windows and the building sways. It's a subtle movement but the effect is terrifying, like gravity has rebelled and we're about to fall off the earth.

"Fuck it," Nora says with wide eyes and starts punching numbers at random.

"I do know," Abram adds like an afterthought, "that these locks have explosives in them."

Nora's finger freezes.

"Three wrong entries and you lose a hand."

Nora steps back. Julie is shaking her head incredulously. "What is wrong with these people?"

I open the interior door and step into the dark, wind-blasted expanse of office space. Papers flutter around like leaves. Chairs roll back and forth. Inspirational animal posters flap against the wall—wolves eating deer and worms eating wolves, all with the same caption: WIN.

There is so much I don't understand about this thing I helped build. My grandfather was greedy and cruel and nearly every other pejorative, but he wasn't quite insane. I'm unable to imagine us designing this building. This city. These experiments with death and these grinning automatons. Where did all this come from? What created this fevered exaggeration of the world we envisioned? We may have drawn the outline, but something else filled it in.

I hear someone calling my name—the one that I've earned and lived in and cared for, not the one pinned to me at birth and stained beyond recognition—but it's far away. Each step I take into the office is a step down a staircase. I descend to my basement. I begin searching the musty boxes.

Where is it? I ask the dirt-smeared derelict chained to the stairs.

Where's what? he snickers.

What I need to get out of here. Show me.

Why should I?

Because you're selfish. You look out for you. And as much as I hate to say it, I'm you.

He considers this. *Fair enough.*

He kicks over a box.

"Excuse me," I say, touching Tomsen's shoulder. She is staring at the keypad and rubbing her fingers through her hair and she jumps at my touch. She looks at me, sees something in my eyes, steps aside.

"What were you *doing* in there?" Julie says to me, straining to push the office door shut. The stairwell has filled with windblown debris.

I look at the keypad. I look over my grandfather's shoulder as he shows me our private family code, which I'm to pass on to my children and grandchildren and—

"R, don't!"

Atvist enters his code.

The door clicks open.

"Mother . . . fucker," Nora says. "I *knew* it." She glances at Julie and M. "I mean, we all knew it, right? His clothes? All those freak-outs?"

Julie is staring at me, not exactly shocked, but shaken. She's waiting for me to say something, and I sense that the right words right now could fix all this, bridge our chasm of secrets and finally bring her back to me. And the words she's expecting are easy: *I remember my old life. I was an Axiom employee, just like M and Abram, a deluded cog in an evil machine, and now I'm not.*

If that were the truth, I would blurt it out and be done with it. But the truth is a much longer confession, and it allows no simple handwashing. It invites no sympathy or supportive back-patting, no assurances that I'm among friends and safe from judgment. It's too big for that. It's not a few regrettable mistakes; it's a *life*, a *person*, woven inextricably into the person I am today.

My secret is myself. How can I confess that?

I step through the door and descend the staircase. Freedom Tower sways beneath my feet like a woozy dream.

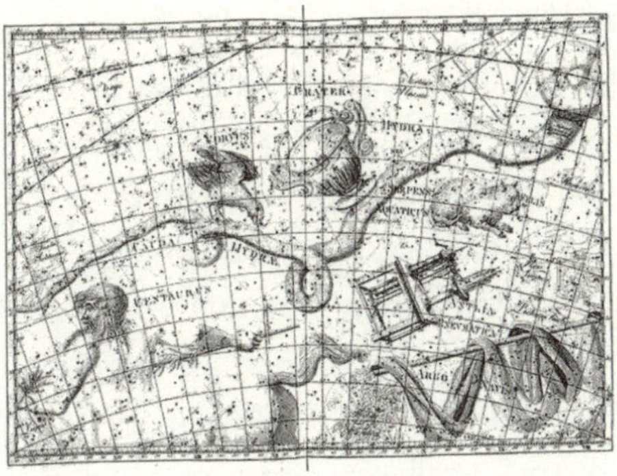

WE

We are reluctant to watch the school. The things that occur there penetrate veils and creep uncomfortably close to us, scrawling fragments of sentences into disparate books on Higher shelves and Lower shelves and strange hidden nooks never meant to be found. Such intrusions have not been possible for many centuries, since before the world became solid, and now that it has softened again—or perhaps cracked open—we are no longer sure what can happen.

So we watch with caution, but we can't look away. The boy, hovering over the chasm, is our closest link to the living, and more and more with each revolution of this burning, melting sphere, we feel a desire to be known.

The boy retreats into us for shelter as the sensory assault continues. He roams our dim halls, climbs up and down our living ladder, perusing other lives and other ages while the noise beats against the walls. He wishes he could bring his friends here. Joan and Alex are outside in the storm, grimacing as these unfathomable lessons attempt to rewrite their souls.

Then the lessons stop. The silence is so abrupt that some of the students shudder like an organ has been ripped out of them. A man in a beige jacket bursts into the room and converses with the two lecturers, but the boy does not listen to their words. He looks through the open door out into the hallway, where a group of children wait in a line. At the front of the line is a girl. She is about the age the boy was when his life was halted. The boy sees her black hair, her tawny skin, her single dark eye, then he blinks and sees her cells, her genes, intricate collages of fathers and mothers throughout history, endlessly combined and reconfigured. Then he blinks again and sees beyond cells. Beyond molecules. Roaring yellow light.

"Hi," he says.

He is standing in the hall in front of the girl, his IV dangling from his arm.

"Hi," the girl says. "I'm Sprout."

We recognize her. We have felt her presence in our halls. Our familiarity leaks into the boy and he smiles.

"I'm . . . ," he says, then his smile fades into astonishment. *I'm who? I'm what?* It's the first time he has asked these questions.

"Your eyes are pretty," the girl says.

"Thanks," the boy says. "So is yours."

"Wanna see my other one?" She reaches for the blue eye patch with the daisy painted on it, then the wind slams a piece of trash into the door at the end of the hall and she jumps. "There's a storm," she says, forgetting whatever she was going to show him.

The boy stares at the window. A square of light. And then he's outside, walking behind the girl, and Joan and Alex are behind him and many others behind them, all tied together at the wrists. Men in beige jackets are marching them somewhere, and the wind is trying to tear his hair out, but the boy is gazing at the city around him and watching it change. There is another city behind it, visible in patches as if through worn fabric. The ruined high-rises are polished and full of people and lush gardens sprout from their tops.

Canoes and ferries traverse the canals that fill the streets. And the black cloud that looms over the city is splitting apart, opening like a curtain to reveal the sun.

The girl looks over her shoulder and smiles. "Do you see it?"

The boy studies these shifting, translucent layers, trying to choose his answer.

I

OPENING THE DOOR is like popping a champagne bottle. Wind and rain explode into the lobby, knocking me back a step. We are caught in the middle of an act of God, but whose side is he on this time? Is this the parting of the Red Sea or the ruination of Job?

A red-and-white triangle spins out of the sky and sticks into the trunk of a courtyard tree.

YIELD

I ignore this message like I ignored the other and I push out into the storm.

The hurricane has revitalized the city. Panic has returned its plodding populace to pre-apocalypse levels of exuberance as every last Manhattanite scrambles to move out. The organized evacuation efforts we witnessed earlier have devolved into the age-old game of every man for himself, with Axiom troops making little effort to direct the mob or curb the eruptions of violence.

The crowd seems to be flowing toward the Jersey Bridge, but I have no doubt we'll be going against the current.

"Where did they take my daughter?" Abram shouts at Tomsen, and Julie nearly overlaps him with, "Where's my mom?"

I might as well join in. "My kids!"

Tomsen glances from face to face, overwhelmed, then points south. "That way."

We take a narrow side street to avoid the crowds, but the concrete canyon squeezes the wind into a face-peeling blast. M and I move to the front to break the force for our smaller companions; I imagine Julie blowing away, spinning off into the sky like a leaf. And as I watch the sky, imagining this and other horrors, I see the top of 432 Park Avenue in the distance. I see a helicopter hovering above it: a huge, dual-rotor beast built to haul mountains across oceans. What is it hauling now as it spins and sways above the tower, tilting almost horizontally against the wind?

A box.

A metal shipping crate is rising off the roof of my grandfather's penthouse, gaudy red against the dark sky. What could possibly be inside? There is no possession in that building that he valued enough to save. He didn't love wealth, he loved getting wealthy. He nibbled the meat but what he craved was the hunt. The only thing I can imagine him saving is himself.

A wad of trash slaps into my face, reeking of rancid beef, and by the time I pull it off and wipe away the vile grease, the helicopter is gone. I give up contemplating its cargo. There is enough terror around us already.

"Pace University," Tomsen says as we emerge onto an open highway and the wind lulls a little. "That's where they take the fresh Dead and the Living potentials."

"My mom's in bad shape," Julie says. "She's fresh but she's . . . hurt."

"If she's work-worthy they'll try to salvage her at the hospital. If not, she'll go somewhere else."

"Where?"

The wind kicks up again, roaring over the discussion. "It's a mystery!" Tomsen bellows. "Need to run now!"

Abram is already half a block ahead, having bolted the moment he heard the location. I realize there has been no moment in our acquaintance when he has stood with us for any reason but necessity. What does he want from his life? Does he want anything?

We run after him, but after two blocks, Tomsen suddenly veers off onto a side street.

"Hey!" Julie shouts.

Tomsen stops, looking puzzled. "What?"

"Where are you *going*?"

"Have to finish it!" she shouts, already running again. "Whole reason I'm here!"

"Tomsen, *wait*!"

"Meet on the Brooklyn Promenade!" she calls back. "Barbara will throw us a party!"

With that, she disappears into curtains of rain.

Julie growls curses that are lost in the wind. We run toward the college.

• • •

Pace University is a utilitarian concrete box that looks more like an insurance company than a hallowed hall of learning. I would never have guessed it was a college if not for the weather-beaten metal letters on its central tower, several of which have come loose and are spinning crazily in the wind. The effect is oddly mesmerizing, like the building is struggling to decide what it is.

A desperate shout startles me back to attention. I see Abram sprinting toward the main entrance, where a few Axiom guards are loading a crowd of children into an old city bus. The bus is covered in faded decals from some old Discovery Channel promo, the doors made to look like the jaws of a shark. I see two familiar heads of hair disappearing into it: curly blond and straight blue-black. Then the jaws snap shut.

I run faster than I have since I ran to stop a disaster, to save my home and my friend from the madness I helped create. I wasn't fast enough then. My cold, stiff joints resisted my efforts, and I arrived just in time to feel the explosion like a slap of rebuke. I am faster now, fast enough to overtake Abram, but will the result be any different?

I stop my sprint by slamming into the door. "Open it!" I shout at the driver.

"Hey," one of the guards says, striding toward me with his rifle swinging at his hip. "This bus isn't for citizens. Back up."

"My kids are in there."

"If they're in that bus, they're *our* kids."

Abram slams into him from behind, sending him sprawling onto the pavement and his rifle spinning under the bus. The engine grumbles and the bus moves forward. I hear Abram wrestling with the guard but I can't help him now. I hammer my elbow into the door until the Plexiglas panel pops out of its frame. I reach inside and fumble for the door-open lever, but the bus is accelerating. It's either let go or be dragged.

I wriggle my arm free and fall to the pavement. I catch a glimpse of their faces pressed to the windows as the bus rolls past me, Joan and Alex and their new friend Sprout, and then they're gone.

What must my children think of me? Since the day they were thrust into my care, I have abandoned them twice: first to go out into the world and follow my heart, to fall in love and learn how to live, and then because their needs overwhelmed me. Because I was too busy fighting myself to protect anyone else. And now that I've come back, now that I'm doing all I can to give them the life they deserve . . . nothing but terror and peril, again and again.

Is this the mind of every parent? This storm of guilt and uncertainty in spite of all good intentions? Did my own father feel this heartbreak as he sat in that chair sucking in smoke, feeling past generations of failure coursing through his veins? Wondering dimly what could break that heavy chain?

I hear Abram screaming obscenities as the bus disappears, as the guards back away with a gun pointed at each of us, as they climb into their Hummer and screech off after the bus. For a moment, all five of us stand motionless, trapped in the space between courage and suicide. Then I realize there are only four of us.

"Julie!"

I whirl around to find her running down a side street toward what must be the hospital. I should have expected this. She will run through the halls screaming her mother's name until her bronchial tubes seize, until she collapses or the building does. The promise she made her mother is the very one her mother broke all those years ago, and I have no doubt she'll throw her life away to keep it.

I run after her, my long legs eating up the distance. She sees me coming and looks ready to struggle, but then she notices I'm not stopping her. I'm not trying to talk sense into her or convince her to give up what I know she can't. I'm just running alongside her, ready to catch her if she falls.

A hint of gratitude warms the panic in her face. Gratitude and more. Then a blur of white roars around the corner and we are underwater.

• • •

I'm spinning, rolling, battered by chunks of debris, then I'm scraping along the street like it's a stony riverbed. The wave finally spreads itself thin enough for me to plant my feet and I stagger upright. The filthy froth boils against my thighs as I scan frantically for Julie.

I can't find her.

I can't find anyone. I have been washed into some unknown

avenue in the shadow of some unknown high-rise, and I feel the weight of it pushing down on me, thousands of tons of concrete looming like a gravestone with no name. *Here lies a body. Here lies nobody.*

"Julie!"

We were side by side; how could we have drifted so far? Did she grab hold of something I missed or did she tumble far past me?

"Julie!" I call again but the wind stuffs it back in my mouth. I hear a crash behind me and I turn, and that's when I see the wall.

I feel an insane urge to laugh.

Manhattan's defense against the siege of inevitability is a layered hodgepodge of increasing desperation. The base is professional: six-foot slabs of concrete mortared tight at the seams. The middle looks like a volunteer effort: freeway barriers stacked atop the slabs, their gaps stuffed with sandbags. And the top: plywood and tin. Frantic gestures of a panicked populace, about as effective as superstition.

The crash I heard was this layer collapsing under another wind-blasted wave. The force of this rush pushes the freeway barriers off the slabs, and the New York Sea spills into the street, its raging whitecaps darkening as they scoop up decades of human grime.

I open my mouth to scream Julie's name, and it fills with black soup.

I tumble and spin, hands and feet flailing for purchase, but this is not a preliminary wave testing the defenses. This is the flood. As I spin in this icy void, I feel the presence of the wretch in the basement, but to my surprise, he is not laughing. He is not gloating.

Is this it? he murmurs sadly. *Is this all you do with our third chance? A few friends, a few kisses, a few boards to build a home?*

The water isn't deep, but my disorientation makes it an expanse without bottom or surface. Garbage wraps around me like tentacles, dragging me down toward some vast maw.

It's not enough, he says. *You've barely touched our debt.*

But I am not listening to him. I'm thinking about Julie, hoping she's far away yet wishing for her presence. All the endings I've imagined for my third life, no matter how dark and violent, involved her at my side when I closed my eyes. I never imagined it like this.

Something hits me hard, and as the black water fades to a deeper darkness, my thoughts become wordless. Simple impulses of love that I howl into infinite halls, hoping someone hears and writes them down.

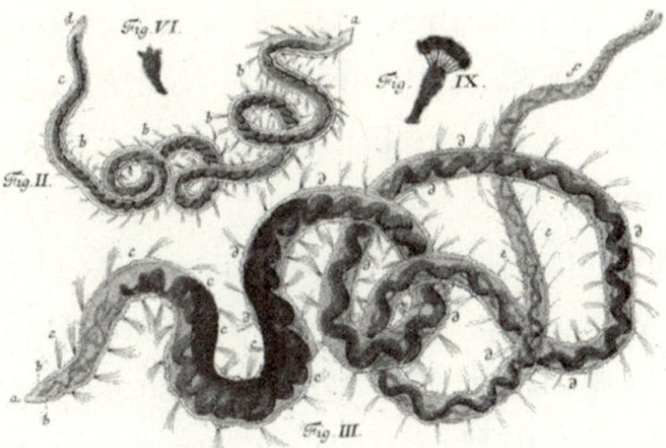

THE END OF IT.

I wake up next to a woman. I'm not sure which one. My eyes burn and my head throbs; even the pricey stuff does it. No matter how much you pay for the drink, you pay again in the morning.

"Hi," the woman whispers, and I recognize the voice. My assistant. "Are you alive?"

I groan.

"Are you working today?"

I groan louder.

"Do you ever stop?"

I turn my head on the pillow. My assistant is giving me that look again, the one that feels like a home invasion.

"There's a war," I say.

"Is there ever not?"

I sigh through my nose, smelling my own rotten breath. "Don't. Not right now."

"I just wonder if you know you have a choice. Everyone does."

"If that were true, you wouldn't be here."

I watch her eyes withdraw from me. The tender curiosity gives way to the loathing that belongs there, and I feel myself relax.

With a stiff smile she starts touching me, and though I'm tired and sick and in pain, I respond. We kiss with flaky lips and acrid tongues. We rub ourselves raw. My stomach churns and my head pounds with each miserable thrust, but I continue. I am expected to continue. Expected by whom, I'm not sure, but I feel the imperative all around and inside me.

After much sweaty effort, I reach the goal. My brain gives up its reward grudgingly and in miserly portions, a few jolts of pleasure on par with a good sneeze, and as the sensation fades I grasp at it, reaching into the darkness of my mind to seize it and pull it back, unwilling to accept that this is all I get. But this is all I get.

I collapse onto the bed, eyes closed, mouth open. She is whispering something intended to be sensual, greatly overvaluing what we just did, but I am sinking through the bed. I am sinking through the floor and the ground and into a dark chamber full of dust and dead worms, endless shelves of damp, fungal books on paper and parchment and stone and clay, cuneiform lines and ochre smudges and unknowable pre-lingual scrapings.

I experience a different kind of climax. I vomit onto my pillow. Then I get up and go to work.

• • •

"I'm sick of it," he says. "Working out of this old shit-hole surrounded by sandbags in the shadow of those midtown towers. Getting our asses kicked by a bunch of thugs in graffitied tanks. It's fucking embarrassing." He paces around the echoing expanse of his office, sipping Scotch from a crystal tumbler while I sit on the couch, swaying and sweating. "We need to expand."

"Expand?" I swallow back the taste of acid. My face feels hot and sore. "I thought we'd already bit off too much."

"No such thing as too much. You ever see a dog walk away from food? Everything in nature knows to keep eating."

"We're losing workforce. We can barely hold Manhattan. If the boroughs join together, they'll outnumber us."

"Which is exactly why we need to expand. Listen, I'll tell you a secret." He sits on the couch across from me and leans in close. "We're going to take the west coast."

His voice sounds muffled, like a radio fighting through static. I struggle to make my throat work. "We can't do . . . how would we do that? How would we . . . maintain control across that much territory?"

He grins. "We're going to take over the LOTUS Feed."

"*How*?"

"We've been closing in on the source for years. We know it's somewhere in South Cascadia. So we just flood the region with our people, acquire every enclave, and start squeezing heads until the secret squirts out. I guarantee within a year we'll be shouting from the rooftop of BABL."

The room is rippling like I'm underwater. My forehead is wet.

"Yes, we have our hands full with the boroughs right now. Things might get bad here. But if we control the Feed, we'll be in every home and bar and bunker. We'll be a familiar face and a household name, and we won't have to fight anymore because they'll *give* us what we want. Whatever we say will be the truth, because we'll be the only voice."

I open my mouth to ask a question or perhaps to express a doubt, but all that comes out is a retching noise.

His grin widens at my struggle. "Go ahead, R—. Puke on my floor. It's an exciting moment and you're a sensitive kid, so do what you have to do to get over it."

I lean over the edge of the couch as my body prepares to accept his invitation.

"But when you get it all out, let's talk specifics. I want you to head the first wave."

I feel a vibration in the floor. It's faint and my grandfather doesn't react to it so I assume it's just my throbbing head. The ripples in his liquor are harder to explain, but my stomach soon heaves these thoughts out of me.

• • •

I am not on Earth when it happens. I am a thousand feet above it in a twin-prop plane, swallowing a double dose of Dramamine. It's been weeks since I've had a drink but I can't shake this nausea. The company doctors chalk it up to anxiety, and that's plausible enough. We are, after all, in the middle of losing a war.

Mr. Atvist is sending me west, and though I do have a mission, I suspect there's a larger purpose to getting me out of New York. I suspect it has something to do with the fire and smoke rising from the streets of lower Manhattan. The reports of branches being broken. Executives being executed. The distant booms of tank shells. Mr. Atvist knows which way the wind is blowing, and he wants his heir elsewhere when the tree falls.

It's tempting to feel touched by this gesture, to feel *loved*—no, I can't even think the word without chuckling. I know what I am to my grandfather. I am not a person, I am Family. I am DNA and legacy, a vehicle to carry him into the future. Nothing more.

So when I see dust rising all over the city, when I see high-rises swaying like trees, the older ones breaking and buckling—when I press my face to the window and see the Atvist Building beginning to crumble and flood, I am not sure what to feel. When I hear his voice on the radio, fading into BABL's bubbling screech but audible until the end, I am not sure how to take his words.

"So it's all a dream?" he snarls over the sound of cracking glass. *"No rules, anything can happen? Fuck this place. Fuck this new world. All of you keep doing your job, you hear me? This isn't going to end us. I'll never stop. I'll never—"*

A grim silence hangs in the plane. The crew looks at me. My assistant looks at me. I don't say anything, so nothing changes. We keep doing our job. We fly away from New York while it writhes and shudders beneath us, and as we glide into the empty expanses of the Midwaste, I see that strange but increasingly familiar sight: ripples on the horizon. Subtle changes in topography. Glittering forms hanging in the blue, glimpsed in my periphery and gone before I can describe them.

Is it really a dream? If anything can happen, can't it be something good? I look down at the metal briefcase in my lap, this instrument of death and deceit, and I feel the urge to cry mixing into my urge to vomit. Who's going to make it good?

• • •

My sleep is empty. I wake with the same thoughts, the same feelings, the same nausea, as if no time has passed though it's dark now and the crew is asleep.

I have often wondered if we can feel the approach of important events. Objects of great mass can distort time; could events of great significance do the same? Could the weight of a moment make an indentation that's felt from both sides, remembered before it happens?

When I wake up on the day of my death, will I feel a tingle and a shiver? Will some small part of me know?

I wander the cabin, looking at the sleeping faces of my crew. The soldiers in their new beige jackets, so wonderfully plain and benign. The negotiators in their silver shirts and colorful ties, a little creative indulgence of mine, unprofessional and due for an overhaul if Axiom survives the night.

And my assistant in her red dress. Another indulgence. Why did I bring her? I am not a man of sentiment. I wrung that out of me years ago. What do I want from this woman beyond a quick fuck to calm my nerves?

I look out the oversized viewing windows. There are no cities below. No gleaming beacons of civilization dotting the landscape. The earth is dark and empty of humanity, and if it contains any beauty, there is no one there to witness it. I feel another sensation I can't explain. Loneliness slithers into my stomach to join the nausea and melancholy, the newest guest at this horrible party. I head for the cockpit to find the one person I know will be awake, feeling weak and helpless and absurd.

The pilot gives me a nod. The copilot is asleep.

"Why is he asleep?" I demand, bracing my softening spine with the thrill of authority.

"We're on auto, sir," the pilot says. "Weather's good, course is set, I thought I'd let him get some rest."

I look at the copilot. He is old. Older than he should be for this job. He must have been an emergency selection.

"Wake him up."

The pilot reaches across the instrument panel and nudges the copilot's elbow. "Hey."

The copilot doesn't move.

"Hey. Doug." The pilot shakes the copilot's shoulder and the copilot's hands flash out and grab the pilot's arm and there's a ripping and a spray of blood and a scream and then the copilot is on top of the pilot and the plane is diving and I am tumbling forward.

I feel a tingle. I feel a shiver. I feel teeth pierce my calf and instead of a scream, a hideous laugh bubbles out of me.

Today! It was *today*! An old man named Doug!

There is a muffled gunshot and the copilot goes still. My assistant pulls him off of me and points her pistol at the pilot.

"Land it."

The pilot looks at his bleeding arm. He shakes his head with a weariness that borders on relief.

"Please!" my assistant says. "You still have time!"

A long sigh whistles out of him. He settles into his chair and pulls up on the controls. I stagger to my feet. I see high-rises on the far horizon, a city, maybe even our destination, and I find myself hoping, believing we might make it—

A pulse of pain from my leg.

Black worms crawling up my veins.

A reminder. What happens next is not my concern. I am standing outside the circle while the Living discuss future plans, their shoulders a wall with no gaps, their message loud and clear: *You have overstayed your welcome. You are not invited to tomorrow.*

I hear distant voices shouting. I see the city floating like an island on an ocean of dark trees. And then all I see is the trees, filling every window.

Noise. Pain. I'm flying freely now, no need for a plane, flailing through the air among shards of shattered Plexiglas, and then I'm underwater. On instinct, not desire, I kick my way to the surface and force myself to breathe. I kick until my feet hit ground, and I stand up.

I am in a forest. I am standing in a river whose gentle rushing is the only sound. The sky is clear and rich with stars, not veiled by any human lights, and I wonder if this is the forest of the Dead. When they wander away from the campfire of the Living, perhaps this is where they go. I have always wondered what they see while they stumble through the ruins; could it be this? Visions of trees in place of buildings, berries and honey in place of screaming meat? Is this where I'll spend my second life, roaming these quiet woods?

Thick, viscous pain thuds into my leg as if to mock me for this fantasy, and I am suddenly aware of bodies all around me. Who are they? I know that I know them but the effort of digging up their names is overwhelming. Their limbs twitch and their lungs inflate wetly, preparing to shatter the silence with meaningless moans, so I pull a revolver out of one man's jacket and shoot him in the head. I repeat this for each one until I come to a blond woman in a red dress, lying on her side and bleeding from almost everywhere.

"So this is it," she says.

I went straight through the window. She didn't. It won't matter. I feel the worms creeping up my thigh and into my groin. A brief agony and then numbness.

I sit down next to her.

"Infected?" she asks.

I nod.

"Looks like I'm going, too."

Why did I hide? Why was it always fight or flight? Why did I choose the hellish world of beasts when I had the privilege of being human?

"Got enough bullets for us?" she says.

I nod. The stars are beautiful but I'm holding my eyes on the dirt. "Rosa."

Even in her fading state, she manages surprise at the sound of her name. "What?"

"I'm sorry, Rosa."

She squints at me, a mixture of incomprehension and incredulity. "You're sorry?" She coughs up blood. It matches her dress. "For what?"

The worms enter my belly and the nerves go dark. My nausea finally vanishes, along with everything else. I am disappearing.

"For your life. My life. Everything." I release the tears. I need them to come out before they disappear too. "I can't think of anything I'm not sorry for."

Rosa stares at me for a moment, watching my eyes pool up. Then she spits blood in my face. "Fuck you, Atvist. Fuck your deathbed confession. You think you can be a monster your whole life, take everything you want, and then wipe your debt clean on your way out the door? Fuck you."

The worms creep into my chest but seem to avoid my heart, leaving it to feel everything. I look down at the gun in my hand. "What if I don't leave? What if I stay long enough to pay it back?"

She laughs through a ragged cough. "Pay it back? If you stay, you're going to double it."

"What if there's some way—"

"There is no way. The plague makes *good* men into monsters. Imagine what it'd do with you."

The worms seem to be in my throat now. My lungs. The urge to breathe is fading.

"Listen to me," Rosa says. Her icy blue eyes lock on mine, tearing me away from my desperate fantasies. "You're going to shoot me, and then you're going to shoot yourself. Do it right now."

The gun trembles in my hand.

Rosa's glare isn't just loathing; it's disappointment. The embarrassed disgust of misplaced faith. "You were always so sure no one could ever love you." She takes my hand and pushes the gun to her forehead. "Well, you're finally right." She squeezes my finger on the trigger.

I'm ready now. Oh God, I'm ready. I raise the blood-soaked gun to obey her final wishes, but as if following some primitive survival instinct, the worms rush into my arm and numb it. The gun sags against my hip.

I am almost gone. I am a head and a heart floating in space, surrounded by cold stars. And as my heart gives its final, frantic thump and disappears, I hear my thoughts like a loud voice, splitting away from this disintegrating mind to give one last command:

You will come back. You will find a way. You will repay what you stole and more.

• • •

Deep in some black void, drifting motionless like the shoals of trash around me, my legs twitch. My feet kick. I rise toward the light above me and thrust an arm out. I breach the surface and snatch a gasp of air. I shout. But my limbs are useless things. I sink again, as corpses do, my hands drifting limply above me.

Someone grabs them. Someone pulls me out of the water and onto something buoyant, and then I'm kneeling on hard pavement, coughing and gagging and breathing, and when I finally get enough air, I collapse and roll onto my back. The sky is dark. Her wet hair dances in the wind. There are tears in her eyes and her nose is bleeding, but she is smiling.

"R," Julie says. "We're not dead."

THE BROOKLYN BRIDGE sways like a hammock as we run across it, clinging to the railing to keep from blowing off. I feel weightless and disoriented. I see familiar faces through the rain and spray, but I have lost all context. I am a man running in a storm next to a woman who saved me, and this is enough for now.

Once we're across the bridge, Brooklyn's old brownstones take the force out of the wind and I feel my weight return. Some of my awareness comes with it, and I realize our group is missing a piece.

"Where's Tomsen?" I shout over the howling.

Julie is breathing hard and can't seem to form words. She just shakes her head.

She is leading us somewhere; everyone follows a step behind as she darts through the streets and tunnels and parking lots of her old neighborhood, and then we emerge from a staircase onto the flat expanse of the Brooklyn Heights Promenade. Beyond the railing should be a tourist-trapping view of the New York skyline, but there is nothing. The rain has erased the city from reality, leaving only a gray void.

M kicks open the door of a souvenir shop and we stumble inside. He pushes the door shut and props a postcard kiosk against it and suddenly—silence. The wind howls and the rain rattles against the windows, but it's a monastery compared to the chaos outside. I can hear myself breathing. It's steady and rhythmic without my even thinking about it; a miracle. I hear the others, too, all different speeds and pitches, but Julie's is the loudest, that dry wheeze so horribly corpselike. Her pack is gone, her jacket, her inhaler . . .

I take one of her hands and ease her down onto a bench. I rub her back as she struggles for air. "We're okay," I tell her. "We made it. You can let go."

She clutches at her throat, eyes wide.

"Just think about air. How good it feels in your lungs. Soft and cool." I take a slow breath and release it: a clean, perfect respiration like a lazy breeze. "Think about breathing. The pleasure of it. The privilege. You're swallowing the sky."

She closes her eyes and purses her lips and the wheezing begins to soften. Nora gives me a nod, approving and perhaps a little impressed. Finally, Julie lets out a shuddering sigh and shakes her head. "A zombie telling me how to breathe," she mumbles. "What next?"

She drops her head onto my shoulder.

• • •

An hour later, the storm is spent. The rain stops and the wind calms. We emerge from the shop and walk to the edge of the promenade. We stand at the railing; all the benches are occupied. Withered skeletons in clothes that no longer fit, some sitting alone, some with a partner, all with guns in their hands, holes in their heads. A good place to say good-bye.

From this distance, the damage looks minimal, but I can still see the change. The new stillness. The glimmer of water where there should be crowds. Manhattan has become Venice. Lovers will cuddle in gondolas while cabbies row them down Broadway. If anyone ever lives here again.

"They were on the bus," Julie says, staring into the city. "Sprout, Joan, and Alex. The kids were on the bus." I follow her gaze; she's looking toward the hospital. Toward the mountain of watery rubble where it used to be.

"I'm sure they have Audrey too," Nora says softly. "She's a Mostly. She's a valuable specimen."

Julie watches the mountain erode as currents carry it away.

"They do have her," Tomsen says.

"Jesus," Julie gasps, clutching her chest. "Where the hell did you . . ."

Wherever she came from, Tomsen is standing against the railing a few feet away from us with her face pressed to a view scope. "I saw her earlier, behind the hospital. They were loading the Dead into trucks. Valuable specimens."

She grips the scope with one hand and a portable ham radio in the other. Either she found it wherever she just came from, or she had it in one of her many pockets and the guards never bothered to confiscate it. What threat is a radio when you control the only channel?

She clicks it on and Fed FM shatters the stillness.

"*Now is the time to gather our strength,*" says a gravelly voice over a pounding action-movie score. "*A branch has broken in the east, but our roots reach all across this great nation. Living and Dead will eat the same fruit as the sun rises in the west.*"

"They're going to Post," Julie murmurs, staring into the flooded streets of Manhattan. "They're going to bring all this to Post."

"So . . . we go after them, right?" Nora glances from face to face, looking for confirmation. "Catch up with the convoy, grab our people, and get the hell off this continent. Right, Jules?"

There's a desperate decisiveness in her voice, like she's refusing to acknowledge how unlikely it all is. And to my surprise, Julie doesn't leap to support her. Julie just stares at the city like she didn't hear the question.

"The plane's probably safe in the hangar at JFK," Nora continues, slightly fazed but undeterred. "Abram, if we could round up a few more mechanics, could you repair it?"

Abram stands apart from everyone else, his face blank, his hair dripping into his eyes. "Are you forgetting something?" His voice is cold and calm. He taps the bandages on his arm and shoulder, soggy and brown with city grime. "I was your hostage." He looks hard at Julie. "And you lost your guns."

Nora sighs. "Well shit, I guess I figured we were past that by now. After everything we've seen, I thought you'd realized—"

"No." He shakes his head. "I can use your help dealing with the convoy, but the minute I have my daughter, I'm done."

"And then what?" Nora demands, her posture turning aggressive. "Another cabin in the woods? Maybe try your luck at the Mexico wall?"

"We'll find somewhere."

"Seriously, Kelvin?" She throws up her hands. "After Helena, Detroit, Pittsburgh, and New York, you still think you can hide?"

"What do you call flying to Iceland?"

"I call it *escaping*. Big difference."

M watches the argument like it's a boxing match, smiling whenever Nora gets in a good jab, but the person I'd expect to be most involved remains absent. Julie faces the city, her jaw tight, her eyes squinted, like there's a louder argument happening in her head.

And Tomsen . . . I have no idea what Tomsen is doing. She peers intently through the view scope, but she doesn't sweep it to survey the destruction. She watches one spot in lower Manhattan, and as I try to find what's caught her interest, I notice something peculiar. The whole city is blacked out, solar panels blown away, infrastructure flooded, and in the evening gloom, every building is dark—except one. A short office tower glows like a lighthouse amongst all the dark high-rises, its bright windows reflecting off the newly formed sea that surrounds it.

"What is that?" I ask Tomsen.

"That," she says, "is the tower of BABL."

Abram and Nora stop arguing. Julie snaps out of her reverie. "What did you say?"

Beneath the view scope, Tomsen's mouth widens into a toothy grin. "Muter of mouths, choker of throats, confuser of pigeons. The only reason *this*"—she hefts the ham radio—"is not a box full of friends. And in exactly several minutes—"

The building flashes white. There's a muffled *thump*. Then the entire structure collapses, sinking into a pit that the water promptly fills, erasing all evidence that a building was ever there.

I feel a shift in the air. A tingling sensation. Or perhaps a sudden lack of one.

"*Yes!*" Tomsen screams so loud everyone jumps, and I step back to avoid her swinging arms. "Burn and drown! You're done! You're toppled!"

"That was it?" Julie says with wide eyes. "*That* was the jammer?"

"Yes!" Tomsen screams again, then drops into a low, rapid-fire babbling. "At first I thought it'd be Freedom Tower but if Axiom knew about the facility they'd have hijacked it by now so it had to be better hidden and probably improbable, not some big obvious antenna but something built to hide forever like maybe an *inverted* tower, some kind of geologic induction to make the earth itself a transmitter or maybe—"

"Tomsen!" Julie cuts her off, and points to the radio in her hand, which is still jabbering propaganda. "*Try it.*"

Tomsen freezes, nods, and twists the frequency knob away from Fed FM.

A scratchy, warbling tone like microphone feedback. Like a police whistle calling STOP. It's a little quieter. It cuts in and out, leaving half seconds of silence. But it remains.

Tomsen's face slackens. She clicks the transmit button. "Hello?"

Noise.

She twists the knob, listening, searching. "Hello?" she says. "Hello?"

A few muffled voices. A few ghostly outlines of syllables. Intercepted walkie chatter or just Fed FM bleeding through the bands, staining all the airwaves.

"Hello?" she says, quieter with each repeat. "Is anyone there?"

Julie shakes her head and sags against the railing. "Fuck."

I look at the ground. I feel knowledge pooling in my head, weighing it down. I sink onto a bench next to a skeleton in a Brooklyn Cyclones shirt and I watch the storm drift out to sea.

Nora puts a hand on Tomsen's shoulder. "You're *sure* that was the place?"

"I stood right in front of the machine!" Tomsen shouts, and Nora steps back, startled. "It looked like a Hadron Collider turned vertical, huge and horrible like the mouth behind everything! The bomb was still right where I hid it, I set the timer and dropped it in and watched it blow up so it should—there should be—" She hits herself in the head with the radio, hard enough to hurt. "I don't understand."

She keeps twisting the knob. Everyone is silent, listening to the squeals and screeches of a smothered world.

Nora lets out a long sigh and looks around for a place to sit. She finds a skeletal couple holding hands on a bench, shoves the woman to the ground, and plops down next to the man. "It's weird that Old Gov called their isolation machine 'BABL,'" she says, almost to herself. "Been a while since I've read Genesis but wasn't the Tower of Babel supposed to *unify* people?"

"'And the whole earth was of one language and one speech,'" Tomsen recites as she wrestles with the radio. "'And they said, "Come, let us build us a city and a tower whose top may reach unto Heaven, and let us make us a name, lest we be scattered abroad upon the face of the whole earth."'"

Nora nods. "Right, so how does—"

"'And the Lord came down to see the city and the tower which the children of men built,'" Tomsen continues, jerking the knob through the same channels again and again. "'And the Lord said, "Behold, the people are one and they have all one language, and this they begin to do, and now nothing will be withheld from them which they have imagined to do."'"

Nora shoots Julie an amused look, but Julie is staring at Tomsen, listening intently. I am listening, too, letting this familiar tale from my past echo loudly in my basement, waking its lonely occupant.

Tomsen adds a prankish snigger as she quotes the Lord: "'"Come, let us go down and confound their language, that they may not understand one another's speech." So the Lord scattered them abroad upon the face of the earth, and they left off building the city.'"

"It was the exact *opposite* of a jammer," Julie mutters. "It was communication and cooperation. A common cause to unite the world. Why did that scare God?"

"Why did it scare Old Gov?" Tomsen says. "Why does it scare anyone who wants to sit at the top? Because hierarchies are lies. Because no one needs the alpha. He gets to the top by puffing and bluffing until we all believe he belongs there. When your power is built on ignorance, you don't want people talking to each other."

The wretch is watching me from the bottom of the basement stairs. He is holding out a box. *Take it*, he says. *Do something good with it.*

What if they don't understand? What if they hate me?

He climbs to the top of the stairs and sets the box at my feet. *You've survived a dozen suicides with these people. What's one more leap?*

I close my eyes and pick up the box.

"Do you know what BABL stands for?" I ask no one in particular.

"Never met anyone who does," Tomsen says. "I've always guessed Buried American Broadcast Lock."

Nora thinks for a moment. "Big Apple . . . Barrier Language?"

"Butt And Breast Lover," M offers.

I release a slow breath, tensing for my polysyllabic confession. "It's Bicoastal Agitation Blocking Lattice."

All eyes fall on me.

"There are two generators. One on each coast. Airwaves won't clear until they're both gone."

"*Where*?" Tomsen nearly shrieks, tensing like she's about to pounce on me. "Where's the other one?"

"Somewhere in Citi Stadium. It's part of the LOTUS broadcast station. And Axiom is sitting on it."

I feel their eyes trying to peel my layers and expose my secrets, but I'm not hiding them anymore. My new life is young. My past is most of me. If I cut it out, I'm a thin and hollow skin.

"They planned it all years ago, before the hiatus, before the quake." I let it pour out of me in a stumbling rush, leaning on my knees with my head in my hands. "They died, but they came back, and they won't stop." I peek through my fingers at the drowned city, trying not to see how my friends are looking at me. "They already have the Feed. Soon they'll have the Dead. Then the Living. Then everything."

The breeze ruffles my hair. A few rays of orange light pierce through the tattered clouds as the sun goes down, its daily routine undisturbed by the chaos here on Earth.

"What are you talking about?" Abram says in a low voice. "How do you know all this?"

I don't answer Abram. I answer Julie. I look into her face and tell her: "I remember who I was."

Her eyes are vast and terrifying, like icy meteors hurtling toward Earth, but I resist the urge to look away. This time, I won't run. I will let her pierce me and dig around inside me, and whatever she finds there, she can have.

But the trial doesn't come. Not yet, at least. Instead of demanding answers and interrogating me on my sins, she turns to the horizon and says, "We have to stay."

I realize I haven't been breathing. I inhale gratefully.

"Stay?" Nora says. "What do you mean?"

"We keep arguing about whether to hide or escape. When did those become our only options? Two different ways to give up?"

Nora frowns. "Um, Julie . . . you've been pretty insistent on that second option."

"I know." She shakes her head. "I was so scared. Told myself we were going to find help and bring it home, but everything was so fucked . . ." I notice a glint of moisture in her eye. ". . . and then Mom showed up, and I just . . . broke." She looks at Abram through the welling of tears. "I'm sorry. I really am."

Abram says nothing. His face is stony.

"But you were right, R." She looks at my feet for a moment before raising her eyes to mine. "I can't save her." She turns to Nora. "And *you* were right. She wouldn't want me to try if it means giving up everything else." She wipes her eyes on her arm and clenches her jaw. "We can't hide and we can't escape. We have to stay and fight."

For a minute or two, the only sound is the squeal of Tomsen's radio as she absently roams the stations. I would expect Abram to have a lot to say about this, but he just looks from Julie to me with that strange blankness.

"Fight Axiom?" M says, pinching his forehead like he's getting a headache. "How?"

Tomsen has landed back on Fed FM, and Julie jabs a thumb at the radio with a disgusted grimace. "I say we start with that."

"The Axiom Group provides certainty in uncertain times," says an earnest female voice while the soundtrack swells. *"How can you rely on your fellow man when he's just as desperate as you? Only Axiom stands above the crowd. Only Axiom is prosperous enough to be trusted."*

"It's not like they have an unstoppable army," Julie says. "They're not taking the country by force. People are giving it to them because they think it's the best way. Because all they know is what Axiom tells them."

"In our thriving modern cities you'll find food, shelter, and work for the whole family. You'll sleep peacefully surrounded by thick walls and trained soldiers while helicopters float above your head like guardian angels."

"I'm so sick of listening to this," Julie growls. "Old Gov or Axiom, it's always the same voice. One loud asshole shouting over everyone."

"Rapists," a man intones as the music turns dark. *"Serial killers. Pedophiles. Terrorists. Inhuman monsters who want to eat your family . . ."*

"It's time for him to shut the fuck up." She grabs the radio and flicks the off switch. Tomsen doesn't seem to mind.

I heave myself up from the bench. With my spine straight, I am almost as tall as M. I fill my lungs with the rain-scrubbed air, and I release an imperative sentence:

"Let's destroy BABL."

A wide grin is spreading across Tomsen's face. Nora's lips are pursed, her jaw stiff, but she begins to nod.

M shrugs like I've proposed a trip to the corner store. "Works for me."

But I see something building in Abram. His eyes are on the ground, weary and sad. He is shaking his head as if caught in some bitter inner argument. Then he stops. He looks up at Julie.

"Good luck."

He starts walking.

"Where are you going?" Nora calls after him.

"I'm going to find my daughter."

"So are we! Get back here!"

I see his head shaking as he walks. "No, *you're* going to destroy BABL and expose Axiom and build a better world. *I'm* going to find my daughter."

"We're going to the same place, dumb-ass! If we don't find her on the way to Post, we'll find her *in* Post!"

"You're not going to make it to Post. The world's going to eat you alive."

"You said yourself we can help you!"

"I was wrong."

Nora throws up her hands. M looks uncertainly from me to Julie. "Should I stop him?" He cracks his knuckles. "Don't need guns to take a hostage."

Julie doesn't seem to hear him; her face is taut with overlapping emotions as she watches Abram recede, so I answer for both of us.

"Let him go."

I feel a rush of guilty relief as the words leave my mouth. We've dragged this man across the country hoping he would emerge from his stupor, see the light leaking into his life and walk toward it, but instead he walks away. He says, "It's too far, no one will ever reach it," and he walks away. And I am tired of him. I am tired of him and the people who made him and the people he will make if he can. I am tired of the tradition he carries, the legacy of a low existence, and if he wants to carry it far away from us, I say let him.

But as always, Julie is warmer. As always, she's the last to give up.

She bolts after him.

"*Abram*!"

I follow at a distance, just in case this escalates.

"Abram, *wait*!"

"You know what's funny?" he says without slowing down, and without a trace of amusement. "You keep saying you're sorry for shooting me, for taking me hostage. But that was the closest I ever came to respecting you."

Julie's hands clench at her sides.

"That was the one time I saw you look past your ideals to do what you had to for your family. And now you're going back. Giving up on your mother and running off to save the world."

"I'm *not* giving up on my mother," Julie says through gritted teeth. "I'm going to find her and be with her for as long as I can. But there's more at stake here. We might be the only people outside Axiom who know where to find BABL, so we—"

"Good luck!" He quickens his pace. Julie starts to fall behind.

"Abram, *listen* to me!" Her face is all dogged determination, but her voice is getting hoarse. "I know what it feels like to lose your family. Like you're cut off from humanity, like you're *meant* to be alone?"

He turns onto a dark side street, gaining ground with every step.

"I fight that thought every day, but it's not fucking true!"

He finally stops. He spins around, and his blankness is gone.

"Then what is true, *Julie*?" he snaps in a voice like acid. "What do you believe if you don't believe your own thoughts?"

"I believe what my mother always told me." She stands straight and meets his anger with soft immovability. "That humanity's a family you can never lose. No matter what happens."

I stare at the side of her face. Is she aware that I'm listening? Is she speaking to me too?

Abram is looking at her like she's from another world. An impossible shape speaking alien tongues. I expect a burst of cold laughter, but he just squints at her, dragging his escaped emotions back into the prison of his head. Then, safely blank once again, he turns and walks away.

Julie doesn't follow. The fervor drains out of her; she seems to shrink three inches. Abram shrinks too as he increases the distance between us. Then he slips around a corner and he's gone.

IN THE CORNER of a shadowed parking lot, surrounded by stripped cars and heaps of trash, something big sits beneath a brown tarp.

"Is that it?" Nora says. "It's huge."

"Please tell me it's camo painted," M says uneasily.

Tomsen approaches with a hand outstretched like she's calming a frightened animal. "I'm so sorry, baby," she coos as she unfastens a corner of the tarp. "I didn't mean to leave you for so long."

Julie has been quiet since Abram left. She walked the six blocks from the promenade without a word to anyone, and I imagine her wandering gloomy halls of memory, perhaps reliving the last time she failed to save a Kelvin. But I glimpse a faint spark of interest as she watches this unveiling.

"They caught me right before I could do it," Tomsen says, unhooking the last tie-down, "but I did it anyway. I did it today. But I guess there's more to do." She yanks the tarp to the ground. "Barbara," she says, "this is our new crew. They're going to help us finish."

Barbara is, as promised, not a van. She is over twenty feet long, rounded and bulbous like a cartoon submarine, riding low on three sets of wheels like a retro vision of the future. A forest of antennas sprouts in the cracks between solar panels, and a roof rack holds three plastic barrels marked NOT GAS DON'T STEAL. Other than a red stripe running along the sides, the whole length of the thing is bright, unapologetic yellow.

M sighs, but I see a smile creeping into Julie's face.

"1977 GMC Birchaven," Tomsen says as she pulls a key from a box under the chrome bumper and unlocks the only door: a curved hatch remarkably similar to the one on the 747. "Finest motor home ever built, made even finer with a few apocalypse mods."

As we file into her strange little home on wheels, she rushes around trying to tidy up. It's a comically lost cause. The RV's interior resembles a merger of a newsroom and an eccentric artist's studio: documents and photos and collage clippings piled on every surface, maps and sketches pinned to the walls and drawn on the windows, and of course, plenty of actual trash.

A beat-up old copy machine occupies the kitchen counter, surrounded by reams of yellow paper.

"So this is where the magic happens," Nora says with genuine wonder.

Tomsen looks embarrassed as she struggles to stuff the chaos into the already overflowing cabinets. Every seat is piled high; there is literally no room for anyone but the driver.

Julie puts a hand on her shoulder. "Tomsen," she says. "Do you still need all this stuff?"

Tomsen stops stuffing. She looks at Julie.

"It was for your search, right? For the tower?"

"And the Almanac," Tomsen says. "For writing and publishing the Almanac."

"You just toppled one tower. We know where to find the other one. So isn't all this . . ." She gestures to the chaos around her. "Isn't it finished?"

"Are you suggesting she should discontinue the Almanac?" Nora says, aghast.

"Of course not," Julie says. "But once we kill the jammer, the Almanac can go on the air. It can go worldwide if you want it to." She wades through the trash to examine the sun-darkened copy machine. "It's amazing what you've done with a single copier . . . but maybe you don't need it anymore."

Tomsen looks at the copier. She looks at it for a long time with what I assume is fondness and nostalgia. Then I have to rethink that interpretation when she grabs the machine and throws it violently out the door. It bursts apart with a satisfying crunch, and she dusts off her hands. "Good-bye, exed world."

• • •

We all assist in the purge, scooping up piles of research and tossing it into a huge pile on the pavement. It's a strange feeling, dumping out someone's life's work, but this work is finished. Soon she can begin another.

When the publishing house is gone, what remains is a surprisingly spacious home complete with a restroom, a kitchen nook, two sets of couches that fold into beds, and plenty of orange shag carpet. The cabinets are filled with a treasure trove of canned food, tools, car parts, and survival gear, except for the one occupied by some kind of oil filtration system. Through the gigantic rear window, I see a scooter hanging from a rack.

The RV isn't a home on wheels; it's a self-contained city.

"H. Tomsen," Nora says, spinning slowly in the passenger seat, which sits like a throne on the elevated cockpit platform, "you are the coolest person I've ever met. Where the hell did you get this thing?"

"My dad," Tomsen says as she darts around shutting drawers and securing loose objects, battening down the hatches. "He was always a step ahead. Saw it all coming. Spent his life savings future-proofing Barbara, right before the currency crash." Everything is secure but she keeps moving around, looking for more to do. "Had a few good years together. A few good trips. First five issues of the Almanac were his."

I open my mouth to ask where her father is now, then I remember Julie's lesson and I close it.

"His writing was beautiful," Julie says softly.

"How would you have seen those issues? You're not that old . . . are you?"

Julie smiles sheepishly. "I, uh . . . bought them off a traveler. For my collection."

Tomsen looks perplexed. "You collect my zine?"

"I have every issue."

"Maybe we're a little weird," Nora says, "but the Almanac meant something to us. There was nothing else like it, no one else trying to reach out. There might be a few other explorers out there, but when they find something good, they sure as hell don't share it with the world. You'd have to be crazy to do that."

"It wasn't just news for us," Julie says. "It was like . . . an artifact from some other universe. A universe with different rules. Different possibilities."

Tomsen looks back and forth between them. Her confusion gives way to deeper emotion; her throat clenches. She climbs into the driver's seat and buckles up and sits there for a moment, staring through the huge, wraparound windshield. Then she flips a few switches and checks a few gauges and turns the key. The antique engine—or whatever customized contraption her father installed—coughs a few times, waking up from its long nap, then roars to life with a deep diesel rumble. The air fills with an unexpected odor.

"Is that . . ." Julie sniffs. "*French fries*?"

"Vegetable oil," Tomsen says. "Fryer waste."

"Wow," Nora chuckles. "I haven't smelled French fries since . . ." She thinks for a moment. Blinks a few times. Her smile falters. "Don't know. Can't even remember." She spins her chair to face the windshield and it clicks into position.

I glance at M and find a similarly unsettled expression. He looks at the back of Nora's head with a gravity I rarely see on his jocular face.

We all fall back onto the couches as the ancient RV surges into motion, and by the time we're onto Brooklyn Avenue, the shadow has lifted from M's features and Nora's too. But it lingers in my mind. I glance at Julie and find her lost in her own preoccupations, some of which I can guess while others remain obscure, and I am suddenly conscious of a fact I often forget: I am not the only one with locked doors. Everyone around me is full of hidden hurt, but the hoarded heap of my own has always blocked my view. What's in their forbidden attics? Their boarded basements? Are their monsters a match for mine?

Julie is staring out the side window, oblivious to my gaze, so I let it wander her face and body, from her matted hair to her stained clothes, fresh wounds and old scars. Despite my romantic flights of fancy, she is no spotless angel. She is no standard of perfection by which to measure myself. I think of her rage in Detroit, gunning down three people with barely a blink, the ice in her eyes as she shot Abram once, then twice, looking ready for a third. I remember all her tales of drugs and razors and blacked-out fucking in alleys, ugly truths she was never afraid to share with me. Was I afraid to listen? Have I ever really known this woman, or did I paint an image that inspired me and prop it up in front of her? Did I glamorize her defects, give her pain a glow of noble tragedy, and cheerfully omit whatever I couldn't beautify?

I feel something dissolving between us. A hazy film of mythology and abstraction. I see her in the unflattering sharpness of reality: a fragile human being with neuroses and psychoses, smelly feet and greasy hair, who acts rashly and contradicts herself and fumbles her way forward in the dark.

She has never looked so beautiful.

Still unaware of my slack-jawed stare, she stands up, testing her balance as the RV accelerates onto the highway, and moves to the rear bedroom. She presses her fingertips to the huge window, watching the ruined husk of New York recede behind us in a red-orange blaze of sunlight. Then she sits on one of the couches, looks at me, and pats the spot beside her.

I sink down next to her on the brown plaid cushion, wondering if she's aware of the storm in my head, the lump in my throat. For as long as she's known me, I've insisted I was no one. Now that I know I'm someone, she deserves to know who.

"I'll . . . tell you . . ." My tongue fights the words like it's my first day among the Living. "I'll tell you . . . everything."

Her eyes are guarded. She looks young, vulnerable, but not quite afraid. "Do you *want* to tell me everything?"

I hesitate. I let her see all my turmoil and terror. Then I say, "Yes."

She nods. "Okay." She leans her head against my shoulder. "But not now."

"Not now?"

She releases a long, slow breath and closes her eyes. "Not now."

Her face is pale with exhaustion. Her eyelids are puffy from recent rivers of tears. Of course not now. There will be time for confessions—and their consequences—on the long road ahead. For now I'll let her rest. For now I'll be grateful for her head on my shoulder, for each remaining moment of trust.

Behind us, the city shrinks against the sky like it's melting in the sunset's fire. I watch until it's gone and imagine everything I did there melting away with it. Then I dismiss this useless fantasy. My past is not behind me. It's in front of me, marching west with a vast army. And we are chasing it.

WE

THE EARTH TURNS EAST. But beneath the surface, there are different movements. Earth's molten rivers flow on strange whims, sometimes counter to the crust, and as we float deep in its near-solar heat, we feel a shift. We are a prominence pushing up through the fabric of everything, and the earth responds to our pressure. The heart of the earth begins to flow west.

Thousands of human beings are flowing the same way. Some are fleeing a disaster. Some are obeying a voice they heard on a TV or a radio. Others, like the boy and his three friends, have no choice in the matter. They are sitting in the back of a bus, wrists cuffed in their laps, wondering where they're going and what will happen to them when they get there. But these questions are low on the boy's list. The more urgent ones are the ones he directs to us:

Can we change this?

His body is restrained but he runs free in the Library. He races down our halls and digs through our shelves, skimming pages of paper and crystal and warm living skin, the memories of countless lives throughout time.

What can we do while we're young and small? How can we grow bigger?

He climbs our ladder of living bones, each rung a generation, and pulls out Higher books. He strains to read them but not even the authors know the language of these glossolalic poems, these sigils and hieroglyphs scrawled in strange ink, visible only to a rare kind of eye.

What can we become?

Packed into the back of a cargo trailer, cold and gray and confused, a woman in a dirty lab coat is asking similar questions, and she is not alone in her turmoil. She is surrounded by others like her, in this trailer and elsewhere, all across the unstable landmass once known as America. They gather in the streets of forgotten cities, in forests and in caves, standing motionless to suspend their hunger while they wait for the answers to come.

And how we wish we could give those answers. How we long to emerge from the hush of memory and shout into the present. To reveal our secrets to all these desperate searchers and finally tear the veil. But though a library brims with a thousand eloquent voices, it can't speak a word until the world learns to read.

So we wait.

We wait with the Dead, moving through their ranks like spies or maybe allies, and we share their mood: restless, hungry, ready to go to war. It's been years since any attempt to count them, and this is good, because the Living are fearful enough without knowing they're outnumbered.

The Dead are a larger army than any ever assembled, and they follow no leader, fear no threat, and accept no bribe or compromise. The Dead are the silent majority, and should they ever decide to say something, it will be the new law of the land.

The mantle flows beneath their feet like the nudge of a warm hand, and one by one, they begin to wander west.

Acknowledgments

I'd like to thank the 108 billion people who lived and died throughout history to make this book—and other things—possible, and the even larger number of nonhuman creatures who helped. Much appreciated. I should also probably thank my editor, Emily Bestler, and my agent-editor, Joe Regal, and everyone else at their companies who guided this hubristic ship of a book away from various icebergs. Justin Guild helped me make David Boeing as realistic as possible within the needs of a ridiculous story. My sister Nurse Christa Wheeler answered many disturbing medical questions. Stephen McDonnell helped me build a horror that will lurk in the phone lines forever. The baristas at Fremont Coffee Company gave me a warm corner in which to write and caffeinate. Nathan Marion and Jared McSharry engaged me in the windy philosophical debates that shaped the ideas of this story. And final, ultimate thanks to my readers for their outrageously generous support—for spreading the word about this book, for handing out cards and putting up posters and other stunning displays of passion, and just for reading the damn thing. I'd be alone in my head without you.

A road trip across the wastelands of an unraveling world. A search for lost family and a cure for poisoned love. When the past finally erupts, R finds himself alone at the edges of his hard-won humanity. But all roads lead home, to a final confrontation with the avatars of the plague.

And in the ancient vastness of the Library, something is stirring. . . .

The story concludes with

THE LIVING